2024:

A HISTORY

OF

THE FUTURE

CHRIS OSWALD

NEWMORE PUBLISHING

Second edition published in 2017 by Newmore Publishing.

ISBN 978-1-9997868-8-5

Cover design by Book Beaver.

Book design and layout by Heddon Publishing.

Chris Oswald has lived in America, Scotland and England and is now living in Dorset with his wife, Suzanne, and six children. For many years he was in international business but now has a little more time to follow his love of writing. His books have been described as dystopian but they are more about individual choice, human frailty and how our history influences the decisions we make, also about how quickly things can go so wrong.

For Suzanne, my love.

2024:

A HISTORY
OF
THE FUTURE

The Procession

G eorge Unwin-Smith had been waiting all night, without
knowing why: waiting with strangers, magnetically-
bound polar opposites. Waiting at the barriers erected across
each entrance to Parliament Square, as if chalked into a
pavement picture; waiting for the rain to wash out and merge
the very colours that made them. He felt as if he knew them
now, ten hours of winter darkness, little wind and light drizzle,
giving him an acquaintance, a comradeship, he could not
otherwise claim. Not that he knew their names, just as they had
not learned his. It was a comradeship of silence. But he knew
them - for instance, the tall chap in front of him. Hood up, legs
bowed backwards as if he wished to hide his height from the
world, the cord of his anorak hanging low on one side as he
stooped against the barrier that barred their way into the
square. Sometimes, when he shifted his weight, the cord would
sway, brushing across the girl sitting at his feet before coming
to rest on her shoulder. At first she had brushed it off; that much
George could see in the watery, orange lamplight, but sleep had
worked into the young body on the pavement so that the
anorak cord was free to flutter and perch where it would. Was
she the man's girlfriend? It was hard to tell. Throughout the
long night they had ventured little conversation, like a
submarine crew used to operating with minimal sound. But as
dawn diluted the dark they became alive, surfacing and then a
yawn that rippled across the pavement. Each individual
movement became another chalked scene; magically moving as
distinct colours emerged in the winter sun. The girl struggled
to her feet and George saw how much younger she was - early
twenties at a guess - half the man's age.

"She'll be here at eleven," The man said, his words meant for the whole group. "We can expect the crowds from nine onwards." His voice sounded technical, a Geology teacher on a field trip, yet it carried authority. The shifting and stretching continued across the small crowd. There was a pressing towards the barrier, which carried George along, as if the tall man had issued an order to close up ranks. Now George could see more faces, more bedfellows of the pavement. But who were these strangers with whom he had spent a cold, damp night? And why had they been here?

"She'll come up from St James' Park and stop there between the abbey and Parliament." An older man pointed out the route, adding, "See the platform? That's where she'll stand." Somebody else produced coffee from a flask and pushed a mug towards George with a gloved hand.

"Here, drink this, it looks like you need it."

"Thanks, it's been a long night!"

The coffee-bearing girl was older, rather un-pretty, with an oversize chin and pockmarks dotted around her pale face, but magnificently brightened by flame-coloured, curly hair. She gave George a weathered, eroded impression, like some well-known feature of the landscape, or a squat, bleached tree on the edge of a windswept beach. Now that he thought about it they all seemed sprung from the ground. He looked into her eyes. She looked back: clear, sky-blue, intense.

"Whatever it takes," she said simply but with commitment. Then she turned back to watch the empty square.

The man in the anorak was spot on. The crowds came from nine onwards; the perimeter to Parliament Square was packed by ten, still with an hour to go. After the luxury of space all night, George was now crushed against his comrades, inevitably forced to greater intimacy. As eye contact became more common, the more he sought to avoid it. He felt a false comrade now, only willing to commit when darkness covered him, shrinking back as daylight brought true relationships out into the open. The barrier moved with the crush. It toppled, steadied itself, and then gave way under a new influx of bodies pressing from the rear, pushing George against the young girl he had speculated was the leader's girlfriend. Now he was not so sure. She stumbled and George caught her. She looked briefly in gratitude at him. Her whole face was lit with the bright fire of enthusiasm, turning the raindrops into steam around her, it seemed to George. Then two policemen, wearing their riot gear with ease, moved towards the fallen barrier.

"Stand away from the barrier there!" Nobody moved. Nobody could move. "Come on, move along at the back." In drill fashion, two right hands dropped towards their holsters and the pressure instantly relieved in the crowd. George felt himself less crushed. The barrier was righted again. The policemen walked on, efficiency chiselled into their features, dark glasses hiding their eyes, American-style.

"I haven't seen you before." The blue-eyed girl stretched around a pair of rain-coated shoulders to address him. Her hair was bright carrot red making the contrast with her pale face vivid and eye-catching. For some time now George had been aware of her interest in him but had pretended not to notice. "Where are you from?"

"Oxford originally, but I have lived all over the place. I have a flat off Ladbroke Grove."

"I meant which branch?"

"Branch? I don't understand." She had thought him one of them. But he was not. And who were they, anyway? Why did they wait so patiently for the Queen to arrive?

"You're not..? I thought you were with us. Never mind, my mistake." She looked deliberately away, her body language silencing George's questions before they could be asked. So he was not their comrade, he shared no purpose with them. He was an interloper, passing through the craggy, windswept landscape; a townie in the wilds. He had no reason to be with them, no purpose. He was a loiterer; someone they should challenge.

It suddenly struck George what it was that had drawn him into this all-night vigil – the intense aura of purpose that hung about them like the smell of the sea. But purpose for what?

The police had been forewarned and were well prepared. Minutes before the carriage arrived, they moved in, targeting the all-nighters with ruthless efficiency, as if they stood out from the whole crowd as a different breed of humanoid: Neanderthals amongst Homo Sapiens. They did it so neatly that the day-trippers, those that had not even earned their place at the barrier, were not aware of the round-up, seeing instead just a minor scuffle followed by an agreeable opening up of prime real estate. The police were not harsh, no bones were broken; they were just good at their job. George was shunted off with his new comrades - only they were not his comrades. From pavement to van and from van to reception and then to a police cell, he was managed and processed as though he were on a packaging line.

"I don't understand." The anorak man crossed the cell to squat next to George. There were a dozen of his male followers spread around the room, which was actually a large empty training room on the second floor. The female comrades, being fewer in number, had a proper cell in the basement. "You are not a member yet you were there with us all night. We all thought you were from another branch." He looked at George, the only evidence of his arrest being the lengthening of his anorak cord so that it scraped against the cell floor as he talked. "You are not a reporter, are you?" The mild voice became briefly overcast, threatening thunder, but it might pass. Who were these people?

"Well, as a matter of fact, I am a sort of journalist, but not the kind you're thinking of and that wasn't why I was there with you. I am editor of a history magazine, that is all, or I was until yesterday." As George spoke, he became aware that the entire cell was listening to him. In the seconds of silence that followed, he read the soul of each of the dozen disciples who were staring at him. The anorak man broke the silence, dispelling the storm clouds with a gusty squall that cleaned the whole sky.

"You're not... I mean... you can't be - George Unwin Smith - can you? I mean, not the..."

"Yes, I am actually."

"Good God, I think I have read everything you have ever written! I can't believe it is you! And to meet you like this! I must say 'The History of the Future' is quite magnificent; so inspiring, so challenging. I have always wanted to meet you. I can't believe I have spent all night ignoring one of the finest minds in Britain today. Wow!" The Geology teacher had gone back to his own childhood and met with a boyhood hero, a superman! They stood and shook hands, George genuinely surprised to be recognised, suddenly very self-conscious, the other man evidently in awe.

"My name is Mark Borden. This is amazing to meet you like this. Why, your father was my tutor, Professor Unwin-Smith, at Oxford! I am really, really honoured, Mr Unwin-Smith!"

"Call me George, please. So you read History at Oxford?"

"Yes, I graduated in '02. Your father was, and still is, I am sure, a remarkable man and a very fine teacher."

"Thanks! I'll pass that on next time I see him. Actually, he is all but retired now, just teaching one or two classes to keep his oar in. But tell me, what is your organisation? What were you trying to do this morning? Are you some kind of an anarchy group?"

"No, far from it! Let me explain..." But George would have to wait for the explanation for at that moment the cell door opened and his name was called.

The questioning was brief, the processing speedy. George, suddenly alone on the London pavement, felt strangely cheated; a boy sent firmly to bed at the climax of the late night film. The whole affair was deeply puzzling. Yet the irony was that he felt let down by his quick release, rather than by any threat of retribution or injustice. Can it be an injustice, George wondered, to be let off the punishment for something you did not do? And then to feel deflated?

"Do you have any connection, Mr Unwin-Smith, with the people you were arrested with this morning?" A thin office-bound chief inspector, whose large glasses dominated his soft, lowland face, had asked him, barely bothering to look up.

"No, I was just standing next to them. Who are they?"

5

"How long had you been there?" Although bent over his papers, George could see the eyebrows working as mini engines, chugging up and down, ploughing the paperwork. His collar was too large for his neck, as if his mother had expected him to grow into it.

"All night."

"All night! Why?" Now George warranted a direct look, the faintest trace of enquiry drawn onto the inspector's procedural features, the engines in neutral, uncertain as to direction. This did not fit a pattern and the Chief Inspector liked his patterns.

"I wanted to see the Queen…" He knew as he answered that this was not true. The strange crowd, not the Queen, had sucked him in and earned him a few hours in a temporary cell in a police station he did not even know the name of.

"Oh, is that all?" He returned to his file, wrote in a careful, slow but neat hand, and snapped it shut. George now fitted in and the world was right again. "You are free to go, Mr Unwin-Smith. My apologies for detaining you unnecessarily."

"Chief Inspector, who are these people? What organisation do they belong to?" And why was a chief inspector involved with petty misdemeanours concerning crowd control?

"You are free to go, Mr. Unwin-Smith." A second look up. The head moved to the door, indicating George was to leave. George noticed that when the chief inspector moved his head his shirt and tie stayed straight forwards, uncoupled from his neck.

"Just a minute, you have marched me away from a public space, bundled me up in one of your vans, transported me here and held me for several hours without any explanation. All I am asking for is some information on who they are and what they were arrested for. I think you owe me that."

For a third time the head raised, the eyebrows worked through the processes. The soft head then wavered back to the paperwork so George quickly added: "And if you don't tell me I will have no alternative but to bring this up with the Commissioner, who I know rather well and dined with just the other day." He had, indeed, dined with the head of the Sector 8

Police force but it was a large gathering and they had only spoken for a few minutes. George noticed the similarities with this policeman; the office-bound nature, the importance of procedure. When had either of them last chased a shoplifter?

But it worked. With a sigh to show procedures were being set aside, the chief inspector clipped out an "alright" before the briefest of explanations. As he talked, George noticed his uncaring, soft features. How could anybody be more different from Mark Borden and his followers? In a few moments, when Mark was bought before the chief inspector, it would be rock meets cake. Who would win? George found himself wondering what had become of the great British bobby. When had the change occurred? It probably dated back to the directive setting up the Pan-European force.

"They are just some crackpot organisation that wants us to get out of the Super Union of European States. They are a dreadful nuisance." Hardly anyone called it the official name anymore. It was just U.S.E.

"Is that a crime?"

"It is, yes; actually several: creating public disorder, resisting arrest, blocking the highway. And then there is the serious stuff."

"Which is?"

"Undermining the Super Union and its institutions, questioning the constitution."

"My God, Chief Inspector, they wanted to see the Queen, our Queen. Is that so bad?"

"Mr Unwin-Smith, I really must be getting on now. The constable will show you out."

George wandered along the river for 20 minutes. The late November day had already given up, the weakened winter sun no match for the all-emboldened dark. The sun set on the Embankment behind him as he walked. Something bothered him. It had been an uncomfortable night but it was not that, nor the tiredness that had descended upon him as he stepped out into the street and realised that they, the police, had confiscated the already shortened day from him entirely. But it was not indignation, nor hunger, nor fear. It was something he could not put his finger on. As he strode on, oblivious to the crowds, Thames on the left, traffic on the right, he went back methodically through the last 24 hours from when he had left his last meeting with the magazine's supervisory board and happened across that strange group, readying for their all-night vigil. He lived briefly again through that night; alone but not alone, following a cause he was not part of, wondering what troubled him so badly.

No answer came to George that night; no enlightenment or grand realisation. His darkness remained with him. Yet something was at work for, after twenty minutes of steady pacing, he crossed the road and caught the Circle line from Westminster. At Paddington he would get the train to Oxford.

By the Age of Thirty

By the age of thirty, George had completed his education. Of course, nobody ever really finishes, but there comes a time when the balance tips and the individual starts to give back. Again, of course, the formal stuff had ceased some time earlier. First the minor but well-thought-of private day school in Oxford. Then a year off, working for a few months in the City, followed by four glorious months on an apple farm in Somerset, sleeping in a caravan on the edge of one section of the vast orchard, he and his two co-workers walking each evening to the absurdly named village pub, The Fisherman's Rest. Nine years later George had gone back, intent on taking his then girlfriend to lunch in the pub. But the pub was closed, now a private house, the acres of apple trees long gone, turned into an 'executive village', as the poster proudly advertised. This mad compaction of roundabouts, 'Tudor' houses and prim but deserted play areas had received a commendation for excellence in modern planning. Why, George wondered, did it just not seem right? He tried to remember where his caravan had been, but it was hard to be sure with so much change. He wandered over to the central Community Centre, drawn to a huge, steel-framed notice board growing tall against the concrete beds outside. It was crowded with notices and George, aware that his girlfriend was getting bored in the car, scanned just the bolder ones.

'The Orchard Gardens Executive Sub Committee on Safety wishes to advise all residents that children are not allowed in any play area without adult supervision. Play Area Supervisors are always present but are there for the purposes of fairness and overall security. They are not trained for other than emergency first aid and are not to be relied on. They have been instructed to deny access to all children unless a responsible parent is in attendance at all times.'

Below this the Parking, Pavement and Paths Committee had stern words to say about cars left on the road overnight while the Entertainment Section (surely a lighter read?) complained of poor attendance at a recent Culture Night.

"Bit of something for everyone," George heard a voice behind him and turned to see the owner of the board, a man a few years older than George with 'Community Centre Janitorial Services' stitched onto his brown overall coat.

"Yes, I suppose so. But there are so many rules."

"I maintain the board myself; nothing stays more than 30 days except for these here long-standing stuff." The man heard only appreciation; no criticism entered into his neat, janitorial world.

"I must go," George mumbled and retraced his steps, still no clearer as to where his caravan had once stood. All the hedgerows had gone, replaced with neat suburbia.

He had later traced the owner of the orchard to a semi in Yeovil and found a bitter man.

"We couldn't compete with the Frenchies. They bloody flooded the bloody country with cheap apples - tasteless too - and then they gone and paid us peanuts to uproot the trees. It's a bloody way of life that's gone now, it is. And look at what you pay now for apples in the supermarket! And what did I get for all my hard work, a compulsory purchase order and a two-bed semi in exchange for my old farmhouse."

George had written a piece for the magazine but the supervisory board had to pull it as there was a risk it was too critical of the Common Agricultural Policy. They had asked him to turn it into a piece about vanishing heritage but instead he commissioned an article about ancient Britons and their tribal organisation. He often thought of life in the past, that there is a past, sometimes glorious and sometimes pitiful, but it had all been the present before it became the past. Apple trees had blossomed, had probably blossomed in that same orchard for centuries, but now were gone and replaced with tidy houses and tidy lives, denying future eighteen-year-olds the delights he remembered, like the bittersweet apples he had helped ripen. He had been much saddened as he left the ordinary semi in Yeovil. Everything had suddenly seemed so modern, so organised, constructed for today rather than grown up out of the past the way a hill that has always been there is just there. He sometimes mused that nature was really history, because things evolved, thus chequered fields were chequered because countless generations had slowly created them. Humans influenced nature so very, very slowly, gradually imposing themselves until one day they feel so confident that they brush it all away, destroying their very selves in the process. What are we without our past?

His choice of university, like the subject he had read there, had been an act of rebellion, one that seamed ridiculous now, a deliberate spurning of the old for the new. He could easily have gone to Oxford or Cambridge. He had known that then, yet had chosen the brand new, futuristic University of Cumbria. The top-heavy, modern glass University Village, stuck so oddly in the ancient hills of the Lake District, had pleased him at first. When it had opened he had been in the fourth form at school. It was topical because the Prince of Wales had been heavily critical of it in a speech to the Royal Society of Architects. What were they called now, subsumed as they were into the pan-European organisation, fattening steadily on government new builds? Whatever the new name, the Prince of Wales had not been asked back and the university complex had gone ahead, funded by the benevolent Super Union.

So George had turned his back on the establishment, but also on his father, his only parent, and the celebrated 'Father of Modern Historical Thought'. He read Media Studies rather than the History he had always loved. Professor Unwin-Smith had raised it several times as George's perverse path became clearer. "Why turn your back on the subject you love?"

"It's your subject, Dad." But said without conviction.

"You know you could go to Oxford."

"I don't want to be bound up in the past. I want to look to the future."

But thank God on three counts. First, George's stand against everything he was came early. Second, it passed quickly. And third, education does not stop on graduation. The euphoria of modernism faded like cheap veneer; an erosion that would have delighted any geologist. In a matter of weeks, he was disillusioned. In a matter of months, he had admitted his mistake to himself. Before the end of the Christmas holidays, he spoke to his father and things moved rapidly.

His application to Oxford was in the system before the deadline and he was on a flight to Boston, heading for an internship as a research assistant with an old colleague of his father who had come to Oxford years before, when a young man. January to June was spent in the coffee shops and libraries of Cambridge, Massachusetts, first penetratingly cold and then hosting gentle sunshine and light showers. He lodged with a group of History PhD students in a top floor apartment of a tall, narrow city building. The youngest was five years older than George and their conversation a little falsely erudite, as if they needed to impress their intelligence on everyone around them. George could not get a beer in a bar so they drank at home and discussed their theories late into the night. A few were original, hidden amongst the rehashed concepts of youthful minds. Maybe original thought was lurking there in quantity but could not burst through the shield of youth. However, George found himself enjoying it and his confidence grew as he realised he could play his part and hold his own. In fact, he came to realise that many of his ideas contained more weight than an entire clutch of PhD students'.

His work, too, was fascinating, although he knew his was a minor part. Professor Jay Stuttermann had devoted his life to the study of the holocaust. His father had escaped Germany as a teenager, along with Jay's grandparents and aunt - who

George met when invited back to the Stuttermann home. Aunt Jessica was an engaging narrator of the drastic events of over seventy years earlier. Her veined face shone like highly polished old china as she related their near entanglement in the early stages of the Final Solution. She delighted in pulling up her skirts to show the still evident bullet wound in her left leg that had left her unable to run, yet run for her life she had; there was no choice. It had doomed her to maidenhood, plus looking after her young nephew, Jay, when both his parents died in a train accident in 1964 while commuting back to their newly purchased home in the Bronx. Now Jay returned the favour and took care of his elderly, crippled aunt. He had never married so she naturally kept house for him from her wheelchair.

Aunt Jessica never tired of telling her story. It was a classic case of major excitement followed by seventy years when nothing particular happened.

"We had to leave with almost nothing." Her heavy accent caught everyone's attention, regardless of how many times they had heard it before. "Papa throws some clothes and jewellery in a canvas bag, not dissimilar to a kit bag, then we left. It was the dead of night. That is often when they come for you." Her muddling of tenses, past and present, had a way of bringing the story to life, as if the past could happen now, alongside the present. Then she would stop, feign tiredness, or perhaps the reliving had really exhausted her old frame? The story would wait for another day, another invitation to the Stuttermann home.

Thus George heard the whole story several times over, some parts more than others. He knew the incredible race for safety in all its detail, experienced the suspense, the fear and the exhaustion, and never grew tired of it. To someone growing up in safety it was a world apart; a world he loved to dip into through her words.

He learned it in parts, first the mad rush across the border to Switzerland, bullets zinging through the air, the stumbling as the metal sheared through her leg, the mistiness and the slowness, time on its own time. First they were running for their lives then everything was so still, the shouts and cries moving back into another world. Then the ground came up to meet her, she struggled to stand and fell again as the second bullet hit her shoulder. Her father had come back for her, scooping her up and turning on his toes to sprint for safety. She remembered her mother's anguished face that said it all – was the price of her family's safety her precious daughter's life? Then she remembered no more until the hospital in Zurich. Another time, George heard about the desperate journey from Berlin - where the family had lived and worked since her grandfather had been a boy - to the border with Switzerland. The trip in a butcher's van, concealed behind carcasses of pigs, the heart-stopping moment when the van was searched, but the soldiers were too lazy to go right into the cargo area, accepting the driver's assurances that no Jew would hide in a lorry-load of pig meat.

Other times she would talk of the kindness they met along the way. Although only eight, she was struck by the decency of some people, especially when lying in a loft one night she overheard her parents and her hosts talking of the Donnersmidts down the street, who had been arrested and shot for safe-keeping a Jewish family only weeks before.

"Now their millenary shop has been taken over by the wife of the SS sergeant who organized the arrest so we go to one on the other side of town." She clearly remembered the young mother who was harbouring them saying.

Her father had replied: "I recommend you return to their shop so you do not attract attention. Sooner or later they will wonder why trade is down."

Very early the next morning, long before the sun was up, their mother had shaken them awake and they had climbed down the loft ladder, yawning and hungry. The lady gave them porridge and hot chocolate. It was their last meal for four days. They had left when still dark and walked quickly in the deepest shadows from the lamp lights out to the edge of town, where an ancient man waited with his taxi that did not look much younger. It lasted only 16 kilometres before giving up on life, just as the sun rose on the new day. The old man shrugged and started to walk to a garage. He had not said a word until he mouthed 'Good Luck', as he disappeared around a corner. After that, they had walked and hidden, walked and hidden some more, crawled, waited silently still in ditches, mainly moving by night, always on edge, never anything to eat.

Then, they were caught. A police car drove by on the morning of the fourth day, before they could run and hide. It stopped before the bend in the road and roared back in reverse so that Jessica's father had to bundle them onto the verge to avoid being hit. There was nowhere to run to. They had been on the road eleven days and were 80 kilometres from the Swiss border. The door opened and a huge man emerged to ask curtly for their papers, before bundling them all into the back seat of the car.

"You Jews?" were the only words he said on the journey. Her father nodded miserably. The policeman drove on.

Only suddenly the car turned left off the road and stopped in a yard behind a butcher's shop.

"My brother." This was the only explanation given as the policeman got out of the car and left them alone, walking into the rear entrance to his brother's shop. This was their chance, but before they could react the policeman was back with his brother in bloodied apron.

"My boy will take you to within ten kilometres of the border in the van." He was as big as his policeman brother but more talkative. "There has been too much suffering. Come first and eat. We have cold beef and bread and potatoes. Quickly now, my son has to leave in fifteen minutes."

Fifteen minutes later they were trundling along, sharing their van with eight-dozen pig carcasses, but their tummies full so they dozed as the lorry wound its way up into the mountains. It was like a dream with a happy ending. Their captors were their saviours. The world was turned upside down. Civilised people turning to cruel acts as if they were playing bowls on a Sunday afternoon, while the hard face of authority had shown such compassion.

George's work was mainly involved with tying up records of lost and separated families, nearly all long dead. He loved the neatness of finally piecing together each component into a full family. The father transported to a distant labour camp, the mother dead from hunger, giving her only scraps to her frail, shaking daughter. Filthy son and filthy daughter gassed in Auschwitz two days apart and thrown no doubt into the same grave, finally together after eighteen months of desperate separation. At least, he thought grimly, they could enter the next world holding hands. The grandfather and grandmother both shot down in the street of their native Warsaw, considered too old for the labour camps, or perhaps they just did not move fast enough out of the way - or perhaps the soldier was just bored.

And into the dry world of past facts, every so often would come a slow, hesitant interview with a survivor speaking what was still a foreign tongue. This, in George's opinion, gave the colour to the pencil drawing of a nation at shame, a world gone completely wrong. It slammed it home to the nineteen-year-old would-be historian that each and every fact he filed away neatly was actually a bottle brimming with pain and sadness. Once he met a man, a survivor, who thought George was his brother. He did not seem to know that almost three quarters of a century had passed since the Nazis had brutally tortured and murdered his beloved Helmut. They were still young men with the world in front of them. Life was promising. Life was good.

And then, in the last week of Harvard's year, he met a girl. She had very long, very straight light brown hair with a healthy sheen that could be seen across the street. She came from California on a scholarship. Her teeth were uneven but she laughed a lot. They loved each other for a while and she took him back to the slums of LA where her mother lived with three younger boys, then on to a mobile home near Bakersville where her father had two girlfriends who were sisters. They spent the summer bumming rides around California and visiting as many beaches as they could. As the heat increased, so their passion cooled, and they both knew by August that it would end with the summer. They flew back to Boston and said their goodbyes at Logan Airport. It had become the sort of relationship that would survive the forgetting of names and be remembered with warmth and nothing more. George flew into Heathrow and got the bus back to Oxford. Always back to Oxford.

The three years George spent at Oxford were the fastest, most blurred of his life so far. The first-class degree was expected and achieved with relative ease. Chairmanship of the History Society took a little to manage, fighting an election against Maria Wilberforce, a formidable opponent and a claimed descendant of the anti-slavery campaigner. George won by sixteen votes and swore it would be his last election ever. Maria responded with a warm kiss and the resolution to be the best deputy chairperson. This they had agreed in advance: whoever lost would be the deputy to the other, and together they would be a team. For half a term after that they dated until Maria fell madly in love with a first year PPE student. George and Maria thus slipped with minimum awkwardness into a deep friendship and mutual trust. They would still kiss and touch each other from time to time, but as friends, almost brother and sister, both being only children.

Maria had an intellect equal to George's, framed in a slightly round, olive-skinned face, long jet-black hair and a five-foot-five-inch skeleton on which hung the remnants of her puppy fat. Her eyes were almost as dark as her hair and George could see the intelligence in them, almost bouncing around, trying to get out and be free to roam the university and all that it offered. It became apparent that she spoke several languages fluently and had a knack for picking up new languages, which amazed George, who had never excelled at anything linguistic. Her memory was fantastic; she only had to read something and it was there somewhere in the vast mind to be dragged up sometime when required. Her mind was like a library condensed into a small oval football.

When Maria looked back at George she saw someone not

unhandsome. His nose was slightly too large, his mid-brown hair looked as if it could retreat early in life but was still at present in abundance on the twenty-one-year-old, slightly diffident man standing an inch short of six feet tall. She liked what she saw; there was something honest about him that was attractive in a general way.

The first History Society evening they arranged was a coup and a great success. Professor Stuttermann flew in and gave a compelling insight into the world of mass displaced and disenfranchised people.

"Imagine the polar opposite of you'll," he began quietly. "A great number of persons, like the student population of this great city, but lacking a single purpose, a common age range and also mostly of average not higher intelligence. Here all further comparison breaks down. You have tradition, more even than we have at Harvard! You have an establishment that frames your existence and assures you of continuity and purpose. You have a set term, typically three years, after which you go on to another world, taking with you memories and contacts to assist you. Thus it is a seamless flow from childhood to studenthood and on to adulthood. At each intersection you decide which way to go and what you take with you of the previous road. Now look at the Jews in Europe in the 1930s and 40s. All their props were whipped away by a viscous, vindictive political and military machine. Their establishments and traditions were ripped from under them. They were separated from friends and relatives and thrown in with strangers who, oddly, often became surrogate family by reason of their being thrown together. They were sent on a journey, like you, but they had no control over the mode of transport, their fellow travellers, or even the destination."

Professor Stuttermann looked around the room and deliberately made eye contact with as many of those listening as he could.

"Just... try... and... imagine... what... it... was.......... like." His words settled slowly on the audience and then he sped up. "Extremes happened, of course; extremes of selflessness and

18

extremes of selfishness. Great acts of kindness, bravery, deceit and cowardliness became everyday occurrences as the veneer of civilisation was stripped away. Good and evil became naked."

Like the dumped bodies of the victims, thought George.

This was the professor's central theme. Good and evil are both cloaked in ordinary life by some vague things we can call convention, manners, tradition and civilisation. Such aspects act upon us to rein in the extremes, thus we plough as we have always ploughed and the chequered fields remain chequered. When those things are knocked away the good and evil become open and honest for all to see.

"What is the best example of the removal of the veneer?" he asked his audience.

"War."

"Bigger than war."

"Occupation by enemy forces."

"Bigger than that, think back through history."

Great minds, including the dozen professors attending, searched back through history. It was Maria who came up with the right answer.

"Slavery."

"Go on, be more specific."

"Well, the transatlantic slavery trade."

"Exactly, and why is the transatlantic slave trade the greatest example of this phenomenon?"

"Because it took people from one complete society to another about which they neither knew nor could understand anything. They were wrenched apart from all their traditions and everything they were familiar with and sent on an awful voyage, chained in the hold to emphasise the drastic change. Plus, it introduced captivity to people who, while they were aware of slavery, had never experienced anything but freedom. And to use your analogy of a journey, they went on a dreadful journey over which they had no control, not even any knowledge as to when it would end."

"I see I am soon going to be out of a job!" said the professor to obligatory laughter, tinged with regret, each audience member asking why they had not thought of the answer. But George was thinking of that journey that Professor Stuttermann's aunt had travelled, like the journey to slavery only there was freedom perched at the end of it. But how would anyone know? How does it feel to be forced on that journey without knowing the end? Can you work out the end from the experiences? Can the past and present assure you of the future?

"Professor, do you think this phenomenon you describe is absolute or relative? I mean, does it kick in at a certain point or is there a sliding scale?" Maria was with George and Professor Stuttermann and a few others, lingering over the last of the wine and refreshments.

"An excellent question, Maria." George had introduced them earlier. "My supposition is that it is relative, it is your sliding scale. I excuse my talking of polar opposites, suggesting it was absolute, as a gimmick to make my point. But in reality I believe it is relative in two ways."

"You mean on a societal level and individually," someone volunteered.

"Precisely. My argument is that as society moves away from the established norm so the veneer slips. The more it moves away, the more veneer is removed and the more the underlying good and evil emerges. For example, take a fierce political election where two or more people are desperate to get into power. They don't usually commit murder but there is a lot of temptation to carry out lesser acts they would not be proud of on greater reflection. Or even take a family vacation. This family, being confined together, will naturally exaggerate the basic trends of behaviour in each person."

"And some more than others, which is where the individual aspect comes in," Maria said.

"That is my theory; each individual has a different threshold to the level of change as well as a differing amount of goodness or badness – and most of us have both of course."

"So," Maria summed up, "individuals behave in a vast array of different ways, creating a mass of fluctuating reactions resulting from a simple change from the norm, but the direction will all be similar, reflecting the events everyone is experiencing. Thus you get people with superficially similar backgrounds engaged in, say, a war, and one behaves heroically while the other behaves shamefully, but they are both reacting outside their normal behaviour because of the war conditions."

"You make it sound so scientific," commented George, "as if none of us have any say in anything."

"The only say I want right now is to take you both out to dinner, as my treat," the elderly professor quipped, but the serious conversation lasted throughout the meal and on into the early hours.

University raced by. Both George and Maria achieved firsts. They stayed firm friends and had dinner together on the last evening before graduation. Their diverging paths were set; she to the Foreign Office where she hoped to use her languages and her specialisation in Diplomatic and Political History; he on the fast-track graduate training scheme at Ergen & Bell Inc., an American media giant into newspapers, internet, publishing and much more besides. His father had wondered why he had not stayed at Oxford to pursue an academic career, or maybe gone back to Harvard to assist Stuttermann, but decided not to intervene. Even with his son, his only flesh and blood, he had learned to be patient.

From Ergen & Bell, George moved on to Radiant, which was purchased by Henkel of Dusseldorf, who only wanted the manufacturing part and sold the rest on to Hinsui. From Hinsui he was headhunted to help create the new media division at Arlington Investments and then, becoming increasingly restless with each move, he tried Ergen & Bell again, at six times the salary he had started on four years earlier. But E&B the second time was even worse than the first so George left quickly with a negotiated pay-out and, at 26, found himself unemployed.

On advice he 'looked to the future' and took a government

job in Brussels. Even better pay combined with long holidays and all expenses paid. It worked for a while, but not for long.

"What do you want from life?" his father had asked.

"I don't know, I really don't. Sometimes it all has meaning, and then everything reverts to the trivial and meaningless. There must be something more."

It was his father who came to the rescue, with his contacts. He was a founder and major shareholder in the publication *The History of the Future,* but he insisted that George apply for the editorship in the normal way, sending in his CV and attending the interviews alongside the other candidates.

"Tell me, Mr Unwin-Smith, with no direct editorial experience, what do you think you could bring to this position?" The questioner, one of a panel of five, clearly enjoyed his work, looking at George over the rim of his spectacles; a ridiculous overacting parody of self-importance. George had, of course, prepared an answer for this question. It went something along the lines of his varied background in modern business and government, his media experience, and his interest in history. He would expound, with a little drama, along the theme of editorial experience being less important than energy, ideas and an interest in people. He straightened his posture and opened his mouth to answer.

Yet the answer was not what he had rehearsed. It was spoken suddenly from the heart. It was as much a revelation to George as to the panel, who were immediately impressed by the honesty and insight.

"I know history, it is in my family. It is part of who I am. But more than this, I have learned the value of history, the use of it, thus I can apply it to life. I understand the aim of this magazine being to influence the future through the lessons of the past. I am young, 27 years old, with my life stretching out into the future. Yet, thanks to my background and my interest, I am steeped in the lessons of the past like an old crooked man weighed down with the wisdom of experience. I have a stake in both aspects of this magazine. I am of the future but I bring the past with me."

"Go on." The chairman of the management committee prompted George in the silence that followed his words.

"Well, a magazine like this should point out themes, show direction and leadership, open up debate, and get people questioning. We should all be asking ourselves whether we have it right, whether the past is leading us in the right direction. But most of all it should convince people that, just like they own their past, so they own their future."

The decision was unanimous and George was offered the editorship that afternoon. He seemed to all of them the embodiment of the magazine's theme. His words were changed slightly and, by insistence of the management committee, incorporated into every edition of the magazine:

'Understand the past and you will own the future' was printed in George's own handwriting just below the title from his first edition onwards.

The three years George spent at the offices of *The History of the Future* were the happiest he had spent since his apple days. For the first time, his job had purpose. Each day, even the more mundane, he felt as if he achieved something. He loved his work. And his love grew as the circulation expanded. It had been a specialist publication before George took over. Now, without any deterioration in intellectual standards, it became popular, well known, talked about and profitable. The editor was also the business manager so George was thrown into a whirlwind of activity: hiring staff, building up a network of contacts for articles, interviews and opinions, dealing with suppliers, strategizing with the management committee and learning how to run a commercial venture that was growing. Soon, his reputation was made. He was called upon to take part in *Newsnight* and *Question Time* and a host of other television and radio programmes. It all seemed to fit so well: each strand of thought, each thread of argument, each piece of research. They all built themselves, like a colony of ants, into a coherent, popular and easily defined philosophy. And it was clearly apolitical, bigger than spending plans and social engineering, perpetually asking, 'How do you want your future to be?'

Personally, George also flourished. He was using his intellect. He was an academic and businessman combined. His salary was a third of what it had been in Brussels but his sense of purpose soared. His confidence grew with his stature and fame. But, more importantly, his wisdom grew. He found he could apply thought and history to practical problems every day. He was doing it better and better.

So, by the age of thirty, George's education was largely complete. It was at the tipping point where one gives out more than one soaks in. But he knew he needed to move on once again. There was an unexplained restlessness within him. He would always stay in touch with the magazine. He was moved to tears when they asked him to join the management committee when he handed in his resignation. Something indefinable drove him on to the next stage, the next task.

But what should that be? And was that strange organisation, peacefully passionate, part of his future? Would Mark Borden and his fellow campaigners play a part in his next role? Why were his thoughts always coming back to them? Again, therefore, at a junction, George turned once more to his father and caught the evening train to Oxford.

The Modern World

David Kirkby had a long-standing weakness. His mother had noticed it first, and then hidden it, hoping long into adolescence that she would be able to cure it with love and attention. But by the time the young graduate prepared to leave home for his first job and a bedsit along the burgeoning M4 corridor, she knew it was incurable. Her son simply did not have the character to surmount it. Was he even aware that his sense of perspective fell away whenever things got difficult? His judgment melted. Anchorless and rudderless, he drifted with the opinion of whoever last spoke to him. This was David Kirkby: a bright young thing with a serious character flaw.

It was nothing to worry about for those who knew him well. They could step in with a few calming suggestions and disguise the panic and anxiety as anger or passion.

It would have been nothing too much to worry about for the average man. An occasional storm in an otherwise still life, a tremor from time to time to shock those around but not to cause permanent damage. Perhaps if he had stayed with the electronics firm throughout his career, working his way up to Senior Manager and then Director of Research, and then even Managing Director, it would never have hindered him. Indeed, in the six years David spent in industry things never once went sufficiently wrong to cause him to lose control. All the omens were good: a couple of promotions, one remarkably early, the stability of marriage and then two children in rapid succession. In 1981 they had moved, leaving behind a decent, ordinary detached house on the edge of Bracknell and taking on a barn conversion deep in the Berkshire countryside. Life for David Kirkby and his family seemed set and secure, as rhythmical as the seasons.

But David Kirkby had ambition; too much ambition for an electronics engineer in a shrinking economy. He saw his boss and his boss's boss and even the Chairman and majority shareholder when over from the States.

And what he saw was Dead Man's Shoes and it did not inspire him.

It was 1982, the year of the Falklands, the year when despondency and depression turned like a slick frigate in open waters towards hope and optimism. Thatcher was in her ascendancy. The city loomed with its aura of success, its statement of modern Britain.

"Industry is crumbling," David explained to his wife, Marjorie, the spirited daughter of a retired Brigadier who was now MP for Oxfordshire South. "The future is in services. What does it matter if we import all these consumer goods from Japan, so long as we pay our way in other fields? Insurance, banking, consultancy, investment, big, big money! Doesn't it sound exciting?"

"But what would you do in the City?" Marjorie asked with her practical slant. Five years into her marriage, she knew his limitations. She knew she had not married wisely, but loved him all the same.

"Marjorie, they are crying out for people like me! They need people with sound industrial experience yet able to see the future. I am going to see a chap next week." He rightly took her doubtful expression to be disbelief. "Marjorie, the salaries are double, the bonuses even better! And it is a meritocracy, people rise on their ability rather than length of service." That was the very point to Marjorie, but she let it drop; things would work themselves out.

The City had loomed in David Kirkby's life, entrancing and engulfing him. It claimed twenty-six years, eighteen in successive merchant banks working on privatisations and euro loans, raising ever more heady sums for ever more questionable projects. Then eight years as a partner in a small but prestigious firm of consultants with a double-barrelled name that everyone has heard of but no one can quite place. He thrived on merging and cutting, acquiring and selling. Words like 'synergies' and 'reorganisation' peppered his everyday language. He generated an air of self-importance that, sadly, left his children behind. Sally, the eldest, became a schoolteacher and married a miner she met during a march. Hugo took four successive gap years before extending it to a permanent sinecure at a celebrity-filled ski slope in Switzerland. But David's chosen career paid the bills and funded both children until they could stand on their own. It gave them a lovely country house home to come back to, where their pompous father and serious, loving, practical mother held court through gentle summer days and blustery gales by the fire.

So what drove a change? Why did David not slide gently into a comfortable retirement, grandchildren eventually replacing children, stress slipping away like evaporating mist? Why, quite suddenly, was the thought of golfing holidays with fine wine and even finer Scotch so much less appealing?

The answer came in one word. Marjorie instinctively knew the answer. David did not and she would never tell him. The answer was Vanity. But she still loved him. The capacity for humans to love frailty is extraordinary.

David was beckoned by bright lights and fame, a born-again teenager making their way to Hollywood. His political launch was in 2009 when Britain suffered from recession and uncertainty. The cheap veneer applied by the Labour government was wearing thin, displaying the acres of rotten decay like faulty valves and hardened arteries around the country's heart. In 2009 much happened to compete for the news headlines so a minor, predictable by-election result in Herefordshire barely made the news at all. It had been expected that the Conservative candidate, a well-to-do City consultant of maturing years, would maintain the comfortable majority of his predecessor. Even when a young hack raked up the fact that

Kirkby refused to commit to moving to the Border Country, it raised barely a murmur.

So David Kirkby arrived in politics with no fanfare, no great announcement, no shaking of Heaven and Earth. He was another of many and nobody saw what would happen next. That is nobody except, perhaps, Marjorie.

That had been fifteen years ago, the unheralded beginning of a meteoric career. Historians are queuing up to explain this rise with caustic phrases such as 'accelerated through a vacuum of talentless yes men'. He was now at the top of British politics, but often wished he were not. Most men his age were on the golf course or, perhaps, enjoying a much younger wife. He was Prime Minister and it was wearing thin. His innate, unsolvable character flaw surfaced much more frequently. In his effortless life to date he had not realised that stress and character weakness are in inverse and exponential proportion.

"Are you ready for the off, PM?" Another one of those thin, reedy types. Where on earth had all the hale and hearty chaps gone?

"Yes, I think so, Charles." It was Charles, wasn't it? His new parliamentary private secretary did not object to being a Charles. "Tell me who is along for the ride." The jollity was a front, but so much in use that it was now natural, like good old boys and buffers and chaps. Sometimes he even found himself talking to Marjorie in this way. Marjorie! What would he ever do if he lost her?

"It's not a big do; Foreign Sec., Home Sec., their PPSs, yourself, myself, and a clutch of civil servants. Oh, and Bertie Graves."

"Good, we need the best brains around, circle the wagons and all that." Evidently the best brains around thought in perpetual clichés. "Tell me, Charles, what is your reading of the sit? Pretty serious, don't you think?"

Kirkby had been lucky, exceedingly lucky. Or was that unlucky, he sometimes pondered. He had stepped into the disaster of 2019 with a clean sheet, yet just enough ministerial experience to persuade others he was the horse to back. As

Moor's government had collapsed in what became known as 'The night the lights went down over Britain… literally!' Kirkby had seen his chance. He campaigned on the slogan:

'It's not that we can't beat them, but why fight them at all?' Actually, it was Bertie Graves' slogan. He was the Slogan Man. It had been Bertie's idea to completely reverse the previous Conservative government's policy of resistance to monetary union.

He reversed it, claiming logic, but, as the historians will tell you, he won the leadership campaign on vanity. Not his this time, but the vanity of those who thought they had a right to govern and could see no other way forward.

He often remembered his Victory speech, re-ran it in his mind:

"Like Canute, we are too wise and too experienced to stand against the tide. We are standing here today because we see the Future and that Future is good. We embrace change and the modern world and fight our corner for the best deal we can secure. Thus, we build the best position for the people of Britain. Remember, Europe is the tide and it is coming in. Europe is happening so we might as well ride the waves rather than drown amongst them." Bertie was proud of the words, David was proud of the deliverance. When George Unwin-Smith heard them, he thought of the Orchard Gardens Village rising up out of the ancient landscape, complete with rulebook and committees, and a shard of ice struck deep within him.

Behind the scenes, when the great men of government discussed their new policy, there was less certainty.

"But the price, they are demanding so much."

"It does not matter, David. We just need to present it as a new deal for Britain, a partnership with Europe, that sort of thing. You know, taking Britain into the future. It is all a matter of presentation." Bertie could turn out clichés like a production line. And, to extend the run of clichés, David swallowed them hook, line and sinker. He swallowed everything Bertie had ever said since the slick young PR consultant had hitched his wagon to David's seven years earlier.

And, David reasoned, what other option was there when the pound sterling was worth less than sixty eurocents, inflation and government borrowing were rising in parallel, and the trade deficit had far too many zeros on it? Something had to be done and he, the Right Honourable David Kirkby MP, was the man of the moment.

***

"Class, for your homework assignment you will write a 1000-word essay on the correlation of vanity with historical change. Take any time in history except the present. Dismissed." Perhaps Sally, miles away in South Yorkshire in a grimy ex-mining village, had inherited the perception of her mother rather than the pride of her father.

***

"We ought to hold a general election," David had announced to his first cabinet, but the chorus of disapproval had convinced him that this was just a sounding, not policy. "I just thought it would seal the new direction." But, you poorest of thinkers, the direction has already been sealed and for a decade or more the people, the citizenship, had not mattered.

"And give the Socialists another chance to ruin everything!" someone snorted with, what David thought was, less than the required amount of respect.

"But that is not the real threat though," Dennis Shepherd, Minister for the Environment, had said quietly. He did not talk much but was listened to. "The real problem is the Liberal Democrats. Now that they have merged with that European party, what do they call themselves now?"

"The European Alliance of Progressive Social Democrats."

"That's right. With this drastic policy change of ours we have put them in a very strong position. We now are advocating everything they stand for."

"The only difference, off the record, is that they believe it!"

That was the Foreign Secretary, Terry Rose; a jovial, cunning man who knew how to raise a laugh. David was scared of him but envied the weathered, red Yorkshire face of sixty-odd years as it fronted a razor-sharp mind. He was so straightforward and casual with people, but not a man of principal. He was the polar opposite to David, David thought. But why did he oppose Dennis Shepherd at every turn?

They had not voted on the general election proposal. They were all against it, even Kirkby. He had, after all, only lobbed it into the meeting to provoke reaction, ever the master of the discussion. Instead, they would concentrate on making a bright new future for their tired, confused nation, forging the way ahead. They knew this was right.

Progress from the change of heart of 2019 to the eve of the Intergovernmental Conference of EU States in 2023 had been difficult, often impossible, in David's view. There had been some steps forward but also many in the other direction. It was Bertie's job, of course, to present every reverse as an advance and at this he excelled. They were sticking to their unenviable task of re-writing the Future. Now, however, was the opportunity to take a big step forward and right the many wrongs of the last four years. He, David Kirkby, has managed to persuade Hilda Rheinalt, the German Chancellor, to set aside thirty minutes for a personal discussion of all such matters the evening before the conference began. David pondered that, like a general, it is not the long, hard slog through the mud that earns him a place in history but it is the quick, decisive move to outflank the enemy. He would be remembered as the Man who had carved a Future for Britain in Europe, the Creator of the Future, the Defender of the British Way of Life, the man who finally said, "Enough is enough." He could hear the speech on his return to the Commons, a speech that would set the seal on the terrible European debate and set the course for Britain sailing steadily off into the Future.

"Are you sure about going it alone?" Bertie cut into his six-second fantasy. It had gone on too long.

"Yes, of course I am," he snapped. Bertie was a useful fellow, but a hanger on, while he, David Kirkby, was the PM.

"What are you going to ask for?" Bertie was sitting upright like a soldier, always a bad sign.

"Recognition of our way of life, an agreement to consult with us on future constitutional matters before they go to the council. And my absolute rejection of the Common Armed Forces Directive…"

"David, a word of advice…"

"What is it? I have to be there in a moment so spit it out."

"It's just that she is a cold fish, is our Hilda. And she has something against the British. It is clear to most people. She looks at us in meetings as if we have collectively committed some horrendous crime against her. What I am saying is…" Kirkby had stood up and was making his way to the office. Was he even listening? He had to try. "If you go in there making demands left right and centre, you will get nowhere. It takes…"

"A soft approach? You are suggesting a soft approach?" That would have remained the extent of his outburst and the word of caution would have lodged somewhere in his mind as he strode out, anxious to be there on time. But a sudden thought came to him. "Did Churchill take the soft approach? Did he tell our grandfathers to go so softly, softly when they went up to smash the Luftwaffe out of the sky? I think not, Bertie." Face-reddening muscles twitching, the PM strode out of the room, a little late for Hilda, so hurrying to catch up.

Softly, softly, be damned.

But he did not want to be late.

Strange Bedfellows

The anorak cord was in perfect balance, an even six inches on either side.

"Mark…" His hood was down, despite the light drizzle, displaying his ragged dark hair, offset with an invasion of silver. George could not remember his second name.

"Hi George! Do you remember we met last November? Westminster Square followed by the nick?"

"How could I forget? Come in." Borden was the name; Mark Borden. George recalled also what had struck him about this man. Mid-forties, severely weathered, with one deep line, a crack in the rock face, running up the right-hand side of his face beside the twin features of mouth and nose. It could almost be a battle scar. Very tall with an almost embarrassed posture, as if he did not know what to do with that extra nine inches. There was something elemental about his appearance but, for all that, he could be one of ten thousand, lean and tall types; a geography teacher, a research assistant in a pharmaceutical laboratory but with a passion for cycling or canoeing, at home in a canoe. It was not his appearance but his manner that singled him out and had partly drawn George to spend the night with strangers last November. He was a quiet man who expected to lead. Not that he appeared peaceful, but confidently in control, unfazed. His gangling height, his casualness, his lack of attention to his appearance… all belied the fact that Mark Borden knew where he was going.

"Thanks. This is Mandy Friar."

It was the girl from the barrier, dressed, as before, in similar style to her mentor: anorak, thick jumper, jeans, trainers. Yet here the likeness ended.

"Hi, George." She extended her hand, her self-possession belying her youth. George got the impression of someone who had skipped the awkward, questioning years between thirteen and twenty, someone born to a purpose. But there was something else. She had energy, undiluted; a pure mountain stream in springtime, in need of strong, steep banks to funnel the rush of water headlong down the hillside.

"It's good to see you again, Mandy." George looked into her black eyes as they shook hands; eyes that danced like puddles in heavy rain yet had a depth to them that seemed never-ending, the deepest of wells. "Would you like some tea or coffee, perhaps?"

"Tea, please." They were too earthy for coffee.

"We heard about your resignation. Have you taken on anything else yet?" Mandy's youth was displayed in her direct question. Mark would have laid the groundwork first, dug the beds over rather than scattering the seeds on unprepared ground. Why did George feel that he knew them? He had only met them briefly. Briefly but strangely, he reflected as he considered his response.

"No, not yet. I wanted some time to think things through. I am contemplating what to do next." George's mind was working on a multitude of levels, asking: why did he sound so pompous? Why was he concerned at sounding pompous before these two? What did they want? Why did he so want to know what they wanted of him?

"Good, we wanted to put a proposition to you."

"I'm all ears," George groaned inwardly at his clichéd speech. "I'll just pop the kettle on." There he was again. Why clichés? Why nervous? Why did he care so much what they said?

Why had they come back into his life at such a crucial time?

"We tried your flat in London." This was the first time Mark had spoken since the introductions. "But it was closed up."

George had continued to pay the rent on his Ladbroke Grove

34

flat all through the winter but had not lived there for months now. Once he had been up to pay the bills, arranging with a neighbour to forward the mail to the family home in Oxford. Quite why he had done this he did not know. Except something was driving him to seek the company of his father, to learn something of the man who for so long had been a figurehead, someone wise to turn to. His father was more than semi-retired now, cutting his teaching to the bone, just a handful of advanced tutorials a week. This gave George the opportunity and he had taken it. Yet Mark and Mandy had found him here, as if they knew he would be here, belonged here. George felt the liberating yoke of fate as he walked to the back of the house to make a pot of tea.

He and his father had slid into an easy bachelor existence over the last few months. They rose at a reasonable hour, all things catered for by the housekeeper his father had employed when his wife had died over thirty years ago. They worked all day, sometimes voicing ideas, often in concentrated silence. A lot of contented purpose like sands quietly slipping through fingers. They worked late into the night. It was not work. It was a labour of love, for father and for son.

"Will there be enough material for a book?" George had asked. The tacit agreement, lead and assistant researcher, had been made. No need to risk a natural understanding with the straitjacket of words. They were working together for the first time ever. And it was so appropriate that the historian father and wayward, now reformed, historian son should work on what was probably going to be their only project together: a subject so close to both of them – the wartime exploits of the father's father, the wartime general so little was known about.

"If anything, it is too much. It will take months, maybe years, to weed it down to the pertinent sections. This is why I wanted to get on with it now, why I cut my classes to a minimum. I want to get this finished before I die."

That always hurt. No child can bear to contemplate the end for his or her parents. Yet George, as an historian, knew better than most that all things come to an end. The present becomes the past. History is created every day, every second of every day. It is like a self-sustaining energy source, a stream that never runs dry.

Just as George was thinking about streams again, Mandy was at the kitchen door.

"Hi George, can I help? Mark is deep into old times with your father."

"Oh yes, I'd forgotten that Dad had been his tutor at Oxford. The tea is just about ready, if you could just take the cups through. Do you take sugar?"

"No, nor Mark."

"So, what is this great proposition you have for me? Should I be charmed or alarmed?" She was so young, surely just a hanger-on. Perhaps he should not have asked her. But the answer came back straightaway.

"We want you to work with us. We're really impressed with the views and ideas you espoused as editor of *The History of The Future*. You have a lot in common with us, like… well, Mark will explain further."

"He's in charge then? Of your organisation, I mean."

"Yep, I suppose he is. Not elected, not even chosen, just sort of naturally. He started it all in '18." The admiration was clear. She picked up the cups and led the way back to the sitting room.

"George!" His father bellowed with his best parade ground voice – George often joked that it was his father's chief inheritance from his own father. "I had no idea that you were acquainted with this young chap. He was in my European History tutorial class of, when was that now?"

"'01, well over twenty years ago. But I won't complain about being referred to as a young chap!"

"Well, it's all relative, although I dare say I looked ancient then, too." The professor stood up and offered his hand to Mark. "We can't let an old man and his reminiscences steal the day from the younger generation. I'll leave you to your discussions but it was jolly good to see you again after all these years. Perhaps you will drop in again sometime?"

"Professor Unwin-Smith, please don't go. What we have to say to your son is a little unusual and we would be glad of your opinion, that is if you don't mind, Mr Unwin..."

"Call me George. And I don't mind at all if Dad hears what you have to say."

"Well, if you're sure, I would be glad to stay." The professor settled back down in his half-vacated chair while Mark stood up; the two ends of a see-saw.

Mark's voice exuded calmness, bathed in that quiet authority that George had noticed three months earlier on their first encounter on the edge of Parliament Square. He spoke for five minutes, easy-flowing words, like an ancient storyteller reciting a well-known myth. His accent spoke of the north somewhere, but it was too faint, too swept away by many winds, to be sure of the exact location. It was easy to listen in that hushed sitting room, warmed by the fire with an audience of two experienced listeners. But somehow George could imagine him being heard on a bare, frosty hillside amongst a babble of school children on a field trip. His charisma was so silent, confident rather than showy. Like the best spots in nature, his charisma was undisturbed and had to be sought out. Mark's world was not a pushy world.

"George, you must be wondering why Mandy and I have come to see you today, staking a claim on our very slight acquaintance. The time we met before, I started to tell you about our organisation, but did not get very far." A slight smile broke at his reference to their brief time in the police cell together. "It is called The Society for the Preservation of the British Way. We are a peaceful organisation, dedicated to the preservation and, in some cases re-establishment, of the many institutions, characteristics and peculiarities that make us who we are as a people. It is not anti-anything, rather welcomes the input from all areas of the world and just preserving what used to be." Mark paused briefly, a lull in the wind. George stared into the fire, then at the back of his hands.

"Well, frankly, we need your help. Our membership has been falling steadily over the last few years, it is almost as if

37

people are getting used to the lack of tradition. At first we had a lot of momentum but something has happened." Another pause, Mark willed George to look at him but, if George were aware of the silent request, he would not consent.

"George, you could help us reverse that decline. We don't know how else to do it." It was out now and George looked directly into Mark's eyes, then to those of Mandy. Her dancing, shimmering eyes were the spring brook babbling over the rocky ground. But Mark was the ground itself.

"Go on." George was compelled to fill the silence. But Mandy then stood up, the words rushing out.

"George, we love your work. We've followed it all, I mean all the writing and thinking and editorials and we've been to your open forums and discussions. I mean, you are the embodiment of what we believe in. We think your intellect with our passion will go a long way." George wondered how they could both have passion, being so different. Yet they did. Hers was all movement, while Mark's was stillness, permanence. "George, we don't have much money but we could offer you something. Maybe you could do a magazine for us and keep some of the profits or…" Suddenly the brook ran dry. Mandy stood a moment longer, looking even younger than her twenty-five years, before a flush of self-consciousness sent her back to her seat. She sat on her hands, as if restraining herself.

There was a long silence. George wondered whether Mandy and Mark slept together. Then he became aware that they were waiting for an answer. But they had numbed him.

"Thank you, that is very flattering. I need to think carefully about it." What else could he say? He needed some time to absorb the idea. Were they a bunch of eccentrics? Should he steer clear? Then Mandy jumped up again, her five-feet-two-inches suddenly seeming much taller. She had become the sharp crag that stuck out above the lie of the land, visible for miles around, stubbornly resisting erosion. Her words soared on their simplicity. They soared again on the passion so evident.

"Please don't dismiss us out of hand. We believe fervently in what we stand for. So much is going wrong in this country. Every day, we lose a bit more control. We must stop this process and show the world it is not inevitable. We can be a free people again and honour our traditions while absorbing new ones and letting them evolve. We can be alive as a society, open and confident of the future, open to new ideas and cultures, instead of besieged and attacked on every front. Why is it that our justice system, our currency, our weights and measures are all gone? We are driven to resist this, to restore some balance, but we cannot do it alone. We need to harness all the forces we can. George, you are looking for the next step in your life well, what could be more logical that joining us in our endeavour? What could possibly have more meaning?" Again, she sat down abruptly. Again the silence, but this time it was the silence after a storm. She held his eyes in hers in a Herculean grip to force her point. He had to look away; it was too compelling. Then the silence suddenly became an ordinary one. George shifted awkwardly in his chair and Mandy knew that they had failed.

The conversation flickered on for fifteen more minutes, but it was a pale shadow of what went before. At the next pause, Mark stood up. George thanked him again for the offer. George noticed the anorak cord quite uneven again now, as if jerked on one side by the force of the words now dispelled into nothingness. George would consider it carefully and get back to them. It sounded like the closure of a not particularly successful interview.

The truth was that George was frightened of these free thinkers, yet he had carved a reputation as a free thinker himself. Were they just a bunch of latter-day hippies or was their free thought a degree of magnitude beyond where George had ever taken himself? Had he ever really broken away? He felt as much a fraud that late January day by the warm fire as he had in the damp, cold November night when he had first bumped into these strange people. He wished suddenly that he were Robert the Bruce in his cave with the spider, or Alfred the Great minding the cakes. How easy to make a decision when there is nothing to lose. But what exactly did he stand to lose?

"At least he said he would think about it," Mandy said as the door closed behind them, defiance colouring her face quicker than the cold that descended upon them.

"He won't, Mandy love, his mind was already set. I've seen it before. He was being polite."

"It was a daft idea. I'm sorry, Mark. I should have guessed that he would never throw his lot in with us."

"No, it was not daft in the slightest. It was a brilliant idea, it is just that sometimes even the most brilliant of plans don't work out." Mark put his arm around her and they walked on together. "Now we have to move on and see what to do next."

"I suppose so." Mandy pulled his arm even tighter around her. George, closing the curtains, saw them in the street and was in no doubt now that they were a couple. They were like the children's game where paper defeats rock and water puts out fire. Yet they fitted together, the rock and the water, in defiance of the game's rules. That was it: they were united in their defiance. She was hungry like a cougar and always in motion. He was still, permanent, his wisdom older than time. But both, in their different ways, were true to themselves. George looked away from the window and felt a deep disappointment with himself.

George's curiosity had been aroused but the proposal seemed wrong. He felt no affinity with protest. He was an historian and a journalist, he told himself. His tools were debate, reason and analysis. He could not see himself hard at it for long weekends, painting banners and marching through cold, wet streets. He had been drawn to this strange society that night in London but, he told himself, that was journalistic instinct rather than a potential career move.

However, the meeting with Mark and Mandy would not leave his mind. Little snatches kept returning, sometimes Mark's plain statements, other times Mandy's passionate pleas. On occasion, while in the shower or getting dressed, he would rerun the whole act, scene by scene, turning it into a one-man play by jumping from role to role. The most striking thing was Mandy's passion. Most girls her age would be having fun: first job after university, flings with boyfriends. Yet he could see her shining, earnest face as clearly as if she was standing right in front of him.

But as the days wore on and the events moved slowly to the back of his mind, time steadily circling around the flock and shoe-horning the scenes into deeper pens of memory, he came to realise that Mark's face held an equal amount of feeling, just so different, like a valet working steadily in the background. The contrasts intrigued him: different generations, personalities, physical size, voices. Only their dress was similar, but George knew that to be a form of flattery from Mandy to her mentor.

What bound this strange couple together? Why did it matter to him?

"I did the right thing in declining."

"So you keep saying," his father replied, watching his son closely.

Throughout the balance of January and into February, George worked with his father. Father and son were indulging in their shared interest, seeking out information on the father's father, looking neatly, George mused, a generation back. They worked at feverish pace, distilling and collating, sorting and categorising, methodically retracing the steps of Major General Unwin-Smith as he advanced across Northern Europe and into Germany almost eighty years before.

"I don't really remember my father," the professor volunteered during one pause in their work. They had taken steaming cups of instant coffee outside into the back garden and were sitting, as always, on the rough log bench they had made years ago when George had been a child. The day was bright with brilliant snowdrops promising a vibrant spring. The sharp sun hit the building in front of them, the family home, turning large patches of pale stone to a warm orange colour. "He died in '58, when I was thirteen, but he was hardly ever at home. Your granny, my mother, used to travel with him to such dreary places like Kenya and Hong Kong while I was lucky enough to go off to wonderful boarding school!" He always made that little joke and then paused for the appreciative response.

"Of course, I remember what he looked like and I remember his voice, at least I think I do, and some of his mannerisms. But there is so much more. What about his humour, his beliefs, his temper and his fears? What did he like and dislike?" He sipped his coffee, kicked idly at a nettle that threatened them on the bench, then added, "I lost a chunk of my own past when he died. One needs that continuity through the generations in order to be a whole. We are a product of what came before us. My father married late and died young. These two occurrences combined to cut me off from my past. I became not the end of an evolutionary chain but a single broken link. Or, to be more precise, a broken chain, for I still had my mother. Then I suppose everything is distorted, the past comes to us through only one perspective. Of course it happened all over again when your own mother died young." George held his breath and waited for his father, who hardly ever mentioned his wife, the mother George had never known, to continue. "Everything you have learned about your past, George, you have learned from my perspective. Your mother's perspective died with her. How fragile it all is. And when a child becomes an orphan, countless generations of the past are wiped out in an instance." George thought about his university choice, his deliberate turning away. What if his father had also died young? He would be lost without the parental anchor so firmly wedged in the past.

"I suppose that's one reason why you want to do this book now, to get to know your father a bit better."

"Yes, I imagine so." He finished his coffee and stood up. "And if we don't get back to it we'll never get it finished!"

They discovered a lot that January, with their methodical approach. By early February everything was classified and catalogued for future examination. They did not try and read everything but every so often something would claim their attention.

"Look at this!" George would cry, flourishing a personal note from Montgomery, or a diary entry that spoke of a diversion to some ancient chateau. The general had obligingly kept two diaries, official and private. From the first they pieced together his movements, the problems he encountered, and how he overcome them. But the second was the treasure as it illustrated his personality in black and white, as if etched on canvas. It showed how he worried for his men, the internal debate that foreshadowed each apparent snap decision, the confidence, the fear, the intense loneliness of command and, ultimately, the determination so necessary for success.

"Yes, that is the man I remember," the elderly professor would proclaim with pride, indicating that he had innately known something of his father.

It was in this way, working solidly together, that they came across the first great discovery. It must be remembered that most of his movements of 1944 and early 1945 were well known. There remained, however, a shadowy area between fact and myth. It had been debated over and over. Numerous historians had formed theories and counter-theories but never proven one way or the other. Until, that is, George stumbled across a torn report on a blustery morning the first week of February. His father was giving his tutorial. The report was hard to read but proved to be a concise summary in his grandfather's own hand of the surrender of the Nazi General Frank Stein.

"So it did happen. It actually happened." The professor's eyes shone with joy when George shared his discovery. No Klondiker could hope for a richer find.

"But why," George wanted to know, "did he never send the report to Montgomery?"

"I don't know, just don't know," the old man replied, thinking deeply. "Something must have prevented him, or caused him to change his mind. The puzzling thing is Stein was dead three days later, killed either by an aide or by his own hand in his tent back in his camp. If he surrendered to my father why was he back behind his own lines shortly afterwards?"

"And why did the aide shoot him in the head, if he did? Or, more interestingly, why did he kill himself?"

"And why was the aide shot that same day without even an attempt at a court martial?

"Did your father ever say anything about it?"

"Not a word. He refused to discuss it and walked out if anybody tried to raise the subject." Something had sealed his lips forever.

"So," George concluded, "we have this report and two untimely deaths. We just have to get to the bottom of it."

"Yes, Sherlock," joked his father, saying suddenly more seriously, "and with the historian once more in the role of detective, rebuilding the painful past one small clue at a time."

A History of the Recent Past

Change sprang from 23rd June 2016. The government of the day had thought fit to promise a referendum on membership of the then European Union. No doubt the government later regretted it for the people won that referendum; that is, the ordinary people won. They did not win by a huge margin but they did win. And nothing would ever be the same again.

Where there is a winner there is also a loser. In this case, the establishment lost. Dazed at first, incredulous because they had never expected to lose. The winners never expected to win and the losers never expected to lose.

But the establishment was not a good loser, far from it. In fact, in some ways they did not lose at all because they did not let the people win. So perhaps they were the winners after all. Perhaps the real campaign only started the moment the result became clear in the early hours of Friday 24th June.

The new campaign took many forms. It was a grand alliance to fight the misguided winners. They had been misled and they were misguided. It is logical, therefore, that, if properly educated as to all the facts and the right way to consider them, they would have voted the other way. Hence the losers set about winning and the winners became the losers.

The establishment had everything going for them: media channels, education, parliament, overseas leaders, international organisations, the civil service, the Bank of England, trade unions, employers' federations, comedians, actors and sportspeople. They were the establishment. They worked the system and made the winners look small, mean-minded and closed off from the world. What enlightened person would ever vote to leave?

They worked together, the different arms of the establishment, in a way they never would before or after. Theirs was a great mission and all other differences had to be put aside. Thus, television presenters launched an avalanche of facts and opinions from every conceivable source. But always the facts and the opinions came down to the same central tenet: the people had voted unwisely and needed to be guided on the true path. But it was never said in naked form, rather always wrapped in a cosmetic of what the people had voted for.

"Brexit means Brexit!" the establishment cried, while working efficiently and quietly to remain.

Thus comedians ridiculed the common man and his 'bigoted, racist' opinions, while the trade unions berated their members for stepping out of line. The Bank of England told us repeatedly that it had to make the best of a bad decision and the pound sterling sunk below the surface until, struggling for breath, it finally drowned and was laid unceremoniously to rest. The establishment welcomed the euro with open arms because it meant a significant step down a one-way street.

And what of the civil service during all this? They had two roles, both unwritten and unsaid, but acted upon with a relentless purpose. The first was to slow down any Brexit possibilities. The second was to hurry the country down that one-way street that led from London to Brussels. And they excelled in efficiency during the eight years that started on 24th June 2016.

And what of the BBC during all this? Well, they led the charge to European subjugation but they termed it 'co-operation' or 'working together'. The very makeup of the BBC made it abhorrent to do anything else. Those at the BBC who saw it differently were in a tiny minority in 2016 and they shrank further, rooted out by lack of promotion and opportunity. Thus in 2020, Directive 20/191 made each national broadcasting service a part of a pan-European organisation, separate but under an umbrella committee that dealt with standards and policy. The unofficial poll amongst BBC employees later that same year registered 100% approval on 94% turnout for a name change from BBC to EBC.

Surely the other television and news and opinion channels spoke up, providing a contrast with the newly named EBC? Some tried, of course, but 20/191 also contained a clause establishing EurComm as the body designed to set standards amongst all media forms. Some went pirate but were hunted down. The big American corporations went along with these changes at first but quickly found that running two of everything was too expensive and they steadily withdrew. They could not afford news for the free world and separate news content for the USE so they contented themselves with the free world.

While the establishment in Britain was shocked, that of Brussels and across the continent felt shaken to the core. Their gravy train was threatened. One of the bankrollers of the EU had voted to leave! It was time for change and that change happened very quickly as it was motivated by fear: if one left, so could others. It was time to close the stable door. It was time to create Fortress Europe.

At first the changes were undetectable. A minor change in balance between the different segments of European government went barely unnoticed but the power of the bureaucrats increased a bar or two, while that of the elected slipped down the scale. A few more quangos followed. Then in October 2018, following a disastrous election the previous year, they played their first big hand. Each subsidiary country was designated a European delegate to sit in Cabinet meetings and be the 'voice of Europe'. A short while later, Bertram Grandee turned up with several aides in a long, snaking line behind him. A life-long European politician, Grandee was an affable overweight man with a smile that hid a calculating mind. He quickly established himself in an expensive town house close to Downing Street, although also claimed a right to use Chequers as and when required. He had an expansive office in the French Embassy, where many European officials were housed, but also a pleasant office in No 10. This was the reality behind the façade of Brexit negotiations.

A Brexit the Establishment never meant to happen.

And the weak government in Britain made their task so much easier. The leave talks spluttered on, hesitant, U-turns most weeks, setbacks, problems to fill each headline.

This was followed three months later by the Directive dictating the creation and approval of political parties, under the guidance of EurPol. From then on the slope of change was dramatically steeper. 2019 saw the creation of the European Police Force, termed in a crude attempt at endearment as EurPo. That same year also saw the first organisation behind a European Army. Directive 18/1254 detailed the conduct of elections and set up EurVote. A useful by-product of this directive was that Dusseldorf, selected to be the HQ of EurVote, became the centre for all ballot paper printing and, hence, control across the EU; a lucrative contract that meant major new investment in printing presses. Then in 2020 there was a simple name change. The European Union became first the Super Union of European States, then for simplicity changed to the United States of Europe.

And with the name change came a relentless drive to subsume national identity within a European nationhood. In 2021 it became illegal in public documents to refer to words such as British or English or Scottish, or Danish for that matter. The following year saw the great taxation reforms, designed for justice and fairness across the USE. Taxation was approved in Brussels but application could always be made for local variation.

The pint was the culprit of 2023, along with miles, yards and every other traditional form of measurement. It sounded ridiculous to hear people talking of someone being 1.82m tall or having a quick half-litre in the local pub. But such was the price of the reckless folly of the British people on 23rd June 2016.

The Financial Transaction Tax was introduced in 2021. It started as a tax of 0.01% of every transaction; share sales, bank loans, foreign currency transactions, futures, metal and commodity trading. The law was set in Brussels, so logically the funds raised went there too, and were used to subsidise communities across the USE. The tax was controlled, however, in keeping with the 'benevolent uncle'-type image the USE was so eager to establish. It could go up but only tenfold and only with the approval of the ECB.

Control only ever went one way and it kept accelerating.

An external observer of these times might also have noticed the subtle drive to pay back the foolhardy that had voted for change. The leadership played a long game. There were some who wanted to wade right in with wholesale change, but wiser heads urged caution. Chief amongst them was an up-and-coming politician called Alois Verdun, A Frenchman by birth but from Alsace-Lorraine, hence fluent in German and with much sensitivity for that great country. He argued clearly and intelligently for the long approach.

"By rushing change you risk losing everything in a great reaction to progress," was one of his favourite sayings. Another was, "Slow change brings certain results." He argued that appropriate treatment of the foolhardy should be stretched over a generation or more and should consist of a thousand, thousand tiny changes, each one too minute to worry about but as a whole building the progress they so wanted to see. Verdun's arguments won the day and he was rewarded in 2019 by being appointed the first ever President of the USE for an initial period of twelve years.

From 2019 Verdun was firmly in charge and the pace of change slowed but certainly did not reverse. In fact, historians later pointed out that the changes remained relentless, but under a subtle cloak of deception, Verdun being utterly determined to make them stick. Hence, while there were plans for all sorts of things, the Queen was decidedly left alone, as was the House of Lords. Rather than tackle sensitive issues, he claimed credit for the magnificent flexibility of the USE in leaving them extant, while making many changes instead to the fundamental structure of what had been British society through changes in education and social policy. It was an approach that Verdun, a vain man, congratulated himself on each night before he went to bed.

The harvest of the British people provided the fuel to keep the experiment going.

2019 was also a sea change in terms of British politics. The Conservative government of Moor collapsed in October when overseas-controlled power generators turned off the lights in Britain. They simply instructed their power stations to halt production of electricity. The lights went off twenty minutes later. The cause? A disagreement over Britain retaining the pound sterling. A common currency was held by the international community to be eminently sensible, as it would complete the fourth great global currency block, with no major or middling economy outside their control. Nobody cared which block they joined, just that they did join. There was talk of joining the dollar block, but geography won out in the end. Within a week there was a new government headed by David Kirkby and the power was back on to light up the plans to convert to the euro. Historians would later debate the turning point and identify several possibilities but, without doubt, one contender was the Conservative flip-flop of 2019, racing into the Euro to get the lights back on.

Another thing all historians would agree is that the eight years from 2016 saw enormous change. It is extraordinary how long periods of relatively light change can be followed or preceded by short periods of complete upheaval. Not just revolutions, but all ferocious change. But then perhaps all change of that nature is, in truth, a revolution. Certainly, if you could find a British citizen willing to go on the record in 2024, they would recognise very little about their lives that seemed continuous with the period prior to 2016. Superficially, no problem; they drank the same coffee, went to the same gyms, read some of the same newspapers (although some had been closed down) and ate similar food, although much more of it was imported as farmland was ploughed up for housing. But go an illegal inch deeper and you would see a very different picture. There were four times the level of rules and a quarter of the possibility of making a change to those rules. There seemed to be a mass, a weight upon the land from some other place. It was called Authority. It was called the Establishment. People quietly, amongst their families and closest friends, said it was Dictatorship, but never out in the streets or shopping malls, where you never knew who might be listening.

President Verdun congratulated himself on one other thing each night. He had spearheaded so much change but always with his precious USE depicted not as aggressor or oppressor but as liberator and saviour, enhancer and guardian. It was the establishment in full throttle and no one could stand in its way. Sometimes, at small private dinner parties, he described his role as avuncular, a kind older relative who guided the young in their best interest. Nobody could argue in his circles because it was against the constitution, ironically negotiated and concluded in the Treaty of London of 2022, which set up EurCon to govern and interpret the treaty.

And it left a mass, a weight upon the land.

From Uncertain Past to Uncertain Present

"Bertie, what's the best way to approach this? It's a bloody mess, that's for sure!" David Kirkby MP, Privy Councillor, First Lord of the Treasury and Leader of the Conservative Party, liked to scatter his sentences with a few bloodies. He slammed the thick burgundy file down on his desk and strode to the drinks cabinet. Did he give the impression of one in charge?

"Have a drink, Bertie, and let's discuss the options. With the elections no more than nine months away we need to be spot on with this one." He poured two whiskies, larger than was sensible, but did they not say Churchill was a heavy drinker?

"Terry Rose will be here any mo, PM, and I've telephoned the Home Office for Morris. He was on his way to open the new Prisoner Rehabilitation Centre at Dunstable; you know the 'New Approach to Crime' initiative we started last year after Directive 23/7654. Anyway, he has sent his deputy in his place. Julia Freeman should love playing billiards with the criminals." Too late, David registered the humour and guffawed appropriately. Big players joked when the chips were down.

And the chips were certainly down for Bertie. It was the worst of luck that had put him with this rabble that called itself a government. But how could he back out now with his whole consultancy business, everything he had worked for, dependent on his relationship with the PM?

"It's not right, Bertie, it's just not right. We had her damn assurance that they would not act without first consulting us. She said that to me personally when we got together last November."

"To be fair," Bertie replied, "it was not her. It was the ruling from the European Court of Human Rights."

"Do you think I don't know that? That bloody ruling is carved in my mind." Kirkby walked to the window, a shot of whisky, then another. A deep breath.

"We've got to work out how to turn this to our advantage. What do you think the attitude of the other parties will be?" That was better; become aware, analyse, then act. They would not find it easy to drag him down.

"The Socialists will welcome it," Bertie Graves replied, both an observer and a player in this unfolding scene. "It's no more than what they tried to do with the Lords in '10. Another year in office and they would have succeeded as well."

"I know that, but the Socialist Labour Party, for all its grand past, is no threat to us today. They are yesterday's men." *Good phrase*, he thought, *punchy*. "It's Blayton and Appleby who worry me. What stance will the Libs take?" A top-up for his glass; Bertie declined.

"They are for Europe all the way down the line."

"Then we must be against it; this ruling, I mean."

"But David, can we afford to fight it? Pick your battles and all that." When Bertie wanted to get through to the PM he employed clichés, they seemed to work. "There is so much happening on that front at the moment; devolution, the old colonies, the Euro-army. We have to choose our ground carefully. That is the whole point behind our approach. We have to be seen to co-operate in order to get the best of a bad job. We cannot afford another ill-chosen confrontation that leads to an embarrassing climb-down, just like the currency fiasco."

"I see what you mean." David shuddered, despite the lingering warmth of the whisky. The currency disaster had put him in office; another such calamity would certainly put someone else in his place. "It will, of course, have to be a cabinet decision. I'll have a meeting called this afternoon."

The rumours were already flying when the cabinet collected together at Downing Street just before two-fifteen that afternoon. A huge knot of journalists filled the space behind the cordons, camera crews crowding out the pavement space. Experts were rushed in: experts on Europe, on the constitution, and on the government. Layer after layer of opinion and discussion filled the air, building suspense as if crafted by a Hollywood screenwriter. But there was no news from the cabinet. Four o'clock came and, with it, the steady descent of darkness. As the temperature fell, the tension rose, as if to compensate. Then five o'clock struck, but still no news. The strain on the faces of the television producers told a story. Would there be anything for the Six O'clock prime news slot? Everything had to be passed by the EurNews first and that could take some time.

Then the door opened and Morris, the heavily-moustached Home Secretary, walked out to the bank of microphones.

"Why no PM?" Several reporters shouted but to no avail.

"Ladies and gentlemen, and you, Bert Hurst." But the joke fell flat; such was the urgent need to get copy in front of the authorities and back to the news desks by six. Morris brushed his moustache and launched into his prepared text.

"As you are aware, the cabinet met this afternoon to consider the latest ruling from the European Court of Human Rights, namely that all forms of non-elected participation at regional and local levels of government constitute a breach of citizens' basic human rights. The cabinet discussion was a lengthy and lively one..."

"Bit like the press briefing, long time coming!" The offending reporter was instantly flanked by two policemen and fell silent.

"And we prepared the following statement." Morris cleared his throat and looked briefly at his audience. He would have to allow a few questions.

"This government laments the ruling by the European Court of Human Rights but recognises its jurisdiction in all matters concerning the status of USE nationals. It believes the decision to be hasty and calls upon all member territories to convene urgently in order to try and resolve this issue in a manner which accords with both the rights of the individual and the long-held and respected traditions of the different regions. Ladies and gentlemen," he continued, folding the paper decisively, as if that could be the end of the matter, "rest assured that at this very moment the Prime Minister is talking with the heads of other USE administrations to convey our concern and press for an immediate delay in the implementation of this decision. In addition, the Home Office is setting up a telephone hotline to reassure the public and to pass on news of developments as they arise. Thank you, everybody." Now the questions.

"What is the legal position in the meantime?"

"Has the Queen been informed? What is her reaction?"

"How far are you going to take this issue?"

"Is the cabinet split?"

"Will the Foreign Secretary resign?" Terry Rose was well known for his opposition to too much Europe, as well as for his personal ambition. David had only included him in the cabinet because Bertie had suggested better to have the enemy within.

Morris endured the questions for a long four minutes, all the time backing towards the door to Downing Street then, thankfully, slipping in.

"How did it go?"

"Tough!"

"Well, we did the best we could." Kirkby was irritated again. "We had to show our displeasure at the ruling while, at the same time, not alienating our partners. Bertie's right on that score."

"Did you get hold of the other governments?" Morris asked.

"We are still trying. Berlin's a devil to get through to. Ah, that might be them calling back now."

"No sir, it is the EBC, asking if you would be prepared to do an interview on the Ten O'clock News."

"Tonight?"

"Yes sir, to be there at 9.15 for make-up and briefing."

"Well, tell them we will get back to them. Where is Bertie?"

At 9.50, David settled himself into the chair. The makeup session had been strangely soothing. He knew they had taken the right road. It would all work out. It was the rational winning over the extreme. And if Terry Rose could not accept that? Well, that was a personal decision, but he, as Prime Minister, could not be diverted by one stubborn and patently ambitious minister.

The lead-up to the interview, a minute and a half of clear and impartial background, made an excellent introduction. Across the table, shuffling sheaves of paper, was that young, friendly chap who had questioned him before during the last election campaign of 2019. What was his name? James Baker? No, it was John Baker. That had been a good time, those far-off days of glory when he had been opposition spokesman on Foreign Affairs under Moor, watching the Labour government, barely two years in office, crumbling before their eyes, splintering into faction after faction, the core retreating to their socialist upbringing. That interview had gone well.

"Prime Minister, it is jolly good of you to take the time to talk with us when everything must be pretty hectic back at Downing Street."

"Yes, well John it is, I mean, no… well it is always a good idea to make time to explain the government's position."

"Quite, Prime Minister. A tricky situation, is it not?"

"Well, things are finely balanced but we have the interests of the people at heart and we're not going to do anything rash. We need clear heads and clear discussion with our European partners."

"I see." His speech was slow, overly thoughtful. Then, like the sudden rattle of a Gatling gun, "Tell me, Prime Minister, exactly what are you going to do?"

"Well, we're going to insist upon an inter-governmental conference to discuss in some detail, I may add…"

"But several of our 'European partners' have said there is no need for such a discussion. To them it is black and white."

"What? What the… I mean who, who said that?" David sat up suddenly.

"Italy, Belgium and Luxembourg, to my knowledge, there may well be others."

"I can't, eh… comment on that, we've received no official communication, I mean, take…"

"Prime Minister, why do you not stand up for your country?" Rapid fire again.

"I am; I mean we are. You have to look at this in the round, taking all views and entering into rational discussion and…"

"And meanwhile, surrender our last vestige of sovereignty? Tell me, have you spoken to the Queen about this?"

"That's a matter for Her Majesty."

"Do you accept the jurisdiction of the European Court of Human Rights?"

"Its jurisdiction: yes. Its rulings: not always."

"Is that not a little childish, Prime Minister? Selective adherence, like selective hearing?" David thought he heard a sweep of laughter ripple across the live audience.

"Let me please explain. We accept the authority…"

"Right, I get that. Now what about the fact that so many European positions are not elected by the people? Can you explain that?"

"Well, as you know full well, Mr Baker, the European Government is controlled by Directive 19/1242 which specifically excludes the jurisdiction of the whole EurCourt system. That means…"

"That means one rule for them and one for the rest of us. But let's move on, Prime Minister. Can you explain the position of the Monarchy when this ruling is put into effect?"

"That is a hypothetical question. At this stage everything is open to negotiation."

"I understand that so I only expect a hypothetical answer."

"I cannot give you a direct answer right now as that would… compromise our negotiating position. I can't and won't indulge my time in looking into every possible outcome. Suffice it…"

"On the contrary, I would have thought a debate on all the implications of this remarkable ruling quite essential. Maybe we will get that from our next guest. Thank you, Prime Minister."

David mumbled his thanks and made to shake the interviewer's hand but he had swung his chair around and was already on the next introduction. David had been dismissed.

The days that followed, the early days of February 2024, were confused and directionless, or rather multi-directional, with each one conflicting with the last. A conference was talked about, then plans were made to tack it on the next meeting of heads of government in April, but this quickly degenerated into a squabble over the agenda. Morris, the Home Secretary, flew tirelessly around Europe, desperately seeking support where support did not exist. And the rumours continued to spread. The Queen had abdicated: quickly denied. The PM had resigned: hotly refuted. The Prime Minister had been invited to Berlin, then on to Paris, one of the more enduring rumours but eventually strangled by inactivity. Amidst it all the government wavered, first a show of defiance, then quick reconsideration leading to retreat. One spokesperson said 'Yes' while the other said 'No'.

Still, Morris flew on, by sheer persistence, eventually gathering together a bare skeleton of support for the hoped-for conference. But still no definite plans. The editorials clamoured for action, almost any action. The government was a shambles, more concerned with finding someone to blame than finding direction. David Kirkby longed all day for the blessed release of sleep and then could not get to sleep when it came time. His headaches increased alongside his intake of Scotch. Bertie seemed strangely reluctant to air his views.

Into this increasing shambles, Alois Verdun timed his intervention perfectly. The call came on day nine.

"David, my dear friend, I hear you are having some little local difficulty." Between the heavy French accent and the crackle on the line it was impossible to discern the integrity of his address. "May I please find some way to help my dear colleague?"

"Alois, thank God. It's this damned hereditary thing. Quite frankly it's hit a nerve with the electorate and put us in a dreadful mess."

"You deserve better, my best of friends. They are such a fickle lot, are these voters not? I assume you would like to be in a position to announce a postponement of this ruling? Well, I think I may be able to help you there. But David, I must have some things to offer to them in return. This standstill on the Euro Army, for instance?"

Quite suddenly the problem had gone away. Alois Verdun, the business-like USE President, had everything sorted out within a couple of hours. A series of phone calls with European leaders set up a large committee, three participants from each region, to examine the issue and report back in due course.

"David, I would not expect a conclusion from this committee before three years and maybe even longer." The words flowed over the telephone, rich with Gallic warmth, but they could have come to David from Heaven itself. "Of course, in return I had to pledge the complete support of your sector for the Central Armed Forces Directive, which will, as I know you have always been aware, be of enormous benefit in enhancing our European role and influence on a global scale."

"I understand. We were never against the concept in principle, it was just some practical reservations…"

"Don't worry, David. Although implementation is to start immediately it will be a staged, consultative process with many chances to iron out the concerns we all share over this matter. But there is one more thing."

"Oh, yes?"

"Yes, my dear David, it concerns - how shall I put it? - the other main stumbling block of recent months. That is a good English phrase, is it not? I refer to the question of the remaining colonies. You surely now agree, do you not, David, that the other members of our illustrious union cannot continue to accept the geographical diversification of administrative authority which your unique and special history has endowed on you. This, my friend... no, please wait, David, while I make my point... this, my friend, is a truly historic event in the making and you, David, will be at the very centre of it. Now is not the time to look backwards, clinging to some outmoded theory of empire. We must go into the bright new future uncluttered with the assemblances of the past."

"But please, Alois, what of the Spanish colonies?"

"But David, you know full well that these have already been catered for through the Treaty of Seville. They are independent protectorates of Spain. They ceased to be colonies when the treaty was signed. Likewise, with France."

"But could we not do the same with our colonies? Strictly they are protectorates, anyway."

"David, the time for that has passed. You should have spoken up before Seville. Really, this is why it can be so difficult working with you lot. You are on the sideline all the time and then step onto the field at the last moment and want to be scrum half! There was a time for tolerance of protectorates as a way forward; now times have moved on and they should rightly come under the direct control of Brussels, except Gibraltar of course."

"Why Gib?"

"Well, you know, David, what goes around comes around. Don't cry over spilt milk now, David, let us look to the future, holding hands in our new Europe."

The announcement by the Prime Minister on the Ten O'clock news was presented as a triumph of diplomacy. A hastily installed map of Europe set the background as David Kirkby performed his piece. The concentration, inevitably, was more on the solution that the price paid. Here was an example of a strong government holding out for what it believed in, retaining sight of their objectives during the difficult days of negotiation, the course steady, the hand firm.

"What of the concessions?" Bertie asked, suddenly back in the thick of it.

"There is a price for everything," Kirkby snapped, irritation born of the questioning of his judgment once again. It was so easy to criticise from the touchline. "You see, Bertie," a wave of paternal emotion suddenly affecting his tone, "we achieved what we set out to achieve. In politics it is the impression that counts, the substance is secondary." He felt sure he had heard those words spoken to him at another time, could they have been from Bertie's lips before? Before what? Before he damned well started questioning the PM all the time. He, David Kirkby, was the statesman, not one of these tiresome hangers-on. Had he not just demonstrated his skills to the whole world? Just wait for the Sunday paper opinion polls.

The Hourglass Theory

David Kirkby was spot on. The opinion polls registered an immediate swing, reversing the five percent lead the liberals had held consistently since the month after the last general election. The Sunday papers were full of the deal, nudging opinion a column inch to the right, reflecting a resurgent Conservative party. David wanted to have the *Sunday Times* leader framed for his study at home, bold letters stating 'A Real Leader at Last'. The party machine had been in overdrive, never considering that if they put as much emphasis on policy as presentation they may have some genuine successes to boast about. For inevitably the truth started to eke out by mid-week, although the newspaper leaders followed the European line a little longer, explaining that it was a bold government that embraced reality and made the most of it. And were not the 'colonies' just relics standing in the way of progress? Surely every European Citizen would welcome these noble changes. Yet rumours circulated in a way only rumours can and, despite the ringing endorsements of the mainstream media, the opinion poll lead slipped back into deficit once again.

Only one free handout paper spoke a different story. *The Spider* had long since lost its Public Information Licence, preferring like its publishers to go underground rather than conform to the best standards of journalism directive of 2021.

Gibraltar Give Away

The desperately sad situation is that after 300 years of British participation, the rock can no longer fly the Union Jack. Despite being won in battle and kept by treaty, this unique part of British soil now flies a Spanish flag alongside the hated Union stars. This day should be known throughout history as The Day of Shame. The British Nation should hang their heads low and crouch along like the beaten folk they have become. If you, the British people, read this then consider how far your nation has fallen into subjugation. When they beckon do you really have to run and bend your knee? Can you not for once stand tall as your parents, grandparents and countless generations before them did? And if this is not sufficient to drive you to distraction, think on the miserable lot of the Gibraltarians, their nationality stripped from them by deceit. Yes, the British Government has deceived the British people. And yet there can be no accounting for it.

But the *Spider* print run was not above 30,000 and many were abandoned on the street corners when the police approached. Only a handful of copies made their way to Oxford, but not one to the Unwin-Smith household. If it had, they may not have even noticed it on the hall floor, so closeted were they with their historical discovery. Not that they were cut off from events. They stopped work at ten each night for a whisky and to watch the news, registering it but not taking much in. Their world, the immediate world of 1945, was too close, too exciting and too evolving, to allow much diversion for their combined intellect. Yet diversion was everywhere and eventually succeeded in breaking the hold that the past had on these two, or sometimes the three of them; it seemed often that the old General was there with them, his character gradually becoming known to them.

"George, this is a bloody mess if ever there was one!" the professor exclaimed as the headlines chimed into their sitting room one night. "He is no more fit to lead than I am to head the

General Medical Council!" George had not answered that night, his mind firmly in February 1945.

Yet even George was roused to anger, tinged with the irritation of being dragged back to the present, when three days later the full details of the deal engineered by the French and backed by the rest of Europe emerged in the newspaper he picked up at breakfast.

"This cannot be true! Gibraltar, St Helena, the Falklands, every single remaining overseas territory stripped from us. 'Administrative authority to be transferred to the European Council, Foreign Section, with immediate effect.' And the audacity of the government and the media claiming this to be a resounding victory! Dad, this country is heading in completely the wrong direction. We are surrendering everything we have built up and learned over the years, the decades, the centuries. And what do we get in return? Some sort of shadowy, semi-existence with our identity subsumed into a mass product, the dream of a clutch of Eurocrats."

"Where did I put your soap box?" Professor Unwin-Smith put aside the document he has been reading and looked over at his son. Thirty-one years old, a fine mind, an even finer personality. There was profoundness about him that the father had long recognised and admired. There was an honesty and clarity of his thought patterns. He was like an aristocrat of the intellect, so like his own father who he had known so slightly but whose character was striding out of the documents they studied. Yet there was something else, something missing. It was almost as if George was perfect, yet somehow untried by life. He was a vintage car discovered in a barn, unused since the day it was delivered. What was it exactly?

"What post have you got, son? That looks like a letter from America."

"It is," George replied, expecting a missive from Professor Stuttermann.

"Maybe it's an offer of a job."

"No, not a job, but something quite interesting. It is from the American Society for the Advancement of Liberty."

"What do they want?"

"A lecture tour." George was still reading the letter. "They want me to do a series of six lectures in Washington the week after next: six consecutive nights on the theme of 'Man's role in securing the Future of Freedom'. It seems they think quite highly of my work on the magazine. My God, look at this! They are prepared to pay $5,000 plus all expenses."

"Not bad for a week's work."

"Dad, it is five thousand a night! Thirty thousand in total. But what on earth am I going to say? What words of mine could possibly be worth $30,000?"

"Hey, don't question it if they are prepared to pay! If you intend going, send the acceptance immediately. Then you can spend the time between now and then in preparation. If you hum and hah about it, you will end up not going because you will have not thought what to say."

Although their work over the next week and a half remained centred on General Unwin-Smith, they returned often to the intended theme for the lecture series. Their thoughts often collided, or missed each other completely, yet gradually a consensus emerged.

"Firstly," George's father begun one evening, summing up the progress they had made so far, "it is clear that you cannot give them the same blurb each night. Instead, each lecture needs to build on the previous one, while being capable of standing alone. We need a theme that can progress over the six nights but someone going to one evening will get a full and interesting lecture and not an unfinished work."

"That's fine as far as it goes, Dad, but what is the focus of this grand journey to be? At ninety minutes a night I have to come up with nine hours of enlightened and thought-provoking comment, all of it tied to one central idea. That is a tall order! There are some things I have thought about but nothing yet with that continuity, no thread running through the whole week."

"One central idea," the professor mused, concentration

written deeply on his wrinkled face. "One thread running through it all." So they worked and thought and developed their ideas so that at the end of ten days they had something. It was good, they both knew that, but it could be better and that irked them.

"We still haven't hit on the perfect central theme," the professor said one evening, throwing himself into his favourite armchair with a sigh. The flight was booked for the day after the next. "Let's go back over it one more time. What is it that we are trying to say?"

"That every individual can and should own their future, that it is the responsibility of every individual to own it and that an understanding of the future is achieved by looking into the past."

"Correct! Now, we will go over each section."

And so they did. Each word was analysed in turn, the frustration mounting as they approached the end of George's statement.

"Finally, 'looking into the past', well that is history, pure and simple."

"History... History... How History helps us to own our future. That is what it's all about, isn't it? That was the whole purpose of the magazine. It has been staring us in the face all the time! We have been so damn caught up in complicated theories and the blindingly obvious has been there all the time! By God, George, I think we may have it!" The professor rose, disappeared into kitchen, and returned a minute later with an old hourglass.

"Look at this hourglass, George, it says it all. The sand runs from top to bottom in a continuous stream. It ends after a while because the glass is small, made with a particular purpose in mind. Now, imagine an hourglass on an enormous scale, a scale befitting the size of the universe. The sand runs on and on, for all practical purposes it has always been running and always will. Now, the narrow waist is the present. The top half is the future, the bottom half the past. What is it that first strikes you, George?"

"The relationship between top and bottom. The same sand sits in each half, it is just a matter of time that determines whether the sand is in the past or the future."

"Exactly, so here we are sitting at the waist and we want to do the best things for the future but cannot see what is to come. So where do we look for help in making those decisions?"

"Logically into the top half," George replied, picking up quickly on the beautiful simplicity of the theory. "Except that we cannot look up directly into the future, only down into the past."

"But it does not matter. The past is no more than the future of yesterday."

"That is fine, Dad, as far as it goes, but isn't it little more than the old cliché about history repeating itself? It would fill the first evening but not the next five."

"George, that is easy. You develop the theory in stages. Why is it that the future equals the past? Because it is the past that has formed us and it is our decisions about what actions we take in the present that influence the future. Those decisions are made because of the sum of what we are from our past. Thus taking man out of the mix it is the past that forms the future."

"Provided people are true to their past."

"Exactly! The next stage of the theory and really the essence of everything you should be trying to say. Only by being honest about the past can man hope to own his future. When one disowns the past, or tries to cut it away, then the difficulties arise: the dictatorships and the genocides. It is similar to the thoughts we have had about the influence of parents. If, for whatever reason, that influence is not there or is distorted in some way then the chain from past to future is broken. Man is the sum of what went before him. It follows, therefore, that the future is the sum of the past and man's actions in the present."

"So he is adding his life, his contribution to the chain that extends from the earliest days."

"That is right, my boy, and hopefully the chain will continue on into the future."

"So, if individual chains can be broken by the premature

death of a parent then the equivalent for society is a revolution."

"You have to be careful there, George. You do not want to be dismissed as an advocate of no change. This is not about change. Change has happened in the past and it will always go on. This is about honesty, clarity and direction; responsibility, even."

"Or in other words; ownership. But what I meant was not out of line with your thinking. What about all this nonsense over Europe, for instance? The continual retreat from the way things have been? The abandonment of traditions? The transfer of power to an artificially contrived authority based in another bloody country? Surely what all this amounts to is a deliberate attempt to remove a number of highly developed and individualistic societies away from their past and straitjacket them into a future that has no past attached to it? Like this." George picked up the hourglass and neatly snapped it in two at the waist. "A past with no future and a future with no past."

"I think you have just happened upon the theme of lecture number six, George. Only honesty about the past can make for the right decisions in the present and only the right decisions in the present can bring about a future consistent with who and what we are. I knew we would get there. By Jove, George, I think we are in business!"

A Week in Washington

A week in Washington: the coldest week of the coldest winter in living memory. Snowfalls measured by the yard, competing with each other for a place in the record books. Sub-zero Fahrenheit in the early dawn, climbing to low teens at best; icicles spurting off icicles, vast areas of virgin snow with most people staying warm indoors. Most television sets tuned to the Weather Channel, forming a backdrop of constant reporting on the cold, like background music in a mall. Ice-cold but very, very still, no wind to blow the weather away, Europe-bound, across the warming ocean, not even enough to whip up a haze of fluff from the ever-harder packed snow.

George, travelling alone, First Class, is met at the airport. She is obviously intelligent, with an open face and eyes that bounce with the vitality of ideas. She is beautiful, with the richest, darkest hair he has ever seen, falling way beyond the shoulders, no doubt, were it not tied firmly and clasped at the sides and back. She is friendly with a smile and immediate conversation, uncluttered, fresh and warm. Yet she is formal, dressed in a dark suit and white blouse. She is, so she informs him as she offers a slender, olive hand, his personal host for the duration of his stay. How American! How pleasant!

Her badge gives George the vital information:

Miss G. Matthews
Deputy VP: International Affairs
ASAL

But George prefers her version:

"Hi, I'm Gerry Matthews. I'm gonna be your personal host while you're visiting with us. Did you have a good flight, Mr Unwin-Smith?"

"Yes, thank you. Please call me George."

The remarkable, fascinating thing about Gerry Matthews, George discovered within the first day of their acquaintance, was that she was a complete person. She was more than educated, having that rare quality of fullness or natural wisdom about her. He sensed it superficially in their first hour together, taxi to the hotel, the drink before a light supper. Then over the next two hours, while they sat across the table and let the conversation roam, his airline-tired mind trying to stay up somewhere at her altitude but usually diving back to a crash-land, he learned of the depth to her character, the substance behind her thoughts, the gentility with which she held her intellect. A good education is just a start.

"My father always believed that every person has a destiny which was mirrored by their potential," she explained, encouraged by his interest. "The secret to success in life is to understand that potential, the strengths, the limitations and the possibilities. A proper understanding and honesty about it will naturally lead to one's intended path."

"It sounds like the theory of pre-determined destiny, everything mapped out ions ago!" he commented, half joking, but keen for her to continue talking. He was coming to love the way she used her hands to act out her story; sometimes delicate and subtle, often with considerable enthusiasm so that she brushed against her wine glass several times, more than once making it wobble precariously before settling back on the starched white table cloth, a deep red stain spreading from the stem.

"No, no!" She laughed. "Not predetermination at all. Predetermination is set before the person reaches rational thought and adult behaviour. It has nothing to do with finding one's way and making choices as an adult. Perhaps destiny is not the right word. I think he meant that everyone is a complete individual and has a number of paths to go down, some are right for that person, some are wrong but could be right for others. It is the duty of every individual to find a path that adds to their success, their enjoyment, and the common good. That way everything you do is pointed in the right direction. You feel at ease with what you do. Sometimes you see this in its extreme – you meet someone and what he or she does in life just seems to be a natural extension of what they are. Then there is no delineation between work and relaxation, career and home. They just are."

"My father," George said, suddenly realising this to be the case.

"Really? I think my grandfather too found it eventually but not at first."

"Tell me about him," George said.

"No, you tell me about yours first," she replied. Then they had a minute and a half on 'No, I asked first' and 'You are the guest, you should go first', until, with a grin, Gerry gave way.

"My grandfather, my mother's father, was an ordinary storekeeper from Kansas. When he was young it seemed like his future was going to be a settled life in small-town America. But thousands of miles to the east Adolf Hitler had other ideas. He was consolidating his position in a country and a continent that might have meant nothing to Kansans. But then the letter came. It was an open letter from the newly-formed Society for the Advancement of Liberty, set up in the mid-thirties to try and rescue as many Jews from the Nazis as possible. Reverend Peters read it out in Church in place of his sermon and Grandpa's life was never the same again."

Gerry paused for a sip of wine and to collect her thoughts.

"Three hundred forty-nine Jews were rescued by him between that date in 1938 and the outbreak of war in Europe eighteen months later. Six times he travelled to Europe, mortgaging his store and begging for donations from all sources. Six times he met top Nazi officials, attracted by his jingling pockets. Six times he haggled and bargained for the lives of a few more Jews. You can imagine the corruption with every official out to make a packet."

"And he brought them all back here?"

"Every one of them, except a baby who died in transit. Three hundred forty-eight settled in Fairlow, Kansas, his hometown, where he pleaded for houses to be built at cost and begged for jobs for all who could work. Many of them are still there, many still live on Morrison Street, the road they named for him. The townspeople called the whole thing 'Morrison's New Deal' to differentiate it from Roosevelt's of the same name!"

"What was his full name?" George asked, the historian coming out. He would look him up later.

"Gerald B. Morrison."

"Were you named after him?"

"I was. I am his only grandchild. But in many ways he had hundreds of children. He gave his whole life to those poor refugees, snatched from the evil clutches of envy and hatred. I remember him in his nineties, still arguing in the town council for a scholarship for his Jews." She paused for more wine then continued, as if moving to another level of frankness. "It was his story that made me determined to do what I do. It was the Society that started him off and it is through the Society that I want to continue his work."

"I understand," George replied, his tired mind seeing the ragged bunch of refugees arriving at the Church Hall and a young spindle of a man with a clipboard and pencil at his ear, making arrangements for whom they should all stay with. He saw the despair of the refugees turning so neatly to hope and security because one man had followed his destiny.

"Gerry, I think you should be giving these lectures, not me. That is quite a story!"

"Nonsense, George, everyone is itching to hear you. But you must be tired. What would you like to do tomorrow and what

72

time shall I call? I thought you might like to do some sightseeing. There is a function tomorrow night after your lecture so you can meet some of the other members then. That leaves the day pretty free." Was there a smile behind her eyes as she said this?

"Sightseeing sounds great. Shall we say about ten?"

"Fine, ten it is. Goodnight and thanks for being such a good listener." They shook hands politely and Gerry was gone.

George sat on with a whisky, thinking lazily of her father's theory and her grandfather's story, thinking also of her and how she was.

The Hourglass Lectures, as they quickly became known, were an instant success. They delivered a message on two different planes: society and the individual. But the two planes crossed over continually, aircraft doing acrobatics in the sky, their coloured smoke trains mixing over and over again to build up a picture on a splendid scale. The early lectures in the series just hinted at the themes, streaks of pure reasoning gradually standing out from a cloud of generality. But from the beginning the suggestion of insight was there, capturing the audience's attention and taking them on the journey with him. The critics described it as a great piece of spoken literature, mixing carefully thought-out ideas with the inspiration of a poet. This was certainly something to remember.

"Real good work, George." The President had slapped him forcibly on the back at the first-night reception, perhaps sensing the direction George was to take or perhaps just predicting an entertaining series of speeches. "It's a pleasure, George, a real pleasure, to have you here with us this week." He raised his glass and knocked it hard against George's as he spoke. A strange man, well into his seventies, with the appearance of another age, as if dropped by mistake from the early twentieth century. He had more hair than George, despite his age, and looked like a hard Texan rancher, but apparently had grown up in Rhode Island and never been beyond the Mississippi.

"Thank you, Mr Pearson, it is a great honour to be here."

"Call me Ted, George, and the honour is all ours. Here, let me introduce you to some of the folks. I hope Miss Matthews has been taking good care of you."

"Very good care, thank you. She is a marvellous and engaging companion."

"Excellent, excellent! We're real lucky to have her on the staff. Now, here we have Alfred Horrington, our Secretary, and this is Josh Peters, about whom you have probably heard..."

George met many people in his week in Washington, probably several hundred in total, most of them deeply committed to the cause of freedom. Many had particular concerns and favourite issues; the right to speak your mind, personal information in the computer age, the implications of European federalism, the right of man to organise as he sees fit, even the right of man to be disorganised and to embrace chaos. Theories and causes ranged from deeply conventional to wild, the intellect stoking them from average to brilliant. George was pressed into speaking in debates and discussions every day. In fact, it rivalled even the height of his editing days at the magazine for involvement in pure intellectual pioneering but always with a practical bent, Gerry's grandfather's story reminding him that even intellect has a master and that master should be the common good. He often found himself centre-floor, arguing with an abandonment that created pure joy yet barely aware of the profound developments within him.

It is strange how one person can change steadily all their life long while another will seem unchanging for decades only to suddenly alter beyond recognition in a heartbeat.

The theme hatched in the Oxford sitting room had become something far greater, and with far greater implications for all involved, than George and his father had ever imagined.

"Ladies and gentlemen, I think it hardly necessary to draw your attention to the marvellous insights we have witnessed this week thanks to the generosity of Mr Unwin-Smith," Mr. Pearson summed up on the last day. "I have been a member of the Society for over fifty years, since long before some of you were born!" That always got a polite laugh. "I can safely say that in looking back over that half-century that never before has one individual inspired our movement so emphatically and clearly. As we face many uncertainties over the decades to come, I know you will all remember the themes and the delivery of this week and it will sustain and nourish you as we press the cause of liberty ever forward." Here he paused, perhaps sensing that his own contribution was reaching a climax; looking slowly around the room he took the microphone in one hand and read from his notes. "Remember always the words verbatim from George himself: 'Just as man needs society as his link with the present, so he needs history as his link with the past. Look into that past; really understand it, for there you shall find your model, your blueprint, for the future. We are a product of what went before us. Just as we must be honest with ourselves so we must be honest with our past, for it is our past that becomes us and governs us.'"

"Ladies and gentlemen," the stiff-backed old chairman got ready for his final words, "it only remains for me to express regret that we had to trawl abroad for such a fine mind and to thank Mr Unwin-Smith for a truly fantastic experience."

It was over. The next day came with no change in the weather and no sign of change on the horizon. The capital city seemed locked in ice. The delayed flight gave George and Gerry, barely alone together since the first evening and subsequent rapid tour of the city, a few moments in the half-deserted airport building at Dulles. Words after so many and so much excitement seemed hard to come by.

"What are you going to do now?" she asked, fingering her scarf and allowing only an occasional glance up from the Formica table-top.

'I don't know." Then, after an awkward silence. "Gerry you know what you said the first night about your father and his ideas?"

"Oh my God!" She laughed. "To think I thought his grand theory might impress you!"

"It did. No, I mean it. It helped with some of my thinking. Listen, Gerry, remember what you said about being in tune with your potential and so on? Well, I feel that I am almost there but something is still missing, one link missing."

"George," she spoke just as the flight was announced on the Tannoy, "you were completely there, nothing missing. All this week you have been living proof of the old man's theory." Then, as he stood up to go. "Just believe in yourself and trust in the future. Live your theory and everything will work out for you. I know it will."

"But I don't see how. I am motivated to do something but I keep trying things and they are good but not enough. Take *The History of the Future*, for example. Many people would consider that a dream job. It was a dream job! But it wasn't enough. I can't explain it."

"George, follow your instinct. Let yourself be guided by the heart, by gut feeling, rather than analysing everything. Instinct rather than intellect is what you need. What about that crowd you told me about – the Preservation Society?"

"But what sort of job would that be?"

"What sort of job was it for a storekeeper to go to Germany and rescue Jews? Those were real strange times and these are real strange times, too. You need to think outside the box. Frankly, it seems to me that you are just waiting for the next nice, interesting offer to come along. Life does not work like that. You have to make choices and live with those decisions. Think about commitment."

"Wow! I feel suitably chastised! But seriously, thanks, Gerry, thanks for everything. I have really enjoyed this week."

"Listen to the expert!" She joked, but now with her dark, shining eyes fixed firmly on his, "Here I am, trying to tell you what to do when you've come three thousand miles to a veritable freezer to do just that for us! Good luck, George, it has been great…"

"Goodbye and thanks." They almost kissed.

"Goodbye." Softly spoken, so quietly, but George would never forget it.

George slept superbly on the aeroplane, the comfort of First Class engulfing him. He was exhausted from the rigorous debate and interchange of the last week. The time on board was time for everything to sink in, settling to form a natural perspective. Seven hours of continuous lulling motion in first class seclusion gave him the rhythm he needed. He had one whisky after take-off, rinsing it slowly around his mouth to savour every drop, and then slept soundly until the descent into Heathrow.

A quick few taps on the phone as soon as he was allowed to switch it on and he had the information he needed to dial the number. There had been no conscious decision, it just happened.

"Hello, could I speak to Mark Borden, please?"

"Just a mo, I will get him. Mark? Call for you." That was Mandy, he was sure.

"This is Mark Borden."

"Hi Mark, it is George… Unwin-Smith."

"Hello, George. Are you calling from Washington?" It was almost as if Mark had been expecting him to call. But that was not possible.

"No, Heathrow, just got in. Look, can we meet this morning? I'll come to your place if that is convenient. I know it is early but this is important."

"Don't worry, do come. It is 14, Leicester Gardens. The nearest tube is Paddington. I'll see you in an hour." Mark put down the receiver and smiled at Mandy in her pyjamas. "Mandy, that was George. He is coming here this morning."

The Future Perfect

" A new political party?"

"Exactly. We shall have to move quickly to build up a position by the October elections."

"But George, I mean it is a great idea but can it be done? The approval process and everything and we have so few resources."

"Approval process?" This was new to George.

"Yes," Mark replied, "surely you are familiar with the Political Participation Directive 2019?" George's blank stare led Mark to continue. "Every prospective political party, or any movement like a trade union or a pressure group, requires a licence. To get a licence you need to go through an examination process with the office of the Commissioner of Political Relations, otherwise known as EurPol."

"So we do that."

"George, it takes years. It took us two and a half years and we are a stated apolitical group. Besides, to become a proper political party you have to ascribe to the values and principles of the USE."

"Wow, I had no idea."

"Don't you remember the by-election in 2019? The last time UKIP stood? They were shut out of the election and their votes were disqualified. They actually won that vote but the Conservatives got in."

"But it was never reported that way. I remember the television coverage at the time. They just showed the Conservative victor."

"George, because nothing can be reported that is contrary to the principles and beliefs of the USE. That was the Public Information..."

"Directive!" George added his voice to Mark's, suddenly understanding what he was up against. He was a product of the system, whereas Mark and Mandy lived just outside it. He knew all about the Public Information Directive, it was the regulation that had so often stopped him from publishing what he wanted to publish at *The History of the Future*. At the time it had been an irritation, but then he had not met Mark and Mandy, or Gerry. Now it was different. There was silence for a moment as George jumped through the possibilities. Finally, he said slowly, "We will just do it anyway. We will create a movement that will turn the world on its head. We will win the moral argument."

"I have a better idea." Mandy stood up, as she so often did when she spoke. "We don't create a political party at all."

"What?"

"We don't create a political party because a political party has to be approved by the USE and they will never approve our party. So we don't create one."

"Then how?"

"Easy, if we are not a political party, not an organisation of any sort, we cannot be disapproved. We can be a grouping of 'like-minded fellows' or a discussion group. We can be anything provided we are not an organisation that requires approval."

"Yes, of course!" George's face was alight with excitement. "And then when we win the moral argument, we can demand a change in the rules because the people will back us."

"Exactly, so all those in favour of NOT forming a new political party, raise your hands!"

Mandy's proposal was audacity itself. But as George and Mark listened to the developing plan they too felt a certainty.

"You have an organisation." George started. "How many members?"

"Over 8,000." Mandy replied.

"But it used to be treble that," Mark added.

"So it is not what it once was, but it is a start. How many of those are committed members? How many can we count on to support us?

"Two thirds at least." Mandy spoke again, the words starting to rush down the hillside, bouncing against the steep banks. "You saw the numbers at Westminster Square. That was just one cell and they all got arrested. Twenty-four of us spent thirty days in prison for that." George had not known about the sentences, closeted as he had been in his Oxford sanctuary, immersed in the project to discover his grandfather. "We have our share of commitment, George."

Then Mark spoke. "George, we followed the Hourglass Lectures on the internet. We could get them although the connection was not good. They were not reported here, of course. George, you see the USE as a surrender of history, just like a common dictatorship only far subtler, but just as sinister in many ways. You see it as a wholesale turning away from our history and our traditions and from our liberty as a result. Well, we are just the same, a little less history and a little more tradition, but we are splitting hairs. We broadcast the Hourglass Lectures to our organisation and, yes, we broke the copyright rules as well as the broadcasting rules, but for a higher cause! It fitted our philosophy exactly. Not every member will go the whole way with us but I agree that most will. We are your bedrock, your disciples, your followers."

I bet you are, thought George, reflecting again on how solid Mark was, how permanent, how like a rock. He should have been named Peter.

"But we need a lot of organisation to not get a new party going! Seriously, we need to do it properly," Mandy offered. "We need officers, a constitution, some rules… yes, I know, but seriously we do need them! And nothing in writing, nothing that can lead them to a new political party."

The rest of the windswept February day was spent in Mark's flat, making plans and discussing ideas. They brought in Chinese mid-afternoon, George amazed to see that they were both rabid carnivores, tugging energetically at the spare ribs. He has expected them both to be vegans, or at least vegetarians. They completely dispelled that myth when at close to midnight Mark cooked bacon, eggs and sausages, which were gritty and burned as if cooked on a campfire. They drank bottles of beer, George nipping down to the off licence to get some more. As he turned the corner he felt the wind and wrapped his coat around himself. He suddenly thought that he was stepping out into the cold and who knew when or where he would next find a warm shelter. This was going to be very different to working with his father in front of the roaring fire.

They argued a lot, differing on many aspects, but at Mark's insistence, voting on each point and sticking firmly to the consensus, even when he was the loser. Although George was from the start their nominated leader, he felt it was Mark who was the chairman of their meeting and the true leader. Towards the end of their midnight meal he raised this point: "Mark and Mandy, hear me out a moment. We have been discussing things for well over twelve hours now. Well, one thing is clear. Mark, you are the leader of this new organisation, not me."

"No way."

"Mark, you cannot deny it. You are the natural leader."

"But George, you are so well known, you will attract attention that we cannot hope to achieve. We need you."

"And you will have me, no doubt about that. I will be the spokesperson if you like but you need to be the leader." When Mark continued to shake his head, George added, "We will put it to the vote. All those in favour of Mark Borden Esq. being the leader of the 'movement that is not' raise your hands." Mandy's hand shot up and held rigid in the air, as if the force and magnificence of her effort added weight to the argument. Mark was outvoted and was now the leader.

They settled on Mark as Chairman, George as Director of Policy and Publicity, and Mandy as Deputy Chairman and Spokesperson on the Environment. Nothing in writing and all unofficial.

"We have a lot to sort out, that much is clear!" George stood up from the kitchen table and stretched. "This is the first time in my life I've felt totally in tune with a purpose." He thought of Gerry, back in Washington. Everything seemed to fit.

They talked on into the early hours about Europe, sovereignty, local democracy, the environment, education, policing, and touched on many more subjects. "The theme is emerging," George concluded. "Choice because we have always chosen, democracy because it is deeply rooted in all of us, as old as the hills." George looked at the tall, craggy Mark, their democratic leader. This was going to be something good.

After a short sleep on their sofa, George made his way back to Oxford in the morning. It was late February, suddenly warm for the time of year, so there was a spring-effect everywhere, people sitting on doorsteps or lounging against railings, talking to neighbours. Even the policemen smiled on their rounds, their white teeth visible behind their helmet faceplates. They seemed to be everywhere, making George wonder whether he had missed some big alert or a visiting dignitary from the USE. He felt the sun as he walked the short distance to Paddington for the Oxford train. It was heartening to feel it penetrate the overcoat he had taken to Washington and spread through his back muscles, which were slightly aching from two nights on makeshift beds. Gone was the damp, windy cold of the first night he had spent with Mark and Mandy last November. Gone, too, was the so very still cold of Washington, so cold that nothing seemed to move; a silent cold which belied the debate and discussion that had filled the week. Mark had told him that the Hourglass Lectures had not featured in Britain, not even been reported on. As far as the authorities were concerned the lecture series had not existed: history was already being rewritten just days after the event in question. Mark, Mandy and a clutch of the faithful had had to listen to George on an unlicensed, distorted internet site, risking another thirty days.

Knowing he had a bit of time before his train, George lingered to watch a family: father, mother and two teenage children, joking and pushing each other as they walked down the street. They carried bundles of brochures, perhaps advertising a sale in one of the chain stores? Yet they were held beneath coats folded over their arms. Why hide them? They were coming closer and now George could see that most people hurried past, only a few taking the brochures and then quickly pocketing them for future review or because, perhaps, they had taken them by mistake and wished they had not. As they came closer, George became determined to take a brochure. He crossed the street, feigning his sudden change of direction on being lost by looking at the blank screen of his phone and then looking at the street names. Something told him not to approach this family directly. He reached the pavement and stopped, again looking at his phone just as the father came up to him.

"Here you are, my friend," he said, pushing a cheaply printed newspaper towards him. "Keep it out of sight but make sure you read it. It is worth a bloody read, mate." George sought the face first. A livid scar ran down the left side, joining eyebrow to lips and onto the chin. It was a captivating sight, no doubt with a story behind it. George was suddenly reminded of Jessica Stuttermann and the jagged scar on her leg. He badly wanted to ask this stranger for his story, but knew he could not. Instead he glanced down and saw a copy of *The Spider* in his hands. His first instinct, like the others, was to thrust it deep within his clothes. But he was not ready to let the man move on yet.

"Thanks, how do I get in touch?" He heard someone talking. It sounded like him but seemed to be someone else. He felt sweat springing up everywhere, suddenly making his shirt uncomfortable and clammy, where just moments before he had been relaxed and at ease. Yet his throat was as dry as the desert. His peripheral vision located a police patrol moving up the street, taking an inordinate interest in the people on his side of the road, the side the family had moved up as they passed out the leaflets.

"Do the crossword, friend, we need to move on. Watch out for yourself." George shoved the newspaper under the coat he carried on his arm, unconsciously mimicking both the donor family and the other recipients all around him. He started to say something but the family had moved on. He watched them for a minute as they worked their way down the street. Now he realised that their jollity was a cover – they were probably not even a true family.

"They causing you any problems, sir?" It was a policeman; dark glasses, stacked belt of equipment, standard helmet, no smile. He raised his phone and clicked on George, twice. George felt a shiver despite the sun as he faced authority.

"No, not at all," he replied quickly. "Just advertising some sale or something. I didn't take a copy because I don't live around here."

"Papers please, sir."

"What?"

"ID, sir, papers. sir, document what identifies you as who you are, sir, usually located in the wallet often found in a pocket, sir."

George handed over his ID after fumbling it from his wallet. The policeman looked at him carefully, sensing his fear. He scanned it back and front with a device from his belt, then looked at the picture carefully before returning it.

"Did you see what it was, Mr Unwin-Smith, sir? We have had reports of unlicensed material being distributed around here, nasty stuff by all accounts. We don't want that do we, sir?"

"No, Officer, I did not take in what it was. I have a train to catch so I need to run."

"Run along then, sir. And don't worry, we will catch them." When, George wondered as he re-crossed the street for the entrance to Paddington, did the police start getting so damn cocky with the general public? And when had they started taking photographs on their phones? His heart was beating like pistons, the engine at full throttle. Was this what his life was to be like now?

The crossword took George from Paddington to Reading, not to complete it, but to work out what the man had meant. He soon realised that the answers were very easy and irrelevant but the clues held the answer, in that their numbers gave a few sensible sequences of mobile phone numbers. As George was alone in the First Class carriage, courtesy of the American Society for the Promotion of Liberty, he got out his phone and called several variants of the number, reaching first an old lady then a recorded message from a youngster singing a rap song as his greeting. Third time he got a quiet, serious voice saying just one word: "Hello."

"I did the crossword." George said.

"Name, please."

"George Unwin-Smith." Now he was committed. Now who could tell what the future would bring? It was one thing to make plans, quite another to enact them. Sitting in his comfortable First Class carriage, George felt a chill at the clandestine turn of events. He thought about the policeman who had questioned him and reality hit him hard. He was an intellectual stepping out into a dangerous world where anything could happen.

"Not *the*?"

"Yes, it is. I want to talk to someone."

"Someone will call you." The phone went dead.

Someone did call just as the train left Didcot.

"George?"

"Yes," he almost whispered the word despite being entirely alone in the carriage.

"Memorise the number I am about to give you and call when you are entirely on your own. Don't ever call the crossword number again. Understand?"

"Yes, I understand." George was staring at danger. But danger somehow makes everything clearer and decisions, after the first one, more automatic. How would he react when he really faced danger?

George had a short bus ride from the station to his father's house but instead he walked and rang the number the moment the crowds were left behind.

"Yes."

"This is George Unwin-Smith. I was told to…"

"Are you alone? Can't be overheard?"

"I am alone and on my own."

"Good, I'll put you through."

The phone went silent for a brief moment and then a brusque voice, foreign accent, came on the line.

"George, let's get to the essentials quickly. This is Francine L'Amour. I am very pleased to hear from you, delighted in fact." George drew in his breath as the rich Gallic tones reached his ears and made him look around for fear of being overheard. Could it be the old leader of the Spiders on the phone with him? But that was impossible.

"But I thought you were killed."

"That was propaganda, my dear man. I had to go underground along with the rest of the Spiders. Then the USE put it out that a splinter faction of our group had me killed back in '19. They tried to make it seem like bitter infighting to discredit us further."

George and Francine talked for over thirty minutes, with George walking on past his family home up to the parade of shops at the end of the road twice before the conversation finally was brought to a close. George had launched into his plans and his motivation and found Francine L'Amour quick to pick up on everything.

George had a hundred yards back down the road after the phone call finished. He walked slowly. Each step along that hundred yards seemed to him to be a step he was taking into his own future. It was fraught with danger and he was very scared. This was like nothing he had ever done before; everything else had followed on one step after the other in a natural rhythm. Now he was breaking from the past, defying his own hourglass theory.

It was George who named the new movement later that night. He called Mark and Mandy and got their agreement for the Future Perfect.

The Funding Review

"Tax cuts," said David, "we need tax cuts."

"But Prime Minster, without corresponding reductions in public spending…"

"Tax cuts are the answer. Whatever the polls say, we know from experience that the majority really want cash in their pockets, whatever they say."

"It seems as if we have become the party of whatever the majority wants." That was Dennis Shepherd. The clamour to be heard suddenly died away, everyone turning to face the white-haired Minister of the Environment. He continued into the silence. "Perhaps we'd get more respect if we stood for some principles. Sometimes I think it does not matter what we stand for as long as we have some principle somewhere. We could state that every lamp-post in the country has to be painted pink provided we do not say a week later that they should all be orange." That frivolity was his mistake.

"Dennis, if all you are going to spout is nothing but facetious trivialities it might be better to keep your thoughts to yourself."

Terry Rose never missed an opportunity to put Dennis Shepherd down. But then aggression was his trademark. Everybody knew that.

"So we are agreed, by and large, that tax cuts are the answer?" David tried to restore order. "The next questions are which tax should we cut, how much to lop off, and, of course, how we should pay for it. Peter, it is your floor, lead us on."

The Chancellor of the Exchequer rose to his feet, thought better of standing, and sat back down again.

"Well, as you know, things are not looking too good. Under the EurRegs on Government Debt Ceilings, we are maxed out on borrowing. The tax cut will need to be substantial so we have to mirror it with substantial cuts somewhere else. That is not going to be easy or popular. I've prepared a paper that I will hand out in a moment. The other question of which tax we cut is quite simple. EurRegs state we can make reasonable changes to any rate of tax except the following taxes: VAT, excise duties, social security contributions and corporation tax. I suggest income tax..."

"Don't we need approval?"

"Yes, the Standing Taxation Committee of EurPol will need to screen all proposals first and they could forward it to the ECB in Dusseldorf if they suspect the numbers do not add up. Of course it helps to be seen to co-operate in other areas."

"So Peter, just remind us, what would each euro cent in cut cost us?"

"About ten billion, Terry, but to be effective we should be thinking of two or three cents."

"OK, let's work on the need to find thirty billion. All agreed? I know you are not happy, Dennis, but then when are you? Pass out the paper, Peter."

"We'll make a final decision at the next cabinet meeting and announce the tax cuts before Whitsun. Peter, can you get them through the various approvals by then?"

"Like I said, PM, it all depends what we can give them in return. "

"What is topical?" David asked. What, he wondered, did he really think of his Chancellor of the Exchequer? He was young for the job, wavy blond hair showing no signs of whitening. He seemed uncertain of himself yet had a brilliant mind, almost too clever. If anybody could get these tax cuts through to final approval it was Peter Burrows with his bleached, pudgy young face sitting so oddly above the bold shirt stripes, a mass of vertical tramlines ending abruptly at a destination nobody needed to visit.

"Well, refugees, for one."

"You mean we take more in exchange for permission to reduce our own taxes a few percentage points?" Dennis could not help himself interrupting.

"A hundred thousand will do it." Peter sounded like he had done the deal already. "That is a drop in the ocean."

"But Peter, we are going to be cutting health, social services, education, transport. These are all full to overflowing with demand and we will be cutting funding and imposing another 'hundred thousand will do it' on top?"

"PM, I will jump on it." Peter calculated that Dennis was best ignored. You can beat a radical by not hearing their arguments. And it was not as if he had to persuade the others. They were already in the tax cut camp.

"Right," resumed David Kirkby, secretly envying Peter's effective put-down, "that is the morning's business completed. Remember, all members of the Security Committee of the Cabinet, that we have a special meeting on Tuesday morning to discuss the antics of Unwin-Smith. Thanks, everyone. Oh, Dennis, could you stay behind a mo?" This was not going to be easy. But Terry Rose, for all his obnoxiousness, was right on this. Dennis was out of line and had been for some time. And it was his job as PM and leader of the Conservative Party to do something about it.

Half an hour later, David was alone with Bertie Graves. It was Maundy Thursday and David was looking forward to a long weekend at Chequers. It was unfortunate that the EU High Representative for England and Wales would also be in residence now that government houses were shared with EurPol, but it was a big house and Bertram Grandee was a perfectly reasonable fellow, charming and easy-going. He had never caused more than a ripple at Cabinet meetings. He seemed a good sort. David needed a good rest as the election was looming and it had been a difficult few months. He was looking forward to the long weekend and had cleared his responsibilities as much as possible. He poured a large whisky for himself and one for Bertie, too. Wait until he had some rest and recharged his batteries. Then they would see what he, David Kirkby, PM of Great Britain, could do.

"The car's here, sir." He had not heard the soft-footed assistant open the door.

"Thank you, tell Monsieur Grandee if you will. There is little point in taking two cars down there." That was a considerate idea, he thought.

"Sir, Monsieur Grandee has already left. His cavalcade went straight after the Cabinet meeting, sir. In fact, it is a little embarrassing but he took some of the outriders detailed for you, Sir. We only have one escort car left, sir."

"What? Well, no matter. He must have been in a hurry."

"He stopped at the French Embassy on the way, sir."

"No doubt forgot his luggage." David got a dutiful laugh. He turned and nodded a goodbye towards Bertie and was off.

It was five minutes to eight by the time he and Marjorie had climbed into the waiting Mercedes. The programme started at eight and finished at nine, just minutes before David arrived hot and tired from his commuter-filled journey to Chequers. Thus he missed it and nobody dared mention it that evening. The buzz was all about how it got through the EBC Programme Approval and Selection Panel.

David, too, when he saw a replay at 8am on Good Friday, wondered the same thing. He made a few phone calls but, frustratingly, could not get more than a duty manager who could not add much.

"So, what is this I hear?" Bertram slurped his hot chocolate as his head hovered above the bowl. Marjorie pretended to be occupied with a napkin ring that had fallen on the floor. "How on earth did that programme get through the approval process, Daveed?"

"I am trying to find out," David replied.

"I spoke to the EBC - England and Wales Chairman this morning." Bertram had got straight through.

"And?"

"He said it had been an 'almighty cock up'. He suspects someone sympathetic to their cause has wormed their way in to the top of the EBC, at least the English and Welsh section. He has started an enquiry."

So David, longing for a well-earned rest, instead spent the weekend fretting and calling Bertie, who saw it not as a disaster, but as a brilliant publicity coup. If only it had been his idea! It was a fraught David, close to the edge, who chaired the Security Sub-committee of the Cabinet that following Tuesday.

"Before we settle down to our normal business," Terry Rose angrily demanded, "I want to know what we are going to do about this latest mess."

"I have a short presentation on the Future Perfect." Bertie replied. "It's actually extremely interesting…"

"I'm not talking about some poxy group of radicals. I'm talking about the damn EBC. Here they are raking in the profits from our commercial broadcasting policy while still collecting the lucrative licence fee. And this is the way we get repaid! I think it is high time those self-important twats in the eeb get brought down a peg or two."

"Bertram, tell everyone what you told me at the weekend, about the infiltration at a senior level." Bertram rose and took centre stage for thirty minutes, detailing all his office had been able to find out so far.

"So," Terry concluded, as Bertram sat down, "what do we do about the EBC? Let's tackle that first and look into the bunch of radicals next time."

The proposal came from Peter Burrows, hinted at first until he grew more certain of his reception. "The EBC – England and Wales has a charter, but in essence it is a business like any other."

"So?"

"Well, Terry, a business has value."

"Go on."

"Well, I was just wondering if we could kill two birds with one stone."

"How?"

"Well, we are looking at ways to fund a tax cut but are pretty tied up with what is acceptable to the STC – EurPol. At the same time we have a few trouble-makers in a large public body which has a great deal of inherent value."

"You mean…"

"Exactly, we privatise it."

"How much are we talking about?"

"It's hard to say. It would depend to a great extent on how we tackled the licence side of things…"

"Turn them into subscriptions," Terry interjected.

"Precisely," Peter replied, wishing he had thought of that twist. "You would have a business overnight with fourteen billion in revenue."

"There's the backlog of programmes as well. The US media giants would fight to the death to get a stake in that collection."

"You're right, PM, I would conservatively place the value at fifty billion euros."

"Well, I like it." Terry was as much behind it for the opposition he knew would come from Dennis. "What do you say, David? This could be a quadruple bonus – privatisation, media reform to bring it in line with eurostandards and tax cuts without any corresponding cuts to expenditure."

Dennis rose, noticing all the faces suddenly sloping down as if drawn by puppet strings to examine the shiny table-top. His argument was rational and cohesive but, like the parable, it fell on stony ground.

"Yes, Dennis, but that is a pretty old argument about it being a great British institution," Terry interjected.

"But just because it is an old argument does not mean it has any less merit. Do all arguments have to be new to be valid?" Again Dennis had fallen into the trap laid by Terry.

"No, old fellow, but if the old solutions don't solve the old problems you need to look to new solutions rather than staying stuck in the past. Quite honestly, we have to look to the future, not to the past all the time. I don't give two hoots for any institution or organisation that claims validity by presenting the past as its justification. Tear them down, I say, and let new institutions rise up to replace them, ones that are relevant to us today. That is how we build a future, certainly not by linking ourselves tamely with whatever happened a hundred years ago!"

"Well, Bertie, what says the great advisor on presentation? Can it be done?"

"I'm not sure, David, it is just such an institution, rightly or wrongly. It survived euronisation, it is part of our soc..."

"Poppycock!" Terry's dismissal thundered across the room. "On the contrary it is a tremendous opportunity. I get really fed up when everyone keeps on clinging tamely to the past, terrified of making changes. Clinging on as if these outdated anachronisms will somehow protect us. They hold us back, dear fellow. We need to sweep them away." He paused, sensing he already had the balance of the argument. "If we don't grab this opportunity we have no right to be sitting around this table. We certainly won't be in a few months' time after the election."

Ten minutes later, the decisions were made. The EBC would be offered up privately to the trade, the whole organisation split into three: the broadcast operations, a quickly separated news and current affairs division, and the coveted library of old programmes. The Home Office, with considerable Treasury input, would work swiftly to gain the necessary approvals and complete the sale. A media bill would be presented to parliament to help give it a cloak of planned policy. The funds raised, probably fifty billion euros, would be used to cut the basic rate of income tax from forty to thirty-seven eurocents, while also leaving some over for a popular, headline-grabbing increase to the health and education budgets. The price of approval was set by Bertram at 100,000 refugees and all was agreed, just paperwork to follow.

"It's the prefect strategy in the lead-up to the election this autumn," David summed up. Once more, he had pulled something out of the hat. Nobody could say he was not a survivor.

"David," Dennis had stayed behind at his own choosing this time, "I have to express my complete reservation concerning this decision."

"We know, Dennis. You put your views across and then we voted." The vote had gone sixteen to one, Bertie being just an observer.

"David, surely you can see it's not the right thing to do. I'm all for privatisation, you know that. Good Lord, I was working on the first wave of sell-offs back in the Eighties! But this is wrong, hopelessly wrong. I urge you to reconsider. It gives totally the wrong message about us as a government."

"What on earth, Dennis? I would say it demonstrates our resourcefulness and imagination and therefore is an excellent boost to our image!"

But Dennis was firm and suddenly much clearer. The whole arrangement smacked of a quick City-type deal, something dreamed up by some clever merchant banking boys to create instant wealth without effort. His problem, he realised, as David drummed his fingers on the table and looked up at the ceiling, was to take the Prime Minster with him. He was, after all, very much the City type himself, easily impressed with slick and flashy solutions – neatly wrapped, as if problems could be resolved in the real world with no bad repercussions at all. It reminded him of the old arguments from his first days in politics, over forty years ago now. Coming out of recession, traditional industry limping from crisis to crisis, crippled from underfunding. But really crippled because all the bright bods had gone, not to rejuvenate the old factories, not to fight a war, but to the multitude of city offices rising like ghosts in a graveyard, promising a fortune from nothing and fat bonuses along the way. "Who needs industry when we can live off services? We are entering the post-industrial age." Those had been the cries across the City of London's dealing floors and echoed in the same cabinet room he was now sitting in. First it had been shipbuilding, then locomotives, automobiles and a host of others, until finally steel had gone the same way. All that potential, all that investment, lost in redundancy payments and offers of early retirement. And David Kirkby had been one of those bright lights following that City-bound road, seeking his fortune like Dick Whittington. How could a man like that ever understand what Dennis Shepherd was about? Yet he had to try one more time.

"I think it is financial engineering and the public will see it for that. I don't believe in the long run it will do us any good at all." It was a limp attempt but Dennis had already given up on a hopeless task. He needed to think carefully about his future. Unlike Terry Rose's brash demand to step from past to future with a clean break, his would be a carefully considered move, taking his past, who he was, along with him.

Some Lessons in Education

When expressing his original intention to retire in the summer of 2019, Professor Unwin-Smith had hoped to devote himself completely to the family research he had wanted to pursue for so long. He had, however, been persuaded to retain his two most promising classes a while longer.

"We need you, Edward," the Head of History and a life-long friend had said. "We desperately need your influence in the department as well as your fine mind in the classroom. Besides, it will be lonely around here without another old-timer to bump into in the corridors. Won't you at least consider remaining with us for a few hours each week?"

So the decision was made; a decision that the professor at first regretted but later came to be increasingly grateful for. He now had three platforms to his life. Taking up most of his week he had his research, the long hours closeted alone, yet almost not alone, for the more he delved, the more he learned about the fascinating general who had been his father. Sometimes, after a good, thoughtful session in which the professor had completed page after page of notes in his private shorthand, he would say things out loud, odd comments and observations that could only make sense between son and father.

Then he had his own son; a similar relationship in reverse, taking on some of those same characteristics he was discovering in his research, but actually happening now, as if time, having reached an end, had started to loop backwards. He was a mirror, he realised one evening as he closed up his papers and turned on the television to catch the news. A pivotal mirror that swung on its axis to reflect the future in the past and the past in the future, highlighting in revolving flashes what it is that continues down the generations. Thus he could be both a father to his son and a son to his father, using his research to re-create how it could have been.

At first, given the discoveries he was making, the twice-weekly interruption to teach had been an irritant, something that only served to break his pattern of thought. He had taught all his adult life and loved the time spent carefully inserting knowledge into young minds, so acutely aware that knowledge is the bedrock of wisdom. Yet he felt that he could not give his remaining students the dedication they required, his attention being so fixed elsewhere.

"I think I'll have to call it a day at the end of the year, Robert. I can't seem to give it what I used to and it's not fair on the students. You know, the more I read about my father, the more I realise that this research is something I've got to do."

"I understand," the Head of History replied, now five years closer to his own retirement. He swept his long grey hair back to cover the small but growing bald patch. "But I'll be sorry to see you go."

Then, quite suddenly, the classes had changed. It started one Thursday afternoon in early March, close to the end of term. The sun shone through the closed windows, giving an illusion of summer with just enough strength to give an air of lazy distraction. They had been discussing the interwar years in Europe and the resurgence of nationalism that led to the Second World War. The essay had been a complicated one, dealing with the diplomatic aftermath of the Abyssinian Crisis but the day, with its echo of early summer heat, was conducive not to detail but to themes and ideas on a much grander scale.

"Professor, do you believe that the Second World War was

really avoidable?" The questioner, Timothy Jays, was one of the finest students Edward could remember. Tall, thin and thoughtful, he seemed to soak up everything thrown his way with the enthusiasm of one allowed to indulge, at long last, in whatever was his chosen passion.

"Yes, certainly it was avoidable. One thing I have learned in my sixty-plus-year love affair with history is that nothing need happen. People say that history repeats itself, but that is nonsense. What they mean is that people repeat the same old mistakes, the same old misjudgements, over and over again. And why? Because they fail to learn from history. There is one principal lesson that is always valid: strength breeds strength. One only has to look at nature to see the truth in that. Nature is a product of history, an environment and ways of life built up over generations. Of course, there are many different kinds of strength. The lion is strong, as is the elephant and the ant. Hitler's armies were strong. The British spirit stronger still. Individuals are strong and sometimes whole countries are strong, too."

"So we have to ask ourselves what it is that makes something strong."

"Exactly, Tim." It was the sort of fascinating debate that lasted throughout the rest of the academic year. Each week with Tim and the professor in the vanguard, but the other students able to contribute, they opened a new chapter, discarding and distilling until happy with the conclusions. It was a flowering of teaching and a flowering of learning, two fine minds streaking ahead. It concentrated on history but quickly became something more.

Together, as the summer term sped by, they split strength into its component parts: physical ability, sensitivity, knowledge, confidence, humility, compassion and perspective. They examined each ingredient, sifting, mixing ideas, but all the time learning.

"In essence, what we have been saying...." It was the last class of the year, the last of Edward Unwin-Smith's teaching career. He felt the need to sum up, "... the essence is that the future lies in the hands of those willing and able to grasp it. And by able, we sometimes mean physically, but more often through awareness. Every conceivable outcome is possible because there is no repetition in history, only a lamentable repetition of man's response to uncertainty. And this is the crucial point – the awareness comes from true strength and experience. But experience will take a lifetime and still not be complete so education is vital. Education is the concentrated form, the real legacy left to us by previous generations. Hence education is the essence of success, of being in control."

"So says the educator!' Chimed the class comic from the back. He got his laugh and so ended Professor Unwin-Smith's long career in education.

***

David Kirkby strode through the open, cracked glass door and smiled at the headmistress, holding out his right hand. He was trailed in order of importance: first Michael Spotting, the fat, bespectacled and hairy education secretary, who some said looked more like a music teacher than a politician; then Bertie Graves, ever a watchful eye for both opportunities and threats. Behind Bertie were various aides, then journalists, camera crews, and hangers-on.

"A quick pose for the cameras," Bertie suggested. He was in charge on occasions such as these, the publicist in his element. "On the steps would be best. Thank you, stand back, please. No, not now. The PM will be glad to address your questions after the presentation in the gym. That will be in about forty minutes, after a tour of the school. We can have one journalist from each of the preselected organisations accompanying us on the tour: each should have their passes on display. The rest of you, please make your way around to the back of the main building where the gym entrance will be found on the left."

"I hear you are something of a record holder," David knew how to conjure up the personal touch.

"Well, I have been here quite a while," the headmistress

replied, her stride and swishing skirts giving Bertie an indication of the strength of character. "Over forty years, in fact, with the last twenty-four as headmistress. Before that I was a teacher, then head of department and deputy head. Apart from three years at Bloomsby Junior, which was closed a couple of years ago, I have been here my entire career. We are the only English primary school in Chingham now."

"Excellent, concentrating resources, economies of scale, excellent." It always seemed more business-like to talk in stunted form; a technique he had developed over the years. It worked just as well in City boardrooms as in the cabinet office.

"Strange, because Bloomsby had a higher rating than us when it was closed. It also had better facilities."

"Mr Spotting, why did Bloombsy close?" One of the journalists at the back asked the Secretary of State.

"It was deemed unnecessary by EurEd. Chingham is little more than a village and one school for foreign speakers and one for the indigenous population was deemed to be sufficient."

"So where is the foreign speakers' school?"

"At Bloomsby, of course, it was deemed to be logical. There would be no point in building a new school, would there now?"

Meanwhile, the conversation at the front of the entourage had moved on to a safer footing.

"How many pupils here, Headmistress?" David could not remember her name.

"819, Mr Kirkby."

"That's a pretty good size."

"Yes, as the prefab classrooms will attest. We make do because we have to. Now, Mr Kirkby, here is a reception class. Unfortunately, Mrs Gilmour is ill but Miss Evans is filling in. Miss Evans is our librarian."

David looked around: colours everywhere, from bright green carpet, patterned darker from years of spills, to dozens of red sunsets pinned around the walls and animal alphabet characters in suits of clothes looping around the whiteboard. David could not see the D, presumably for Dog, but no, there it was, a Dragon in a red shirt and trousers, breathing fire over the E for Elephant. Bertie noticed how many children there were, mostly staring out of the windows at the host of cars and camera vans in the car park.

"Good morning Mr Kirkby. Welcome to Roselands," the children chanted, some forgetting to stand up.

"Good morning, children. I hope you like your lovely school. I certainly do. Tell me what you are learning today." Again the personal touch, he was a natural.

So they went on through classroom after classroom, then to the library, squashed to overflowing, and the dining hall in which the youngest children were already eating their lunch at 10.45.

"It's to fit everyone in," the headmistress informed him. "We have twelve sittings for lunch, fifteen minutes a sitting."

"Very efficient," David commented.

"Hardly conducive to digestion," came the acid reply.

David moved on. Bertie tapped him on the shoulder and whispered that they needed to slow down: it would not look good if they arrived at the gym early.

"Tell me Mrs... eh... Brown..."

"It's Browning."

"My apologies, Mrs Browning, I cut your name short!" A little humour worked wonders at easing the way. "I just wondered what the average class size was here?" Not the cleverest of questions.

"Thirty-eight."

"Really, I thought..."

"At Bloomsby they are down to twenty-six."

"Then why not transfer some pupils?"

"Mr Kirkby, they do not teach in English." David felt foolish when he heard this. Why had Spotting not briefed him properly? "But we have plans to build an extra classroom block."

"Excellent, excellent, that is what I like to see; the good schools expanding at the expense of the weaker ones." He would use that phrase with the press afterwards.

"But the cash was not forthcoming."

"What? Did you try...?"

"We went all the way through the Department of Education and even appealed to EurEd. Apparently only schools that support diversity in migrant populations are fast-tracked. We are on the waiting list."

"Ah," David breathed a sigh of relief, "these things take time."

"Seven years, they said, that would make it eleven from the granting of planning permission. Of course, EurPlan may not allow us to renew the planning permission when it expires next year."

"What about PFE?" That was his saviour. The Private Funds for Education initiative had been a personal brainwave of his, a supplementary source of income for schools, coming directly from the local community. The pupils had to draw up the business plans and marketing strategies, thus gaining valuable experience for their future as well.

"We tried, Prime Minister. EurEd has blocked our application until an equivalent amount is raised by the local community for each school in the district. Bloomsby appears to have no interest in such fundraising exercises."

Another tap on his shoulder, Bertie again. "Change the subject, PM. Move on to something less controversial. You can see she has a thing about funding."

"So which class did these fascinating nature projects?" David, always quick off the mark, spun on a cent coin and changed the subject as suggested.

"Well, Mrs Browning, a most interesting tour of your school, thank you very much. Shall we move on to the presentation now?"

"But there is still a lot you have not seen! The toilets need urgent attention and the playground desperately needs money spent on it, then there are the computers..."

"I know, Mrs Browning, but it is always difficult with a tight schedule. If you have any concerns, please put them in writing and send them to my office."

"We did!"

"Good, good. I'll get someone on to them first thing in the morning. Now, we must move on to the presentation. Bertie, where is the award? Good, fine, let's be on our way, then."

The Triple X programme had been another bright idea of the Kirkby administration, bringing competition to the staid world of education. Each year, every school in the country was awarded grades across the areas of traditional academics, social acceptance and community responsibility. Grades ranged from fail to excellent, with X being the abbreviation for an excellent grade. Hence a Triple X was the rare occasion when a school scored the highest marks across the spectrum. Usually the award was presided over by a school governor or an official of the Department of Education. More promising success stories were allocated to EurEd and once or twice Bertram Grandee, as the senior USE official, had presided. This was the first time the Prime Minister had been authorised to carry out the task, but then it was an election year. In response, the journalists crammed into the gym, shoes scuffing the already scuffed floor.

David's speech was short and to the point. It dealt briefly with Roselands, admiring the efforts and the clear motivation of the staff, stemming from the headmistress and her leadership. It was a successful school and was the product of successful education policies. These were sensible, well-thought-out policies that targeted the resources where they could do the most good. Good schools would flourish under a Conservative administration, taking over their weaker brethren because money in education, just like in the real world, followed success. It gave him great pleasure to present this award for achievement of Triple X status to Mrs Brown, all her staff, the pupils, parents, governors and the whole community. They could all take great pride in the school they had helped create.

"Thank you, Prime Minister." Mrs Browning took the trophy and stepped over to replace him at the podium. "Mr Kirkby is absolutely right. This award represents a tremendous achievement by the staff, pupils and all those with an interest in Roselands. I thank them all wholeheartedly for the efforts they have made." A pause here, a sharp look at Kirkby, sharper still at Bertie sitting next to him; a warning, perhaps? "Efforts," she continued, holding up the shiny silver bust of Shakespeare sitting at a computer, "made under heroic circumstances. I believe you all know the sickening scenario well enough by now. Cuts one year followed by cuts the next and the next, until cuts are established in the school calendar like Whitsun or Easter Sunday. Ladies and gentlemen," Bertie was on his feet now, reaching for control of the microphone, but Mrs Browning anticipated his lunge and whipped it away from his grasp, "what is remarkable is not this award but that my school can provide a passable education at all. Prime Minister, on behalf of the staff, pupils, governors and parents of this school I would like you to accept back this award as we need money not trophies and…"

"Thank you, Mrs Browning." Bertie had managed to grab the microphone now, a pleasant smile etched on his reddened face. He had to breathe deeply for a moment, his breath amplified to the whole audience. "Your comments are most interesting although sadly ill-informed. As you are no doubt aware, the argument you employed is rather an old one." My goodness, he thought, he was sounding just like Terry Rose. Was nothing true? Could everything be bent one way or the other? "As most of you will be aware, while the overall level of direct funding is set by the UK Government, the actual allocation of funds is made by the European Office of Education, more commonly known as EurEd. They add their own funds to ensure fairness across the board. I believe therefore that it is a little misleading of you, Mrs. Browning, to lay the blame for cuts at this administration's door."

"You agreed to the setting up of EurEd," someone called from the back.

"Precisely so that funding of education could be taken out of the political see-saw. This was no more, nor less, than the decision with health and the police and justice system. I think it was a brave move to stop politics entering our schools."

"More like to stop discussion and start brainwashing." Mandy's voice rang pure and cool across the room. She was holding Mark's hand while Mark leant against the broken rails that ran up the side of the gym. "Education is our future. It is the future of our economy and our culture. We should never have given up control to EurEd."

"We did not give up control. We…" Despite the advantage of the microphone, Bertie was no match for the clear, true voice of Mandy.

"We gave up control and well you know it. Why is it that Euro Schools in this country get almost double the per capita funding? Why is it that on average every religious school gets less again? Why are there 819 pupils in this school and only 254 in Bloomsby? Why do you pay lip service to education and short-change it every time? Why do you pretend?"

"That was a close escape." David, safely back in his BMW, gave a deep sigh of relief. "You should not have stepped in, Bertie, I was just about to stand up. I could have handled her. That is what politicians do." He was thoroughly annoyed with Bertie for taking the limelight. That was not his job. Maybe Bertie was losing his judgment. This whole trip had been a disaster.

Close escape? thought Bertie. If that was a close escape then what would a disaster look like? Did he really want to be around to find out?

"Where's Stopping?" David demanded.

"He took his own car back."

"Get him on the phone now. We need to sort this out. Set up a meeting for tomorrow, 10am."

"Yes, sir." The aide rushed to do his bidding.

Michael Spotting came from his hastily arranged breakfast meeting with Terry Rose and was shown straight into the PM's study at No 10.

"Easy," he said, after allowing Kirkby to rant for several minutes, "I have the answer."

105

"Well, what is it, dammit?" It was too early for the Scotch routine.

"Mandy Fryer, the youngster who gave you the hard time yesterday…"

"Gave Bertie the hard time, you mean. If I had been at the podium it would have been a different story."

"Of course, the girl, Mandy Fryer, who gave Mr Graves such a hard time yesterday. She was a pupil at Roselands."

"So?"

"She is also a founding member of Future Perfect."

"That rabble led by Unwin-Smith?"

"Actually it is run by her boyfriend, Mark Borden. The point is, we kill two birds with one stone here. We put it about that she is a founding member of a shady organisation that has not even received EurPol approval. Then we raid their flat, well we suggest to the police that they raid her flat and I am sure we will discover something illegal.'

"I don't know, Michael." David turned to seek Bertie's opinion but remembered he had not been invited to this meeting. "I tell you what, I'll think about it."

"You must do, Prime Minister, this has done the Party a lot of damage already and with the elections coming up…"

"Yes, yes, but what of the underlying problem? How do we get the funding eased on good schools like this one? Can we use the money we earmarked from the EBC sale?"

"Unfortunately not, Prime Minister." David's Principle Private Secretary spoke up. "That money is reserved, Prime Minister; part of the deal that was done with EurComm."

"What deal?"

"The deal to get approval for the sale of EBC and for the consequential tax cuts."

"I thought Bertram said the deal was 100,000 new immigrants?"

"That too, Prime Minister. The sale of EBC looks set to raise sixty billion euros. The size of this approval meant we had to give something else."

"And what is that something else?"

"Well, Prime Minister, the seven billion we had put aside for education is to be spent on education but not exactly on the things you might want. Just over half is going to fund the new app, *Europe and the World*, including a free copy for every person under the age of twenty-one. Some of the rest is going to the Awareness in Education week and the rest is going to Central Euro Reserves for emergency education funding throughout the USE."

"My God! What have I done?" David slumped back in his chair, his head in his hands. Where was Bertie when he needed him?

The Trees

It always soothed her nerves. Twelve minutes at the correct temperature. Her doctor had explained it once, something to do with muscle relaxation, but it was the result, not the theory, that had sold it to her.

The whole place soothed her; the rising hills around her, the peace and quiet, the lack of interruption. But mostly it was the deep green woods and the shade they gave. That shade, so cool and luxurious! Sometimes, when caught in windowless conference rooms day after day, tied into tedious negotiations in two dozen languages, she ached for the shade, just to get away from the glare that was her profession. At times like this she wished she were not a woman, not a politician, not even the Chancellor of the Federal Republic of Germany, but a simple tree, provider of shade and generator of peace and calm.

Of course she knew she could not be a tree, at least not for more than a long weekend. She was a leader and it was the thrust and struggle of politics that made her sap rise. Still, between ten and twenty times a year she got away to the little wooden house in the foothills of her favourite mountains, just a mile from the old border.

Very few people came to her house. Sometimes the whole year would pass with no more than a handful of guests taking the turning off the main road, following the dirt track over the rusty iron bridge and on to the clearing that framed her little wooden house. There they would sit quietly on the porch or walk along the side of the stream until it joined the river, just up from the rusty bridge. The guests were ever mindful of the peace and calm, waiting tensely for Hilda Rheinalt to open the conversation, ears pinned back whenever the muted telephone threatened an invasion from the world outside, drawing a sigh of relief when the cases were back in the car and the iron bridge was safely behind them again.

David Kirkby was honoured, deeply honoured, to be invited, especially at such short notice. And the only guest as well! If he had been able to find Bertie, he would have instructed him to make maximum publicity out of the invitation to the Chancellor's sanctuary. But Bertie was on holiday again. And in an election year?

Like all the other visitors before him, David trod carefully, eyebrows raised every time he passed her, expecting something profound, some purpose for being summoned here. But Hilda seemed alone with the trees, her conversation minimal and perfunctory. Surely he had not been asked here in order to be ignored? And why hadn't Marjorie been invited to accompany him? Marjorie would have known how to break the deadweight of silence that hung about the place like the presence of a ghost.

"You are curious, no doubt, as to why I asked you." She spoke English perfectly.

"Yes, as a matter of fact, I was wondering." She would weigh about the same as him, he thought. Nine inches shorter at five-foot-three, but broader at every stage, from ankles upwards. Yet he suspected not an ounce of fat. With her sixty-nine years and her pinned back grey hair, she could have been a retired Soviet era athlete, muscles and brawn from neck to feet. He pictured her in training, minimal perspiration as she strove steadily towards the declared objective.

"I wanted some chat with you."

"Oh, yes?"

"We have been sparring partners for some time now, do you not think?" Her eyes were a reflection of the perfect summer's day: no cloud, no mist, just a tangible hardness that could be steel if it were not the brightest of blues.

"We haven't always seen eye to eye." What was she getting at? "But please, be assured…" But her interruption saved David from ingratiating himself.

"However, I believe we understand each other. This is important when so much is at stake." She paused and looked over at the trees. Directly in her gaze was a small copse of untrained saplings, thick with vigorous young undergrowth, establishing itself in a part of the open area between porch and stream. Finally, she looked back at David and then nodded towards this cheeky outpost. "Two years ago there was little there. At first I thought it would not grow much. Then last year I meant to speak to the caretaker about having it removed but I forgot."

"I know what it is like, hectic schedules and everything."

"Yes, exactly. My point, however, is look at it now. It is a wild mess of unruly brambles. One can hardly see the stream from here at all."

"You could still take it out." Had he been called all the way over here for a discussion on gardening? There was so much to do at home.

"We could, you are right. But the work is increased considerably compared with even last year." She looked at him closely, unable to trace any understanding on his face. "I am sure you see the parallel."

"Eh?"

"The Future Perfect."

"Oh, yes, of course." David recovered quickly. Now that he had something to hang her words on they made more sense.

"It would be a great pity," she was explaining, "if our broad, collective and essentially liberal and accepting view on Europe be obscured by some rebel growth. This is growth that quickly infests the whole scene with unsightly offshoots springing out in all directions. Especially a pity to sit by complacently when early action could stop it ever getting established."

"I see." Dare he ask what she proposed? Would he have to?

"I think you know what I mean. They are an idealistic lot, are they not?"

"Yes, bunch of do-gooders as far as I can see."

"You have, I take it, made a study of their aims and methods?"

"Yes, yes, of course. Well, one is being prepared right now. It will be ready for when I return tomorrow. "Could Bertie manage to beef it up in time? He would have to leave Bertie a message.

"I would like very much to see it." A return to silence followed her polite order. David watched the sun sinking behind leafy treetops, falling steadily into the western sky and sending out thin pencils of light and shadow up the grass and onto the porch, one stronger block of shadow cutting between Hilda and he so that one could imagine a canyon between them.

It grew a little colder as the sun dragged its rays across the distant Atlantic Ocean, but still outdoor weather. David refilled his glass, noting that Hilda never seemed to drink anything, still less good Scotch. It was almost seven. At seven sharp they would go into eat. By nine she would be in bed.

David sat out long into the evening, long after Hilda had retired and darkness had descended with all the noises of the night rising up to replace the light. The soda had run out but the decanter had three inches left. What had she meant him to do? Had she meant anything sinister? Or was that his imagination? Should he be doing her bidding? What was the best course of action? Not for the first time in recent days, he wished Bertie or Marjorie were there to help him work it out. He carefully re-plotted the route of their broken conversation, trying to find her purpose like ships in the sea, recalling where they had tacked and turned. The problem was she had said so little, her real intentions hidden behind clever metaphors. Yet he felt as if he had received distinct orders, crisp and clear, parade-ground fashion. Was this deliberate? What should he do?

"Dammit, these Europeans are too bloody difficult for words."

The morning brought little enlightenment. Hilda Rheinalt, Chancellor of Germany, was once more in her chancellor's cloak. The car arrived at five-thirty, dropping David at the airport before sweeping off to Berlin. She saw no trees that morning, just a schedule involving meetings, conferences and private audiences.

"Thank you, Hilda, a most relaxing weekend." They were now buzzing along the autobahn on their way to the airport. The newly-risen sun, now shining over the low hills to the east, could offer David no more for its night-time trip around the other half of the globe. There is no progress in space, no 'doing things better next time'. Things just happen amidst the endless routine that runs the universe, timeless and silent, like the best machinery, seeking no purpose, no improvement, just running. Perhaps there was some other being, quietly mocking the human effort it witnessed. Perhaps it had seen it all before, over and over again.

"My pleasure."

"And a very interesting discussion last night." No word from Hilda in response. "About the Future Perfect, I mean."

"Yes, very much so indeed. You will send me the report?"

"Of course, the moment I get back."

"Good." Was that to be it then? But not quite. With the airport building in sight she spoke once more. "I can depend on you David, I know. You will not allow such a splendid view to be selfishly destroyed. We are all acting for something greater than ourselves, something greater than our individual nation states. Some things must be done in the name of progress; difficult actions but very necessary for future security. You do understand? Good, then we shall talk of it no more."

Hit Hardest When Least Expected

Terry Rose knew exactly what to do. "We hit them hard before they develop into something to really worry about."

"How?"

"Two ways. First, we ridicule their policies. As you know, I am no lover of Europe, but we have to expose their half-baked ideas of independence, let people see the danger of opting out of the future."

"But Terry," Dennis spoke up, "you are on pretty thin ice here. You have often argued for getting out of Europe."

"Better a Conservative administration in Europe than a bunch of gibbering hippies trying to go it alone." How could he dismiss principle as if it was no more than the wrapper of a child's new toy? Dennis was sure Terry took pleasure in the trivialisation of things other people took seriously. Beliefs were targets to be shot down with barbed arrows.

"OK, so what is your second proposal?" Terry allowed twenty seconds to pass as the smile spread across his florid features, every bit the bluff Yorkshireman he acted out in town. It worked; he could see the anticipation shining on every face around the cabinet table.

"Scandal," he said at last, so quietly that those at the far end had to strain to hear. "A little association with something bad, probably drugs. Combined with the ridiculing of their policies, it will completely undermine them. They are a bunch of idealists, exactly the sort to smoke dope for breakfast, dinner and tea. We need to expose such tendencies. It is our duty, even if it does require a little invention. Look at it this way, gentlemen," another pause, used to great effect, "all we'd be doing is pointing out the obvious truth. Those dirty hippies have to be knee-deep in marijuana. How else could they come up with such garbled policy initiatives? Now, ask yourself, what sort of policy contribution can we expect from a doped-up bunch of radicals hanging out somewhere north of cloud nine? Gentlemen," seventeen faces glued to his, "I can guarantee the result you need. Take my word for it, the Future Perfect has just peaked, long may it enjoy its glorious downward path." Weaker faces smiled and nodded, some chuckling at the vision etched out by Terry. Stronger faces looked away. They were outnumbered, better to live and fight another day. Bertram Grandee sat impassively at the other end of the table. He would abstain in the pending vote, of course, but would report favourably back to his bosses in Brussels and with a side note to Frau Rheinalt.

So Terry Rose knew exactly what to do. Dennis Shepherd was unshakably opposed, but Terry had expected this and, anyway, Dennis was on his way out, the next reshuffle would see to that. It was the Prime Minister's agreement that Terry really sought for that would make it official, backed by someone more senior than him. But David would not meet his eye, nor anyone else's. He seemed lost in his own world; trying to find his own way, perhaps?

Dennis was opposed, very opposed, yet lacking in focus, seemingly also lost in thought, but striking out in fits and starts. Other worries clouded his mind that bright June day. Who was it his wife was seeing, his wife of thirty years, the woman who had shared most of his political career? What had happened between them? Was it either of them at fault or just the crude insertion of someone else? Had he neglected her? More to the point, what should he do about it? Should he confront her or bide his time? Maybe they had become too used to each other but, by God, this hurt! The prospect of existence without her was like a great ugly cancer eating into his side.

"What's up, Dennis?" David asked. The cabinet table was empty save the two thoughtful ones. "You don't seem your normal self."

"Nothing, David." It wouldn't do to let anybody know the truth. You never could tell in politics. "I think I am just a little tired. I'll be OK in a day or two."

"Good, we need you, Dennis." Was this an overture? His political instinct took over.

"But I oppose Terry's plans, David, I think they are twisted, evil..." But that was his mistake, where his instinct was not what it had been. David pushed back his chair and stood, leaning over the table in Dennis' direction.

"Dennis, this was a cabinet decision. If you cannot take collective responsibility then maybe it is time to bow out." This said with the force of someone who was not convinced but wanted to be. If Dennis had not been so preoccupied he would have sensed the Prime Minister's reservations about Terry Rose's plans. They could have built an alliance to fight back against the shifting balance of power. But for Dennis the opportunity slipped by unnoticed, one of the many turns a person might make but did not.

"Are you saying there's no room for my opinions in the cabinet?" he replied too sharply.

"I'm saying there is nothing to be gained by fighting every decision." David too was missing the obvious opportunity. At that moment, Bertie walked in.

"But David, this latest idea is blatantly dis..." Dennis tried again but without a proper mastering of the argument it was a lost cause.

"Nonsense! You know what Terry is like with his rich language. There is nothing wrong with the police carrying out an investigation, is there? And if this damned new outfit is not involved in drugs or other shady things they have nothing to worry about. It's just the test of politics. If they come out smelling like roses we will have done them a huge favour! Now, listen to the advice of an old friend, Dennis. Take a few days off and consider your position and your contribution to the government. We don't want to lose you, Dennis; your efforts over the years have been invaluable. You are the last link with Mrs Thatcher. But times move on and if you cannot put the party first then it might just be time to move aside and let someone else take the reins. I'll see you next week."

Hard words. Yet it was not his boss's warning which struck him as he left Downing Street and, declining his car, wandered vaguely in the direction of his City Hall apartment across the river. Not the warning from the PM at all, rather the look on Bertie's face as they had crossed at the threshold to the cabinet room. He had never seen that mixture of sympathy, collusion and confusion before. It was as if Bertie had suddenly seen Dennis for everything he was and, in return was trying to open himself up to Dennis. Yet he did not know how to do this, his own confusion pooling with that of Dennis.

Dennis' options were several and conflicting and he needed to think. Walking always helped, especially with the quiet, under-employed Thames at his elbow. The river was, he considered, like the country it flowed through, their destinies tied closely. Even their histories were similar in splendour. But now the Thames rested on that glorious past; an angry young man grown old, seeking stillness where once it had made waves, yet secretly wishing for one more storm, one more headlong rush. It had natural advantages but it no longer exploited them, passing by the opportunities as they arose, resigning itself to a course for simple pleasure boats, up one side and down the other, red and white awnings above stubby craft that would never know excitement or adventure. True, it was cleaner than it had been for years, the exclusive fishing piers gave evidence of that while the reports on his desk proved it. But what else had it achieved in his lifetime? How did it compare with the great rivers of Europe? The Seine, for instance, seemed somehow infused with Frenchness, mixing majesty, culture and fierce national pride into one distinctive body of slow-running water. And was not the Rhine called the artery of

116

Europe? And the Danube the Rhine of the East? For one brief, escapist moment Dennis saw himself as the Rejuvenator of Old Father Thames, tracing the river back through modern England to its source and, in doing so, magically rediscovering some of the characteristics of a nation that could be so much more, that had been so much more for so long. But wait a minute. Why all these crazy thoughts when his wife was cheating him, his wife of thirty years?

"Sir!" The porter cried, slamming down the telephone and rushing to intercept him. "Sir, could you spare a moment for a word - some advice, I mean? It's about my son, sir. You see, he's a bright youngster, very interested in the environment and nature and all, keen to make a difference. I thought Mr Shepherd, he's the one, as Minister for the Environment, he'll know what was best." Dennis was tired, despite the relatively light day and early hour; too tired and ill-positioned as the porter moved around him, to notice the black BMW that slipped quietly off from the front of the building.

"What's his name?"

"Who, sir?" The porter looked around anxiously.

"Your son. I'll see what I can do."

"Oh, thank you, sir. But I can see you are tired, I'll catch you another day, sir."

Two flights up the back steps, no fast breath for, by habit, he always used the stairs. Then along the thick carpeted corridor to the door to their modest but expensive apartment. Not a home exactly, but made comfortable through the years.

"Hello Den, Dear, I'm in the bathroom, out in a sec." That was how he knew. Nothing tangible, just the extra tone of endearment crafted into her voice. Her voice was lush and tuneful as always, but to Dennis it made a sombre chord, set in a minor key.

The telephone rang, breaking his thoughts.

"It's for you, Den, Bertie Graves. Don't talk long." The same tone of confirmation.

"I'll get it in the study."

117

What on earth could Bertie Graves want of him? Besides, they had been together not thirty minutes before. Then Dennis remembered the expression on Bertie's face.

Secret Liaisons

Bertie Graves had that middle-aged feeling. A successful business, a beautiful daughter at Cambridge, the other still at boarding school, and a pleasant country house on a long, tree-dotted slope outside Winchester. The house gave a spectacular view over the chalk downs but nothing on the vista offered by the Hideaway, the tiny cottage they had found together, quite by accident, when touring the Highlands some years before.

The name had been his wife's choosing; a neat, if stereotyped, choice he had allowed her, for it was here they came whenever possible, quite literally to hide away from the world they were tied into. They could have extended the clichéd name to recount what they did, what all busy executives do to wind down – taking things easy, great drafts of fresh air, working with wood, peace and quiet, walking, always walking, recharging batteries, avoiding the hustle and bustle. Yet Bertie knew, as Felicity knew, that they really came to be alone together. No other reason.

They were happy, had always been deeply happy. Yet Bertie, the consultant and adviser on image to the famous, had that middle-aged feeling. He experienced the dreadful questioning; the wondering as to purpose, the perpetual conflict whereas when youth had dominated there had only been one way. A working life is a hill climb. Some try and circumvent it; others sit and look at the distant top. Some start well and then take different side paths, running parallel to the ground rather than rising. But for those that make it to the top, what faces them?

Yes, the view, but from there every path leads downwards, back down to those that made much less or no effort to climb at all. The fresh wind of exhilaration proves to be a mere gust or swirl, returned to deadened stillness, provoking loneliness and then despondency. And the law works like this: the steeper the gradient or the higher the hill, the greater the feeling of hopeless despair. Hence the crisis in Bertie's mind for he had risen high through hard work, creating others into bigger people than they really were and now the questioning, the doubt, ate at every prop he had created along the way.

Bertie had that middle-aged feeling. But Bertie was lucky. He had Felicity Graves, his ever-loving wife. Felicity was a highly intelligent journalist with a leading Sunday paper. And they together had the Hideaway. Between these contrasting supports, flesh and stone, warm-blooded and cold, active and ever motionless, every view would fall into perspective in time. Every worry and concern would find its solution.

"What on earth is it all about?" He would ask as they tramped along fern-fringed lanes, the purple world stretching out to the sky that formed a clear blue dome above and around them. And she would explain as best she could, a superior kind of agony aunt deeply involved with her only reader.

"There must be more to it than this," he would declare, his essence crying out to know the way, as they crossed the north end of the tiny loch and approached their Hideaway by the back gate. She would go first, over the stile and through the swing gate; she always did. Inside, he would stoke up the fire, perhaps fetch some wood from the stack he replenished each morning with axe and saw. She would fill the big kettle and put tea bags in the pot. It was the same routine that countless generations of previous occupants, long gone and forgotten now, would have followed. Bertie reflected they were like planets and moons that moved around the sun; all ambition, all seeking for change, gone, vanished into the vastness of space, ordered by forces as old as time, in fact part of the creation of time itself.

"But something has to change," he would state as they sat,

late at night, blinded by the fire. "Something must have meaning."

"You must change," came the reply, her feminine voice a breathless waterfall of understanding for the man she loved. She could, she thought, live her whole life in one minute of his, a career reporting to her readers on every inflection of his voice or each tiny mannerism. She could produce a series of highly respected articles on the thousand thoughts that passed through his mind during that minute. "For your own sake, Bertie, change before it is too late. Be truthful, be honest with yourself." She had hit on it, this superior type of agony aunt. Truth. Truth as the bedrock of wisdom, yet also the mechanism that drives progress, the maker of the future yet the guardian of the past. Truth is the only inevitable.

And truth, once spent, the pure energy dissipated like the warmth of the day; truth then reincarnates as the pages on which the clearest history can be written. The past is the future happened. Then the truth comes back to haunt those who denied it, who hid from its glare, preferring the safe shadows where excuses meet explanations and grand theories attempt to distort reality. Felicity could not express all this. She might have said, had the words come to her, "It is those who are most honest and truthful with themselves who achieve great things and really make a difference, a world made better by your passing." But she did not need to form the words for Bertie heard them anyway. As the last log on the fire split into two and slid, both sides, to a fiery death, he heard the words she could not say and he understood.

"I hate my work, what it does, what it means." He spoke quietly, patchy voice mixing with cackle and spit from the dying fire. Now he was firmly in no man's land, the trenches of convention way behind him.

"Then change, Bertie dear, change before it is too late."

So Bertie changed. And the first thing he did was to call Dennis Shepherd, the guardian of principle alone on a hillside of wolves, the one man he knew to be true.

Dennis Shepherd, Secretary of State in Her Majesty's tired Government, Minister for the Environment, lover of the environment, old statesman, cuckolded lover, on his way, alone, to the Highlands one warm Friday in late Spring. Much like his boss going to the clearing in the forest in the foothills of the mountains, wondering why he had been called. Dennis arriving at the station, being picked up by Felicity, marvelling at the beauty, then witnessing the new, changed Bertie Graves, earnestness pouring out of him like a child continuing to fill a brim-full glass. Unlike Hilda Rheinalt, Bertie surrenders the advantage she assiduously cultivated, and spells out his ideas as soon as they can talk. Dennis, badly shaken by his wife's infidelity, notices the obvious love between Bertie and Felicity and is distracted, has to ask Bertie to slow down, to give him time to absorb the barrage of ideas.

But progress is made that first evening and on into the quiet, excited weekend, such progress that Felicity cuts the wood and stokes the fire as well as placing food before them. Two political minds meet, with a third and finer mind still, looking on and approving, happy to be the catalyst she is. The meeting of these minds is extraordinary because they should not agree on anything, yet they do. Dennis and his principles meet Bertie and his ideas. Together, in secret liaison, a team.

Then Dennis is back on the train. Bertie comes to the station this time. The train pulls out, heading south, back to the political jungle: Stirling, Edinburgh, Newcastle, York, Doncaster, Peterborough and London. So the Secretary of State for the Environment is back at his desk, the working week and much more ahead of him.

Investment in, and an Invitation to, the Future

Eight pages, two million copies, total cost 1,432,000 euros plus VAT at 30%: quite an investment, way beyond the reaches of most nascent political parties, more so one that did not even exist. But Sir Terrence, nearing his hundredth birthday, had never been the timid type. Not that he did not know fear: every day he felt again the cold steel of the rifle muzzle, strangely refreshing against his hot, sweaty neck. Refreshing yet terrifying. He had turned very slowly, rising from the shrub that had failed to hide him, until his eyes locked onto those of his captor; warm, frightened, pleading eyes, eyes younger than his own eighteen years. Dangerous eyes for they were only just in control.

He spoke no English and Sir Terrence, then 2nd Lieutenant Scott, knew no German. They communicated with their eyes; a shift sideways indicating a required movement, raised eyebrows for a question. They understood each other just enough. And Lieutenant Scott, seasoned by three months in Normandy, although terrified that death lay seconds away, knew that the balance of terror lay across the rifle in the young German. Those warm, brown, milky, boyish eyes told the story. How he wished that he had not stumbled upon this English officer who he may, at any moment, have to kill. How much he did not want to close the finger around the inch of steel to make the whole world reverberate and one more body crumple to the ground. Joachim Fielder had never been in a position to kill someone, never even pointed a gun in anger. He would be eighteen in October, drafted in the closing act of the war, an understudy who never expected to perform. If only he had remained at headquarters instead of going off alone with the foolish notion of finding the general and trying to persuade him to come back. After all, would he have even listened to a boy?

Gently, very gently, their eyes locked together as if the combat was to be enacted with whites and pupils rather than guns and grenades. After, it seemed to both of them, enough time to fight the whole war over again, Lieutenant Scott placed his left hand around the rifle barrel now pointing directly at his chest. He lifted it at a slant by degrees, never daring to shift his gaze in the slightest, for fear it would break the fragile but mesmeric hold he had established over the German boy. He forced the lock of vision, keeping his gaze and seeing right inside the young German soldier, sharing his own personality in return.

Then, suddenly, there was no fear. Lieutenant Scott had the gun, all was well.

"That was incredibly brave, sir." His platoon was emerging around him.

"I didn't have much choice, Sergeant. You speak German, don't you?"

"Yes, sir."

"Ask him what he is doing here on his own." The questioning did not take long; Joachim gabbled freely in German.

"He says he's been looking for his general, sir."

"His general?"

"Yes, sir. He is General Stein's batman. Apparently the general is missing, not seen since last night."

"But what brought him here, so far from the German lines?" The sergeant quickly translated Scott's question.

"He says he knows he came this way, sir. The general was

124

talking about turning himself in. The boy is concerned his general has lost his nerve."

"A full general? It does not seem possible."

"I think he is off his head, sir. He's only a kid. What shall we do with him, sir? We can't take him with us." Ominous words. But Lieutenant Scott was not the type. And war was not for boys.

"Keep his weapon and send him back." The German boy hesitated a moment when the decision was translated, mouthed his thanks, and shot off the way he had come.

Sir Terrence often wondered about him over the years. He had been a little younger than Sir Terrence, so would probably be ninety-seven now if still alive. He had probably put the war behind him and lived a full life, gone to university, maybe, married and had children and grandchildren. He may never have thought back to those four or five minutes that could have turned out so differently. Sir Terrence could see Joachim as a teacher or garage owner, something very ordinary that dimmed the terror into nothingness.

But those few moments had stayed with Sir Terence over the next eighty years; making him, he sometimes thought. He often said to his children, then grandchildren, then great-grandchildren, "If it taught me one thing, it taught me that if you don't take risks you will never achieve anything out of the ordinary. You take a calculated risk and then look to minimise the downside." It had been the rationale behind a brilliant business career. It was also the rationale behind his decision now, when undoubtedly close to the end of his life, to invest in this new entity, the Future Perfect.

But Sir Terrence was also a man of ideas, it being his suggestion as to the pamphlet's title: *An Invitation to the Future.* "It draws people in, inviting them to be a part and reinforcing also that they can make a difference."

"I like it," George had replied. "It is far more appealing than *The Three E's* idea we had. "

But the operation was on a larger scale as well, reflecting Sir Terrence's energy and vision.

"My whole life has taught me the truth of the philosophy behind the Future Perfect," he had explained in a quiet moment with George. "There is nothing that cannot be shaped and words like 'inevitability' and 'resignation' are not in my vocab."

"So you do not accept the inevitability of the USE and the decline of the nation state?"

"Absolutely not! I know it is treason but they are worrisome myths that tend to be self-fulfilling. There are no inevitabilities in life. Everything comes down to choices made. Take two youngsters starting out in life. The first is taught that certain things are inevitable, bound to happen. The second that success stems from individual choices, right or wrong, but made by real people. Now, which one do you suppose would feel inspired to strive the hardest? And which young person would be more satisfied after a life spent to good, honest purpose?"

"You should meet my father," was all that George said in response.

The pamphlet was organised into three sections covering Europe, Education and the Environment. Each part was a wealth of ideas, so much so that every word had to be valued against others competing for inclusion. It was tight, coherent and informative. It was a winner. And it came from nowhere for Future Perfect did not exist as an organisation, hence it could not be regulated or disapproved. Every day George thanked God for Mandy's brilliant idea to create a party that was not a party, an organisation that did not exist and could not therefore be attacked.

Word spread quickly through the underground. No official poll could mention an organisation that did not exist on the Political Relations Official List so they could not measure for sure their rising popularity. However, the 'Don't Know' category had historically been around 6% and was now running over 20%. Everyone knew that was support for Future Perfect. And it was the European Liberals who were losing two votes for every one the Conservatives gave up, bucking the established trend of governments suffering badly in the polls.

"First we win the moral victory," Sir Terrence had stated. "Stranger things have happened than changing ballot papers at the last minute."

They were meeting to discuss strategy generally but one thing in particular. Francine, the underground leader of the Spiders, was present.

"Friends," she said, stepping up to the small stage at the front of the hall in West Pickering, Mark's home village, "friends, I have a proposal to put to you." She spoke for only six minutes, keeping very much to the point. She wanted to join forces. She said the vote at their management committee had been unanimous. It was matched by the Future Perfect vote shortly afterwards. The Spiders brought 38,000 active members and an underground network that could push out information and ideas throughout the country. It was the perfect distribution method for Future Perfect. So the illegal, underground political party subsumed itself within a wider organisation that did not legally exist and the combination proved three times the sum of the parts.

Francine L'Amour was still a young woman, although had given many hard years to the cause. She was tall, erect, a conservative dresser, always in smart clothes and was astoundingly good looking. She was often gruff but this hid her good humour, as if all the optimism of the world sprang from a well deep within her. She and George quickly became friends, writing and speaking together. Francine seemed to have a knack for staying one step ahead of the law. They used phones they discarded frequently and, like Elizabethan priests, they moved at night from one place to another. The usual arenas such as television, radio and advertising, were not available to the Spiders but they spoke in small halls, pubs and street corners and the Spiders increased and then increased again the frequency of their newspapers, printing more and more copies each run, bankrolled by Sir Terrence.

"George, have you thought much about how this could go?" Francine asked one night on the streets of Glasgow, long after dark. They had vacated the pub they were talking in only minutes before a viscous police raid that had rounded up some of their supporters. "I mean, if the 'Don't Knows' become a majority we basically have a revolution on our hands. We will have to find a way of getting the people's will in place. I don't know how to do that."

"The interesting thing," George replied, yawning excessively as he talked, "is what you bring to the table. You have in the Spiders one of the main ingredients to translate 'Don't Knows' into an election result."

"And what is that exactly?"

"Your network. It isn't going to be easy and I don't know how we are going to do it but at least we have a veritable army of supporters between the Spiders and Future Perfect. Here is our lift, I will explain more later." An old ambulance came around the corner and came to a halt in a bus stop without indicating. George, Francine and a handful of others clambered into the back with the ambulance already moving off. They were bound for Dumfries and then Carlisle. George and Andy sat on a stretcher bed and tried to go over some numbers but George quickly felt car sick as the ambulance swung around quiet city streets on its way south. He closed the books and said he needed to rest. Andy, seeing how strained he looked, swung down to sit on a first aid box, giving George the whole stretcher to lie on.

"Thanks." George yawned.

"Nay bother," Andy gave a passable impression of a Glaswegian accent. But George was asleep, forgetting about the fight. For a few hours he was back in the freezing cold of Washington, being taken around by Gerry Matthews on a whirlwind tour in the cold, still, silent day. This was a time before commitment, where the stillness made time stop and only ideas mattered. In his dream he took Gerry's hand and kissed her as he wished he had done.

The Professor and the Jigsaw

By late spring, as Oxford sought to wind up its year and slide, perversely, into academic winter, Professor Unwin-Smith had his papers in order. Thirty-eight indexed files, bulging and cross-referenced, piecing together a short but intense period of his father's life. Thirty-eight fat files plus one slender volume. This one he picked up and flicked through most often. Yet there were only three pages; the report George had found in February covering General Stein's apparent surrender to General Unwin-Smith during the final stages of the war complemented by two pages of scant notes in his own handwriting. His search had yielded no other reference to this mysterious event and the trunk of inherited papers now stood empty, categorised and filed.

Was this single report an error? Yet it was in his father's handwriting so it could not be. Why did the rumour of Stein's surrender exist when there had been no evidence until now? Why would his father have refused to talk about it, refused even to let it be discussed? What possible explanation could there be? So the academic winter wound on with the professor deadlocked in his study, thirty-nine files on the desk in front of him.

"Listen again to what it says, George." He read the concise report, noting for the hundredth time the expressions of facts and the lack of any external references, as if censored by God to pass on nothing but the essentials. "But are they facts? Why this one isolated report? Nowhere else does it mention anything about General Stein." He waved his arms above the table of files. "Maybe there is a side to Dad I have never known. Maybe it is wishful thinking on his part – the capture of some great Nazi warlord, a dream sketched out in ten lines of fake report. It would be understandable."

"I don't think so," George replied. "I doubt he would have found a single moment for idle dreams in 1945." George had returned to Oxford for a brief respite, like a starving teenager bringing home a bag of washing, his father had joked.

"Well, it is a mystery I do not understand."

"Then concentrate on something else, at least for the time being. We need your help. The election is looming. We have to convert the 'Don't Knows' into a meaningful army of voters with a choice. We are trying to put together a team of very well respected public figures from all walks of life, people who are prepared to back us openly. It is being led by Sir Terrence Scott, the industrialist, who has helped us with huge donations. You don't know him but he is keen to meet you. You'd like him. Can we count on…"

"Of course, son, of course." So the professor pushed his unfinished jigsaw to one side and stepped, with a silent sigh, back from the past to the present. Maybe he would never finish the puzzle.

"We want to let rip with a really effective broadside," George was continuing. "You see we have the awareness. There can't be many voters across the country that have not heard of the Future Perfect and what we stand for. We just need to find a way of breaking into the mainstream without being closed down for being against the principles of the USE. We even have contacts who can get you and others on television and the radio, anything which might convince the electorate that we are a genuine political force, although not legally an entity at all!"

"Glad to help, George. And I do need to put this to one side for the time being." But could he put it out of his mind? It seemed to him to be the culmination of a sixty-year academic career. Could he force isolation between the generations by turning away from his father to assist his son? Was this possible? Superficially, yes, his father was long dead while George was very much alive. But take a step back and look at it again. Was George doing anything very different to his own father? Both were endeavouring to force change in order to return to what had been before. It seemed nonsensical when put that way. It was clear to him that both his father and his son had a nobility of purpose that set them apart. He himself was a leading academic, a highly respected Oxford don, but he knew he lacked that higher vision that sandwiched him on both sides; past and future, father and son.

"It won't be long, just until the election." George laughed nervously, seeing the questions on his father's face. "Besides, it will do you a little good to have a change of scene. I've arranged for you to meet Sir Terrence and some of the others on Thursday evening in London. We will need to stay at my flat because there is a press conference on Friday at 10am. Also, I think Melody has you tentatively booked on the *Today Programme* that morning, apparently to talk about educational standards at university but I am sure you can twist it around!"

"Well, the cannons are charged and the broadsides ready to let rip!" Edward would go through with it. It was his duty.

Promotion

Gerry Matthews looked herself over one more time. The birch-framed full-length mirror presented an image of the young executive. Springy hair tied back, not severely but neatly, the slender metal clips matching and merging with the rich brown colour. Some makeup, but not too much; just enough to accentuate her large, solemn eyes. Then the clothes: smart black suit with skirt three inches below the knees, simple white blouse and matte red tie. The almost coordinated red briefcase was a piece of luck for it was the only one she owned, but it completed the picture. The young executive: purposeful, businesslike and feminine.

She had thought she would take a taxi but walked instead to the metro station. Despite the heat, the sun burning down on her black-jacketed back, she preferred to walk. The motion served to settle her, a little at least.

One more glance at her reflection in a deli window across from the station entrance. She had to look right. How would it go? Was she dressed too sombrely?

Sitting in the train, briefcase on her knees, straightening skirt and tie with clammy hands, watching strangers with new interest as her stomach slowly churned. Four stops to go, then three. In ninety minutes, she told herself, it would all be over. The return journey would be so different, sitting back with loosened collar, briefcase deposited on the floor. Maybe she would even undo her hair. Yes, if it all went well she would take out the clips and throw back her hair.

She knew each member of the panel, had worked with some

132

of them. But this was different. This was promotion, a chance to really make it.

"So, Miss Mathews, you have told us about your reasons for being here today. But what is it you can actually offer the Society in this position?" The light, shooting through the bank of windows along the wall to her right, illuminated the questioner like a spotlight. Yet the day had turned cloudy, hot and humid, the sun making brief visits only. In a moment the spotlight would be dimmed until the next interrogator required lighting up. Six of them, including her boss, lined up along a table of worn mahogany. Firing squad or welcoming committee?

"Two principle things. First, a breadth of experience and understanding you will not find in many people my age. Second, a vision combined with a deep sense of commitment. To me this is not just a job, but a vocation. It has always been a vocation. My father taught me how important it is to discover what you are supposed to do in life; your 'natural purpose', he called it. And then to be the best you can at whatever it is. My strength is that I have found my 'natural purpose'. It's a neat circle because the Society gives me my sense of purpose, which allows me, in turn, to give so much more back to it."

"You mean an individual is considerably more, let's say, productive when focused and doing something he or she is naturally suited to?"

"Yes, on an obvious level but also more deeply. We are talking here about loyalty and dedication. It might sound a little twee but I believe in it."

The sunlight flashed in and out, in and out, as the hour ground on. Questions and answers - some good, others not quite so.

"Tell me, Miss Matthews, about your concept of liberty. Is it worth fighting for and why?"

"What are the greatest challenges you see in this position?"

"Would you break rules in pursuit of your objectives?"

"Your greatest achievement to date?"

"And your biggest failure?"

133

"How do others see you and you see others?"

"How do we know you can build a team around you?"

"And how does politics fit with all this?"

And so it went on, questions and answers alternating like verse and chorus.

"Any further questions?" her boss asked as the clock marked off an hour and ten minutes.

"Yes, just one." The sole lady on the panel spoke up, shifting herself slightly upright in her seat. She had only asked easy questions so far. Was she a natural ally? "I would like Miss Matthews to tell us all what it is that makes her so sure we should give her this promotion when there are a dozen far more experienced people available."

"My outlook..."

"No, Miss Matthews, that won't do. Outlook is like attitude; it comes and goes and anyone can profess to it. I want to hear something more substantial. What is it that makes you so qualified?"

"Well, Mrs Johnson, I believe I have a good mix of experience. I have been lucky to work here in Washington..."

"So have others, including half of those on the shortlist."

"As I was saying, my work in Washington has been real unique, owing to the international context. Take last February, for instance. I worked closely with George Unwin-Smith when he came over for the highly successful Hourglass Lectures."

"You mean you entertained him?" Was that a sneer?

"Yes," a sudden boldness born of irritation, "I entertained him, but I also engaged him, engaged his mind." Sweat made her blouse cling to her skin, her collar uncomfortably tight. If only she could reach up and ease the restriction for a moment. Why hadn't she worn something more comfortable?

"That's true. He told me himself how impressed he was with Miss Matthews." Pearson, the president, confirmed George's opinions with a faint smile. In that moment, before the sun emerged once more and blurred his expression into a mass of orange and pink pulp, she knew she had his support.

"I believe," she continued, a little more certainly, "that this demonstrates my value to the Society. I have the vision, enough said of that." The confidence was flowing back now. "I have the drive and I have the ability. In addition, I have experience of setting up a local branch..."

"Yes, but in Nebraska..."

"Nevertheless, I was instrumental in getting it going. It was my success there that got me my job in DC. And now I have the national, indeed the international, experience so necessary for this position. Others may well be older with more years at the Society behind them. That does not mean, however, that they are better suited. What I have to offer is unique and perfect for this position. Whether I get the chance is up to you. Thank you everybody for giving me the opportunity today to put my strengths to you. If there are no further questions?"

Quick goodbyes, final handshakes, door closed behind her, now galloping through the office she knows so well, seeking the blessed relief of anonymity. Back down to the metro station, train waiting. But Gerry forgets to pull the clips from her hair or deposit the briefcase on the floor. As the train moves out the briefcase remains clutched on her knees. Still watching strangers, her stomach no more settled. Fingers, acting independently, run up to her collar. It aches to be undone, to hear the gasp of released steam once the valve is opened. But instead she only fiddles and straightens as if still in the interview, still under observation. As if, even here on the train where she ought to be anonymous, she can still, somehow, influence the decision. Thus, once home, she moves about the apartment but does not relax. Her mind retraces the proceedings, sending down thrills and frights to make her heart jump and miss a beat. She runs a bath but does not get in. Her roommate returns from work to find her pacing the floor; good suit, hair still tied up. Only the makeup is a little smudged, to mark the passing of an entire afternoon.

"Relax, Gerry, it's over. There is nothing you can do now." But it isn't over, not until the decision has been made.

"I want the job so bad," she replies, still unable to sit.

She had been the last candidate. They had said they would

let her know one way or the other that same day. How much longer was this protracted interview going to last, this besieging of their collective judgment with her single battery of willpower?

The telephone rings. How cruel, it is just a friend.

"No, no news yet. I'm just waiting to hear. It's hard to tell, some parts went good, others not so. I'll call as soon as I know something."

Eventually she is persuaded to have a bath: a hot, steamy bath. But before she even starts to fill the tub the telephone rings again. She scrambles to the sitting room to take the receiver from her roommate, who is smiling.

"Can I come and visit you over there?" she whispers as she passes it over. Gerry does not answer, refusing to allow the tension to disperse until it is official. But she knows now.

"Hello, Gerry Matthews here."

"Hi Gerry," her boss, sounding cheerful, "congratulations! As of right now you are the Chief Operating Officer of our first ever overseas location and the youngest COO we've ever had in the Society. It was a unanimous decision by the panel. You might be interested to know that Mrs Johnson, who gave you a hard time at the end, was adamant that you were the most suitable candidate by a long way. It's a marvellous opportunity to influence the start of a new, international chapter for us and we could not hope for a better person to fill that role."

"Thank you, sir, thank you."

"Don't thank me, you were the clear leader. But you also have let yourself in for a whole lot of work over the next few years."

"I know, sir, but thank you so much. When do I go?"

"As soon as you can, hopefully early next week. Come into the office first thing tomorrow and we'll go see Mr Pearson. He'll run you through everything. Now go celebrate tonight, relax and enjoy. It may be your last chance for a while!"

"I know one thing," she said as she replaced the receiver, turned to her friend and grasped her collar with both hands, "this is one opportunity I'm never going to regret!"

Playing with Dates

Quite why, David Kirkby did not know, but something about Bertie had changed. He could no longer trust the man. He seemed somewhere else, still hungry but for a different food. Still singing but the melody no longer a tune David could recognise, in fact ugly clashing discords drawn from scales the PM had never heard before.

"Terry, I want you to run the election campaign."

"Not Bertie?" Terry Rose was not surprised.

"No, the man has changed; I can't put my finger on it. No, you are the man for the job."

"Complete freedom of action?"

"Yes, just make sure you win the damn thing. Scotch?"

"Please, thanks, cheers! Step number one, get rid of Shepherd."

"Are you sure?"

"He's a liability, David, he'll cost you votes."

"Well, let's think a moment…"

"Nothing to think about, David. If you want me, he goes. Simple as that." David, with his innate political sixth sense, had really known it would come to this. As the whisky swirled down his mouth he saw how neat the solution looked. He could blame Terry this way. The sliver of guilt at sacking the man who had held his hand when he first entered the Commons was washed away by the second slug of Scotch. Politics was, after all, a harsh game where the greater good had to be looked out for.

"So be it." David half-rose to clink glasses with Terry but the gesture was unreciprocated and ended in slight embarrassment, David disguising the movement as shifting in his chair. "I'll do it after Thursday's cabinet meeting. I want you to get your election committee together before that and report to me, say Tuesday evening, on your initial strategy before I send Dennis to the great Commons in the sky!" Terry did not respond to his joke, increasing David's unease. Instead, he simply finished his drink, rose to go and informed the PM he already had his committee ready and would advise on strategy at the appointed time. Indeed, he already had his strategy in place and knew that his committee members would back him completely. He had expected more of a fight to get full control but his boss almost seemed to be abdicating.

On Tuesday evening, Terry and the PM sat together in the Number 10 private flat, a whisky apiece; same as the previous meeting only two floors higher. Bertie was not there. He had gone home or somewhere but was not part of this meeting. David finished his drink and rose for a refill, not noticing that Terry was sipping his. David was on the hilltop, looking down, nervous at the rapid ascent of his cabinet colleague, yet guiding him up the steep slope. Terry spoke first.

"The first essential step we spoke about, that is all in hand? You're going to see Shepherd after the cabinet meeting?"

"Yes, Terry." That did not sound right, not coming from a Prime Minister. He ought to be controlling the meeting. Sitting upright, he took another slug. "Now, what other thoughts have you got for me?"

"Step two is recognition of where the real competition is. It's not the farty LibDems I am talking about. Let's call a spade a spade. We have to beat the shit out of the Future Perfect."

"But they are not standing, not even a political party, no contenders…"

"Lord, David, don't you see what the crafty buggers are up to?"

"Well of course I do," another shot, his glass was empty again, "but carry on. I want to hear your views first." Had he appointed a crackpot to run his campaign? Where the hell was Bertie?

"Think about the principle of democracy and then think about the function of democracy." Terry rather enjoyed the fact that his boss clearly had not thought this through.

"One person, one vote."

"Precisely, now look at the polls." Terry pulled out a notebook from his jacket pocket and continued. "I average out the 'Don't Knows' to be 38% over the last six published polls. That is four times higher than it has ever been before. Why?"

Why, David thought bitterly, was Rose playing with him instead of explaining?

"Just get on with your briefing, old chap. I don't have that much time."

"If you wanted to vote for the Future Perfect, how would you do it?"

"Terry, you can't vote for them. Do I have to remind you that whatever that directive is…"

"OK David, let me put it this way." David had never been able to stand strained patience. It crippled his confidence. "How would you express your opinion to a pollster if asked who you wanted to vote for and there is no box to tick for Future Perfect but that is who you want to select?"

"I don't know… oh, I see. Good God!"

"Precisely! So the real opinion poll averages are as follows: Future Perfect 38%, Conservatives 27%, LibDems 20%, European Socialists 8% and others whatever is damn well left. Hence the Future bloody Perfect is our real competition and Mark bloody Borden stands to be the next Prime Minister."

"Good Lord!" Where was Bertie? David rose for his fourth refill. "So that is step two. What next?"

"We push the investigation. We get EurPo involved. We get EurInfo involved. We get any bloody Euro office who will listen to us involved and then…" Terry fell back on his old trick of pausing to build suspense.

"And then?"

"Simple, we bring the election forward. We bring it forward

by eight weeks so it falls right in the middle of this investigation."

"But that means getting European approval. Directive something or other says the European Commission has to approve all dates for elections."

"In the works, David, in the works. I had a quick word with Bertram first and then applied 48 hours ago unofficially and got their blessing – it is in their interests and no doubt Grandee paved the way! All it needs is your signature on this document and we can announce the new election date immediately. We can do it tonight. That gives us an extra advantage."

"Being?"

"We get Shepherd to back it fully and give him some special but meaningless role. Then instead of sacking him on Thursday you get him to resign and he suddenly loses all credibility, becomes a spent force."

"You have thought it all through, haven't you?" David was grasping for somewhere to hang his authority.

"One other thing, the general approach to our election campaign. The Future Perfect has their three Es. We are going with the three Cs. 'Continuing Conservative Concepts'."

"I like it. Yes, it has a ring to it." Everything screamed at David to reject one part of Rose's approach, just to assert some control, but it seemed impossible to find fault.

"Now, I'd better let you get on with that other pressing business you alluded to. Goodnight, David." Terry left his half-full glass on the table and, with the signed election approval papers in his hand, quickly left the room. David sat back and wondered again where the hell Bertie was when he needed him. Or Marjorie, for that matter.

Resignation

David caught Terry's eye and understood. Then Bertie, along with the others, was gone, leaving Dennis once more face-to-face with his boss.

"I wanted a chance for a little chat." The PM crossed the room and beckoned Dennis into a small antechamber. "It will be private in here."

One desk, large chair behind, small upright one in front, out on its own, a scene prepared. This was it then, the sacking, the end. How would Kirkby handle it?

"Dennis, old chap. We're entering some pretty uncertain times over the next few weeks." The words flowed according to the formula. "I don't mind telling you, as one of my oldest political allies, that I am taking some big risks right now. I'm going to announce it to the full cabinet in a moment but I wanted you to hear it first." Dennis sat up. This was not the script he was prepared for. He looked at David, who looked out of the window.

"Announce what?"

"The election." Said as if Dennis should have known all along. "I've decided to hold it early, September 3rd to be precise. To catch the others off balance."

"But that is only six weeks away!"

"Exactly! Six weeks for the other parties also." Did he come across as supremely self-assured and in control? As Terry had when making the same point to him? "Dennis, I've asked Terry to be my campaign manager..."

"Not Bertie?"

"No, not Bertie. I... I, well, I need a seasoned politician in the job, someone with aggression. I think he will do well."

Well for himself! Dennis wanted to add but did not.

"But so much is at stake," David continued, noticing with satisfaction that he had got his minister's complete attention. "I've decided to split the role. I want you to coordinate all presentation and publicity for the campaign while Terry concentrates on policy and organisation. It's a tough brief, Dennis, I don't mind admitting that I thought long and hard about this. You have seemed a bit off-colour lately. But I still think you are the right man for the job and one of the few who can stand up to our Mr Rose!"

It worked at first. Dennis felt the warm glow of praise mixing with pride and ambition. Of course he could do the job. He was an experienced and capable politician. This was a challenge many would jump at. And he had expected dismissal.

"Yes, of course I could do it..." Dennis started to say, until the colour of the morning sky, visible in the east through the single window, caught his eye. He had seen that sky before, quite recently. A long, invigorating walk in unfamiliar countryside. Sound perspective, renewed senses, old muscles rediscovered like childhood articles in the attic. Then he recalled going inside the stone-built, single-storey building to the welcome of a comfortable chair. He could picture the surroundings now; the bright, energetic fire eating hungrily at freshly-sawn logs, spitting and dribbling in its haste to devour all with its orange tongues. He could hear the gentle sound of voices: one his, the other..? It would come in a moment. The presence, too, of a woman. For a moment he thought it must have been his wife, the stranger he had known for a generation and more, but, no, it was Felicity Graves, adding an occasional, succinctly expressed opinion like another log on the fire. It was he and Bertie discussing the future. He had not realised it at the time, but could see now how she had guided their discussion, the experienced ship's pilot keeping an eye on the tiller while those less knowledgeable learned their craft.

It almost worked, Kirkby's and Rose's scheme to render him

impotent in the coming campaign. Almost.

"I'm afraid I am going to have to say 'No', although I appreciate the offer. In fact…" It was then, just thirty minutes from the announcement of the General Election, that Dennis Shepherd, oldest and longest serving member of the cabinet, Minister for the Environment and a man of truth, resigned, abruptly turning his back on a life devoted to the Conservative Party. But even more abrupt was the alteration in Kirkby's countenance, realisation and dismay swarming in from different directions and meeting, in predictable confusion, in face central. He had no secondary plan! What should he do?

"Dennis my dear friend, this is very sudden."

"It's what you have been expecting and hoping for all along." The truth, glorious in its naked form, stripped of the diplomacy that so often destroys it, so powerful because of what it is.

"But Dennis, it is critical that we stick together, the election…"

"Come on, David, you know as well as I do that this administration has left me far behind. I should have resigned months or even years ago. I've got nothing in common with where you're taking things and certainly nothing ever in common with Rose."

"You'll be on your own, finished!"

"Not at all, I believe I have a lot of personal backing in my constituency. I might stand as an independent."

Terry Rose had shrugged this off, his calm countenance in contrast to David's flustering.

"I'll handle it." He had a plan B even if Kirkby did not.

"Of course we'll have to put off the election." A statement but in question format; asking permission.

"Nonsense, we plough ahead. I said I will handle it. I can keep Shepherd in line."

Terry stood up, a sign for the PM to leave. The others were waiting for him in the cabinet room.

"How?" He hung on Terry's words, a climber well above the

valley floor, way beyond his level, fingers away from death and oblivion.

"Just leave it to me and send Shepherd in to see me."

Dennis did not resign that day, nor did he sleep that night. Terry had the satisfaction of placing sweet plans in action, but Dennis witnessed nothing sweet; only turmoil of heart and mind, conflict and confusion. He wrestled with these thoughts all night, alone in the flat that had never been a home, before reporting dutifully to Terry the next morning for the follow-up election campaign meeting.

What sort of Dennis, then, sat sleepily and sheepishly around the campaign table that morning, the first morning of the election campaign, facing his boss (relieved) and his old adversary (triumphant)? What sort of Dennis took on the mantle of presentation and publicity, summoning up every bit of deceit his honest body could muster? What sort of man, guardian of principles and shepherd of the truth, bows to the weight of blackmail, knowing his career to be in shreds, that same climber hanging on with one fist clenched in a crevice, body swinging freely, waiting for the world to rush up past him? What shepherd will muzzle his dogs when he knows the wolves are moving in?

Terry's view was simple. "If he wants to stay I get rid of him, if he wants to leave I keep him." So Dennis stayed on because he was so alone and feared losing the one non-political thing he valued to the man he hated and feared. So Dennis betrayed himself for half a chance of keeping his wife.

And where was Bertie during all this? Did the truth they explored together in the simple isolation of the Scottish Highlands prove inadequate for the sophisticated city? Happily not. Bertie hesitated only long enough to draw breath before presenting a short, crisp resignation letter to the PM that afternoon. Kirkby panicked and Terry calmed him down. Bertie was not a main player and had been going downhill for weeks. He was a spent force. Now the PM could hire the very best PR consultants this crazy metropolis could offer. David felt reinforced but Marjorie saw that the reinforcements were required too often now, like a drug addict needing more and more frequent fixes while his old friends faded off into other lives. He poured another whisky and then one more before retiring upstairs to his flat and waiting wife.

"David, dearest?" Marjorie watched him tip a generous glass from the decanter. "What is your angle on the election?"

"What do you mean?" David turned around, knocking the decanter stopper onto the floor; Marjorie deftly picked it up from under the sideboard and placed it back on the decanter.

"I mean, what approach are you going to take?"

"That's, I mean, that's for the Election Committee. They've only had two meetings. I am sure they…"

"But David, your instinct must tell you something. What is important?"

"Of course it does. I mean." David fell silent for a full minute and then sat down in an armchair off-centre for Marjorie's view. "I mean I want to be known as the man who carved a future for Britain in the USE. The man who…"

"But David, don't you think you might be a little behind the times?"

"Nonsense! I am the future. There's no point in ranting and raving about getting out of the USE when we stand to lose so much. These idealistic dreamers think…"

"Idealistic dreamers, you say?"

"Yes, the Future bloody Perfect and the bloody Spiders!" When Terry swore it added something to the argument. Somehow, when David tried, it did not quite work.

"These are the same 'idealist dreamers' who appear to have a commanding lead in every opinion poll and the backing of a growing but admittedly still small body of the intellectual elite of this country. The same 'idealistic dreamers' who appear to have sound arguments on the environment, industry, health, defence, foreign policy, agriculture, fishing?"

"But…" David looked down at his glass, swirled the remaining amber around the base and then looked out of the window at the setting sun. "But, well, I mean everyone agrees, don't they? I mean, we have spent all my time in office fighting

145

for the best for Britain."

"Retreating, sometimes in an orderly fashion and sometimes less so."

"But fighting, dammit! Now I am exhausted. One more for the road and let's hit the sack." The clichés were out of their cage again and fluttering freely around the Number 10 upper floor flat.

Around the Table

"Ladies and gentlemen, both in the audience here at Southampton University and all of you watching at home, these are, without doubt, stirring times. Who here has not felt the wind of change? Who here has not wondered if perhaps the original will of the people, expressed in the referendum of 2016, might not after all become the future? Who could have foreseen a new force in politics arising so rapidly? And yet that force is not a force. It does not exist yet it has all the traditional parties scrambling frantically for higher ground. As we face a General Election in just twenty-eight days, how are we going to reconcile this relentless force for change with the fact that you won't find 'Future Perfect' on any ballot paper?"

"We'll let it run for now," said the editor back in London. "I was told to use my discretion so have a suitable documentary programme ready to switch to but let's run with it as is for now."

"John, you cannot. It is against the principles of the USE. We can't let this nonsense pollute the political debate and side-track the real issues. I was led to believe there would be discussion about the benefits of integration, the investment that the USE has made in education and culture, the new education initiatives, the *Europe and Me* app, not claptrap about illegal parties and views which don't serve any purpose other than to incite the people and leave them ultimately unhappy and discontented."

"Eleanor, this is my decision. We have to show that we are

open to new ideas. The backup switchover is confirmed as in place. I just flick the switch and… Jeff, what does it go over to?"

"It's that doc. we did last year on the growth of multiculturalism and tolerance in the USE."

The presenter was rambling, liking the sound of his own voice. "1945… the start of the socialist experiment… the Thatcher revolution… Social Democrats… Brexit."

"This is enough, John, we cannot have mainstream presenters mentioning that word on television. You know very well it is strictly prohibited."

"Eleanor, I know as the Sector 8 Director of EurView you have responsibility for all political and social content but this is my programme. I am the editor, and I have the right to overrule you to see where this is going to go. I have a backup and will not let this get out of hand. You need to relax and trust the people. Open debate, carefully guided, gives the impression of choice and the illusion that people can make up their own minds. So please be quiet and let me get on with my job." Eleanor missed the brief wink he gave Jeff.

"That is it, Mr Baker", no more 'Johns' any more, "I am going outside to call my boss, who will soon put a stop to this." Eleanor stormed out, her greying blonde hair bouncing behind her, Jeff rushing to open the door and close it again quietly.

"Well, John, that will give us thirty minutes until the big boys bear down on us. I hope it is worth it for all our sakes! This really is the point of no return now!"

"Tonight, as the General Election campaign gathers pace, we have a star-studded cast to lead us through the maze of British politics."

"John, this is dangerous," Jeff warned. "He knows he has to call it European politics, not British, and he can't have 'politicians' on a panel unless they have been pre-approved by the authorities. This is heading somewhere very scary."

"Jeff, relax. I feel born again after hearing Professor Unwin-Smith on the radio yesterday morning. I sense we are making real history now, like Tiananmen Square or the Civil Rights marches under Martin Luther King. Don't you see? This could be huge and we could be a small part of it. We have to give it some prime time and this is the only way to do it."

"Our panel of eight has been drawn from the leading political thinkers of our time. For the conservatives we have Terry Rose, often tipped to be the next PM, and with him Henry Morris..."

George was next around the table after the Home Secretary and wondered briefly what words the verbose presenter would throw around the room to introduce him. Certainly, Terry Rose looked content with his description as a Prime Minister in waiting. His red, made-up cheeks, shone under the studio lights, his upper half reflected but distorted in the polished table-top around which they sat. George had never talked with Terry Rose before. He had tried twice on previous occasions to start a conversation but each time had been met with cold stares of contempt.

George felt confident. He had appeared several times on similar programmes in the past and knew he could hold his own in rational debate. It made the desperate moves in borrowed cars late at night worth it. This was what he was born to do.

A ripple crossed the room. Beside George, Mark was blushing and smiling. It must have been something the presenter said about him. That meant George had missed his own introduction.

"Now, enough time on the preliminaries, let us move to the first question, which is from Mr Roberts. Where are... oh, there you are." A tall, thin man with a grey goatie beard stood up and unfolded a piece of paper from his corduroy jacket pocket. "Mr Roberts is a teacher at Cackley Comprehensive. Your question, please."

"Would the panel agree that the recent United Nations report on education, which placed Britain 59th in the world league and was the 15th consecutive year of decline, represents a damning indictment of the government's education policies?"

"Terry, would you agree?"

"Of course not, Michael. No rational person could agree with the questioner. The fact of the matter is that education over the last six years has gone through a tremendous revolution. These things take time but we are starting to see the results coming through already. Our aim has been to put control of education firmly back into the hands of the parents, taking it away from the faceless civil servants." His voice rose as he got into his stride. "It's the parents of this country who know what's best for their children, not some quango closeted in Westminster. Our policies are all about choice, individual choices to match individual needs. This is the future of education in Britain, not some global, wishy-washy, desk-bound theory which sounds plausible but never actually delivers." Sitting back amidst moderate applause, Terry leaned back on the chair's hind legs, pleased with his opening salvo and defying his opponents to do better.

"George, you might have something to say in reply."

"Yes, indeed." He looked at the audience, wondering how many parents there were: sixty or seventy, at least. He could do this. This was easy for him: reasoned debate, the power of the intellect. "Let's go back and ask ourselves what education is. Put simply, somebody pays money for somebody else to impart knowledge and understanding to another. Normally, when we spend money we expect something in return. If we give it that is another matter, but spending is a contract. So what are we getting in return? We should expect knowledge, developing wisdom, understanding, technical ability, creativity, and love of the subject. But, by and large, it is not the spenders who gain directly but the youngsters, the next generation. Thus it is not present consumption but a true investment in the future. Education is like the man who plants oak trees on his estate, knowing he will never see them in maturity. So, sure, choice is important. Any business likes to have a choice of possible investments. But much more important is the quality of that investment leading to the eventual return. Quality is the key word in education. In its simplest form it is a production line, input and output. But it is like a production line where some cars are Rolls Royces, some are Fords, and some are scrapped as not up to standard. The job of those in education is to eliminate the scrap rate and maximise the quality of each car, whether a Bentley or a Fiat. Because this will give us the greatest return out into the future and will ensure that the best teachers and the best resources are available for the next rising generation. Our future prosperity and security depends on getting the very best out of each and every child. So we must invest remorselessly in education. We should never waste money but we should be asking ourselves..."

"Yes, yes," it was Terry, impatient, "fine theory, but the world does not run on grand theories. You can't live up in the clouds all your life, coming down once in a blue moon to spout a little more nonsense."

"I agree, Terry." That silenced Rose. "We theorise occasionally but most of the time we invest heavily in education. We should not be frightened into cutting back and shaving off this programme and that, or introducing a new, sweeping regime every few years, as has been the practice throughout my lifetime. Time passes, which means one more bad experiment and you have a missed opportunity for another child somewhere. And that has a human and a financial consequence for all of us. Every discovery, every breakthrough is not an instant thing but a product of years of combined effort at building knowledge." George looked at the audience: twelve rows with about twenty in each row; twelve-score faces absorbed in his argument. He was pitching it just right. "You cannot deny the findings of the United Nations. Other countries are doing better than us and, as a consequence, have more to invest and more fruits to share. It is a perpetual cycle of improvement and we, instead, are bound up in cuts disguised as policy initiatives! The other countries ahead of us act as if they know what they want to do and how to do it. When we start to act with that confidence we will be hopping up the league tables, not arguing about the rate of decline." His voice had reached a crescendo, something he did not realise until he stopped talking and for fifteen full seconds there was absolute silence. Then, very deliberately, Mr Roberts, the original

151

questioner, began to clap; slowly, as if marking the time it took for the words to sink in. Others joined him, building up to a new crescendo.

"Wow," said Jeff in the London studio, "that was something else." They had forgotten about EurView and the threats from above. No finger hovered above the backup switch.

The subsequent questions and answers flowed in similar vein. The Conservatives were aggressive in defence of their record, Terry trying again and again to ridicule the opposition, Morris more reasonable. The other parties barely got a look in. The clean-shaven Liberals, with their decent, obvious answers but lacking in energy, seemed like a sorry campfire, drenched beyond resuscitation by heavy rain. How brilliantly those flames had once raged and flickered, fed, like the early socialists, with the swiftly igniting, explosive oils of social injustice. But that was buried now in 'eurotalk', a determination to be good Europeans above anything else, above liberty, their very namesake. Then there were the Socialists, now a fringe party, or several parties, but every time they raised their voice they were shouted down by Terry Rose in a blaze of abuse.

To the audience it was rapidly becoming apparent that the election was a two-horse race, only one horse and rider was not even qualified to run on the track, not even registered and at the starting gate.

If it was a battle they fought around the table, then Mark played the part of inspired company commander to perfection. Not as quick to jump in as George, his points were shorter and less emotional, almost matter-of-fact. Yet George noticed that Mark was hardly ever interrupted, despite his quiet voice. He chose his ground well: the environment, transport, training in industry, farming, not much more. He responded to Terry Rose's dismissive behaviour with a remarkable degree of self-assurance and composure. Every word he said, every expression, seemed to underline how important his message was, how principled and full of hope his ideas were.

"Take transport," he said, following a particularly aggressive swipe from the glistening, scarlet-cheeked Foreign

Secretary, "many journeys by car are for frivolous reasons, yet the cost to us as a society is enormous. We should bear all these costs in mind and then ask ourselves whether we want to pay the price. But before returning to the horse and cart, why don't we look at the other options? Why don't we take the best from each era of transport? Motorcars have their distinct advantages, but so too do trains, planes, trams and barges. If we, for example, invested heavily in trains to increase their frequency, reliability, reach and comfort and then priced car travel with the true cost of motoring, we would get many more people choosing to travel by train. The real point is that this is all up to us. Why sit back and accept a damaging trend when we can collectively do something about it? We create the world we live in and we can improve it if we are determined enough."

But it was Europe that made the show and left Terry Rose cursing the Future Perfect, just as John cursed the truncheons banging on the outer studio door as Eleanor came back with reinforcements. They hurriedly dragged cabinets, desks, anything heavy, against the door to buy just a few more minutes of George's words for the airwaves.

"Look at our history," he began; he could not help it, it was the way he saw things, "time and time again we've looked out into the wide world with tremendous results. Then, frankly, Europe has taken away that perspective and dragged us into war. Look now at Europe and what do you see? Not the melting pot of USA but a mass of competing, thrusting, individualistic societies trying to gain one off each other, a vast pot simmering just below boiling point. Not a melting pot but a boiling pot. Time and time again from before the Dark Ages there have been moves to unify and dominate Europe. They tried with force and failed, but caused great misery in their trying. Now there is a new effort, a new push. But the objectives are just the same. They allow no one standing in their way, no competition to the monopoly of thought they ascribe to. Some of you may remember the Spiders, some may welcome their resurgence, others probably always detested them. But at least they represent a choice, a real choice, an alternative to the approved three-line whip."

"Wow," said Jeff as the door started to splinter, "this is really going places!"

"Jeff, take out the backup tape and destroy it. It will give us a few minutes."

"Better than that," Jeff replied as he swung a chair at the switch, breaking it off at its stem, "now they cannot put another tape in until they figure out how to do the manual override!"

"Now turn your attention away from politics, war and diplomacy and turn to trade," George continued, "Look at history one more time. Think of the links our history has given us with the world; the old Commonwealth before it was disbanded three years ago, the USA, the remaining colonial possessions before they were shamefully handed over earlier this year, the new states of Africa and Asia and South America. With such rich ties stretching around the globe, why should we focus so much on one small part of it? Make Europe one more glorious tie of co-operation and friendship rather than be blinkered and unable to see the wider world."

"I have one more point to make and that concerns sovereignty." But the wider audience would not hear this point because at that moment an enterprising employee of EurView found the main breaker and closed down the EBC just as the police burst through the pile of desks and cabinets and dragged John, Jeff and three assistants away in a big black van with high windows. They had played their part but now had to pay the price.

But those in the audience at Southampton University heard a few more precious words before the local police replicated the actions up in London and cut the lights and power, thankfully allowing George and Mark to escape in the confusion. Thus they heard the last few words from George that night: "Sovereignty is not about self-interest or national interest but about the peoples of today taking the hard-won treasures of the past on into the future, to pass on to their sons and daughters. It is a heritage we have no right to destroy because we are not the creators, merely the tenants for a half-dozen decades or so.

We have a responsibility to improve and adapt and not stand still but we also have a responsibility to remember that we are the sum of all that went before us." It was at that point that the lights went out and the debate shut down.

"Bloody Future Perfect!" Terry spluttered, still angry when he had returned by fast car to Downing Street and accepted Kirkby's standard offering of a large Scotch. "It's high time something was done to take them down a peg or two. Theorising bloody bastards."

One Joint

Twenty days prior to the election, strictly speaking it was a clean sweep for the Conservatives as the popular option was not on any ballot paper. But that was before it all went so horribly wrong.

Terry had not been at the scene, he had no official reason to be there, but did not need to be there. The moment the telephone rang and she answered it, looking quizzically back across the bed as if to say 'who knows you are here?' he knew.

"Rose." He took the receiver, avoiding her unspoken question. Several seconds of silence giving rise to more questions from her.

"What's happened, Terry? Why do you have to go? It's something serious, isn't it? I can tell." Interrogative, slightly panicked eyes followed him round the room as he tried to dress quickly.

"Yes, it's bloody serious alright!"

His mind pitched valiantly against a sagging spirit, no mood to address her bank of questions. Besides, he had so many of his own. What had happened? And how? And why on earth had he gone ahead with it in the first place? What had happened to his razor-sharp judgment? But most of all, why, when it happened, was he to be found in this damn woman's bed? He had told himself one more night before ending it in the morning. Now it had to end immediately. Back to the telephone.

"Porter, Terry Rose here. Get my car out front right now."

"Yes, sir. And it's all clear, sir. The subject is in his

constituency tonight, sir." Said with schoolboy delight in collaboration.

"When will you be back?" she asked, drawing the sheet away from her naked body. But all Terry saw was a lonely middle-aged woman desperate for reassurance.

"I'll be in touch." He forced a peck on the cheek, knowing it was far from sufficient, in fact would create the opposite impression. "This is going to take all my time." He still had not told her what had happened in the middle of that hot August night.

Terry Rose makes his way to his car, brushing past the schoolboy responsible for the door, creating more disappointment on the way. His curiosity is all-encompassing, but even he has to wait, a senior member of government forced to pace his fifth-floor office while others below, more junior and more involved, retrace events and piece together what must have happened. The facts filter through, like time slowed right down so that single grains make their way through the hourglass, not future to past but speculation to horrific reality.

"Three shots… in the back… blood everywhere… no chance of survival… no, correction… still breathing but unconscious… almost certainly paralysed… coma." Terry gets the news but not that much earlier than the public, the people he serves, the people he represents. He has to hold fire. He has to be careful. It would be different if we were Home Secretary. But he is not so he has to wait.

One person who saw it all is Mandy Friar. She was there when the police broke in, there amidst the rapid confusion as moving shadows plunged and darted through larger, paler, stationary ones. If that can be called seeing then she saw it all. Certainly, she heard the three separate shots as they rung across night-time London, the three dull thuds as bullet hit bone and Mark Borden's sturdy shadow dropped like the sails of a stricken man of war to wallow hopelessly in the lower, blacker regions that lurked that night by the bedroom floor.

"Lights. For Christ's sake the lights!" Somebody, kneeling by the body, took charge. "He's still breathing, get an ambulance.

And get that bloody girl out of here." One flash as the portable light went on like a flare, rushing through the room and pausing, briefly, at the high point of its trajectory. One flash in which she saw, not so much her bloodied lover lying so perfectly at sleep on the floor, but the embarrassed dark uniforms which encircled her room. Then she was hustled out, the door closed firmly behind her as the light was rigged in a semi-permanent position. She was shepherded into the sitting room, where a female police officer offered tea and then wondered how she would make it with the power cut at the fuse box.

History has, for all its virtues, a clinical approach to matters past, for how else can it operate other than through facts, data, analyses and interpretations? They are recorded, learned and argued over and always will be. But consider how much else there is. Take one relatively uneventful second from any time in history and imagine how many millions of rushing thoughts and sweeping events were crowded into that single Calcutta Massacre of time. Far more than millions. Far more than square inches in the universe. Then consider how many seconds there have been since the world began and how each such event in each such second plays on the others; a million billion unique relationships hopping back and forth across the frontiers of time. Right now there are several billion at least whose influence is not yet spent, decisions and determinations the effect of which may not be felt until close to the end of eternity. Think how dynamic such a structure is, how impossible it would be for the finest, most powerful computer to replicate it. This is real History: living existing relationships of cause and effect which span the barriers that divide the past from the present and the present from the future. This is the virile, never-ending chain that ties the first day to the last; complexity of the highest order and, from this, we note down the merest fraction and call it 'History'. How can we expect to understand the whole when we leave so much out, the blind piecing together jigsaws in a darkened room?

Take Mark Borden as an example. The first 'history' of these terrible events would be in the television and internet broadcasts, a few hundred words of limited, hastily convened facts peppered with conjecture. Next would come the newspapers the following day with sufficient time to check more facts but also time for further conjecture, clever journalists posing 'penetrating questions'. From there mainstream history takes over with analysis and facts in several inches of print. Mark's shooting at the hands of the drug squad would be mentioned in every political history of the twenty-first century. More specialist books would be available, carefully treading an allowable path through Euroregs, seeking blessing pre-publication from EurView. But this is normally no more than a stage in a journey to dry academia, dusty shelves where people only look from time to time. But every so often there is something else. The shooting of Gandhi, the liberation of Mandela, the execution of Charles I, and, most of all, the signing of the Magna Carta which stood solid as a rock for 800 years before being tidied up into Directive 18/126. Every so often something remains and makes a difference, defying the instruction to park itself with all the other facts on high-up shelves of seldom-visited rooms.

And this was just such a case. And the Spiders knew exactly what to do. Within thirty-six hours they had a five-million-copy special edition available at every street corner. Gone was the furtive distribution, quickly moving on when the black-and-white uniforms came into view. Gone was the fear of being caught and jailed. Gone suddenly was all fear, replaced by something new, something unstoppable and with an energy of its own. It was fired up by the Spiders, backed by Sir Terrence, and flamed by Future Perfect until the forest fire got entirely its own momentum. And once going it ripped across the land. Andy even managed to get one of George's speeches on YouTube, gaining fourteen million views in twenty-four hours. George did not consider it a good speech at all.

Terry Rose paced his office floor and wondered what to do as the world around him exploded with hope.

But who has thought of Mandy during all this? The young woman who had witnessed the raid that went so horribly wrong and gunned down her boyfriend and role model? And who considered the agony the police inspector suffered before redirecting his exhaust fumes and leaving behind nothing save a wife, three children and a house with negative equity? And what of the fear that clutched Terry Rose in those hours immediately after the telephone call that rudely interrupted his play with another man's wife? For Terry, each development was like scratching a jagged, rusting saw across his belly, ripping and grating, backwards and forwards; besieged nerves became a ragged ruin. How the arrogant have fallen. And what of Andrea Shepherd, slowly realising through silence that she meant nothing to Terry Rose and then racked as the guilt set in, framed in stark reality? Where, then, is the history of these multitudes of emotions that did not exist, were not thought about or imagined, before those three panic-inspired clutches on the trigger? How indeed can one single second cause so much?

It had all gone so terribly wrong. One inexperienced policeman among a host of seasoned professionals. If only he had gone sick or been reassigned. If only things had gone as intended.

"Good work last night, Terry," was all that Kirkby would have had to say with a wink to show their brotherhood.

"Thank you, PM," he would have replied, matter-of-factly, seriously but with a reflection of the wink in his eye. But instead it was grey, worried faces, more than a dozen, that met mid-morning the next day. More than a dozen faces staring blankly at Terry, a wall suddenly grown up between them. This was the risk that went with reward. The others were not responsible. They each justified their support away. It was not their problem but they would have to deal with the consequences somehow.

"There's to be an enquiry," David had said, ashen cheeks moving with the words like bellows, but the lips barely moving, like a human censor limiting the flow of words of an unpleasant nature.

"To report after the election?" Everybody knew there would be an enquiry and it would report long after the election if at all.

"That's right."

"And in the meantime?"

"Business as usual. We have to limit the damage. "

"Did the police find anything?"

"They found one joint." That was Morris, the Home Secretary. At least they had something.

It is established, then, that what we understand to be our understanding is the tip of the iceberg. We see the crest of each wave but can only guess at the depth and force below it. Or where each drop of salty water was before it rose to head that particular wave. And before that and before that. And how those numberless, never-to-be-registered, particles join and form large constructs before breaking up in search of new adventure. We happily sail or swim across two thirds of the world's surface without troubling ourselves as to what goes on below. So history recorded the tragic events of that August night, but not the multitude of meandering effects that bumped and rippled as they went. Little is recorded of Mandy. Yet she is the one who felt most severely, who suffered so acutely, and who lost and gained so much. George tried to comfort her. So did Mark's parents, quickly summoned from their Lake District retirement.

"I don't want to feel better while Mark is lying there dead to the world," she told them. "I want it to hurt. The anger is so powerful. The more it hurts, the more I want to fight back."

"How?" George had asked, intuition telling him the answer before he even asked the question.

"By carrying on with his work. Give me some of his responsibilities. I know I can do it. You won't regret it."

So Mandy Friar, twenty-five, swift and strong, the river at its most virulent as it comes of the hills and hits the plains below, takes over where her boyfriend had suddenly left off. She fought with an energy that startled, never relenting, ever fierce, yet retaining enough of her wit and charm to remain popular and listened to. And often when it seemed that river was at its strongest, late in the night after fierce debate, she would be found at the bedside of her boyfriend, the granite over which she flowed but would never erode.

And Mandy's energy did great things for Future Perfect so one perspective is it had not gone entirely wrong after all.

A Productive
Friendship

Edward Unwin-Smith had, for many years now, ordered his life around his work, making George's request for support a sacrifice dear in the making. Breaking from research to a thought-provoking seminar was one thing, but dragging a brilliant mind from the past, where it belonged, to the present and future, where it could help George, was hard to do. But such is the nature of paternity, the love that forges the chain linking past to future.

Edward reflected that his sacrifice was no different to, probably less than, many others taken by mothers and fathers every day across the world.

So Professor Unwin-Smith, now an old man with one task left in life, the history of his father, instead dedicated precious days and weeks to the cause of his son, the history of the future. Moreover, he decided not to tell George of the malignant tumour growing in his stomach and the 'only months to live' diagnosis he had received at the consultation that morning.

Professor Unwin-Smith was extremely useful to the cause, most noticeably because he had a gravitas that spoke of wisdom and common sense. The Spider underground movement and Sir Terrence's contacts got him on the air frequently, often on the pretext of historical or constitutional issues. But each time the approved script was torn up and Edward devoted his time to the Future Perfect, adlibbing as he went.

Thus the team heading up Future Perfect changed once more. It had commenced when George set up shop with Mark and Mandy, changed when the outlawed Spiders joined forces with them, changed again when Mark was shot down in the middle of the night, and again when Sir Terrence Scott and Professor Unwin-Smith added business and intellectual emphasis. The team reshaped itself around the newcomers and the momentum kept on building.

"I'm afraid I am exhausted, George!" Edward slumped, so unlike him, into a welcome armchair. "It's terrific fun but the pace is a little too much for my tired old bones." Mid-August, a week after Mark's shooting, seventeen days to the general election. Seven people in a borrowed corner of the EBC television centre coffee lounge in Manchester. Surrounded by glares and affronted stares, they felt like an invading army. George and Edward had estimated that well over 90% of the EBC staff was fiercely loyal to the USE; their paymasters, at the end of the day. Even with the privatisation there was a sense of superiority, as if they had a higher purpose rather than grubbing around making programmes they hoped to sell to the highest bidder. Any time spent in the EBC buildings was uncomfortable but very much necessary if Future Perfect were to get their views across. They relied on the courage and conviction of the 10% of EBC staff who still believed in democracy and everything that went with it. The Spider involvement made the combined operation actually illegal, only you cannot charge an organisation that does not exist. Nevertheless, they were like resistance fighters, in and out quickly, melting into the crowds but doing the damage. All it would take, Edward reflected, was one EBC employee to make a phone call. They were relying on inertia. Their liberty depended on the simple fact that no employee wanted to be distracted by becoming a witness. And certainly, although expressing outward hostility, he imagined some of them were hedging their bets, especially as the 'Don't Knows' were now approaching 50%.

"You were great, Professor, really great. That bit about…"

"Thanks Eric, but right now I need my bed. If you will excuse me."

"You can come in my car with me to the hotel, Edward." That was Sir Terrence.

The two left, Sir Terrence holding the door open for Edward as he stepped into the car outside.

"Your father looks dead-beat, George. Perhaps we should scale down his role a bit?" Sir Terrence suggested when they met again in the morning.

George agreed but Edward would have none of it.

"Yes, I was all-in last night but I am not going to let up right now, not so close to the end. Look at Scott! He has the energy of a wing forward and he is twenty years older than me!"

"You're as bad as each other," George laughed, "not that I want to play nanny to either of you. You have become thick as thieves, you two, as well. I wouldn't be surprised if you were planning some evil coup to get rid of the rest of us and run Future Perfect yourselves! But I really do appreciate it, Dad. Short of giving your life, what greater generosity can there be than the giving of time? Time is, after all, life chopped up into lots of tiny pieces."

But Edward was first and always an historian. To him the past was more alive, more captivating, more demanding than the present. Thus, in giving his last few months of life to his son, he unwittingly started to unravel a past, a story, that had eluded him and directly impacted on his great outstanding work.

Sir Terrence was rapidly becoming a good friend and Edward could not help but ask about his wartime experience as a young officer eighty years earlier. They quickly found common ground.

"You were in my father's command, then? Were you close to him?"

"Not close! I was a lowly second lieutenant, but I did know him. Several times I attended briefings and he spoke to me a few times individually. He made sure I was mentioned in dispatches on one occasion. My CO was not inclined but when the General heard the story he insisted. That was the sort of person he was."

"What do you mean?"

"Well," Sir Terrence drew in a deep breath as if sucking back the years to make it 1945 again, "it was a way he had. Although he was a general and commanded the respect a senior officer should, you always felt that rank did not matter with him. Somehow, he always spoke on the same level as the person he was addressing. But that sounds too contrived. It was more of an incredible, deep-rooted honesty that pervaded him." Here Sir Terrence paused a while, watching his friend and obviously stumbling over something. "Very like..."

"Yes?"

"Well, very like his grandson; your son George. Thinking about it, it must have been that similarity that first attracted me to George and his ragtag of followers! I didn't make the connection at first, although Unwin-Smith is not a common name."

"Do you think..."

But Sir Terrence knew what Edward was asking. "Yes, the old general would have done exactly the same as George were he alive today. I am sure of it. There was such a spirit about him."

"That is very kind of you, Scott. Can you tell me what you did to get mentioned in dispatches?"

So Sir Terrence related again the story of his encounter with Joachim, underplaying the enormous courage that kept him together when facing the wrong end of a gun barrel.

Edward listened intently. "My goodness! So you captured General Stein's batman and then released him? That means it did happen. It had to happen!"

"Were you in doubt?"

"Yes, the whole surrender of General Stein was not in any official report. All I have is one handwritten note from my father. It was hushed up for some reason but I really don't know why."

"Well, there were rumours, of course," Sir Terrence replied. "I suppose the prevailing one was that he pretended to surrender in order to determine our division's strength. But I don't buy that. I think he would have sent a major or a colonel, not go himself. And how was he to be sure that he would get away again? Yet he did get away again and was found dead, I believe, just days later, in his own lines."

"I have catalogued all the rumours and analysed them but not found one to be convincing yet. It comes back to the same mystery. If Stein did surrender, why was such a senior general let free again? Or did he escape? And is his death so soon after his release connected, or just another accident of war? I despair of ever finding out the answers to this riddle."

"You know how to find out more?" Sir Terrence sprang up in excitement, belying his ninety-eight years. "We should go and meet the batman. My sergeant is long-dead but he joked with the boy, telling him to go back to Stuttgart. He must have either told him he came from Stuttgart or he had an accent from there. I think as soon as this election is over we have earned ourselves a holiday. Let's go there and see if we can track him down. We might just find something to fill in the gaps in your work! Of course he would be almost my age but you never know. And even if he is dead maybe he left some papers or told the story to his children and grandchildren."

So it was agreed and, with the agreement, came the start of Edward's withdrawal back to the past he yearned to explore. And it became more obvious that his health was failing, although the professor was adamant with George and the others that it was just the weariness that an old man feels when exerting himself. But Sir Terrence was not fooled.

"Edward, you are not well." Sir Terrence's new friend had collapsed into the bus like a drunk, unsteady on his feet, waving arms like sails on broken spars. "What is it?" But Edward swore perfect health again, fearing it would get back to his son, and blamed the hectic schedule one more time.

***

"Dad, Sir Terrence, Major Graham… all of you, please listen. Francine and I want to talk to you about the next stage. Somehow, we have to get on the ballot papers so people can vote for us. We've been looking into this. EurVote manages the whole process on behalf of the national governments. They check with EurView and other bodies and print the ballot papers for the parliamentary elections. They ensure that only approved candidates and parties are on each ballot paper. The big question is how do we get Future Perfect on that ballot paper?"

"Actually," Francine L'Amour interjected, "it is a problem in several parts. The first part we have solved. We have selected a parliamentary candidate for each constituency so we have a name to go on each ballot paper up and down the country. Andy has that list secure on the internet because if it got into the wrong hands then there would be an immediate police clampdown. Remember, officially we are just a loose body of interested, concerned euro citizens!" That got a laugh from the management committee.

"But the real problem is to get the ballot papers switched. EurVote operate in Dusseldorf under strict security. Those ballot papers will be printed next week and held in a vault until the day before the election."

"So we either break into the vault or we kidnap each set of ballot papers en route to the constituencies. Either way, we substitute our version for the ones they print." Mandy spoke with her usual clarity.

"Either way is going to be difficult. They had a programme on the box about EurVote a few years ago. The presenter was bragging about their security."

"We have to try," George replied. "Perhaps we should do both, try the vault first and then fall back on snatching the ballot papers in transit if the vault option does not work. Major Graham, here comes the big question. To what extent can we rely on the armed forces to help us?"

"I see some problems ahead, Unwin. Firstly, I can't talk about the Navy or the Air Force. Both of these have been totally subsumed within the EurForces command so I really can't say but will find out pronto. For the army I can speak. They hate every aspect of the Directive on European Defence and Command, that being the Euroarmy's constitution, as it were. This is the document our dear PM put his paw to. But the problem is that there is no underground movement within the army, just a lot of disillusioned soldiers. I can't bring you what you need in terms of finding a way of forcing a change."

"Who controls EurVote?" Sir Terrence was thinking in a different way.

"It is based in Dusseldorf because management is 'farmed' out to the German government. So the answer to your question, Sir Terence, is our friend Chancellor Rheinalt, probably our biggest opponent."

"And how are the ballot papers distributed?" George asked. Major Graham told him that they were escorted by EurMilPo to the entry points and then escorted internally by EurPo police. Graham had a contact in EurPo who he would get hold of for further information.

"This is hopeless!" George said after the meeting had broken up and he, his father and Sir Terrence were on their own in Sir Terrence's hotel suite. "To think we have come all this way and can't get any further."

"We will find a way," said Sir Terrence, closing down the discussion by adding, "Leave it to me. I have an idea or two. George, you look as worn out as your father. Both of you go into the two bedrooms and take forty winks. I'll work my magic on this problem."

Police Involvement

"What's happening?" The bus lurched sideways before coming to a halt on the hard shoulder, halfway between Manchester and Leeds, their destination. They were scheduled for a local news broadcast in forty minutes.

"Police!" George said, a sickening feeling overcoming him as he looked out of the window at two sleek BMW police cars, parked at angles front and back of the old bus.

"Good afternoon." The Superintendent boarded the bus on his own. "Our intelligence tells us you are headed for the television studios in Leeds." Nobody replied, wondering if arrests were about to happen or perhaps they were just trying to make them late. "There is heavy traffic ahead, a lorry turned over and is blocking one lane so it is slow going." Why tell us this? "Who is in charge here?"

"I am the spokesperson." George wished he were not, wondering if all their plans would come to nothing. Would they spend Election Day serving thirty days? "But we are not an organisation with a structure…"

"I know exactly who you people are. And you must be Mr Unwin-Smith?" George had stood up and was the same height as the policeman. They looked at each other, tense and watchful both sides; before George looked away and out of the window where the passing traffic was slowing down to see why the police had stopped the bus. Then George saw the Superintendent take off his helmet and expose his eyes. At the same time George realised that he had come onto the bus alone, not a threat at all.

"We are going to give you an escort."

"What?" George did not understand but sensed the lack of threat and felt enormous relief. He kept to simple words, not trusting his voice.

"You have a deadline and there is a problem ahead on the roads. We want to get you there on time."

"Well, thank you but..." George thought, could it be a trap?

"Don't mention it. Do you mind if I come with you in the bus? We will have one car ahead and one behind. Stay on the hard shoulder, Driver."

He darted back down the steps and issued a quick order to the sergeant waiting at the door to the bus. Then back up the steps, his helmet in his left arm like he was cradling a puppy. "Do you mind if I sit with you, Mr Unwin-Smith? There is a lot I want to talk to you about."

Superintendent Charles Musgrove gave a quick verbal CV. He was 37 years old and had trained at the elite school in Paris, followed by a stint in Brussels, before moving back to his native Manchester.

"You are very young for your rank," Edward said from the row behind.

"Yes, I suppose so," Musgrove said modestly. "Now, what I really want to talk to you about must not go any further. Do I have your agreement on that? Can we shake on it? Good, thanks."

Musgrove painted an ugly picture. "The police force has been almost entirely 'euronised'. You can see from my own career. I was considered a high flyer so after initial training I was sent to Paris and then as an inspector I was stationed in Brussels. Now they want me back here as a senior officer to ensure we push through the European agenda."

"Which is?" George already knew the gist of it.

"Uniformity of law and total allegiance to the European Government. That means to the extent of undermining the traditions of British policing and laws to follow the European model. But it also means total and unswerving loyalty to all things European."

"And you don't agree with this, am I right in saying?" Francine L'Amour was sceptical. She remembered a time before when a policeman had befriended her and others in her party. It had ended up in a prison sentence and a lucky escape for her, but others were still behind bars.

"That's correct, Mrs. L'Amour, yes I know exactly who you are and the price on your head also! And I don't expect you to believe me just because I say it. But consider this, I could have arrested you easily today. The unofficial reward for your arrest is immediate promotion. I could be a Chief Superintendent by the time of the General Election; instead I am risking my own liberty and career. Why am I doing this, you might ask? Partly because I have always deep down believed in an independent United Kingdom, even when serving in Brussels like you, George. But it is also because of the shooting of Mark Borden. That shook a lot of us to the core. We don't want to be part of a political system that carries on like that. We don't want to be the legal arm of a corrupt system. But, Mrs. L'Amour, don't accept me at face value, wait and see what I do first."

"That most certainly will not happen because you are not doing anything." Her anger came from six years on the run, six years of the prime of her life spent avoiding the police like a hunted criminal and seeing her colleagues whittled down by capture and imprisonment.

"I was sent here," Musgrove replied. "You need to understand there is a significant movement within the police. We keep quiet but we are working to undermine the system in the name of freedom, just like you."

"Who sent you?"

"You people have a great plan. The idea of the 'Don't Knows' exceeding the actual voters is inspired and a true picture of democracy in action. I admire whoever thought it up." Everyone looked at Mandy, who blushed and looked away. "But all great plans need a little assistance from time to time. What I am saying is that I was asked to make contact with you to ensure you could avail yourself of the network should you ever need it. By my reckoning you probably will need it at some stage over the next few weeks before the election. Now, here we are. I told them to stop a couple of miles short so that I can arrive in my car rather than the bus. George, here are some phone numbers to use if you are really in need. Goodbye for now and remember, I never got on this bus!"

"Who sent you?" Francine was insistent but Musgrove was gone, helmet back on, issuing orders as he climbed into the lead car. George stared after him, standing below the luggage rack so that he was bent sideways, until his father gently guided him back on to the seat.

"Do we trust him?" George half-whispered to those around him.

"*Non!*" said Francine.

"My instinct says yes but let's wait and see," the professor said gently.

Late Broadside

What makes man step out on a seemingly hopeless endeavour? What is it that persuades him or her to buck the trends that guide lesser folk? Where does the strength come from, if not from confidence? And what exactly is this confidence, not brash and aggressive, but calm, rooted in conviction, that eludes the majority? We have seen it in Mark, lying now as passive as the empty fells. We have seen it in Gerry, excitedly preparing for her new role in London. But we have also seen it where it was not expected, in Bertie, the master of fashion and spin, whose roots had seemed sown in the loosest of soils. Who of Bertie's many acquaintances would have foreseen the way that man turned, finding principle and vigour amongst a life full to the brim with empty, pointless creativity?

The scene is London, late at night, twenty-eight days before the election. Dennis is home, alone. The television in the corner runs through prediction after prediction, scenarios mounting like stage scenery. But for Dennis there is only one scenario, only one picture, whichever channel he stares vacantly at. Hour after hour he sees his wife in bed with Terry Rose, a scene obscene, framed by gin and bitterness. Bertie is not offered the usual courteous welcome and is shocked by the change.

"I've been trying to get hold of you. Are you alright?"

"I've... I've been unwell." But the empty bottles tell the real story. And the full story is not long behind.

"So Terry had an affair with Andrea and then threatened to

break up the marriage if you did not, shall we say, co-operate?"

"Exactly. I can't go on without her, Bertie. We've been together since university. I just couldn't..."

"But Dennis, you don't have her anyway while you let that bastard rule your life. Surely you can see that?" Then, after a pause. "You've got to fight back, man!"

"But it's finished, Bertie, all finished! And not just my marriage but my political career as well. I won't get another cabinet post after the election, there's no chance."

"No, you're dead right there, Dennis, at least not with the Conservatives. But they won't win the election anyway."

"What do you mean?" At last something was penetrating the haze. "Who else is there?"

"Future Perfect, of course."

"But they are not standing, they are not approved." So Bertie told him of the plans he had only heard a few days earlier. As Dennis listened, he sat up, daring to hear that there might be another way forward. Like binoculars steadily focusing, the washed-out, misty haze of gin gave way to new vision.

It was too late to contact George and they did not know exactly where he was. They would do that in the morning. Instead, they plotted and planned throughout the night, until eventually dawn forced them to catch an hour's sleep, Bertie taking the sofa and Dennis throwing his body, fully dressed, on the bed he had always shared with his wife.

Bertie and Dennis went together to the Docklands that morning. Dennis had shaved for the first time in a week. They met a gentleman Bertie knew well, who scribbled furiously as they talked. Dennis drank coffee after coffee until he thought the booze had been washed out of him. They left the Docklands office after a couple of hours and went outside into the hot sunshine. Shiny dark glass surrounded them like temples to something very modern. They walked to the end of the next street in search of a cab. Dennis felt like new.

"Bertie, could you contact George or his team for me and set up a meeting?"

"Where are you going?"

"I'm damn well going to see where Andrea is and start talking to her again."

The headline the next day read as follows:

Cabinet Behind Future Perfect "Drugs Bust"

The article questioned whether a joint had even been found, and not planted. Mandy and Mark had a clean record on drugs of any kind. The question was raised: Why risk a joint when everything was going so well? There were lots more questions: who was behind it? Surely not the PM? Would there be any resignations? How could this be legal?

The dailies were swarming all over the Government, determined to find whose initiative it was. On 9th August there was a huge article speculating that Terry Rose was the architect. Suddenly his bluff countenance became much more sinister. On 10th August he tried to read a statement, a half-apology, but it backfired because the journalists kept asking him what he was trying to achieve and what he would do now.

Finally, the following Saturday, less than three weeks before the election, Terry went to see David Kirkby, the boss he had despised as weak. The resignation letter was published in time for the Sunday papers. Historians would later make the case that Terry's hanging on for almost a week had damaged the Conservatives' election hopes even more. But the truth was there was little anyone could have done.

"I would be clueless," Bertie commented as he flicked through the paper that held the resignation letter. "There is no spin out of something like this. It is just wholly bad. Full stop."

"Look," Dennis replied, "the 'Don't Knows' are at 55% in this poll. That would be a landslide!"

And then, in the middle of it all, late on Sunday night, Mark died. Only Mandy was there, dividing her time with scrupulous fairness between Mark and the election. There was no last-minute revival, no sudden awakening, no last-minute gripping of hands and warm, lasting words: just a sudden deterioration on the monitors and death within the minute. So here was Mandy, the swift, strong mountain brook with the land gone from underneath her. The deep solid fells, the immobile, constant peaks guarding fertile valleys at their feet. All gone. How can one begin to measure the potential lost through ill-considered actions, or to write a history of what might have been?

These were Mandy's thoughts sitting alone that late night. But these were not her thoughts the next day as a succession of visitors filed around the dead body of her lover. She felt despair and an immense sadness, wondering where she could find the strength to go on. But all the time she knew she had no choice but to live her life for Mark, thus travelling together again in sorts.

The Visitor

They had laughed about the rain, telling jokes about macs and a good pair of boots. But somehow Gerry has expected a gentle sunshine rather than the misty, undecided weather that filled the sky from edge to edge and denied her a view of her new home. Indeed, it all seemed quite ordinary; the ramp from aircraft to terminal, the long, conveyor-assisted walk, baggage handling, announcements and an ever-shifting crowd; quite like the sands, she thought, that George had talked about. Each grain going on to its separate but interlinked personal future: the future turning with great steadiness to the past.

Gerry showered in the Business Club arrivals lounge and dressed in a new suit she had brought the day before last in an exclusive boutique in DC. It had cost the best part of two weeks' pay but she considered it worth it as she did up the crisp white shirt and then the grey pinstripe skirt. She looked at herself in the mirror. Was it right? It was well-cut and conservative, falling to just below her knees with a medium-length matching jacket. She had to look the part. She was in charge of this nascent organisation.

Then she clasped her bushy long hair back with multiple clips, turning the springiness into a neat contained hairstyle. A little makeup and she was ready.

There was no George waiting for her at Heathrow. Not unless the creased chauffeur who announced his passenger with a placard held above his head shared that name.

"You're Gerry Matthews? Good, come this way, please. You're late."

"That's right. I had to get changed." She pushed her suitcase trolley forward. He did not take the hint. She retracted her arms in confusion. Then he suddenly realised what was expected of him.

"Can I take your trolley?"

"No, that is OK. It is no trouble. No, for sure."

No George to meet her. But then she had not told him of her coming or her promotion, hoping he would just know somehow and rush to the airport. Could she really expect him with his huge workload for the coming election?

No George but also nobody from the fledgling British organisation to meet her. That was significant.

"Do you come from around here?" He was from Surrey, had his own business until a few years ago, was just driving while looking for something better.

"You picked a great time to arrive," he said, jostling a way through the enormous crowds. Gerry could not work out whether he was being sarcastic or not, so she merely asked why it was a great time.

"Well today is Wednesday," he sounded a bit like an over patient schoolteacher, "and pretty soon it's the General Election coming up. Everyone is going crazy with all the excitement and wondering what's what."

"So who is predicted to win?"

"That's the funny thing. No party has more than 20% of the vote, barely that, even. There are more 'don't knows' than 'knows' if you see what I mean."

Gerry did not know what he meant. She had had one phone call with George in the last six months, that being the weekend after he got back from Washington. She had heard about Future Perfect – it was freely reported on in America – and knew that he must be furiously busy. Was that why she was here, because of George? Surely it was the opportunity to lead the first ever overseas branch? What a wonderful opportunity! She could not wait to get started. Gerry, lost in thought, let her driver talk on as the view of London slid past her window.

Deidre, David, Malcolm, Simon, Cynthia and Maria; six in

the head office team, no one employee with more than a few months at the organisation. Indeed, there were only 187 members throughout the USE. A lot of work to do and they were recruiting steadily, seven new employees starting this week. The six seemed moderately friendly, some reserve and some curiosity, they were meeting their new boss from America. What must she seem like to them? Still in her twenties, albeit close to thirty, but obviously young for the position. Had one of them hoped to be where she stood now, with the leather-topped desk between them, stamping rank not personality on the otherwise plain but expansive office? Aware, suddenly, that the desk was a prop, she crossed the room to the far window, a view across the street to St James' park. This was the first view of London that she really took in. She stood motionless, back to the others, for a full minute, as if savouring peace during a long hot summer prior to the inevitable declaration of hostilities. Then, as she turned, she was sure she saw the remnants of their childish signs to one another. She let it go.

"Well folks, we have a lot to do together. Now the first thing to do is to get to know everyone. Cynthia, can you please organise name badges for everyone, me included. I think if they just say name, job title and department that will be fine. Then we can all see who we are!"

"Excuse me, but are name badges really necessary? I mean, we all know each other and, I know we are busy hiring, but it is not that big an office."

"Well, I would like to have them." Gerry was slightly shocked that her first instruction was being questioned. It gave an edge to her voice she regretted. But she was in charge. These were the type of little decisions that would make her leadership of this organisation. "It's not just to get to know names but jobs and departments also. And it is a good discipline to get into as we grow and more, and more new people start. So, yes, we do need name badges and Cynthia will kindly organise them. Now, I have two main objectives during my time with you. We need to grow membership for sure. But the second and greater objective is to lead a campaign to turn back the tide of bureaucracy that has washed over this great country. To do that we..."

"Excuse me, Miss Matthews..."

"Call me Gerry, that goes for all of you." It was Deidre who had spoken again. Somehow she had known it would be Deidre who raised the objections.

"It's just that I don't see that as our objective; the bureaucracy thing, I mean. We see the Society as more of a protection against those who have had their basic human rights infringed. More like a watchdog for the European Court of Human Rights." As she spoke she looked around for support, fingers twitching at her skirt: nerves or quietly counting those who would back her?

"Well, Deidre, thank you for that valuable comment. Of course it is far too early to get into that sort of debate. We hardly know each other. Now I was warned about jetlag but actually I slept real good on the airplane so would be happy to get myself sorted out now and then maybe we can go out tonight and you can show me the sights. I'm itching to see London. How close are we to the Palace?"

Exhilaration and loneliness are often found wed, or at least sharing a bed, before one or the other moves on. Gerry found those first few days at work in London to be a whirlwind of daily activity. But at the end of every day comes the evening and, try as she did, she could not make friends with her staff. Her nights were as empty as her days were full. What she had hoped was awkwardness on meeting their new boss soon showed it to be something much deeper. She could not connect with any of them. Yet she could not find fault either. They were polite and efficient.

Deidre knocked so quietly on a Wednesday afternoon that she had entered the office and positioned herself squarely across from the desk before Gerry had realised she was there.

"Deidre! You startled me."

"Sorry, Miss Matthews."

"Please call me Gerry." Was that part of the problem?

"I just wanted a quiet word. You see, Miss Matthews, I mean, we are not happy about the newsletter. This week it has changed so much. It has become so political, if you don't mind me saying so, Miss Matthews. In our opinion we ought to be impartial when it comes to politics. We should not be taking sides, Miss Matthews."

"Deidre, surely that is what we are all about; taking sides, I mean? Taking sides means coming off the fence and making a stand for freedom. Our purpose is to promote and preserve freedom in all its guises. That is pretty much taking the side of freedom in my opinion." Gerry felt a little uncomfortable with Deidre just across the desk from her. She stood up and moved to the window, same view of the park in high summer, a few leaves scoping out the territory like an advance party before the main invasion. People were crossing the park, some lingering hand in hand. It reminded her of how lonely she was in this foreign country.

"But, well, we might have different opinions. I mean, a lot of people believe in the USE as a benevolent uncle or aunt type of figure. You seem to be set dead against it. I think maybe we should present a more balanced view."

"Deidre, we are not focused on balanced views, that is not our objective. We are here for a reason and that is the promotion and preserving of freedom. A balanced view might not have been so determined to save the Jews."

"Yes, Miss Matthews, if you say so." The door closed as quickly as it had opened as Deidre glided out silently, yet her actions spoke of deafening dissent. Suddenly Gerry was alone again in her elaborate, square office with the wonderful view of the park, wondering what on earth she was doing wrong. A printer ticked in the room next door, sliding across the page as if taking bite after bite. A louder click and the printer came to a stop, perhaps satisfied with its meal. Then, as if by command, all was still and quiet, even the traffic outside merging into a hum that failed to register in Gerry's distracted mind. It was very still and silent. She was very lonely. She needed to get on with her initial report.

But Gerry was not entirely alone that cold, quiet afternoon in

Central London. Not alone, that is, if minds can be joined where bodies are not.

Three thousand miles west and south, Pearson, Society President and her ultimate boss, sat equally quietly alone, contemplating the job he had sent Gerry on and, more particularly, the email he had received signed 'your London staff' that morning. It was not a polite communication, he considered, although it followed every convention, beginning with 'Dear Mr Pearson'. It was cold and he sensed calculating. But it was also straightforward.

"Why, I wonder," he said aloud to himself, "do they so desperately want to get rid of her? She has only been there three weeks!"

And less than three miles through the sun-washed London streets, but far from quiet and contemplative, stood the man for whom Gerry had really come. George was with his father in a last-minute rush for votes, ignoring the fact that nobody could actually vote for them. They were in Hyde Park with a solid crowd around them, Francine at the other end of the park with a similar crowd. George spoke of choice and hope and freedom, while the sun slowly closed in on another day. He had an appointment that night that he had to keep but the local police were moving in fast, helmets and batons, boots and guns, certainly not to be messed with.

"George, it's time to leave," said an aide.

"Go, son, don't wait for me. They won't imprison an almost octogenarian like me! Go and my love go with you."

"Have faith, friends, and read the ballot paper carefully before voting." George waved to the crowd and slipped away at the centre of a small group, wishing he had the faith he urged on others. He was not looking forward to the last night before Election Day.

The small group strode through side streets, pubs opening, cafés closing, making its way east. People did not notice them, which was a good sign. It was vital not to be arrested now, not at this last stage. George looked anxiously around him, wondering why the others could look so calm.

As Gerry locked her office and put on her coat, wondering what to do that evening, George was climbing into the back of a people-carrier marked to look like a taxi. As Gerry stopped at a delicatessen on her slow walk home, George was being sped through more back streets, avoiding the police controls, sometimes backing up and changing direction, trying to get out of the city. George had an appointment he needed to keep. And as Gerry climbed the stairs to her two-bedroom flat in South Kensington, provided by the Society, looking at another quiet evening ahead, George had changed vehicles to a beaten-up old Ford for the last stage of his journey. It was twenty minutes later that Gerry summoned up the courage to call him.

"You're in England? When did you arrive? My goodness, we must meet."

"But you are probably too busy, with the election and everything."

"Well, yes, busy, but this is such good news. Where are you?"

"In my apartment in South Kensington."

"What about tonight?" A sudden idea came to him.

"Tonight?"

"Yes, I am on my way to Southend-on-Sea. I can meet you there. Can you get a taxi to Liverpool Street, then get a train to Southend-on-Sea? Call me when you are on the train and I'll meet you. Remember, Liverpool Street and Southend-on-Sea."

"OK, I'll be there!" Gerry's heart was striking like a grandfather clock. She grabbed her coat, checked herself in the mirror, just remembering to take off her new employee name badge given out that afternoon. She held it up: 'Miss Matthews, Chief Executive'. For a moment she was tempted to keep it on, to show George and the world who she was. She looked at it again and felt a wave of pride. But she had meant them to put Gerry on it, not the Miss Matthews they kept calling her. Never mind, she had to go. She went out of the door, down the steps and outside. Now she had something to fill her evening!

"This is a risk, George," Superintendent Charles Musgrove said once he heard about the change of plan. "We agreed no one except those that need to know as part of the exercise."

"Yes, but she is totally trustworthy," George replied, feeling foolish for having made the suggestion, then stating defiantly, "I trusted you."

"But I came up with the plan, dammit!" Musgrove said.

"I'm sorry, I just reacted. Look, she is totally fine. I met her in Washington."

"Her train gets in at 8.35, just twenty minutes before the ETA at the sailing club. It's going to be tight," Andy commented, adding when he saw George's face, "But we can do it!"

It was hardly a romantic moment. George was not allowed in to the station because there were two policemen walking the platforms, standard procedure, but they knew that George's picture had been circulated so there was a chance he would be recognised. Andy went instead. The first girl he approached on Platform Four was an office worker, coming home after mid-week drinks. "Hey!" she shouted towards the policemen. "This man is trying to get one over me." Andy quickly moved off the platform back to the ticket office. The police had seen him but had thought he was just a commuter trying his luck. Then he saw Gerry. He knew it was she because of the black hair and her smart clothes. She was having trouble putting the ticket into the machine at the exit barrier.

"Let me help," Andy said. "Are you Gerry Matthews?"

"Yes I am. I was expecting…"

"He's in the car. He can't risk coming in."

"But I saw you with that other girl, the drunk one."

"I thought she was you. I've been sent for you. I am the Treasurer of Future Perfect. I look after the cash. You have to trust me." Still she hesitated. So he added, "I know all about your Society and the Hourglass Lectures in DC from February 7th to 14th. Please, the car is just outside. I'll walk five yards in front of you if you like until you can see George in the car."

A minute later, George jumped out of the car and kissed her warmly.

"Jump in," he said. "We have so little time." He felt like a commando officer in a war movie. The police were in the car park now. The car slid out into the street before they were asked for their papers and purpose.

"Where are we going?"

"You'll see."

It is slightly absurd to imagine a heartfelt reunion between a man and a woman jammed between two others in the back seat of an old Ford. Both had to sit sideways to fit in, but at least that way they were facing each other. Nobody else acknowledged her presence, too intent upon their purpose.

"It's 8.50. ETA still 8.55." Major Graham was both Operations Director and driver. Next to him was Charles Musgrove.

"We'll just make it." Charles was irritated by the risk to the operation.

But they did make it. The first launch was pulling into the quay as their car approached. There were eighteen police cars lined up, lights off, engines cut, waiting. As they parked off to one side, the operation began. The first two police cars swung around in a tight circle so their back ends were facing the launch. Two police officers jumped out of each vehicle and started catching bundles thrown from the back of the launch, quickly perfecting their throws like rugby passes.

"Your ballot papers," Musgrove spoke quietly.

"This is the Southeast operation," George explained to Gerry. "There are similar operations going on right now in Felixstowe, Hull, Grangemouth, Invergordon, Belfast, Liverpool, Swansea, Plymouth, Hamble and Whitstable."

"I don't understand."

"Replacement ballot papers."

"I still don't... oh my God! You aren't actually changing every single ballot paper in the country to include your candidates?"

"Exactly, but we have to get them to each polling centres by 4am so the race is on. Look, the first two cars are pulling away. We have to cover Essex, Hertfordshire and a chunk of London.

The other regions all have designated areas to cover the whole of Britain."

"Whose fantastic idea was it to use police cars?"

"That was Charles. Gerry, this is Superintendent Charles Musgrove."

Nobody slept that night. Even though the last pair of police cars were loaded and underway by 9.25, they had much more to do. Each polling centre needed to have a Future Perfect cohort to ensure the switch actually took place; no cold feet amongst the polling officers. From there they would be distributed out to the polling stations for the 6am start to voting. Charles went off with the last police car while others went in donated cars to their designated centres. George was due at Hertford for 11pm before going off to a string of other centres across their region. Charles Musgrove and Major Graham had planned everything carefully, including backups, in case the police stopped any of the civilian drivers. "The real police," as Charles had joked. They used police radios for contact and spoke on a different frequency and in code to ensure nothing leaked out. Secrecy was essential because it was not beyond EurVote to cancel the election if they heard a whisper of these activities.

George and Gerry drove through heavy rain, windscreen wipers working overtime, clunking each time they hit the rest position due to misalignment or slippage. There were few people about, mainly centred on the pubs, although they drove past a dozen that were boarded up.

"Now that smoking is banned in all public places the pubs are having a really hard time. You can't even have a cigarette in the car park!" George explained. "People are staying at home to have a drink."

But mostly they talked about themselves, catching up on the last six months but also exhilarated by the events of the last few hours. They both seemed high on the excitement.

"You mean you actually persuaded a senior police officer to risk everything to help you?"

"No, far from it. He came to us. This was his idea. We were

trying to work out how to switch the ballot papers and he came up with this plan. We were stuck completely."

"Can you trust him?"

"Yes. Francine didn't at first but even she does now. He would have to be an incredibly good actor to be double-crossing us. But, anyway, it hardly matters now. We have done everything we possibly could to change this country. If we can't succeed now then nobody can!"

"Don't say that," Gerry replied. "There always has to be hope. Whatever…"

Her words were cut off by the screech of sirens. At first George thought it was an ambulance and looked for a space to let it pass. But he soon saw it was three police cars, one of which zoomed past and blocked their path so George was forced to stop.

"Papers." The strutting policeman made George think of an old movie he had seen about the Gestapo. He handed over his ID and driving licence while Gerry dug out her passport.

"You're to come with us."

"What shall I do about my car?"

"It's not yours, as you well know. Get out, put your hands on the roof of the car, and don't move. Both of you. Now!"

"What have we done wrong?" No answer.

"I am a US citizen, as you can see. You can't just haul us away without any charge or reading of our rights."

"Miss, we are going to do what we damn well please. This is not some liberty-loving paradise but a troubled region of the USE and right now you two are part of those troubles. Emergency law was declared an hour ago. That means we can do whatever we damn well please."

"George, are you still sure about Charles?" Gerry mouthed over the roof of the car as they were each handcuffed.

"Yes, I am. This is something else. Phone the US embassy the moment you get a chance. They will help you and then you can try and help me. Also, let my father know if you can."

"OK." But at that moment a huge policeman pulled back her coat, breaking buttons and patting her down. He removed her phone while another grabbed her handbag. George and Gerry were bundled into different cars and driven off.

Nobody would talk to George as they drove through the relentless rain, siren sweeping a path before them. They almost hit a man out walking his dog as they screeched around a bend at twice the speed limit. He fell back and slipped on the curb, letting the dog go.

"Damn bloody drunk," were the only words said by any of the three policemen in George's car as they sped on their twenty-five-minute journey to the police station. George asked repeatedly what the charge was, where they were going, and what happened next. The silence chilled him.

Gerry had a little more conversation in her car. The female officer sitting in the back with her smiled a few times when their eyes met. Gerry risked whispering a question as to what was up.

"Emergency law," she whispered back. "But you are not alone. Have faith."

"Silence in the back, Stephens."

"Yes, Sergeant." Thereafter, no more talk until they arrived at Stevenage police station; a new grim building built like an army barracks, surrounded by black iron railings and lots of designated parking spaces with initials for their owners. Bright lights shone outside and in. Gerry saw on the 'Prisoner Reception Sheet' that Unwin-Smith, George Edward, had already been processed and was in cell 42. The female officer took her by the arm and led her into a tiny changing cubicle.

"Strip and put any valuables into this bag. We will give you a receipt. Then put on the uniform and wait for me," she ordered in a loud voice, before whispering, "Sandy Stephens, I'll call someone for you when off-duty. Who shall I call?"

"The US Embassy. Thanks. What is going on?"

"They found a box of fake ballot papers in Manchester. All hell is breaking out. Got to go. Don't worry, we'll get you out."

Cell 48 was Gerry's home that night. She was led by the duty sergeant past 42, where George was staying behind the heavy steel door with tiny flap at head height, and on to her cell where the sergeant made a mock bow as he held the door open for her to enter. He then slammed it with such force she jumped, turned around, and saw, for her first time, what it was like to be imprisoned.

Panic overwhelmed her. She beat against the door and stamped her feet, although knowing that these tiny sounds could not penetrate through the door or the heavy walls to get to another human being. She was locked away, entirely on her own, without any control of her captivity. It was suffocating. Her heart beat like it was trying also to get out of a cell itself. She felt panic rising, starting as bile in the stomach and engulfing her body, affecting her breathing, her reasoning, everything. And the worst thing was in all this turmoil there was absolute silence around her. It was as if she was cut off from the world, cut off from civilisation, and from all reason, all humanity.

"OK," she said to herself, "scorecard time. What do I have? I have Stephens who says she is going to call the embassy for me. I have George six doors down." It did not amount to much. She finally sat down on the narrow, hard bed, leaned over the toilet, and vomited into it. Then she sat back on the bed, gathered her legs up into her body and hugged herself into a small, tight ball. She stayed like this for she did not know how long.

Election Day

Thursday dawned bright and new, the rain having washed away all traces of bad weather. It was blustery, which gave an edge to the temperature, but the sun made a brave effort, as if wanting to be at the polling station early. There was, at many polling stations, a hectic start to the day. In the town hall in Somerton, where Edward Unwin-Smith was registered to vote, there were queues when he turned up at 6.08am. He could have honed in on the town hall without sight for the cries were loud and clear. "Future Perfect is on the ballot paper!" and "Now we are going to get some real change!" and "How did they do it? Were they given approval at the last minute? I wonder if this is everywhere or just us." Then as he started on the worn steps of the Victorian building he was approached by a young man, clearly excited.

"Sir, are you going to vote for Future Perfect? Are you going to vote for George?"

"Well, seeing as he is my son it would be churlish not to!"

"OMG!" the young man cried. "Are you the Professor? Wow! Look everyone, this is George's father going in to vote. You realise you can legally vote for your son now? He has been added to the ballot paper!"

Edward had known of the plans but not of their success. A warm feeling of paternal pride temporarily overcame the constant discomfort in his stomach. But then he recalled that George had promised to call him last night when everything was set, but had not. It was unlike him to forget.

"When is George voting?" They all wanted to know. Edward

felt like a pop star, until his stomach started to grip him in a vice of pain.

"I don't know. Can I please have a little space? I am not that well. He should be along shortly." He started to climb the steps, stumbled, and felt the world turn dark.

"Quick, the Professor has fainted," someone cried. "Call an ambulance." Edward tried to say that was not necessary but nobody could hear him. He so wanted to close his eyes and rest for a moment. His eyelids moved down like shutters at the end of a cold day. He felt bumpy movements and gathered that he was being put onto a stretcher and then into an ambulance. But he had not even voted yet. He tried to raise himself up but was too weak. He collapsed back on the stretcher and fainted again.

The few local journalists who thought it a good idea to track the constituency of George's hometown were onto a goldmine. Phones went wild and, within minutes, two big stories splashed across the internet news sites. The fact that in one constituency at least it was possible to vote for Future Perfect was a sensation. The second story, on George's father's collapse, added a human touch, one journalist going as far as to speculate that in George's moment of triumph perhaps his mentor father would be snatched away from him.

Hilda Rheinalt was briefed within minutes of the broadcasts. It was a tense day for her. Rumours had abounded over the last forty-eight hours of trickery in the election process now underway. She had been disturbed at 1.30am with reports of ballot papers with Future Perfect as a voter option. She could not understand this. Her aides had personally inspected a large sample of ballot papers before they were shipped out yesterday from Dusseldorf. They were flown under police escort to various Sector Eight and Sector Nine airports for onward distribution, all under constant police supervision. She called Edouard Bruges in Paris and spent twenty minutes trying to reassure him that the process was under control. No one could have tampered with the ballot papers.

"Then, my dear Hilda, why is it that we are getting reports

all morning to the contrary?"

"Edouard, there has to be a simple explanation. I will get back to you." She hung up and dialled for her chief aide, Herr Biblestrasse. "Andreas, please find out immediately what is going on. Get over to London if you need to but first I want a full update in thirty minutes, not a second later."

"Yes, Chancellor. I will call you within thirty minutes."

"Where are you?"

"In my office, Chancellor." That was ten minutes by taxi from Hilda.

"Then brief me in person. 10.30 sharp. And then you go straight to the airport."

"Yes, Chancellor."

***

There are some places, however, that the internet cannot reach. One of them was cell 48 at Stevenage police station, where Gerry had unwound her protective ball and was now lying back on the narrow bed with her eyes wide open, staring at a crack in the ceiling. She was imagining she was small and supple enough to get through the crack and out to the room above where she would be free. Maybe it was a canteen or the Ladies? Then she could walk out like any free person. Except her clothes were prison issue. Well, maybe the room above was a locker room the female officers use to change before and after duty. So she would be able to change into jeans, sweatshirt and trainers and stroll out like an off-duty police woman. Perhaps she would smile at the desk sergeant, as if to say, 'Your shift is just beginning but mine is over.' No internet to break into her freedom fantasies.

No internet also in the interrogation room George had spent the last four hours in. His white metal chair was bolted to the floor and was hard and uncomfortable. There was no table, leaving his body language permanently exposed to the interviewer. Four plain whitewashed walls holding up a plain whitewashed ceiling with four bright recessed lights to accentuate every metallic angle of the minimal furniture. The floor provided the only real contrast, being matte-red painted concrete. No extra features such as a window or tape recorder; even the door merged into the whitewashed wall.

"I need names, Unwin-Smith." She could have been straight from a spy novel. She wore an unusual uniform, all black, and was a vast size, bulging out of her clothes. She sweated so that small rivers worked their way down her craggy face. She worked twenty-five minutes on, five minutes off, governed by the nurse's watch she wore pinned to her jacket. During the breaks George was left entirely alone but could not relax. The first two sessions were just questions, a series of five or six repeated endlessly, sometimes in sequence, sometimes deliberately jumbled. In session three the interrogator raised her voice and her body language spoke of more ominous things to come. Before session five started, two male police officers entered the room and expertly strapped George to the chair. But session five passed with just the same questions, leaving George wondering when the pain would start. 'Police Interrogation Protocol', if he had been able to read the manual, would have told him it was session seven, three hours into the standard interview. It came through electric shocks, tiny pads attached to his fingers, the control box on the interrogator's lap, cradled like a new baby.

"I need names, Unwin-Smith."

"Does your vocabulary extend beyond twenty words?" The pain was terrible but it made George strangely reckless. She turned up the dial and proved her vocabulary was a little wider.

"Why make it difficult for yourself, Georgie Porgie? We have names and those individuals are being rounded up right now. We just need confirmation."

"Go to hell!" This earned a much more severe blast. It gave George strange strength to think that he was being defiant in such circumstances. What was the expression – wilful abandonment? Or was that something else? Every pore felt sensitive and his fingers were burning as if held over candles. He desperately wanted to lie down on clean, cool sheets and know nothing for a while of the world.

"Your choice but I will break you." In response, George started to recite the kings of England, not knowing or caring what made him start.

"William I, 1066-1087; William Rufus, 1087-1100; Henry I, 1100-1135; Stephen…" The next shock made him pass out.

George survived through session eight, but only just. By the time he got to Edward VII, his interrogator left for her rest period, breaking protocol again by saying, "You're going to love session nine, Georgie Porgie!" George grinned inanely; somehow the pain was more bearable with silly expressions on his face. She slammed the door in response. He was still grinning inanely at the end of the five-minute break. Or maybe he was counting to 300 too fast as she had not returned, no heels clicking on the concrete passageway outside. He counted to 120 and then another sixty. No interrogator returned. All was absolute silence. What if he was left here entirely on his own? He was gripped with fear. He almost wanted her back. How dare she break the routine? There were no sounds anywhere. George strained to listen for something. Then his head fell forward and he slept despite the bright light, the pain, the hard chair, the restricting straps.

***

Gerry was given a breakfast she could not eat on a cheap plastic tray with a plastic fork and spoon, no knife. She left it on the floor where it had been placed. When the door opened she had hoped it was someone from the embassy but she saw only a leg and boot as it kicked the breakfast tray into the cell.

"How long…" But the door was shut again. The smell of breakfast made her vomit again. There was no soap and no towel and only a cold-water tap at the metal basin so she washed her face as well as she could and dried it on her sleeves. She was very hungry and this added to her desire to throw up.

All she could do was curl up, hands around legs and head tucked in as she rocked and hummed tunes to herself, backwards and forwards on the edge of the bed, blocking out the prison walls around her, making her body a cell within a cell.

Then the door did open, this time widely. Gerry stopped rocking and saw a shadow poking into the cell. It was a man. She huddled back on the bed against the wall and quickly resumed her protective ball position.

"Miss Matthews, my name is Forster." He had an American accent. Surely not? Surely the Americans were not in league with this evil police force? "Miss Matthews, there is nothing to worry about. I am from the embassy. I am here to get you out. You are free to go. Your own clothes are waiting for you and your purse and watch and jewellery. There is nothing to worry about. No one is going to harm you. I am going to take you back to the embassy for a debrief and then drive you home to your apartment."

Gerry slowly, cautiously unravelled her ball. "Really? I can go? What time is it?"

"Almost 10am, we can go as soon as you get changed."

"Which day?" She had lost her sense of time completely.

"Thursday September 3rd."

"So I have been here less than twelve hours? It seems like twelve years." Her voice was small and tired, strained to a dry croak.

"Miss, would you like a cup of tea?" A young policewoman followed the Essex accent and poked her head around the door.

"Get away from me!" Gerry shrieked. "Get away!" The head disappeared.

"You're OK now, Miss Matthews," said Forster, "you can stick with me."

"Where is George?"

"Who?" Forster was starting to worry that Gerry Matthews had lost her mind.

"George, my boyfriend." She had said it, her boyfriend.

"Is he American also?" Forster asked.

"No, he is British but…"

"Then I can't help him, I'm afraid, Miss Matthews." When he saw her face he added without thinking it through, "But if you go into the cubicle and get changed I will go ask a few questions."

Gerry let Adam Forster swing his left arm around her and guide her out of the cellblock; into cell reception and to the same cubicle she had stripped in the night before. Was that really just twelve hours ago? She had served several long sentences crammed into half a day. The female officer discretely stood outside the cubicle while Gerry changed with shaking hands. Finally, she had to ask for assistance in doing up the zip to her skirt.

"Sandy Stephens is a friend of mine," WPC Browning said as she pulled up the zip. What did she mean? "We joined the force together. We have the same ideals."

"I think your friend helped me," Gerry said. Then regretted saying it. How could she trust a police officer?

"She did," agreed Browning. "She warned me that you were here. She wanted me to be the one to help you process out."

"Where's George?"

"Is he another prisoner? Did he come in with you? Give me a minute and I will try and find out." She left Gerry alone to put on her shoes and disappeared through another door.

"What, alone?" Forster was back. "Where is that cute policewoman?"

"Did you find out anything about George?"

"They wouldn't tell me a thing. Something is up because there is hardly anyone around. It seems like an emergency going on. Perhaps it is this election confuffle."

"Of course, it is election day. We must get George out. He is in the election. He is a candidate for election!"

"Well, I just don't know how to start," Forster replied, shaking his head. "But we will think of something."

"He's here, Miss Matthews." Browning came back through the door she had just used. There was nothing of her West

Indies origin in her accent, pure Estuary English.

"Where?"

"He's in Interrogation Room 2."

"Where is it? Can you take me there?" Browning hesitated a moment, as if checking her chances against the odds chalked up on the opposite wall. Then she nodded and said, "Follow me." Back through the same door, first Browning then Gerry, Forster bringing up the rear. Along three deserted passageways making a U shape so that they were doubling back on themselves behind the cellblock. They went past a whitewashed door marked '4' on the left, then another marked '3' and then Browning stopped outside '2'.

"Let me go in alone first, in case there is someone in there with him." She pushed down the door handle and stepped into the room. "Oh my God!" Gerry barged past her into the room, Forster right behind her. George sat strapped to a chair, seemingly unconscious; his head slumped against his chest. Then Gerry saw the electric cables neatly clipped to his fingers and she screamed and ran to him.

"George, George, are you OK? Talk to me please, George!" She lifted up his head to see bloodshot eyes and the evidence of much pain in his face.

"Miss Matthews, this is not George Unwin-Smith, is it?" Forster asked with sudden realisation.

"Yes it is," Gerry spoke over her shoulder as she tended to George.

"My goodness, they will be mad if we walk right out with him!"

Browning took charge. "Mr Forster, please go back down the corridor, fifth left is the men's changing room, grab a pair of trousers and a shirt and shoes if you can. Miss Matthews, carefully take the cables off his fingers. When Mr Forster gets back, try and get him standing up and then change him. I'll be back in a moment. I'm just going to scout out our exit. Mr Forster, where is your car parked?"

"In the visitor slot right outside."

Inside six minutes they had George dressed in some borrowed clothes that were not a bad fit. He could stand but was unstable, needing support. Browning was back. "Here's the plan," she said in a rush. "You two will leave normally, back through the passages to the cell reception, and then through to the main reception. Mr Forster, you can check Miss Matthews out at the main desk and then get into the car like everything was normal. Drive out of the gate and turn left and go round the corner and the next corner, two lefts, to the back of the building. Stop where the rubbish bins are, the trash cans, silly!" She smiled, a gorgeous and generous smile, white teeth against skin as dark as her uniform, then looked away when they both stared at her. "I'll come out the back door with Mr Unwin-Smith and we will be away! Any questions? No, OK, see you in a moment. You leave first. I'll wait five minutes."

"Thank you, Officer, I will sign for Miss Matthews. She has had a bit of a shock. That's all right. Have a good day." They were out of the building. Stage one complete. Stage two was simple; a quick drive around the block. Only not so simple because after the first left corner they came up hard against a parked lorry blocking the road outside a side door. There was hectic activity as police officers carried stacks of papers to the lorry, throwing them into the open back. Forster had to reverse up and go past two more turnings to find one that allowed a left turn, then double back, waiting at the lights. They finally arrived at the back of the building twelve minutes after they had got into the car. There was no sign of Browning or George. Forster stopped the car, kept the engine running but stepped out to look around.

"Help me." It was Browning, somewhere in the shadows. Forster and Gerry leapt forward. There they were, hiding behind two huge wheelie bins. "I thought you weren't coming," Browning said.

"English traffic!" Forster displayed his sense of humour for the first time and was rewarded with another of those beautiful black and white smiles.

"You two in the back," Browning said, "I'll sit up front with the chauffer." There clearly was some attraction between them. Minutes later they were away.

"What is your name?" Gerry asked, breaking the silence of relief.

"WPC Browning."

"I meant your first name. We can't keep calling you Browning!"

"Well," sudden shyness, "my parents liked a good joke. My first name is Brownie."

"Brownie Browning!" Forster and Gerry said in unison. The laughter was long and loud, as they swept past police cars in their diplomatic car. Eventually Forster said,

"And I am Adam. Adam B. Forster."

"What does the B stand for?" Brownie asked, but before he could answer she knew. "Not Browning?"

"Yep, my mother's maiden name." And the laughter was off again.

Outside, the world around them looked grim. There were police cars everywhere, both EurPo and increasingly EurMilPo, stopping and searching. Looking out of the window, Gerry was reminded of an old black-and-white movie with steamy mist rising off the streets from last night's rain while police officers tramped the streets, batons swinging. One officer, she noticed, had her baton crashing against her palm as she walked, as if practising. She saw a young mother cross the street to avoid a patrol, bumping her stroller onto the road, only to get called back and asked for her ID. Gerry turned away and looked at George. His eyes were closed, mouth slightly open, as his head rolled with the movement of the car. She put her hand on his. He opened his eyes and tried to smile. The black and white movie faded away and, for a moment, it seemed as if some clever cameraman had zoned out everyone and everything other than George and Gerry. He toyed with her fingers and she gripped his hand tightly. No words were spoken. Soon, the exhaustion overtook him again and the eyelids dropped and his face went passive again. She shifted slightly as his head rolled onto her shoulder. He gave one last squeeze of her hand and was out again for the rest of the journey.

They arrived at Grosvenor Square just before midday. George did not want to wake and, once woken, seemed confused and unaware of who he was with and the importance of the day. Gerry guided him up the steps and stayed close to him, her own terrors at imprisonment fading next to her imaginings of what he had gone through.

Adam had a large office on the second floor; clearly he was senior. He asked his secretary for hot coffee and sandwiches and led them over to an area with two leather sofas and a long, low table in between. George slumped on the sofa and closed his eyes again. Brownie stood hesitantly and said. "Sir, I need to get back to work. They will be missing me."

"I don't think so. Not right now," Adam said. "George, Mr Unwin-Smith, in a moment our intelligence section would like to give you a briefing. Are you OK, sir? It seems like you have become real famous in the last twenty-four hours! I thought you would want the briefing first then some medical attention, just to check you over, but we can switch that around."

"What's happening?" George asked, opening his eyes and seeing the mass of Gerry's hair, clips long lost and forgotten.

"Chaos!" Adam replied. "Utter chaos. Wait a moment for the briefing. I called ahead from the car and told them who you are. They will be ready in in a moment. Let's have the coffee and sandwiches, take it easy a moment and then go into a conference room to hear what they have to say." He and Gerry shared anxious glances. Would George need to be hospitalised? Would the hospital then just return him to police custody?

George closed his eyes again and Gerry requested they give him twenty minutes. She could not eat a thing but sipped at the coffee. It tasted excellent. Brownie ate a few sandwiches, perched on the edge of the sofa, as if she did not belong there. Adam sat next to her and loaded up a plate. "Hard work, pulling criminals from jail," he joked. "Even with inside help!"

Brownie suddenly slid down the arm of the sofa and placed

her hand on his knee. Relaxing with an engaging grin, she stuffed a ham sandwich in her mouth and said, "I agree, but now I'm a criminal also. Would you spring me?"

"You betcha!"

The Head of Intelligence was a grey-haired colonel in an expensive suit, white shirt and red tie – a bit like a politician, Gerry thought. He smiled broadly, almost a boyish grin, saying, "Welcome, ladies and gentlemen. Please take a seat and we will get started. Now, I know Mr Forster but can we do some introductions? I will start. I am Colonel Benton, US army intelligence, head of intelligence at the US Embassy in London. I report to the head of US intelligence in Brussels who, in turn, reports directly to the Pentagon." Gerry introduced herself, then everyone turned to George who, again, had his eyes closed and seemed unaware of the focus on him.

"This is George Unwin-Smith, leader of Future Perfect," Gerry quickly said, then adding, "he was tortured by the police. Can you believe that?"

"I can," Colonel Benton replied gravely. "Unfortunately it has happened under EurPo increasingly."

Then Brownie shyly said she was just a WPC who got involved by chance.

"Nonsense," Gerry said. "Brownie, you took charge back there. You were brilliant. We would not have gotten out without you. You are a sympathiser, I suspect, for Future Perfect?"

"Well, I am a Spider actually, always have been, but we are not supposed to mention it normally."

"You're in good company," Colonel Benton said. "You may not realise it but we have been concerned by the movement away from democracy in the USE for a few years now. When the Brexit vote in GB led to nothing we decided to support the democracy movement in an indirect way."

"But," George interrupted, "you never said that, something else about having a strong Europe."

They had all thought him asleep. Gerry moved her chair

closer to him and took his hand in hers and squeezed.

"That's better!" she whispered.

"Yes, that is the official version of events," Adam spoke up, "but we have backed the democracy movement for all the time I've been stationed here. We've just done it quietly. Now, Colonel, can you please give George the update you have for him."

"Certainly, sir. Mr Unwin-Smith, we are receiving reports from almost all over the country that Future Perfect is on the ballot papers and, furthermore, exit polls are indicating a heavy vote for the party. I suppose it is now recognised as a political party as it features on the ballot paper. Mr Unwin-Smith, I don't want to tempt fate, but the indications are that you could very well be the next prime minister of Great Britain."

George met this announcement with deep breathing making a regular rhythm.

"George?" Gerry said, suddenly worried.

He woke slowly, a 78 played at 33. His fingers were numb, headache like a perpetual avalanche, thirsty like he had a hangover. He reached out for a glass.

"Let me," Gerry said as George fumbled with the glass and broke a lopsided V-shape out of it.

"Sorry," he mumbled, dropping the glass on the table where it broke again, the bottom shearing right off. The noise hurt his ears and he put his hands up to protect them, only he missed and hit the back of his head instead. That reminded him of his headache. It was unbearable and it was hard to focus his eyes on anything.

"Sir, did you have official notification from EurVote that you would be included in the election? It is highly irregular. I don't know of another instance where there has been a last-minute change like this. You must have weighed in with some heavy arguments." Colonel Benton's aide, a keen-eyed female lieutenant with sharp blue eyes, asked the question.

"Yes, heavy, eyes so heavy." George's eyes were closed again; it was the only comfortable way.

"What about the exit polls, Colonel?" Adam asked, trying to

take attention away from George.

"Yes, of course it is early days yet but indications are that there will be a close to 60% vote for Future Perfect. Now, assuming this is correct, the United States Government very much wants to work with you to achieve the restoration of democracy and the re-establishment of the defunct special relationship."

No response from George, whose head lolled again and was only inches from the table-top. Adam stood up and gently lifted George's head to look into his eyes.

"Sorry," George mumbled again. "I can't quite get it together. I'm OK for a few minutes and then I pass out."

It was Brownie who took charge again. "Sir, he needs to rest," she said to Adam. "Can you let him lie down for a while? He is suffering from shock." Then she added, "I've seen this sort of thing before with other victims of torture. They need rest and quiet. If you let him sleep a couple of hours, he'll be alright." Then to the shocked room she explained, "Like I'm not into torture but I've seen the results on other people when they were taken back to the cells."

"Consider it done," Adam replied. "Gerry, you stay with George, while Brownie, Colonel Benton, Lieutenant Sayers and I go to the Ops Room they are just setting up, although I am not sure there is much we can do without George, other than get updates. I'll check on you both regularly." He called through the door for an admin assistant, who led George and Gerry away, Gerry staying right by his side, like a prop. Her police cell ordeal felt pathetic next to George's.

"My God," said Adam, shocked by the effects of the torture.

"Sir?" Brownie addressed Adam as they trooped out of the conference room, headed for the borrowed office that turned out to be even larger than Adam's, and in a corner position. "Sir, could I possibly stay with you?"

"Brownie, you could be in big trouble if this turns out badly. They will throw everything at you. Already you have helped a prisoner escape. Do you want to add treason to that?"

"Yes, sir, I do." Her smile was so engaging. "I was the

custody constable so I will be blamed for the escapes anyway. If I go back now I will be arrested."

"Colonel, she is on sovereign US territory. I am sure the ambassador will be happy to grant asylum should it prove necessary. Do you agree?"

"OK Mr Forster, you're the boss. Browning you can stay, as long as you understand the risks," Benton replied.

"On one condition," Adam added mischievously.

"Sir?"

"You stop calling me 'sir' right away, or else I will call you WPC Browning until my dying day, even when we have eight beautiful children and you are old and toothless!"

"Yes sir!" Her grin reflected appreciation of his joke and his friendliness.

They did not have to wait too long for George and Gerry because the same admin assistant brought them back an hour later. They had slept for forty minutes, had showers and changed into some borrowed clothes. Gerry grabbed coffee and sandwiches for them both and they sat down by the phones. George looked fragile but more rested and aware of his surroundings.

"Feeling better?"

"Much better, thank you. Is it nine for an outside line?" George dialled a number and listened to the recorded message, scribbling frantically for several minutes. "Our way of securing numbers," he explained when he put the receiver back down. "Never put them in your phone, just memorise one number and a code like a pin number and then we have all the contact phone numbers as a recorded message and it is updated regularly."

The next two hours were frantic with phone calls. As soon as George made contact with a few of his colleagues, word started to get out about where he was and calls started coming in; a trickle growing to a flood. The others were kept busy answering the phone repeatedly.

"This is like a bloody call centre," Brownie said while grabbing some more sandwiches.

"Earning your living finally," said Adam. "As opposed to strutting around in that impressive uniform!"

"What a cheek, Mr Adam Bloody Browning Bloody Forster!"

Around 3.15 in the afternoon, George finally got hold of Musgrove for an update.

"Only four constituencies cannot vote for Future Perfect, three in the north west, where two of our cars were stopped by roadblocks. Their discovery of the merchandise caused the initial alarm. Then one car in my area had a nasty accident and came off the road on its way to Colchester. Both of my police officers died and the papers were burnt beyond recognition."

"Charles, I am really sorry to hear that. They died in pursuit of a worthy cause. Did they have family?"

Charles confirmed they had both had young families. It was a sober moment in a drunken, mad rush of distribution.

Just before 4.30pm, George got hold of Francine. She was ecstatic. "It seems we did it, George! I thought we had done it in '16 but we were tricked by the establishment. Now it has to be unstoppable!"

"I agree. Have you heard from my father? I tried him at home but there was no answer."

"Oh *merde*, I thought you knew. George, he was rushed to hospital this morning while trying to vote. I heard an hour ago that he seems OK."

George put the phone down and said. "I've got to go. Adam, is a car going to be possible?"

Thirty minutes later, George and Gerry were speeding down the A40 with an expert driver at the wheel. "I used to be a cabbie in NYC," he stated cheerily as he pressed the horn to warn off others from his lane. The stars and stripes on the bonnet assured no police car would stop them, but there were many about. As they left London behind, they saw a half-dozen tanks and a troop lorry parked on a bridge over the motorway. Things were getting serious. They had left Adam and Brownie to man the office in the embassy. Calls were streaming in from around the country, the important ones relayed on to George in the car on a borrowed phone.

"Sir," Adam said during one call, much more formal now, "I thought I should warn you that the US government has come to a decision to express publicly our good wishes and co-operation for you and for Future Perfect. We can't officially endorse one political party against another, of course, but this is as close as it gets to positive support."

When George rushed into the ward at Oxford General he saw his father sitting up in bed playing cards with the person in the next-door bed. "Hello, son," he said, "you took your time."

"Are you OK, Dad? What happened?"

"Just a little stumble," Edward lied. But the doctor did not.

"Are you his next of kin?" The doctor asked.

"I am his only close relative, his son."

"So you know about his condition?"

"Condition?"

"His stomach cancer. I am afraid it is not good news."

"Tell me," said George. And he listened intently, Gerry at his side, as he learned that his father, who had always been there for him, would not be there much longer.

After the doctor had discharged him and Edward had dressed, returning the borrowed hospital gown, George could not contain himself any more. He hugged his father, something he had not done since he was a young boy. "It's alright, son, it's alright. I didn't want to tell you during the campaign. But," and he drew back slightly to look at his son, "I'm not planning to go to that great library in the sky quite yet. I still have a book to write!"

"Dad, meet Gerry Matthews. Gerry is the girl from the Society in DC. She's working over here now."

"I'm pleased to meet you, Professor." She offered her hand. They shook formally and then something made Edward lean forward and give her a hug.

"Welcome, Gerry, George told me all about you. You've come over in interesting times."

"That must be your British understatement! I would say more like wild, dangerous, crazy, frantic."

"I can't argue with that, but I would very much like to have a few quiet moments to ask you about your grandfather. George told me the whole story."

"Where now?" the driver asked, flicking out the illegal cigarette when he saw his passengers coming out of the hospital door.

"Home, 18 Chesterfield Street, then after settling my father in we need to go to Buckingham to meet with Francine and then back here for the count. It's going to be tight on time."

"I'm coming with you," Edward said. "I wouldn't miss this for the world."

"Dad, you collapsed this morning. You need to rest."

"George, this is history in the making. I am not going to miss it."

"Sir, can I make a suggestion?" the driver asked. "If you and Miss Matthews would be OK traveling in the front with me on the bench seat, the back seat converts into a bed. We could make your father quite comfortable for the drive, sir."

"Done, agreed," Edward said quickly. "I would love a rest right now. How do you set up the bed?"

"Let me, sir."

The Count

One consequence of Future Perfect not being a legal entity was that it had no headquarters. In fact, it had no offices other than the flats and houses of volunteers. So, where others held election night parties in their various head offices, Future Perfect's celebrations did not look like being centred anywhere in particular. Phones buzzed and popped all evening long as the results started to come in. Early declarers were still socialist, but the majorities were hugely down and Future Perfect jumped to second place in quite a few northern working class constituencies. Then came Bristol West, socialist since Maggie's day and now the first breath-taking win for Future Perfect:

"I, Winifred Jones, the acting returning officer for Bristol West declare that the final totals of votes cast were as follows..." She seemed to enjoy her dramatic pause: "Bentick, Trevor, European Socialists - 15,452; Carrington, Mark, James, European Liberals - 2,387; Corby, Michael, Peter, European Conservatives - 6,434; Stanton, Mary, Deidre, Future Perfect - 15,589... I hereby declare that Mary Stanton has been duly elected to serve the constituency of Bristol West."

The roar was deafening, but there was total cold silence in Rheinalt's spacious Berlin office. Broken by the telephone.

"Could I speak to the Chancellor please? This is Edouard Bruges, President of France. I see, so she won't be available at present? Please tell her to call me back as soon as she can. I understand, but I will be waiting by the phone."

"What do I say to him?" Hilda asked her aides. "He was relying on me to get a good vote in the British election and it does not look that way. How on earth did the ballot papers get switched?" They had received only half answers. Andreas' intense questioning all day long had suggested trickery of some sort but every lead became a dead end. Perfect ballot papers left Dusseldorf the evening before and corrupted ones arrived at every voting station, except a handful the next morning. The escort of European military police from EurMilPo had not taken their eyes off the packages, from leaving Dusseldorf to entering customs at the different airports, and then had seen them handed over to the UK division of EurPo, the civilian version of the USE-wide police force.

"Let's go over it one more time," Andreas said.

"No, Andreas, you go over it a hundred more times but get me an answer."

"Yes, Frau Chancellor, of course." He backed away to an anteroom, his staff in attendance.

At 10pm the EBC was in denial of the exit polls, as were most other broadcasters and internet sites. The ETN was the first to break ranks, at twelve minutes past midnight:

"Future Perfect predicted to win a small majority." The veteran election watchers would have noticed a scramble to find suitable people to interview. There was a disconnect at ETN for forty minutes, almost like two scripts merged into one. It took until almost 1am to get some co-ordination and direction back into the programme. Those flipping between channels would have noticed the emerging contrast with EBC, still predicting a majority for the European Conservatives, still failing to field any Future Perfect spokespeople. Of course if John Baker had not been serving thirty days he would have seen the signs and reacted much more quickly. As it was, he watched what he could on the small television set in his cell, risking being discovered long after lights out, feeling a kind of satisfaction mixed with intense frustration: he wanted to be a part of it.

The early hours saw one or two websites also breaking ranks, first the American ones, then a couple of newspaper sites. They were entering into the daring world of implied treason, rubbing up against the desire to find truth. How should they conduct themselves when it seemed like a revolution was happening through the voting system, a revolution with pen and paper rather than guns and bombs? It was not possible to accord with the European Broadcasting Directive while reporting the truth that was unfolding all around them. And more and more sites and shows risked conjecture on how this could have happened. One interviewee declaring that it had to mean approval by EurVote, otherwise how on earth could the ballot papers reflect the option of Future Perfect? By 2am the consensus was for a modest Future Perfect majority and even the EBC was talking about the possibility of a hung parliament. An hour later the potential majority had doubled, and doubled again by 4am. Finally, even the EBC now scrambled to catch up with the news and to find Future Perfect people worth interviewing. Previous hostility towards them from the EBC was suddenly forgotten, one presenter even declaring: "I always said this could happen. Sector eight was a time bomb waiting to explode and it seems from this view that that explosion happened a few hours ago."

Without headquarters, there was a natural gravitational pull to Oxford, where George was based. Sir Terrence was there by 2am, Musgrove soon after, then Adam Forster, Brownie Browning, and a host of others.

"There's quite a gathering in Buckingham as well," said Sir Terrence. "I just came from there." Edward wondered how someone who was almost ninety-nine years old could have such energy. He was almost twenty years older than Edward but looked and acted twenty years younger. "Are we still on for that trip to Stuttgart?" Sir Terrence asked.

"I'm for it if you are. Mind you, I might need to lean on your arm a bit!"

"I heard you had a fall. Are you OK, Edward?"

Sir Terrence never heard how Edward was recovering, nor did he hear about the stomach cancer, for at that moment the acting returning officer took the stage. 120 seconds later George became the 73rd MP for Future Perfect. Even the EBC felt compelled to put that on their screens, along with a caption that read 'Could the rank outsider win the race?'

The Sun put it more succinctly under the main heading of: 'The World Turned Upside Down!' It quipped, 'A Perfect Future with the Future Perfect', then more seriously, 'Top Oxford Toff in Radical Revolution!'

Then Andy Durrington, Future Perfect Treasurer and newly-elected MP for Birmingham South, arrived. "So far we have 49% of the vote," he said, standing, feet apart as if needing a sound base for the laptop, but also bending back his legs to bring his six-foot-six frame down to the level of the others. He balanced the laptop on one arm and tapped into it with the fingers of the other, somehow always hitting the right keys with his massive fingers. "And we still have some good potential areas to come, for instance apart from Mary at Bristol West there have been no results from the South West yet."

At that very moment Andreas was going through the chain of events one more time. "So, Commander, you were with the boxes in your charge from the moment they left the printers in Dusseldorf to the moment they went through customs at Stansted and then you saw them passed over to the local police force when they emerged from customs? Any observations, Commander?"

"No new observations, Herr Biblestrasse."

"Were they changed in customs?" Andreas pondered.

"No, Sir, the custom officers are trained and loyal members of EurBorder. They owe their allegiance to us and get paid by Brussels. Besides, we checked the seals coming out of customs and each box was untouched. Also, we opened one box in ten but at random. They contained the correct ballot papers in every case, Sir."

"OK, Commander, that will be all for now. Get a good night's sleep. Despite the uncertain outcome you did an excellent job. I think you and your boys are going to be pretty busy for the next little time."

"This is a mystery, friends," Andreas said to his staff.

"Everybody remembers the same thing, namely that there was leak-tight security. "

Terry Rose won his Yorkshire seat at 3am, but his majority was considerably reduced. He was not celebrating much, either. He was 64 years old, facing five years at least in opposition. And, what made it particularly hard to accept was that Shepherd got in to his Lincolnshire seat with a commanding majority. Even Bertie got elected for Winchester and the South Downs, a two-horse race with the Conservatives that Bertie won by a whisker. Around five in the morning, as dawn threatened, its late summer dart-like rays across the buildings of Oxford, Dennis and Bertie converged on the makeshift HQ for Future Perfect. Bertie had met George a few times during his summer conversion. But Dennis had not.

"Congratulations, Mr Unwin-Smith."

"Please call me George; after all, we are going to be working closely together. I've always wanted to meet you. I have heard so much about you. This is Gerry Matthews over from the States to keep us in check! Then there is Adam Forster over there, another Yank. It's getting a bit like the Second World War all over again!" After some warm handshakes and words of polite introduction, George steered Dennis off to one side. "Dennis, it does seem like we might be forming the next government. I became leader of Future Perfect when Mark was killed. I think that means I am going to be Prime Minister! We have a lot to do, of course. We have to regain our country and extract it from the USE. That is not going to be easy and we can expect a lot of opposition. Now, I know that the environment has always been your love, but I have sort of promised that job to Mandy Fryer, before I knew you were going to be involved."

"Mandy will do an excellent job, George, no doubt about it. I know her. She has campaigned a lot over the years while I have been minister and sometimes given me a hard time! I could not recommend a better person for the job. You don't have to worry about her in that role or about me, either."

"Dennis, I want you to fill another role."

"Really?" He couldn't help but be interested.

"I want you to be Home Secretary. I need someone solid in that role and you fit the bill completely. I am going to be involved with a lot of negotiations with European leaders and need someone I can depend on back home."

"I'm sorry, George, but I can't accept it. Let me explain. I don't want any front bench role at all. I have put politics above everything else for forty-five years now. My wife had, well, let's just say that I have not had the time for her and I will be sixty-nine in September and I... we need to spend some time together. I want to be a backbencher. There is nothing outside politics for me and she knows that. I will probably still be a MP the day I drop, but I have been on the front bench for almost forty years. I want to find my wife again." Dennis fingered his glass incessantly, embarrassed at his personal disclosure yet finding strength in its honesty.

"Damn, I was rather counting on your support." George could not hide his disappointment.

"Oh, you have my support, all the way."

"But..."

"Just not formally in the cabinet. I need to put our marriage first. But that does not mean I am giving up on politics. Andrea, come over here, please." Dennis' wife crossed over from the group with Gerry and Adam in it.

After introductions, Andrea said, "I've just been having the most delightful chat with your girlfriend and now I have the pleasure of meeting the hero of the day!" It was said warmly, with a cheeky sparkle.

"Andrea, I have just been telling George that I cannot accept a cabinet position but that I am delighted to help in any way I can behind the scenes. I said that you and I, our marriage, had to come first."

"Gosh!" Andrea's tone was of embarrassment. "But Dennis, if it is what you want."

"No, what I want is to be properly together and then the icing on the cake is to be useful to the government. George, why don't you let me advise Mandy if she needs it? That way I can use my considerable experience to help her when she needs it. If that is acceptable to her, of course. I don't want to be in her way."

"No, of course not, in fact far from it. She called me an hour ago to ask what role you would have. I told her I was going to offer you Home Secretary and she said you should be Environment Minister as it was in your blood. She wanted to stand aside and let you fill the role but I insisted that she take it on. I know for a fact that she will be delighted to have you as an adviser. She thinks very highly of you."

"I'd like that," Dennis replied. "Now let me go and find her as there are a lot of things we need to discuss. I am sure I saw her here somewhere." Dennis moved off, leaving George and Andrea alone.

"He is making a huge sacrifice, you know," she said simply.

"I sensed it."

"Politics, government, is in his blood. But he is putting that to one side for me." Andrea paused and then suddenly it all came out. "I was very foolish. I had a senseless, loveless affair with... well, it doesn't matter who with. I turned my back on the one man who means everything to me just because I lost my way. I would not blame him if he had walked out on me altogether, but instead he is giving me, giving us, a second chance."

"Andrea, I think he feels equal guilt. He obviously thinks he has neglected you." It was extraordinary how you could just meet someone and talk openly about such private matters. It made George think of Professor Stuttermann's Oxford lecture, the stripping away of the veneer in times of radical change.

"But all the price is being paid by him. He could be in the cabinet but he is choosing not to for our sake. Yet he has not asked me to give up my directorships or my involvement with Cambridge University. All the sacrifice is on his side."

"Hold on to him," George said, taking the older woman's hand in his and squeezing it gently. "I desperately need him in government, if only as an adviser. I need experienced people. I am lost..."

Now it was Andrea's turn for reassurance. "You will have him. He will be there for you. I won't let him not be there in some form. Don't worry, not now. This is the time to celebrate your great victory!"

Gerry forgot she was in a foreign country and moved amongst the growing crowds as if she was a society hostess. She had been nervous when she first entered the room with George but the nerves were no longer there. Adam Forster and she had a long chat while waiting for George to give his victory speech. She was amazed by how much the US government was behind Future Perfect and their objectives. Not officially, of course. On the face of it they backed the USE but, as Adam said, only good can come of a resurgent, independent Britain.

"We need strong partners in this world," he told her. "We need friends who are broadly similar in viewpoint. The extreme socialism and bureaucracy of the USE is a big concern for us."

"Then why not come out and openly back Future Perfect?"

"Diplomacy, Gerry, diplomacy!" He made as if to move on, perhaps not wanting confrontation tonight.

"No, Adam, think about this a bit more. What do you like about Future Perfect?"

"Pure unadulterated democracy, the sweetest thing in this world when it works well."

"Exactly, so it is a high ideal."

"The highest!"

"But still not worth coming out and fighting in the open for?"

"Gerry, I am a diplomat, not a freedom campaigner. I do things my way and you do it your way. I just sense that we are going down different roads but headed the same way."

"Yeah, the difference is mine is the open highway and you are going off on country lanes that twist and turn round fields, streams and mountains! So I will get there first."

"Gerry, we could work together on this. What better way than freedom wins, America wins and Britain wins? That's what I call a deal."

"What did you have in mind?" But Adam's explanation

would have to wait as George's hastily put together Victory speech was starting.

George did not talk for long at all. There was no verbosity, just simple plain language and simple promises. He promised to remember that there was 41% of the population who had not voted for his party. He promised to form an inclusive government with a heart and a soul, one that looked into its people and out to the world with an open mind. And he promised to end the tyranny that went by the initials USE.

What's the final result, Andy?" It was 10am now and still no sleep. A sleepless night in the cells and interrogation room followed by a sleepless night in their makeshift headquarters. George was exhausted and concerned already at the pace expected of him. Everybody seemed to need to talk to him, to ask his opinion.

"Future Perfect: 361 seats; Conservatives: 152; Labour: 61; Liberals: 46; others: 30. The parliamentary majority is 72. Quite a bloody result, I would say!"

More on Trees and Falling Leaves

The word is not often mistaken, whatever the language. There are, it is true, some subtle variations, ways to hint at it or hedge it with provisos. But every so often there is just the bare word, ringing out between bare trees like a huntsman's horn. Whether 'No' or *'Nyet'* or *'Non'* or *'Nein'*, it is a word that, said with force, stops the conversation dead. After 'No' the armies fall back on their prepared positions, sharpen their blades and dig stakes into the ground. After *'Nyet'* the beautiful woman will have nothing more to do with the unfortunate suitor whose aims perhaps were never realistic. So often *'Non'* or *'Nein'* is issued from tight lips as if any movement, any expression, might be seen as a weakening of resolve. This was the wall that George and Bertie met face-on at the clearing in the trees at the end of the track along the river and across from the rusty iron bridge: the hideaway of Hilda Rheinalt.

She had chosen her ground and would fight to the end. The election had been a travesty and had been voided by EurVote as well as the European Supreme Court. If Future Perfect wanted to stand in an election all they needed to do was follow the rules. Step one: form a prospective party. Step two: apply for approval to EurVote, outlining the objectives of the party and how they fitted in with the European Constitution. Step three: pay the Euro100,000 fee. Step four: wait for approval. When and if approval was forthcoming they could stand in any election across the USE, subject to EurVote approval for each and every election, plus the Individual Election Fee. It was ridiculous to expect that an unapproved party could substitute fake ballot papers and 'win' an election.

"Section 616 clearly states…"

"But Hilda, how do you bind a whole people?"

"The people gave…"

"And the people can take away. That is the essence of democracy. And of sovereignty." So the battle raged from Friday night through the long weekend. There was no bed for Hilda at 9pm, no careful manipulation of time to leave her opponents hanging on her words, waiting for her to start talking about whatever the subject matter they had been summoned there for. Instead, there was relentless debate hour after hour, each side trying to wear down the other with a never-ending vocal barrage.

And during this weekend, the third weekend in September, the world immediately about them slipped from long, hot summer into that steady decline we know as autumn. The shady, cooling trees, their shade properties no longer in demand, shed their leaves by the thousand, each one a new colour creation, a million picture stories never to be told, lives lived and forgotten and trodden underfoot where they mixed with previous generations. Frost tinged the mornings with sharpness like new apples. It warned of the long, icy season ahead when the wounded, weakened sun would be unable to hold back the encroaching cold. The temperature, perhaps marching in sympathy with the mood, declined steadily throughout the afternoon on Saturday. Nobody sought to sit outside on the porch that evening, but remained within the main body of the house, where the efficient underfloor heating kept them warm. Saturday's supper was bread and soup, but delicious bread and delicious soup made by the caretaker's wife from the tiny garden she kept behind the cabin. She delighted in telling George and Bertie the local origin of most of the ingredients. The cut glasses they drank from were exquisite but only held tap water; no wine was offered. It was like, George thought, the retreat he went on when he was twelve. They had bread and soup and water then, only they had long periods of silence whereas here it was constant argument.

"Gentlemen," Hilda could say that word as if she meant the opposite; a remarkable feat for someone who was not a native speaker, "let us be realistic. You have no currency other than ours. You have no reserves other than those lodged in Frankfurt. You have no law other than Roman law, which is our law. You have no armed forces other than those that owe their allegiance to Europe. So don't talk to me of sovereignty as if it is anything you know about. You are Europeans now." And later she elaborated, "George and Bertie, you are sensible people, why not fight for a sensible cause? I can give you real power right at the centre of the USE. You could be my lieutenants! I admire your courage and your leadership. But don't throw it all away fighting the tide of history!"

For much of Friday evening and Saturday morning they were soldiers meeting across the killing ground: no hatred, rather a shared professionalism. But sometime around lunchtime on Saturday (cold meet and more bread this time, with a local beer which was excellent but served too cold) they discarded their soldier's kit and went undercover. More and more it seemed to Bertie that they were spies trying to outmanoeuvre their opponent. There was still professionalism but it was a different kind because the soldierly rules, based on honour and respect, were no longer in play; instead, anything went. Bertie tried to appeal to her sense of self-worth, asking her again and again what she would do in their situation, but it backfired because she would just answer, cold as the weather outside: "I would toe the line and work for the common good of all, not just for one small section."

Then late on Saturday night, or rather early Sunday morning, it moved to stage three: outright hostilities. Hilda started it, accusing her guests of being traitors and of ignoring their calling to serve a higher power. Her guests were vain, conceited, power-hungry and unprincipled. The host was stubborn, unethical and a bully. The 'Nein' word sprang up again and again until finally Hilda almost screamed, "I could have you both arrested for treason."

"You would have to arrest 70m other British subjects as well."

"They are not British subjects but European citizens. When will you ever get that? It is so simple! Your funny old Great Britain is nothing now. It is sector 8 and a part of sector 9."

Stage four came after an initially frosty lunch on Sunday. They had eaten a beetroot salad, followed by trout from the stream nearby. Bertie suddenly started talking about the fishing in Scotland, only to find out that Hilda was a keen angler as well. They exchanged notes on flies, reels and rods for the remainder of lunch. There was excellent fishing in the river that made the southern boundary to her property. She would take them there next time.

"George and Bertie," Hilda tried again while the plates were being cleared by the caretaker and his wife, who still had to feed the bodyguards staying in the bunkhouse behind the main cabin, "you must know that it would make sense to join forces and fight the corruption and the bureaucracy together from within."

"We can't do that," Bertie said. "We can't do it because we have a mandate from the British people."

"You have a mandate from 3.7% of the European citizenry. I don't see how that gives you the right to do anything. Join with us and we will really make a difference! I am an old woman. I will retire very soon. I need some good people to take over. I need people with courage and conviction."

"Hilda," George decided to try a different tack, "tell me a little about your background. Where do you come from? Have you any family?" He rose from the table and stretched, going to the sitting area of the one communal room, where he threw himself down on a sofa, giving Hilda time to compose her history. "Wow, it has been a long weekend."

"There is not much to tell you." She too stood up and came across the room, to a high-backed chair with leather seat and spindles that wove an intricate pattern on its back. She could see out of the window as the wind lazily threw leaves about, like a boy idling with a cricket ball. Three groundsmen were trying in vain to sweep them off the porch and immediate garden around the cabin but the wind had just enough force to frustrate them.

"I grew up in a suburb of Berlin with my parents. There were no other children. My father was a doctor, Dr Rheinalt. My mother had been married to a high-ranking soldier in the war but he had been killed and she was devastated. She had loved him like no other. She was content with my father but he could never hope to replace her first husband. I think she only married my father to have someone to support her. I don't think she wanted a child but Father did. So they got me. I went to university in Stuttgart and then to Berlin for my Masters. I then went into politics and have been so ever since." Her eyes were still focused out of the window on the groundsmen; one was now leaning on his broom. Given up?

"I suppose your parents are not alive now?"

"No, my mother killed herself in '79, just after I got my Masters. It was as if she waited long enough to see me educated and then had no other reason to live. My father died four years and four days later. My father was a stern man but not cruel. I never felt like I knew him, but my mother was, well, she was just everything to me. I have never married and have no other family."

Still her eyes were fixed on the trio outdoors. It was the price of divergence into her personal life. If she had looked at George as she spoke she would have been reduced to clichés; meaningless sentences. She could not make eye contact and be honest about her emotions; it was one or the other. Usually she avoided any form of sentimentalism. She paused a moment, lost in the only world that had shown any love to her, back with the only person who had ever shown it.

Finally, as a huge sycamore leaf splashed against the window with the faintest of thuds, leaving several parts of the yellow and brown leaf slowly sliding down the glass, she was brought back to the present. She looked at George directly and the clichés flowed. "I live for my work, for my Europe, for the people around me. So you see I can be passionate about my cause. The togetherness of Europe has been my lifelong work."

"But at the expense of democracy, which underpins freedom. Is it not better to live with risk and uncertainty but to be free to make choices, individually and collectively?" Bertie also rose and, being Bertie, strode about the room with the zeal of a convert, coming to rest right in front of the spindled chair as if saying, 'I win, my fish is bigger than yours!'

"No." It was that word again. It was that single-syllable word that summed up the failed summit. It was two letters in English, double that in German, but as complete a statement as ever could be.

As they were packing to leave, Hilda came one more time to them. "You realise your permits to travel will expire after you touch down at Heathrow. The police will be everywhere looking for you. We cannot allow rebellion in any form. You are not the government, however many meetings you have had with the Queen. We will not tolerate civil disobedience. We have been too lenient these last few weeks, hoping to get some sensible accommodation with you, but that clearly is not going to happen. I will guarantee your safety and liberty for twenty-four hours but if you do not report to me on Monday by 6pm that you will co-operate then there is nothing more I can do to help you. You have made your own beds."

"Hilda..." George started to argue angrily but Bertie kicked him quickly behind the two stacked suitcases.

"That is generous, Hilda." Bertie spoke up hastily, filling the gap in the conversation his kick has caused. "We will consider your proposals and discuss with the others and we will get back to you. It is a massive divide but bigger divisions have been overcome in the past. Now, how would you like us to communicate with you?" To George he mouthed, "Trust me."

The parting was superficially on friendly terms, with obligatory kisses to both cheeks. Hilda did not go with them in the car to the airport. There was no point; everything had been said already. They sat in the back of a Mercedes with heavily tinted windows and a driver who spoke not a word throughout the forty-five-minute drive at top speed. Bertie and George did not speak, either. Even if the driver was dumb he would not be deaf and who knew whether he understood English and would report back to Hilda. It was only when they sat together in the plane that they felt safe to whisper about their trip.

"Why did you kick me?"

"Because the time for arguing has gone."

"But she was giving us an ultimatum!"

"Which we can use to our advantage. Think about it this way. She is obviously nervous of what we can do with the backing we have. Otherwise, why ask us here and try and persuade us to desert our objectives? She fell back on the ultimatum because her arguments did not win us over. So, you ask me, why accept the ultimatum and not just reject it as you were going to? Because it buys us time! Firstly, we get back to Britain safely. Secondly, we have twenty-four hours to work out what to do next. I have learned over the years that sometimes it is important to seem to acquiesce in order to buy time to then come out fighting harder than ever."

"The only problem is…"

"Yes," Bertie spoke for him again. "I don't have the first clue what we do next!"

"Bertie, diplomacy is a minefield. How do you keep up with all the different positions and ideas?"

"You get used to it." To Bertie it was just natural, he had never thought about it before.

"I doubt I will ever get used to it. I am used to thinking about one subject at a time; one interpretation. I can make a good speech, for instance. Or I can argue a point with Hilda until the cows come home but I don't have that flexibility of thought like you have. It's like a draughts player suddenly taking on chess, but three games of chess all at once!"

"Hey, George, don't worry. It takes all sorts to contribute to a government."

"Even a fish out of water?" George closed his eyes and concentrated on his performance over the weekend. He had done well to ask Hilda about her upbringing, but that was natural to him. He felt slow and ponderous and it did worry him. He was a fish out of water.

Hilda was at that moment on a four-way conference call with Alois Verdun, Edouard Bruges, and Andreas Biblestrasse. She knew others were listening in on the Paris end but had not been introduced to them. She sensed much less respect from Bruges these days, as if he had to think for himself and found that freedom really quite powerful. In the background the caretaker and his wife tidied up, determined to listen in and disappointed when Hilda chose French as the language for the call. They understood a little French but would have to really strain to comprehend. To add to their dismay, the conference participants seemed to be talking in code.

"We went to stage five progressively," Hilda reported. "But the leaves stayed green. We watered, we weeded and we threatened to chop the whole wood down. The best I got was a promise to consider dropping in twenty-four hours."

Why on earth was she talking about gardening when she faced a constitutional crisis that threatened the very basis of the USE?

"Hardly a raging success." Edouard replied. "It sounds like a job for the lumberjacks. Are they briefed?"

"Yes, they are on standby," Hilda confirmed.

Then Andreas spoke up. "Frau Chancellor, what will happen to the timber?"

"The timber will be processed in the normal way. We cannot allow anything to hold up progress. I will call you, Edouard, the moment I hear back from the trees tomorrow. Hopefully we won't need to raze the forest. Sometimes the threat settles in overnight. We will see tomorrow. Now, I have had several late nights in a row and would like to catch up on some sleep. Goodnight, Edouard. Goodnight, Alois."

"Until tomorrow, Hilda."

"Goodnight, Frau Chancellor," Andreas added, but Hilda had already ended the call.

"Get my bedroom ready and make a light supper of left overs," she ordered the caretaking team.

"Yes, Frau Chancellor."

"I will leave as planned at 5am tomorrow morning."

"Yes, Frau Chancellor."

In der Nahe von Stuttgart

"*Zwei Weissbier, bitte.*"

"You know the language?"

"Long ago, I learned my beer in most languages! This stuff tastes just like it always used to do."

"Not like our domestic brew."

"Please, Edward, don't mention that. I get suicidal every time I think of the way they destroyed the British brewing industry with their daft regulations."

"So how did the Germans manage to bypass the directive?"

"I don't know but thank God that someone manages still to make a half-decent beer."

Both men picked up their flared half-litre glasses and drank in silence. The froth and the gold below it moved down the glass steadily, as if marking the silence and appreciation on a beerometer; the further down the gauge the better the beer.

"*Noch zwei Weissbier, bitte.*" And only when the replenishments were before them did the conversation resume. Edward and Sir Terrence were sitting on a street café in Stuttgart, raised eight steps above the street, like theatre seating in Roman times. They had a clear view down the rows of expensive shops and rival cafés.

"So we have one lead. Young Joachim came from a small town called," Edward stopped to refer to his notes, "called Waldenbuch. It is just twenty-five minutes by car from

Stuttgart." Sir Terrence had insisted on travelling in his Rolls Royce. His chauffer doubled as a batman and also was a retired ambulance worker so knew first aid. Sir Terrence had been worried all month by the deterioration in his academic friend's health. He knew in his bones that Edward did not have long to live and he desperately wanted him to finish his book before he died. "Most people speak English so we should get by. And I forgot that Paul, my chauffeur, is fluent in German, as well as some French and Italian. Very useful chap!"

"Do you think anyone will remember Joachim?" Edward asked and then answered the question himself, the history training kicking in. "There is a good chance someone will remember the family. Germans tend to move around much less than other nationalities."

Edward's conjecture proved correct. The family of Joachim Fielder was known, although there were no relatives remaining in the vicinity. On making initial enquiries, they were directed by several people to an old lady's house in the centre of Waldenbuch. They knocked on the door, Paul ready to introduce and explain in German. After several minutes of knocking they heard a feint shuffle inside. "*Ich komme!*" came a tired but vibrant voice, fragility mixing with resilience. The door took a long time to open, so long that Sir Terence wanted to step forward and help from the other side. But eventually it swung open and Paul launched into his prepared speech while Sir Terrence and Edward took in the sight of a tiny woman, made smaller by her hunched-over appearance. Her eyes were like mine shafts; deep black, shiny like coal, seemingly bottomless.

"*Ja, ja, Joachim war ein gut Mann, am besten. Es tut mir laid was passiert.*"

"*Frau Finders, sprechen Sie Englisch?*"

"Yes, I was an interpreter during the war. I studied at a college in Berlin. Yes, you be my judgment. Is my English good enough?"

"It is the very best, Frau Finders," Sir Terrence replied. Not having any real linguistic skills himself, it always amazed him how someone could tackle two or more languages with ease, switching between them like flicking a light switch.

"You gentleman must come in and sitting down."

"Thank you, Frau Finders."

The house was a revelation inside. A pokey, nondescript hallway led into a large sunlit sitting room full of memorabilia; memories built up over a very long life. Everything seemed to have its place. There were dozens of photographs in frames on tables, window ledges, the piano, bookcases and the mantelpiece, under which a small fire burnt next to a neat stack of logs and kindling. Edward recognised themes amongst the photographs. One section was dedicated to school pictures across the ages, another to sporting events, team photos and prize-giving events. The mantelpiece contained only pictures of a young man in uniform and a girl in various dresses: ball gown, graduation robes, wedding dress, simple dresses with gentle patterns to match the tresses in her hair.

"Those are my own *Kinder*." She said, mixing the languages. "These are my *Mann* and those over there are the school where I taught as a games teacher for forty-one years after the war. I am ninety-eight, you know!" She said this last bit with pride.

"Same age as me, Frau Finders," Sir Terrence replied. He had just turned ninety-nine the previous week but did not want to upstage her.

"I have been retired for a long time now but so many people come to visit me. I get visitors every day; friends, old school *Kinder*, now some of them are grandparents themselves, neighbours, all types! Now, let me see, you were asking about Joachim. I have somewhere, yes over there, there it is. Gentleman, this is the person you are looking for, Joachim Fielder." Edward saw a dated photograph of a young man, about nineteen, smartly but casually dressed for the late '40s in an open-neck shirt and a blazer. He looked very young.

Sir Terrence had gone very quiet. Eventually he said, "That is Joachim alright."

"You *kenne* him?" Frau Finders was as sharp as ever.

So Sir Terrence told the story again of how he met Joachim all those years ago. Every time he related it he was transported back to France and the desperate struggle to end the war. He slipped back eighty years, as if he was popping back indoors because he forgot his coat. He held the photo of Joachim and could envisage the cold steel pointing at him, held by wavering hands due to intense nervousness, hesitant as a result, but it was war and in war fortune favours the brave, not the timid. So absorbed was Sir Terrence in his story of long ago that he did not see Frau Finders' tears well up, making her coal-shaft eyes look flooded with tiny streams of teardrops, travelling across country to points of no return. But Edward saw it.

"Frau Finders, are you OK?"

"Yes, it is just seeing that picture again. He was…" She hesitated, as if suddenly not wanting to confide in strangers, but then thought she may as well. "It was like bringing him back again." Another brief hesitation, then she spoke on. "He was my boyfriend. I mean, we were very young but we had plans for when the war was over. I joined up the same day as him but I used my languages while he ended up as servant to a general."

"That is what we wanted to ask you about," Sir Terrence said as gently as he could. "If it is too distressing then please let us know and we will withdraw."

"No, please ask your questions, sirs." She wiped her eyes with her tiny hands and stood as erect as she was able. "It was a long time ago and we were so very young."

"What happened to Joachim after the war?"

'He came home. His family lived on a farm three kilometres from here. He was eighteen then and I was nineteen. I was training to be a schoolteacher and Joachim went to study architecture in Stuttgart. He got the train every day and we used to meet before school started. We would have hot chocolate in a café by the train station. The café is still there. You can visit it if you like. It is now run by the granddaughter of the man who served us each day. I taught her when she was at school. Joachim and I were very happy and had all sorts of plans. Then one day Joachim did not turn up at the café. He came every day but this day he did not turn up. I waited for him and then had to leave or I would be late for school. I was worried about him. I could not call his home because there was no telephone at the farmhouse. I thought he must be sick. So I went on my bicycle at lunchtime and saw the police car there in the farmyard. Then I knew something was wrong. He had gone missing. He had just vanished."

"How terrible for you," Sir Terrence spoke very quietly as she paused.

"I never saw him again."

"Frau Finders, would you prefer us to leave now? Or maybe come back another time?"

"No, it is just that even after almost eighty years I still shudder to think of how he died." The old lady sat down next to Sir Terrence and took his hand in her tiny hand, more like a claw through chronic arthritis. He felt her clammy skin, then saw it, so translucent, like a plant denied light; a shadow of what it had been. *We are both very old,* he thought. *We have both lived through such a lot.*

"Sir, I am trying to picture you and Joachim when you met on the battlefield. Can you tell me more about the surroundings? Were there trees and bushes around? Was it chaos and noise everywhere, like in the films?"

"No, Frau Finders. It was not like the films. It was so quiet and still and beautiful. There were bushes and trees but not many with leaves, as it was late winter. It was gentle farmland, much like around here, I expect. It was a bright day but not warm. There were no buildings in sight that I recall. Really only the fields reminded one that humans occupied the land. Joachim was behind a thick holly bush. It was not a good hiding place but the best available. I should have seen him but I was preoccupied and walked right up to him. The only sounds were a bird singing and my clumsy feet. Then he stepped out with his rifle pointing at me. My first thought when I saw his helmet was that my life was over. My second thought was how could a German soldier be so far from their lines and on his own?

Then I looked at him and saw he was just a boy, younger than my eighteen years."

"He was almost a year younger than me," Frau Finders added. "Just a boy lost in a man's world."

"Exactly. He seemed so young and not at all threatening but he was worked up and had a loaded gun. I tell you, Frau Finders, we looked into each other's eyes and it seemed like we did so for an eternity. I can't be sure what he was thinking but it must have been similar to my thoughts." Now it was Sir Terrence's turn to pause through overwhelming emotion. "I was thinking how incredibly stupid it is to wage war. How idiotic it is to attempt to kill as many of the enemy as possible when they are just young farm boys or would-be mechanics, or doctors or engineers."

"You were very kind to Joachim." Frau Finders said, holding Sir Terrence's hand. Edward watched as if experiencing the climax of a great play. Paul had retreated to the car so Edward felt like an audience of one witnessing a special performance. "He... he had the most terrible end."

"If you don't want to talk about it, please don't," Sir Terrence said. The late September light shone through the French windows, spotlighting the pair as they sat on the sofa together. Frau Finders shifted herself forward on the cushion, talking now to both of them. "He was bricked up in a cellar at the university. He... he starved to death. The autopsy said he had been hit on the head, lost consciousness and when he woke up he must have found himself in the cellar, totally alone and unable to raise any attention. It is agony to even think of it."

After a long silence in which Sir Terrence leaned across and gripped the tiny woman in a hug while she sobbed, Edward asked, "Frau Finders, do you know why? Do you have any idea why someone would do this?"

"Yes and no," she replied, wiping away tears, "I mean, I know something of it. It was to do with something he knew about the general he served."

"General Stein?"

"Ja, I mean yes, it was General Stein. Some dark secret that he learned during the war, I suppose, and somebody did not want it to get out."

"Sir Terrence?" It was Paul at the window, waving a newspaper. "Look what it says!"

"You will have to translate, Paul," Sir Terrence replied, opening the window.

"Sir Terrence, it says George Unwin-Smith and all of the Future Perfect have been outlawed and there is a reward for their capture. It mentions you, Professor, although not Sir Terrence. It also says that aiding a fugitive is treason and will result in the severest penalty. It says the army is in control of sector eight - that means Britain, doesn't it?"

"We need to leave." Sir Terrence had paused a fraction to absorb the information before taking charge.

"Edward, do you have anything else you want to ask Frau Finders?"

"Yes, I'll be very quick." The answers were that Joachim did not have any living relatives, there was nobody else who would remember him in the area, and they never brought his murder to trial, as they were never able to find any culprits. He disappeared on 19th June 1947. They found the body by smell sixty-four days later.

"Thank you so much, Frau Finders. I am sorry to have dragged this all up in your mind."

"Do not apologise. It is a pleasure to meet someone who had such an experience with Joachim. Goodbye, and whatever they say about you in the newspapers and on the radio, I know not to be true."

Back in the car, Sir Terrence asked Edward if he was OK. He clearly did not look well.

"Yes... no. I am just worried sick for George. What shall we do?"

"I don't know, Edward. I guess we have to get back to Britain but they will be watching the ports and ferry terminals. And the airports, too."

"Sir Terrence, may I make a suggestion?"

"Of course, Paul."

"We are only 200km from the Swiss border. There was no mention of this story in yesterday's paper. I suggest that we drive there at a leisurely pace and try and cross the border with our passports. With any luck they will not have heavy controls at the border crossing. It has the advantage of being the opposite direction to Britain. And if there are extra checks at the border points we can always try and cross the border on foot."

"That is an excellent idea, Paul, let's do that. Do we have enough fuel to get there?"

"No, Sir Terrence, we will need to stop for fuel."

"Well, let's do that now while we are in a small town rather than trying it later on when more people will know about us. We will pay cash so it is harder to trace us. We will also get a few supplies, some bread and cheese and water. Roll on then, Paul!"

So, unwittingly, the three of them set off on exactly the same road that the Stuttermanns had travelled eighty-five years earlier in the first days of the war. They had gone by pig truck back then rather than in a Rolls Royce Silver Shadow. The new travellers did not fear bullets in their back, as happened to Aunt Jessica, but did equally fear arrest and detention; perhaps trumped-up treason charges.

Like Aunt Jessica and her family, Edward and Sir Terrence were scared for others, most noticeably for George, who they knew had been in Germany at the same time as them, supposedly in talks with the Chancellor. Maybe that had been a ruse to get him to Germany so they could easily arrest him? And if he had got back to Britain by some chance, what would he find there with soldiers on the streets and martial law imposed?

Aunt Jessica was dead now, but if she was looking down on that Rolls Royce as it made steady progress south through Reutlingen and then on to Balingen, she would have known how they felt and what thoughts and worries turned over in their minds. None of the relations Aunt Jessica's family had left behind in their sudden dash for freedom had survived. Would

George and Bertie be similarly rounded up and shunted off to some terrible end? Their world, just like the world of 1939, was suddenly very uncertain. How quickly the veneer of civilisation can be stripped, leaving naked self-interest without the coating of society; without the traditions we have all grown up with and taken for granted.

After the fuel stop, bread, cheese and a bottle of local wine, they made good progress for three hours, not hurrying but seeming like wealthy tourists driving through the Baden-Württemberg countryside and on towards the Black Forest where so many tourists went. In the late afternoon, Paul turned the heavy car left to head for Singen and Lake Constance. It was just outside Singen, just 12km from Switzerland, that the first signs of trouble ahead came to them. The queue to get into Singen was long and they suspected a police check. Paul got out of the car and Sir Terrence took his place in case the queue moved forward. Paul walked on ahead for ten minutes and then returned to find the Rolls Royce just a dozen cars closer to the town.

"It is a police barricade," he told them.

"Then we turn back, try and take a side road closer to the border and then abandon the car when it is dark and walk over the border," Sir Terrence said. There was no better plan than the one the Stuttermanns had executed all those years ago.

The next few hours were a frustrating mixture of about-turns and endless circles. They tried numerous small roads but could never get close enough to the border. Finally, after many twists and turns, they got on the eastern side of Gallingen, just 3km from where a peninsula of Switzerland jutted out into Germany like an invading army on a map.

"It's time to abandon ship!" Sir Terrence joked. "We should hide the car somewhere and just take some food and water, passports and money. I think we should wait until the small hours of the morning. Goodness, this is like being back in the army!"

They drove the car into a wooded hollow, where the shadows would hide it even when the sun rose, at least for a while. They walked on for a few minutes and found a stream and a natural bench of a fallen tree.

"Let's stop here a while. Edward, have something to eat and then try and get some sleep. You look all-in."

Edward did not argue. He settled down on a mattress of leaves with a chunk of dark brown bread and some cheese that Paul cut and spread with a pocketknife.

"Where are we, Sir Terrence?" Paul asked.

"We are south of the Ramsener Strasse that runs through Gallingen and on to the border. That road runs about half a kilometre north of us. Best I can estimate is that we have about a kilometre to go to the border."

Edward woke after ninety minutes of restless sleep. He sat up and used the bench as a backrest. He had not eaten the bread and cheese; in fact, he felt that he never wanted to eat again. He was very thirsty, however, and drained the bottle of water Paul handed him. His stomach was alive with pain and he felt exhausted.

"Edward, what are your reflections on the information we learned today from Frau Finders?"

"Well, obviously someone wanted to shut Joachim up. But why do it that way? Apart from the cruelty being obscene, it opens up the possibility of survival, therefore a chance that the murder does not work. To ensure silence it would have been far better to have killed him instantly."

"Precisely! I think there was much more to it than that. It was a brutal, vicious murder. The silencing of Joachim was a by-product. The main aim was either revenge or hatred. Someone must have believed there was some type of betrayal."

"Betrayal of the general?"

"Yes, possibly. Or perhaps betrayal *by* the general. I don't know."

"Someone's coming," hissed Paul. They fell silent immediately. Two police officer shapes came out of the dark on the far side of the stream, heading east for the border. Sir

Terrence could see the automatic rifles sticking out of left-centre, like short spears in their sides. They talked in semi whispers, as if the darkness of night imposed a silence on all those out in it. But their boots gave them away, crunching through the undergrowth. They walked on, unaware of the three British people hiding behind the old trunk thirty feet away, crashing into a patch of brambles as if they were human strimmers. A radio went and Paul whispered a translation of what he heard: "Our car was tracked here and they are looking for us. They are sending helicopters with searchlights. I think we should move now rather than wait. We might make it now but we won't later."

"Agreed," Sir Terrence said back. "Edward, are you up to a short stroll across the border? Good, we will walk single file, first me then Edward. Paul, you go last. Keep an eye out for trouble but also keep an eye on me. I might stop suddenly. We will pause when we get close, before making a final dash. Let's just give our friends ten minutes to be on their way."

They set off east in single-file, walking thirty yards away from the stream on their left. Edward was sandwiched between the other two, trying not to stumble but the pain shut out most of the features around him, leaving him in a black vacuum. It was not a complete vacuum because he could hear Paul's breathing behind him. Occasionally there would be a steadying hand as well.

After four minutes the stream bent north sharply. They did not have a map but knew to head due east, so they left the stream and walked into the bare night, no longer any cover from the bushes and trees that ran alongside the water.

"There will be patrols but no physical barriers," Sir Terrence said when they paused eighty yards from the edge of a field. "I can't be sure but I think that hedge marks the border."

"So," Paul said, "we walk on quietly, drop down if we see or hear anything, and be prepared to run like hell if we are challenged."

"That's how we will do it. I think for this stage we should go in line abreast rather than single file, so we can all see each

237

other. If one person drops or runs so should everyone else. Are you up for the final stage, Edward?"

"Yes, don't worry about me." Would he be able to run if it came to that?

They walked twenty yards, then twenty more with nothing but night sounds to disturb them. Sir Terrence paused at the forty-yard line and looked to the two on his right. No words were necessary. This was it. Ten more yards without incident. Were they going to get away with it?

Then just after the thirty-yard line the same two policemen appeared again from their left and flopped down on the ground right in front of them and under the hedge. They all froze as the voices indicated more than two were there. Then Sir Terrence very carefully started walking backwards away from the hedge. The other two followed. It was slow going but after twenty minutes they were again eighty yards away from the border.

"Just our luck to meet a damn rest stop for their patrols!"

"I expect they are skiving off.," Paul added.

"So that means we go a short distance to right or left and there will probably be an absence of patrols altogether."

They went right 200 yards and then turned east again. The distance to the border hedge was actually about 100 yards now. Again they made over half the distance with no disturbance at all. Sir Terrence paused again forty yards out. Then they moved forward, just as the helicopter's brash vibrations crashed through the still night.

"Run!" Sir Terrence shouted. There was no point in being quiet now. They ran, Edward stumbled, Paul came back for him.

"Here, sir." He stretched out an arm for Edward to right himself, but Edward wobbled again as a huge draft of pain encased his upper body. Paul bent over and flung Edward over his shoulder. Thirty yards to go now, Sir Terrence five yards ahead but Paul was catching up.

The first rifle shot came two seconds after the helicopter washed its powerful light on them and raced away before coming back to pinpoint them. They were better lit up than by day but still had fifteen yards to go.

The first shot missed but the second and third shots got Paul and Edward, just as Paul threw Edward at the hedge and jumped after him. Sir Terrence dragged him through and they fell gasping for breath into the ditch below.

"Don't stop!" Sir Terrence hissed. "They will be after us still." And, right on cue, a small squad of policeman came running up the other side of the hedge. Paul had been shot in the arm so he used his left arm to haul Edward onto his back again. Edward was unconscious. The pair of them ran across the first Swiss field.

"Zigzag!" Paul shouted and they did so, back and forth into the night again. The helicopter light started a new search with the police, ready with rifles, leaning against the border hedge, but the fugitives were nowhere to be seen. They had made it. Within minutes they were with a Swiss police patrol, rushing to investigate the shots. Twenty minutes later they were all in an ambulance, heading for a hospital in Zurich. It was not the hospital that Aunt Jessica had stayed in for three months in 1939; the old hospital had been taken down after the war but it was the same site.

Like Aunt Jessica, they should have feared bullets.

Twisted Trails

So what was the twisted trail that saw Terry Rose rise to become the next PM? How did the thrust of power push him to the top? Was it opportunity grabbed by the individual or the tide of events, the forces sent from far above to shape and turn our world to some other purpose. Is there even a purpose at all? Such questions are the spine of history; the same questions could apply to any century, any period, any event. Maybe the answers vary or maybe they are always the same.

And was it the same twisted trail that saw George Unwin-Smith a hunted man? And Bertie, too, and all the others? And what made it so rough a path? What emotion caused the potholes and craggy, vertical edges screaming danger at every turn? Why were they even ascending through mountains?

That emotion was fear, of course. Fear strips away the veneer faster than any other emotion, even love or hate, which must come in second and third. For fear plays on the mind. Fear is the great instigator.

Fear was behind it all.

On 4th September 2024, David Kirkby took the same route as all the others from Downing Street to Buckingham Palace. He had sometimes wondered how he would feel at this moment. Would he be relieved, dismayed, confused, angry, or all of these things? In fact, he felt none of them. He did not even feel a sense of history. All he remembered afterwards was an 'other-world' sensation, like a dying man who steps out of his body at the last moment and then watches his own funeral from a safe distance. It was a blur of opening and closing doors, officials guiding this way and that. He was an object to them, he realised. He was something that had to be processed efficiently and quietly. It was not this way when he had started as PM. It was the mirror-image journey, then starting at his London town home and ending up in Downing Street, now the other way around. But then there had been eye contact and smiles. Only the Queen, matching Sir Terrence at 99 years of age, gave a genuine response.

"Thank you for all your service and for all our meetings, David," she had said warmly so that David had known she meant it. He could not remember what he had said back.

David Kirkby had resigned because he was, at heart, a decent man and because he knew his time had come. Events had moved too fast for him. His props: Bertie, Dennis, even Terry, had fallen away; only Marjorie was still with him. She was worldly-wise but politically naïve, or so he considered her. Besides, he was tired and wished only to rest and have a light view of the world. He ached like an earlier PM had, to be able to go to Lord's and watch the cricket. So, although he felt no emotion during the final scene - the journey to meet the Queen - he returned with an overwhelming sense of relief. He was no longer responsible and he no longer had to pretend.

Convention dictated that the leader of the largest party was called next but here there was a problem. The European Liberals were recognised by EurVote as the next largest party and heated discussions went on between the Palace and Brussels. Eric Finnerly, the new leader of ELP, went three times to the Palace on the instructions of the European Government and was turned politely away on each occasion. It was nothing personal. It was just that Queen Elizabeth II, longest reigning monarch knew, just like Sir Terrence, where the truth lay. Instead, George Unwin-Smith was called often to the Palace and met the Queen and Prince Charles on several occasions but could not gain a foothold in the real corridors of power at the other palace, of Westminster. EurCiv had an iron grip on the civil service and would not relinquish control. Parliament did not sit; or rather it sat as a rump part of the time with no Future Perfect MPs. They were barred entry by a division of EurMilPo dispatched from Brussels: efficient, purposeful and used to control. Uncertainty gripped everyone but it was not the inspiring uncertainty that can be found at the birth of something new, rather a deadened weight of fear and confusion. Where did power lie? Who should be in charge?

Terry Rose thought he should be, or at least saw the opportunity. It was Morris who first pointed out the implications of Directive 19/235 on Emergency Powers in Constituent Parts of the USE. He flew to Brussels five days after the election and again the following week, where he had long meetings with senior people, including Verdun, Bruges and Rheinalt. They debated every aspect in a warm, windowless room, usually used for negotiations on budget deals. It had a long oak table and matching chairs with plush red seats. Waitresses served coffee and biscuits, then lunch. They broke for an hour mid-afternoon and came back to more coffee and biscuits, followed by wine and cheese and a host of tiny edible delicacies supplied from a local restaurant. Rose and Morris were battering out a way forward. Rose did what he did best. He charged forward, red-faced and strident.

"It's dead simple." His strong Yorkshire accent seemed strange in the smooth, functional but comfortable meeting room, as if it were bouncing off the walls and wanting to range much further. "We have an impasse and you have the ability to break that impasse. Kirkby has gone, no great loss. The question is who takes his place. Finnerly is a wimp. I know he supports the USE hook, line and sinker... ah, that means totally and absolutely... but he lacks the guts to get things back under control. I am the only one who can do that. I am well recognised. I am tough. I don't monkey around. I am the man of the moment."

"Directive 19/235," a technocrat called Matrice stood up to speak, "is the instrument that has relevance to this situation. You are quite right, Mr. Rose, in declaring this to be the case."

"Please remind us, Monsieur Matrice, of the relevant details." That was Verdun, the President of USE, the ultimate authority, to whom even Rheinalt bent a knee from time to time.

"Of course, Monsieur President. Directive 19/235 is entitled 'Emergency Powers in Constituent Parts of the USE' and comes in three sections. It first defines constituent parts. Suffice it to say that the area under question qualifies as a constituent part without doubt. It then goes on to state the circumstances under which Emergency Powers could be considered. These range from serious civil disobedience to terrorism, electoral fraud, attempted revolution and treason against the USE. It is our lawyers' considered opinion that the current situation meets three or more of these conditions, most specifically..."

Terry was not listening. He had been briefed separately by the USE lawyers over an informal breakfast that morning. He knew that Directive 19/235 applied to the current situation, in fact was almost made for it. What he wanted to know was who would support him in backing the implementation of this directive. He looked around the long and crowded table. His own civil servants had briefed him earlier on whose support counted and he knew that only two people were essential – Verdun and Rheinalt. If they backed him, everybody else would follow. Verdun's face gave nothing away. It was very hard to guess what he was thinking. But Rheinalt was different. He had sensed the first time he met her that she mistrusted the British, perhaps for some personal reason? She was certainly against the possible breakup of the USE. Would she, however, risk such strong action as overriding the Crown's authority? Would she decide that this posed more risk than ever before? But what of the risk of continued uncertainty, surely that featured in her thinking? It had been over a week since the election and there had been no government in Britain. There was a desperate need for order. There were rallies and demonstrations in favour of Future Perfect every day of the week. The establishment was holding up but there were signs of wear and stress. That damn television reporter, what was his name? The one who had caused all the trouble in Portsmouth, or was it Southampton? He was out of jail now and broadcasting on some damn pirate channel on the internet. That was another thing, somebody high up had corrupted the internet, allowing rebel interests to get on there. There was a tide that had to be stopped and he was the man to do it.

"Mr Rose? Did you not hear me? I was just saying about the decision." It was Verdun. Terry thought he looked more like an actor playing Poirot than a leading politician. His hair was racing backwards, revealing a large olive forehead above shrewd, dark brown eyes, set deep into sockets as if watching the world from a secure position deep in a cave. His suit was old-fashioned and expensive, especially for a socialist, with a waistcoat shaded matte-red and a matching red tie. He was near the middle in so many ways – slightly overweight, a little shorter than average, about half-way through an average lifespan, slightly left of left of centre.

"No, Monsieur Verdun, I was deep in thought on the possibilities." It was too much for Terry to apologise for daydreaming. It was not in his nature.

"Frau Rheinalt has arranged for Mr Unwin-Smith to visit her next weekend to discuss matters in-depth. We would like to wait until we see the success of her efforts. We are, therefore, delegating this to Frau Rheinalt, who will report back to me next Monday."

Six days later the same group of people sat in the same room. This time the meeting was shorter. Verdun led the conversation.

"Mr Rose, how nice it is to see you again. As you know from my telephone call to you, the strategy we followed drew, how do you say it? Drew blanks." He looked across the table at Hilda who sat stony-faced, immobile. "So now we need to investigate 19/235 more fully."

19/235 turned out to be the perfect remedy for the dangerous and deteriorating situation. It allowed the European Government to impose a regional government on any constituent part of the USE. It bypassed the Queen and Parliament. Terry Rose flew back to London with his aides and moved into Downing Street that evening. He was triumphant. He had become Prime Minister. Days ago he was looking at five years in opposition, now he was catapulted onto centre stage.

There were hardly any staff in residence at Number 10 when he arrived. That was to be expected, he thought, as the house had been empty for over two weeks now. He sat alone in the flat with a glass of Kirkby's whisky in his hand, a cigar in the other. How good of Kirkby to leave a bottle of Scotch behind. In a moment he would go to bed, secure in the fact that the civil service would do exactly what their European bosses told them to do. So would the police and the army. They were all part of the establishment and he ruled the lot of them.

The next morning was the first with a heavy frost that autumn. Terry showered and dressed in the same clothes as the previous day. He had forgotten to bring any more with him. He would remedy that later. It was 6am, time for tea and breakfast. He rinsed his face well, trying to shake off the slight hangover he had. This was the first day of his premiership. He would have a cabinet to pick. He needed to meet his staff. He knew them from many previous visits but this time he was their boss.

Terry was met downstairs by a stranger. He clearly had not met all the staff.

"Sir, my name is Jenkinson. I am filling in."

"What do you mean 'filling in'?"

The introduction sounded ominous.

"Sir, the regular staff is otherwise disposed."

"What do you damn well mean? Speak up, Jenkins."

"Jenkinson, sir, son of Jenkins, I suppose."

"I don't give a damn whose bastard son you are, Jenkin – bloody – son. Explain yourself right now." Terry got the explanation and it chilled him to the bone. The entire staff of Downing Street was refusing to accept 19/235. It was absurd! It was unbelievable. It was treasonous. They were staying at home and refusing to come to work.

"I agree, sir, so, you see, we've been drafted in to fill the gap."

No matter how much Terry Rose swore and shouted insults at Jenkinson and the other temporary staff members, nothing could change. He summoned Fernby, the Head of the Civil Service, after he had cooled down a bit. Fernby was sympathetic but told Rose he would just have to get used to the new staff.

"We are getting a lot of fraying at the edges, Prime Minister," he said in the public school tones that drove Rose mad. "My own Under Secretary resigned yesterday, saying Future Perfect should be forming the next government. They had the majority of votes and the moral victory as well. So my Under Secretary said to me before working out."

"Utter crap!" Terry replied.

"I agree, Prime Minister, but fraying at the edges we are. I had someone put together a statistic that might interest you. It says here that the Civil Service is losing up to 1,000 people a day. That is across all departments, sir."

"It was bloody well overstaffed anyway. You could lose 1,000 a day for a year and not notice the bloody difference."

"Yes, sir. In the meantime, I will act as your Permanent Secretary; strictly temporarily, you understand."

"That's against the rules, isn't it? Don't you report to some technocrat in Brussels?"

"Yes, sir, that is correct. I report to the EurCiv Director of Policy and Administration, who has issued standing orders to facilitate the government of this region. I received additional orders last night, sir, instructing me to act as your temporary Permanent Secretary and to do everything possible to assist you in constructing and running an administration as soon as possible."

"Too right! I need to appoint a cabinet. I had in mind…"

"Sir, if you will permit me to interrupt. Brussels has advised that cabinet appointments are a subsequent priority."

"What the devil does 'subsequent priority' mean?"

"Sir, 'subsequent priority' sounds like a contradiction in

terms and, in some ways it is, but practically speaking it allows us to divisionalise priorities and by divisionalising priorities we achieve primary objectives as quickly as possible while also moving on secondary objectives."

"My God, you have this all worked out, even the bloody language to confuse the honest man!" Hardly an honest man, thought Fernby, but he let it ride. "So what are the primary bloody objectives?"

"Simple, sir, although they fall into several categories but they can be loosely collated as security risks requiring attention." Fernby opened a folder he had brought with him and started to explain what his new boss was to do. "The first objective is to secure loyalty. The second is to dissuade dissent and the third is to establish order." It was a list much longer than Terry's patience and several times he rose from his desk and walked around the room, muttering to himself and pounding his right fist into his left palm.

"Sir, can I suggest that we start with the question of the police. EurMilPo has, as I am sure you are aware, infiltrated the regional EurPo and discovered some pretty alarming things. We know, for instance, that the police were involved in some way with the switching of the ballot papers. We can't prove it yet but genuine suspicion is enough under 19/235. We estimate that a sizeable portion of the regional police force has turned tail, perhaps as much as 30%, and this figure is growing. EurMilPo have made arrests but we think the ringleaders are as yet undiscovered. We are in the process of interrogation and the EurPo Extra Training College in Zarbzein is experiencing a heavy flow of new trainees. It is estimated that each junior police officer will require eight to twelve weeks of extra training, if you see what I mean, sir. The senior officers, that is the ranks of inspector and above, are not worth retraining and will need to be otherwise deployed."

"What the hell does that mean?"

In answer, Fernby leant across the desk and said with a small smile in a half-whisper, "It means, sir, a long time away from their families to pay for their naughty deeds." He sat back in his chair and waited for a reaction from his boss. Uncharacteristically, no response came from Rose. He sat very still but with his mind working fast. What had he got into? Finally came a muted, "I see, carry on."

The premiership of Terry Rose lasted on paper for several weeks. In practice, as far as Terry was concerned, it ended after twelve hours. It ended over coffee and chocolate biscuits with the impenetrable Fernby in his pin-striped suit and medium-length grey sideburns shooting down from a forest of white hair. Fernby detailed the requirements to his new boss. It was a thorough briefing, complete with introduction, objectives, detailed execution and a check on understanding. Afterwards, Fernby reported back to Verdun's Deputy for Good Governance that the briefing had gone exceptionally well.

"He started blustering on about setting a cabinet up and policy initiatives and all that. However, after half an hour he understood all too well what was required of him. For all his 'bloody this' and 'bloody that', he is going to be as tame as they come. The situation, Monsieur, is well under control."

"Excellent, Fernby. Keep me in the loop if anything changes."

"Yes, sir," said Fernby, forgetting that he was supposed to be talking in French.

Terry Rose sat alone in his office with several huge stacks of paper. Every so often he was disturbed. Sometimes it was coffee or tea; sometimes it was a reminder about a future date for the diary. Always, Rose now knew, it was to check on him. *I am a prisoner in the place I always wanted to be in*, he thought. But he was a man of action on whom neat irony was lost. His was more a world of head-on charges and 'Take the battle to the enemy' and 'The best form of defence is attack'. *My God, I am thinking in clichés now, just like bloody Kirkby. Maybe it goes with the office.*

Fernby had set Terry Rose to the task of delivering a speech to EurPo Regional HQ that evening. He had been given some heavy pointers along the lines of loyalty, teamwork, sticking together, duty to report others, etc. He also had been left names of suspects and had looked over a few pages at random. He didn't know any police officers by name; they had just been objects to him. But he did find a few unlikely candidates on the list; for instance, Musgrove seemed to be a model of the EurPo system and a rising star. Yet he was on the list with a risk factor of ten, the very highest selection available. Musgrove was being held for interrogation in Terry's hometown of Harrogate.

Rose picked up the phone. "Alex Fernby, please." There would have been a time, in fact just a few years ago, when someone in Alex's position would have been Sir Alex Fernby. But that was before one or other of the multitude of directives since 2016.

"Ah, Fernby. I was looking at the list of suspects you left and..."

"Sir, the speech?"

"Done. I wanted to talk to you about some of these suspects. Take Musgrove. I know him quite well." Terry lied to get his point across. "I doubt very much he is a traitor. He is a product of the..."

"Sir, with the best will in the world, please do not get involved with detail. Your job is policy. I can assure you that Musgrove is guilty. I have read his full dossier."

"You know best." This coming from Terry Rose should have rung alarm bells in Fernby's head as being completely out of character.

Complacency in the enemy ranks is a wonderful weapon, reflected Terry as he replaced the receiver and wondered what to do next.

The Hunted and the Haunted

"You will get used to it!" laughed Francine. "After about half a dozen years, that is." George and Francine were with a small group sheltering from the freezing rain in an old barn deep in the countryside of Dorset. Nothing seemed to get this beautiful, tireless lady down. Every disappointment just meant redoubled efforts next time.

"Francine, I am trying not to let it get to me but this is not exactly what I do best. I am all-in. I don't care if I get caught I just need to sleep in a bed somewhere warm for a few hours. I am not going to get to sleep in this rat-infested barn!"

"If you can find a rat I will happily eat it," Andy commented. Then, ever practical, he said. "There are fourteen of us. We have no food, no real wet-weather clothing and my goodness is it raining! And we have no money to speak of. We know the buggers are all over the place, probably no more than five miles from where we are now. The big question is what do we do?"

"Easy," said one of the Spiders, entering the barn, "first we eat and then we sleep, taking turn at keeping guard of course."

As he spoke, he waved a wicker basket full to the brim with food and covered with a neat stylised red-check tablecloth.

"Where the hell?"

"It was left outside with a note. Shall I read it to you? It says 'Looking to the Future'. You see, it was meant for us!"

"What is it saying on the other side?" Francine asked and it was passed over to her. She continued to read. "'Take heart my lads and ladies. We will set off the burglar alarm if anyone comes near. Eat, rest and fight another day.'"

"Who lives at the farmhouse?"

"No idea, but let's do exactly what they say." George spoke from a pile of hay, his worn face looking cartoonish in the torchlight. Then he was asleep, too tired even to eat.

"Leave him," said Francine when they were putting together a guard rota a few minutes later. "He's all-in. I will take his turn."

In the morning everything seemed a little more hopeful. George woke to see a rat scurrying across his flattened pile of hay. He shuddered and scrambled up, while the rat observed him before running off; clearly George was of no value to it. George pulled on his coat that had acted as a blanket overnight and looked down at himself. He had worn these clothes for how many days now? Six, seven? What he would do for a bath! Looking around for the food basket, he saw it by Francine's side. She was snoring lightly, her mouth moving, almost as if enacting the spoken part of a dream. How could she go on living like this for six years? George had had enough after a fortnight. He looked at the note the benefactor had left and decided that rather than eat the last of the basket food he would walk to the farmhouse and ask for some breakfast, maybe bring some back for the others so they would not see him as a burden quite so much.

Burden? He was supposed to be their leader! But he had not expected guerrilla warfare. He had envisaged a battle of ideas fought from his father's fireside in comfortable chairs, not running through wet woods with dirty clothes and nothing to eat. Who did that remind him of? The running through wet woods and nothing to eat?

Aunt Jessica, of course. Well, if she could do it surely he could, at least for a little longer. He made his way to the barn door but Francine stirred and half got up, wiping the sleep from her eyes with her long, delicate fingers.

"George? Are you going somewhere?" She yawned.

"Just trying to get replenishments, sleep on a bit longer."

He walked in the gloom that precedes a winter day, his mind occupied with the need for an idea to bring this terrible period to an end. He needed a knockout blow. He was not like Francine. The thought of resistance life for the long-term filled him with terror. He had to come up with a plan but the more he thought, the more he seemed to dwell on his inadequacies. What must they think of him?

The farmhouse was actually a small manor; the oldest part probably dating back to late medieval times, the whole so crooked and added on that he imagined the owners finding new rooms every so often. He watched carefully from the rhododendrons before making his way to the back door. It was not yet light but the moonlight was strong. Just as he stepped out to cross the yard with the back door firmly in his sight, a rectangle of darker shade set in the surrounding wall, he felt a massive blow from the left that knocked him over. He had been tackled and was now groping around on the concrete floor while his aggressor quickly pinned him to the ground.

"Who the hell are you?" A surprisingly cultured voice, incongruent with the aggressive rugby tackle.

"Just a hungry passer-by, just came to beg some bread." George thought he sounded completely unconvincing.

"Get up." The man stood, releasing George and then held out a hand to assist him. "Never cross open country if you can help it," he said. "Now who are you and what are you doing on my property?"

"I'm George Unwin-Smith," George replied.

"More like George Bloody Unwin-Fool. Never give your real name. You are with the chaps in the barn?"

"Yes."

"Now you have just given me your entire section's whereabouts. I think it is time for some basic training, George. I'm Major Bellew, Royal Armoured Corps. Let's get you inside."

George could just see now that Bellew was grinning as he slapped George on the back.

Jonathan Bellew was only about George's age, or maybe a few years older. He had been a life man in the army. His father had been a Colonel, his grandfather a Brigadier and his great grandfather a full General.

"So we're dropping a rank or three with every generation. At this rate Mikey, my son, will be lucky to make Corporal!" He had a huge laugh that belied the fact that his sixteen-stone frame moved like a cat, no sound even with heavy boots on. "Training," he told George. "When your life depends on it you are going to be like a ruddy church mouse. Did you like your supper last night?"

"I was asleep, too tired. I didn't have any."

"No matter. I'll fix something in half a tick. Mikey?"

"Yes Dad?" Mikey could not be confused for anyone else's son but the major's; same hair, same build, just his voice higher but starting to work its way down.

"Mikey, run along to the barn and collect - how many is it, George? - thirteen assorted personages, breakfast for the purpose of."

"Will do, Dad." George could have sworn the boy did a neat about-turn before running through the back door and off to the barn a quarter mile away.

"Good lad, is our Mikey," Bellew said as he came back from the pantry with eggs and bacon, bread, sausages and tomatoes. "Now, feast preparation. Well, don't just stand there. Wash the grime and break eggs. We'll do scrambled."

"Are you still in the army?" George asked as he broke eggs into a mixing bowl.

"No, Sir, wish I was but I couldn't stay in once they made the changes. Besides, I'm too stupid to learn a foreign language!"

"Would you go back? If the changes were reversed, I mean?"

"Like a shot, my friend, like a shot. Annie, that's my wife, says the estate, all 2000 acres of it, isn't enough for me and I am only happy when camping on Salisbury Plain."

"Is she here?"

"No, she works as a doctor in Dorchester General. She works nights so after Mikey's settled I tend to spend the night outdoors and then we have forty winks when she gets back."

The others trooped in with Mikey at their head. He showed them where to wash while George helped push two tables together to accommodate everyone at one sitting.

"So, Major, you're a tank man?" Andy asked between mouthfuls.

"That's me, pity the bloody infantry!"

"Can you drive one?" George suddenly asked.

"Not my job... but of course I bloody can! Why do you ask?"

"No reason, just the vaguest of ideas it might come in useful."

After breakfast, George showed Bellew how to keep in touch and took the major's phone number. "I might have a mission for you," he said, getting into the lingo. "Yes, you might just solve a problem for me. Tell me, where would you find a few armoured vehicles - not tanks, faster moving than tanks?"

"Yes."

"What do you mean?" George asked, seeing the grin on Bellew's face.

"I mean yes I will."

"You will do what?"

"Pinch the ruddy armoured vehicles for you. When by?"

"I was working round to asking you, but you went straight there! How about the beginning of November?"

"Done deal, my man. Just shoot me a delivery address and Bellew and Son, armoured vehicle specialists, will deliver as ordered. But when I do deliver you are going to have to tell me what is going on."

"Major, as soon as I know I will be happy to tell you!" It was George's turn to laugh, but the laugh was brief as a wave of low self-esteem swept over him. "I'm trying to work out a plan to get us through this, but sometimes I feel like I am not making much progress. The armoured vehicles just gave me an idea."

Bellew donated two cars so they split into two parties. George, Francine, Andy and a few others piled into an ancient Subaru and drove directly for Southampton, Francine driving because she insisted. "I like to be in control," she explained, her vowels so rich and French, the 'r' rolling to extend the word. The other car, even older, so that it was hard to tell the make, went west, to make contact with supporters there. Before they made it to Southampton they picked up another car in Ringwood, donated by a supporter, and split further with the new car going on past Southampton towards Portsmouth. George expected that the westbound contingent, slightly larger, would split at least twice to head out to the far reaches of the West Country. They were in a hurry. It was 10th October and the rising was set for November 5th. They had set the date, not thinking of Guy Fawkes Night, but because Verdun was planning a visit on that day. But beyond that the details were hazy. They could co-ordinate a general rising and it would involve huge numbers but every day more EurMilPo officers were pouring into the country. There was no guarantee of success. They needed an edge. They had been on the back foot ever since the meeting with Hilda Rheinalt, just staying one step away from arrest for most of that time. They needed somehow to get ahead of the opposition before the whole resistance got ground down by a huge military presence. They needed an idea and he only had a few half-baked ones.

They avoided the motorway and went through lanes and suburban streets. Their destination was the docks, but Andy said they could drop him a couple of miles away and he would make his way on foot to the rendezvous. "It is better that you two take as little risk as possible." So George and Francine drove on, keeping where possible to heavy traffic but always with an eye out for an escape route. She was not a good driver and used the brakes a lot, worrying George that they were attracting too much attention.

They talked much about the country they wanted to liberate and how they wanted to turn it back to how things had once been. At 1pm George fiddled with the radio and got some reception, although the aerial was snapped off like a stunted flagpole. The leading story chilled them, as they knew immediately who was involved. "A leading rebel fighter was captured trying to gain access to Southampton Docks this morning. A spokesperson said it was apparently an attempt to cause massive damage to our infrastructure. It was thwarted by the vigilance of EurPo assisted by EurMilPo who, together, have been guaranteeing our safety and security during these troubled times. It is only by persistence against these terrorists that we will return to normalcy and order.'

"Bloody hell," said Francine, employing the English words deliberately. "The game is on."

"He is one of the best," said George. The truth was that capture had become commonplace, but they needed this one to happen. If it worked it was far more likely that Verdun would come. They had rehearsed what Andy would say. He had to give a genuine impression of a rebel movement on its last legs, although perhaps it would not be that hard a picture to paint, given the reality of their situation. "If he can't do it then nobody can."

"You're thinking of the fun evening you had in Stevenage police station, aren't you?"

"Yes, but also how Andy could possibly have volunteered, knowing what's in store for him. I just couldn't do that." George saw no benefit in pretending anything.

"Did I tell you about my experience?" Francine asked before pulling sharply off the road at a parade of shops. She parked the car, got out and pulled her heavy skirt up and placed her knee on the seat of the car. George saw a mass of scar tissue surrounding her upper leg. "They knew about my fear of fire," she said simply. "That is not the only one, but the only one I am prepared to show you!" That was why she wore such heavy, full clothing all the time.

"My God, Francine. Here I have been feeling sorry for myself after a few weeks on the run and just think what you have gone through over the years. I am not fit to be leader."

"Each person serves a purpose, George, and yours is to lead

intellectually. No one expects you to be a formidable guerrilla fighter but you have collected to yourself a group of intellectuals and people of influence because of your reputation and that of your Papa and this has given credibility to our cause. It has caused the 'establishment' to crack and that means they question themselves. Look at it like this. Six months ago the EurPo underground movement had fewer than 500 members. Now we can count on a third of all police officers. I find the same thing with the civil service. It is too bad we cannot make the same progress with our dear friends in EurMilPo!" Francine got back in the car and drove off, ignoring a car that had right of way. "George, we have got the establishment questioning itself."

"But I can't claim all the credit for that."

"Oh George, you are not listening to me!" Francine swerved as she took her eyes off the road and looked hard at George. The car in the other lane honked and put two fingers up at Francine, who reciprocated the gesture. "Did I not just say that each person serves a purpose? It is your reputation that has made this possible. Sir Terrence could have backed the Spiders and me years ago but he chose not to. We would not have been included in all those radio debates and *Question Times* if it had not been for you and the little bit of the establishment you brought with you. You are not the greatest leader this world has ever seen. You are not supposed to be a Mao Tse Tung or Ghandi. You need to recognise that you are one cog in a machine. That machine doesn't work without you, but it also does not work without any of the other cogs, me included." Francine slammed on the brakes having got too close to a large van in front of their car. "Now you are going to cause us to have an accident," she said, but a little calmer and with a smile.

They turned north and headed for their next rendezvous in Winchester. After a few moments of silence, Francine said, "George, do not try and be what you are not. Just accept that everybody is different and everybody has a part to play. We will get nowhere if you are blaming yourself for perceived inadequacies when all the time you are measuring yourself against some false standard. This is not about being a hero. This is teamwork. We are all in this together and, thank God, we are all different."

George registered what Francine was saying, but kept turning over in his mind the availability of armoured vehicles. There had to be some way of using that to their advantage.

"Francine, why do you do this?" George asked sometime later as they jolted into Basingstoke on the A30. "It is not even your country yet you have given so much to it."

"That is a long story, my friend."

"Then you better start straight away so we get it done before our next stop!"

"Well, it started with my husband. He is English. He studied French at university in Exeter and came to Bordeaux to study. We met there in '07. He was twenty-one and I was seventeen. He was a firebrand, I believe the saying is."

"Was a firebrand?"

"He was a political firebrand and a radical person but he was shot in '12 at a demonstration in London where we were then living. He was very badly hurt, George." She stopped then and did not talk again until they were close to Woking. "He is in a wheelchair all the time now and has terrible mood swings. His parents look after him because he has become so aggressive and only with his mother can he be gentle. I swore to change the system that shot him and caused all this. When it is all over…" Again she stopped while the night closed in, waiting maybe for darkness to frame her confidences. She wiped her eyes many times, her driving even more erratic, but she never wanted anyone to drive her so George did not ask. "When it is all over then I will go back to him and mend it for us. I will mend everything and make it a good marriage again. I love him so much." Then she added, as if it had some significance, "My real name is Mrs Brian Brent. My maiden name is L'Amour. I will be Mrs Brian Brent again when this is all over."

***

Musgrove was taken in for 'routine questioning' the day after the election results and no one had heard of him since. No one except Terry Rose, that is, who knew he was in Harrogate where Terry had grown up and his elderly mother still lived, now on her own. For some reason Terry felt compelled to see Musgrove, a man he had never met and knew only as a name on a list of suspects.

Terry knew that he had acted badly. He knew that his whole life had been a lie, more specifically a race for something that did not warrant racing for. He was Prime Minister, but it was a hollow crown he wore and like the crown of thorns, it dug into him and gnawed away at the wick that was good deep inside him. If God had accosted him and asked him what he intended to do about it he would have said he had no bloody idea. It was more a welling up within him than a plan.

"I have to go to Harrogate to see my mother," he reported to Fernby one morning in mid-October.

"That should be manageable," Fernby replied, sitting as usual in a large wingback chair in the centre of the room. "Things are in good order. We 'dealt' with 343 rebels last week, including the key chap caught red-handed in Southampton. EurMilPo have a good grip on everything. I think we should be able to fit something in the week after next." He leant over to press the bell to summon the Diary Secretary.

"I need to go tomorrow."

"But, that's impossible."

"Make it possible. Fernby, I have done everything you have asked for over the last three weeks. The 'good order' you refer to in such a pleased manner is largely down to my ongoing efforts to achieve the objectives we set. Now I need to go tomorrow to see my mother. You will have to reschedule my engagements and put it down to personal reasons. Perhaps you can arrange for me to do some work up there. After all, I am a northerner and have spent the whole of the last three weeks in the south." It seemed the old Terry Rose was back.

"Perhaps we could do that, it is not a bad idea at all. It might demonstrate confidence to have the PM travel outside of the

Home Counties. Yes, let me work on that."

"Isn't Harrogate the HQ for Yorkshire EurPo?"

"Yes it is, sir."

Terry, on hearing this, reflected that it had been a couple of weeks since Fernby had addressed him as 'Sir'.

"Good, there's your answer. I will visit EurPo and give my tried and trusted speech." It was an inspired idea of Terry's.

"Yes, sir."

One thing Charles Musgrove did not imagine would ever happen was a visit from the Prime Minister in his cramped, narrow cell. As the bed was fixed as a hard platform against the wall there was no room for anyone to sit other than on the bed or the toilet. They chose the bed and sat together, both slightly twisted inwards to see each other. Charles felt embarrassed about his cell, even though it was not accommodation he had chosen.

"Don't waste any time asking questions, just answer mine," Terry said under his breath. "I need to act like I know you so I am going to ask questions about your background, family, etc. Just answer simply and quickly and it can only help you."

"Why..."

"No, don't ask, it will come out later, no time right now. Where were you born?" Terry took out a notepad and wrote each answer in his strange shorthand. "Where were you married? Trained? Educated? How many children, cars, houses?" The questioning went on for fifteen minutes. "Sports? Where did you train for rugby?"

"It is the same man," Terry reported to the Station Commander. "I first met him when he was playing for the Wasps. I prefer League myself but am basically rugby mad so often went to the Wasps games when in London. I was a benefactor of the club and met him; it must have been around 2015, at a do. We became good friends."

"Sir, he is being held on very serious charges. I don't know him professionally, of course," said to distance himself from Musgrove without affronting the Prime Minister, "so I cannot speak of the veracity of them but I do understand that the charges are very serious."

"What are the charges?" More to the point, why was he even bothering about somebody he had never met before today and was just a name amongst a list of detainees? Was it just his way of fighting back against a system that had blatantly betrayed him at his moment of supposed glory? Or was it something else?

The Station Commander opened the file with authority and confidence, flicked over a page or two, returned to the front again and then closely examined each page, sometimes turning back to a prior one. Then he closed the file and stood up so that Terry could see he reached only five-feet-four, even with his boots on.

"Bear with me a moment please, sir. I just have to check something."

"I haven't got all day," Terry replied, his bullying tendency encouraged by the man's diminutive size and sudden anxious behaviour.

"Perhaps you would like to leave it with me, Prime Minister, if you are pressed for time."

"No, just get a damn move on, man." He had almost let the Station Commander off the hook. He was going to have to be more careful.

"I'll be right back, sir."

Terry felt comfortable when those around him showed proper deference.

The Station Commander was gone for over twenty minutes. In fact, he was only tracked down when Terry left the office and found him in the Duty Inspector's Office on the next floor down.

"Oh sir, I do apologise. We have some apparent irregularities we are just looking into. I was on my way back to see..."

"The charges, Chief Inspector, just give me the bloody charges."

"Well, sir, they are at the heart of the irregularities. We..."

"You don't have any bloody charges, do you?"

"No, sir." Said like a schoolboy caught smoking, red-handed.

"I want him released."

"Sir, that is not possible. I can only do that with the Regional Commissioner's say-so." The term 'say-so' infuriated Terry Rose; far too casual for an incident like this. He stood almost a foot over the smaller man and felt the blood racing around his body. He was ready for a fight. Then the most brilliant idea came to him.

"I understand." He said this suddenly, as if capitulating. The Station Commander's relief was immediate. He actually started to sigh and then caught himself and stopped. That was when Terry pounced. "You will release him into the charge of my Police Escort. It is commanded by Superintendent Adams so he outranks you. He will be responsible for a fast-track effort to resolve the balls up you have created. We cannot let word of this get out to the press." As Terry spoke, he maintained his close presence to the Station Commander, keeping up the pressure on him to give way. But at the same time he winked as he used the word 'resolve', giving the impression that the resolution would not necessarily be that enjoyable for Musgrove.

"Very well, sir. Inspector, please attend to the paperwork."

"Chief Inspector, you obviously did not fully get my meaning. We don't want paperwork. Let me spell this out to you. While under emergency law, the police do have increased powers of search and detention, most notably the extension of detention without charge from twenty-four hours to seven days, nowhere can I think of a clause in the emergency law provisions that allows five damn bloody weeks without charge. Let me put it plainly: do you enjoy your job?" It was a rhetorical question and Terry, stabbing with his fingers at the commander's chest, did not allow time for any reply. "I am sure you do. But maybe not if you are busted back to the rank of constable on the beat, and pension provisions are suspended for, probably I would say, a decade? Not such a dream job under those circumstances, hey?"

"Inspector, go and get the custody sergeant and then leave us alone." Then in the few minutes it took for the sergeant to arrive he screwed up his courage to raise another point with the enraged Prime Minister. "Sir, could Superintendent Adams please sign a personal receipt for the prisoner, I mean for Mr Musgrove?" Terry's reply shrank the unhappy commander still further. In any case it would not have been possible because, while Adams was the Police Escort and Security Commander, he was currently in his London office supervising arrangements for President Verdun's planned trip to London in ten days' time. He could not go on every trip for every politician. The senior officer on this trip was Inspector Wright; a competent man if a bit dull. He did all the Prime Minister's security work.

Mirroring George's escape from Stevenage Police Station just before the election, Terry Rose took Musgrove out of the back door, having instructed his escort and car to meet him in the car park: "To avoid the media." Like George, Musgrove wore borrowed clothes. But unlike George there was no skulking behind dustbins, no wait at all as the car was there already. In the back seat, screen window to the front firmly closed and loud, angry classical music powered through the set of six speakers that Mercedes made standard, they could talk with the expectation of privacy.

"Why?"

"I don't bloody well know," Terry admitted in a rare step out of character. "I suppose I wanted to hit back in some way."

"Well, thank you!"

"Don't thank me, if they had not treated me in this despicable way you would still be rotting in that freaking cell." And then after a few moments of Beethoven at its best and loudest, "I know you're as guilty as hell. Your name was on a suspect list about five years ago. You should be in jail. But you can't stay in this damn car. When we go through the tunnel just coming up we slow down for the barrier. Jump out and disappear pronto, bloody pronto. Don't get caught." Terry opened his wallet and pulled out 400 euros. They looked at each other for a moment before Charles made his leap from the car. In that moment he saw many things in the Prime Minister's eyes, but chief among them was a flaming anger.

Back in his office in Westminster, Terry read with approval that the Harrogate Station Commander was up for disciplinary procedures following the escape of a dangerous but unnamed terrorist. He had claimed that the Prime Minister had taken him but no one could collaborate that story and the Station Commander could not show a receipt. Fernby had asked the Prime Minister about it but, like the others, he could add nothing to the facts as they stood.

***

Over a thousand miles south and east, deep inside USE territory, another casualty of the election got ready for the new day. Her damp barracks had no heating and no way of drying her clothes. She shared the room with 101 other 'candidates', as they were called. There were thirty-four triple-layer bunks, seventeen down each side with a foot between each and slim lockers in the middle of the room. At one end were the ablutions; at the other end was the duty sergeant's room. There were no windows and a corrugated iron roof that leaked through numerous nail holes when it rained.

She knew that she was lucky. She had only two weeks to go of 'extra training' and had passed every section so far. Her sergeant seemed to show her a little preference, or maybe it was just acknowledgement that she was obviously trying hard to be a good candidate. Furthermore, since her arrival they had extended the training period from six weeks to eighteen but had not made it retrospective. The passing-out parade was two weeks today. She only had fourteen days to go and then she could get back to her real job.

Today had started much like all the other days before. They had run around the grounds early in the morning, had barrack inspection, and eaten porridge and toast for breakfast. Then after the Commandant's review they had five minutes to get ready for classes. She looked at the timetable on the notice board to double check, even though she knew the rota off by heart. Saturday was her least favourite day. It started with USE Government, double period, then went on to Ethics, then gym for an hour, which was tedious but a relief from the onslaught in the classrooms. After an early lunch of stew and an apple, they had a class on Chain of Command before Loyalties, finishing off with a double session of USE Society and Frameworks. Tonight she had to finish off her dissertation on 'How the USE is beneficially involved in its citizens' lives'. She had chosen this from the list and was particularly pleased with how it was turning out.

Then she heard her name called on the loud speakers that boomed out over the whole camp. "Candidate Browning to the Duty Officer."

"Candidate Browning reporting, sir."

"Come in. Stand at ease. Now, Browning, I believe you knew a corrupt police officer called Musgrove. Is that correct?" Everything about her old life was said by the staff in the past tense, like it happened long ago in a different age. Sometimes she thought it was way in the past.

"Yes, sir. Superintendent Musgrove was my Divisional Officer, sir."

"What did you think of him?" Survival kicked in. Any question asked of her in this place had to be seen through a survival filter.

"Sir, he seemed good at his job but I later heard that he was a leader of the resistance and I don't want to have anything to do with him when I return to duty."

"He escaped two days ago."

"He's not coming here is he, Sir?" she said with widening eyes and a rising voice.

"I should think this is the last place on earth he would want to come to!" She dutifully chuckled at his joke. "Browning, I want to talk to you about your release. Have you thought about what role you might slot in to?"

"Yes, Sir, I would like to do whatever is deemed suitable for me, sir. I understand that you know best, sir."

"That is interesting because for top-performing candidates like you we always try and accommodate their requests. But your request is simply, I take it, to obey orders and do whatever you are assigned to with the best of your ability?"

"Yes, sir."

"It is unusual to see such dedication and faith in a youngster, even after extra training, but we might just have an interesting plan for you, Browning. Off you go now." He handed her a chit for being late for class. She hurried out, pleased to be described as top-performing.

Candidate Browning passed out two weeks later, head of her class. Her final interview had gone really well and the panel of senior officers was convinced that this was an outstanding example of where extra training worked to perfection. The passing-out parade was a fine show with neatly groomed and lined up candidates marching across the central parade ground. They were all faces to her; personality was not encouraged. As she stood to attention through the lengthy speeches she ranged her eyes over the ranks of supporting candidates, those that hoped to graduate next time or the time after, thankful that her own re-training was at an end.

There was one enormous man in the rank in front of her who towered over the others. He was the type who could be from any profession. She could see his rigid frame not swaying an inch. She glanced down and saw that his boots shone to perfection. He clearly was a serious candidate. She wondered what had brought him to this distant training camp, then noticed that he was moving forward out of the ranks, while the candidate next to her was knocking her arm and hissing urgently.

"You're being called up, Browning." She had not been listening, but her training kicked in and very few people noticed the slight scurry as she hustled to fall into step next to the giant.

They were both presented with the sword of honour as the outstanding candidates on their course. The sword was for the day but the sash and the badge could be kept and worn as a constant reminder. Afterwards she was interviewed by the EBC, who were filming the day. She spoke of wrong turns, errors made, and deeds done. She spoke then of her great gratitude that she had been allowed a second chance and of her determination to make the most of it. Then she changed from the academy uniform and became Constable Browning again and got on the bus with the other graduating candidates to catch the flight back to London.

"Congratulations," the giant said. He was not in uniform but wore a light grey suit with a red and yellow striped tie, the type that could be a regimental or school tie, but equally might not. "My name is Andy Durrington, by the way." He gave his hand and shook hers warmly. "I understand we will be working together back in London."

"Nobody told me."

"They asked me to brief you on the journey. We're going to be sitting alone in First Class so we can go over everything." Something made Brownie ill at ease at the prospect.

***

Back in London, Gerry made her way to her office, even though it was a Saturday afternoon. She got a coffee and a take-out bowl of porridge from the café on the corner and carried them precariously, with her umbrella up in one hand and her briefcase in the other, so that the hot cardboard coffee cup made her fingers dance on its casing as she tried to find a painless way to hold it. It was a shallow day, barely light, the leaves from the park opposite now too sodden to fly and jump away. The downpour of the last few days had beaten all life out of them. The wind seemed determined to annoy her, at one point hastening her on from behind so that the collars of her coat and jacket blew up and around her neck. Then it changed direction completely and threatened to lift her coat and skirt so she had to hold them down with her laden hands. She ended up walking with her briefcase in front of her, like a shield against the elements. Then she had to get the key out of her purse. She had forgotten that the doorman only worked on weekdays.

Eventually, she struggled up the stairs to the second floor office suite they were rapidly outgrowing. Another key was needed for this door and, for a moment, she thought she had left it behind. She felt like crying. But each time she felt like crying she told herself sharply to think about what it was like for George. He was a hunted man, never quite sure if he was going to spend the night with a friend, on the street, or in a prison cell. She found the key, lodged behind her driving licence, and let herself in, remembering the alarm at the last moment.

She had planned to come to work today for two reasons. Firstly, she wanted to think carefully about what was going on, why Mr Pearson, her boss, had sent that strange email and was it coincidence that he was not available for a phone call when Gerry tried to call him yesterday? Or was he avoiding her? Silence is the breeding ground of paranoia. It sets the imagination free. She knew this but it did not make her feel any better.

Secondly, she had decided to come into the office because she had absolutely nothing else to do and nobody to share it with.

She read the email again. It was the seventh time she had read it, although the first time today. It had kept her awake most of the night, rehearsing what to say to her boss, how to handle it. She had finally fallen asleep in the early morning, sleeping late as a result.

Dear Gerry, it is with a heavy heart that I write to inform you of grave accusations made by your staff in London. I think I know you very well and feel sure that there is a sensible explanation for this and, following on from that explanation, an equally sensible way forward. I hope we can reach an understanding and direction before it is too late.

"Before it is too late," she said to herself. "Before what is too late? And why?" She rose from her desk and, coffee in hand, now suitably tamed to a drinkable temperature, she crossed to her favourite window, the one with the view of the park. There was a group of Chinese students being led by two older Chinese girls. She could not hear the voices, of course, but imagined them telling tales of the history the park held. At first they would just go through the facts. Who had set aside the land and when, who had given it to the crown and which monarch had that been. Then maybe a divergence into why he or she had given it; in other words, what had been received in return? Then probably some terribly dangerous goings on had happened in this very park, close as it was to Buckingham Palace and the Houses of Parliament, like a buffer between the two, like no man's land when the two sources of authority were in constant friction as so much of British history seemed to be. Maybe Guy Fawkes had met his conspirators here? It was coming up to November 5th, the annual remembrance of the Gunpowder Plot. What a strange thing to remember and celebrate in such a perverse and upside down way! Was it the failure of the plot they celebrated or the punishment of the perpetrators, or even making the underdog of the day into a champion across the ages?

Gerry watched as the tourist group spent eight minutes in the park before lining up to get back on the coach. Where was their next stopping point to be? Maybe they had done the capital now and were heading way back in time to Stonehenge or the Roman villa she had heard about at Fishbourne. She would love to go there, to go to all these places, but she had no one to take her. She considered her private aches – one major one for uncertainty about George, a medium-sized one for uncertainty about her job and a little tiny one of self-pity because she was in an amazing city going through amazing times and she had no one to share it with. Then she shook herself. Self-pity was not a road she was going to travel down. It was still a little early to call Mr Pearson so she would fill the intervening time by writing out the reasons for her actions. She would fight back.

Gerry's fight, of course, was a pale reflection of the fight George faced but it was a reflection all the same. The more she wrote that shaky October afternoon with the wind and rain playing games outside and her coat still on, for the heating only worked Monday to Friday, the more she came to understand what she was living through. And the more she understood, the more she became determined to fight her corner. It was partly, she acknowledged to herself, that she loved George and wanted to fight his fight. But it was also that she saw the struggle of Britain and the iron grip of the USE as a fight she had grown into. It had become her purpose. Deidre and the others would not get the better of her.

'This is the greatest fight or our age.' She tapped away at her computer. 'This is a fight on so many levels; democracy against authoritarianism, reason against rules, the individual against the block, natural society against imposed order, nature against design and history against illusion. But at each level freedom and responsibility are the things being fought for, either to establish them or to deny them.' Her coffee went cold, her porridge also. Finally, the cold stillness got into her bones and caused her to break, stand again, stretch, and return to her window. It was dark now, lamplight and water mixing like a chemical reaction to produce a softened, splashed version of the world outside. She looked for several minutes but saw no person at all in the park or the street. Had the world been depopulated while she wrote her reply to Mr. Pearson? Was she the last person alive, like in some silly movie? Would she move from building to building in search of some human company, always denied the touch and tingle of warm voices, the millions of everyday interchanges, the jokes, the criticisms, the apologies? Could anyone be so all-alone as she was in this city of twelve million?

"Hello, Mrs Pearson? This is Gerry Matthews from the London, England office. Could I please speak to your husband?"

"Wait a minute, Gerry dear, I will go get him." Gerry held her breath and went through a final rehearsal in her mind.

Mr Pearson was a good listener, had always been so. He had to intervene several times to slow Gerry down, however. At one point he just burst out laughing. "Gerry, you are going to have to slow down. It is more than my old brain can take in!"

"I'm sorry, sir."

"Don't apologise, just go a mite slower for me."

Gerry took a deep breath and told herself to slow down. She got control and fifteen minutes of measured speech later she stopped. "That's about it, sir."

"Gerry, thank you for this. I know you to have integrity and honour but I am going to have to hear out the other side before I can make a decision. Miss Deidre Harrington is not available until Tuesday so I am going to have to ask you to sit tight and wait until Tuesday afternoon your time. Can you do that for me?"

"Yes, Mr Pearson. I can wait until then." But how would she? That was almost seventy-two hours of suspense.

"Can you put the work to one side and go enjoy yourself? Have you made any friends? Anybody you could spend some time with?"

"Yes, sir, of course," she lied, staring at a bleak evening tonight, all day tomorrow, too.

"Good, enjoy the sights and don't let things get you down. I'll be on the phone around 3pm your time on Tuesday. 'Cheers', as they say over there!"

"Thank you, Mr Pearson, enjoy your weekend."

Gerry did not have any time to wallow in self-pity for her mobile phone rang, as if choreographed, the moment she put

271

the receiver down for her stateside call.

"Hello, Gerry Matthews speaking."

"Gerry, thank God!"

"Who is this?"

"I need help, Gerry. It's me, I mean Charles Musgrove. You remember election day?"

"Great Scott! Where are you? I thought you were in jail! I wrote an article about you last week. My goodness…"

"It's a long story, Gerry. I am on the run. They might trace this call. Can I meet you? Can you help me?"

"Where are you?"

"Victoria Bus Station."

"Get a cab…"

"I've got no money."

"OK, I am on my way."

"I'll be just outside. There is a theatre, the Apollo on Wilton Road, with a great big crowd outside. I'll pretend to be going in."

"Give me twenty minutes and I'll be there in a cab. Call me if there are any problems. Hold on, Charles."

She was still wearing her coat, forgot to turn off her computer, grab her umbrella, or set the alarm. She did remember to lock the front door. She had to run along Birdcage Walk, almost as far as the palace, to get a cab.

"Apollo Theatre, Victoria, please."

"You running late for the show, Miss?"

"I need to get there quickly. How long?"

"It's just down the road. Five minutes max."

"Great."

She tipped generously at the Apollo and got out of the cab to look for Charles. Her first thought had been to get him to jump in the taxi and they would go together to her flat in South Kensington. But then she thought, what if he was being watched? Better to handle it another way altogether. So when she saw Charles outside the theatre, trying to look as if he was waiting for someone before going in together, but patently not dressed for an evening out in his mud-stained clothes, she walked as if to go straight past him, showing no recognition. The crowd was thick and moving. It was night-time and still raining. It had been raining all day. Visibility was not good, that was an advantage. She dropped her purse just before she levelled with him. He bent down to help her with it.

"21A Burrington Gardens." She slipped a fifty-euro note into his hand before standing up. "Thank you, sir," she said and moved off towards the box office. Another American tourist merging into the damp blackness that was London that night, no sign of anxiety on her attractive, intelligent face.

The Best Place to Hide

Gerry was wondering if it had all been some crazy dream. She had checked her watch on getting back into a cab on Wilton Road. It had been 7.25. She asked the driver to take her to Wholefoods, where she quickly stocked up on groceries, feeling sure Charles would be starving. She got another cab to her flat and was there by 8.40. That had been over two hours ago and there had been no sign of him. She had checked her phone but the number Charles had called from was withheld. She turned up the ringer volume to maximum in case he should ring and she not hear it. She started to prepare a Spanish omelette but stopped at the point where heat was applied. She could get it done from there in a flash but he needed to arrive first.

Then the doorbell rang, loud and brash in the quiet night, as if announcing a criminal. Gerry did not move, then she grabbed her phone, only then realising that it was the door downstairs. She buzzed him in and went to open the front door. Suddenly he was there, standing awkwardly, the man who had made the election a free one.

"Come in," she said, as if welcoming a casual friend in for coffee. "Great Scott, look at you." The better light of the flat showed up the grime and the torn clothes. "Wait a minute." She went into her bedroom and came back with an oversized dressing gown. "See if this will fit. I'll get you some towels. Go into the bathroom and wash and change. I'll get something fixed to eat and then I'll get your clothes into the washer."

"Thanks." It was the first word said to Gerry face-to-face

since yesterday evening, when the doorman at work had said, "Goodnight, Miss Matthews."

"You're welcome." She turned away to hide the tears.

After his second Spanish omelette and two beers, biscuits and cheese, Gerry and Charles sat and talked late into the night. He had not seen George and he had not heard from him at all. He had tried to call various people, including George, but their phones seemed cut off. Finally, he had got through to Gerry.

"I tried everyone I knew in the movement." Gerry did not correct him that she, as a foreigner, was not in the movement. She felt flattered that he had included her.

"And finally got hold of me?" She laughed.

"Yes, and very glad I was too!" He had been robbed in Newark, beaten up in Nottingham, while a couple who picked him up on the A1 seemed likely to turn him in. "They were asking too many questions so when we stopped at a café I slipped off and walked through the night. I certainly know what it is like now."

"What do you mean?" Gerry asked.

"The view from the other side; the criminal side, that is. To be hunted."

She put him up in the spare bedroom and, before he went to bed, he said to her, "I can't imagine what it is like for you not knowing how George is. If I hear anything I will get word back to you. The saving grace is that no news is good news. If he had been hurt or captured I am sure it would be all over the papers and internet in no time at all. I'll have to move on in the morning but keep your phone by you at all times."

"Do you have to leave? Won't you be safe here? For a little while at least?" She felt closer to George with Charles around. Plus, the human contact was something to cherish.

"No, Gerry love, I can't risk staying around. I'll keep in touch but I have to make contact with the others. I have to find out what the plan is. Nobody seems to know what is going on and that worries me. I have to keep moving around until I find answers and then I can be useful."

Charles left early afternoon on Sunday after a long sleep and a good breakfast. He kissed her gently and said again that he would get any news of George to her as soon as possible.

"Thanks. Will you be OK, Charles?"

'I'll be fine. It will take a bit more than EurPo and EurMilPo to get rid of me! I think I am getting pretty good at this!"

But he had not counted on their plan.

And their plan came in the form of Constable Browning, fresh from her extra training and assigned to South Kensington Police Station, her allotted purpose to infiltrate the Society and, through it, to track down members of the resistance. She called at Gerry's office on Monday morning to find the American tense and fidgety. They shook hands shyly and Browning told her what had happened to her since the election.

"But they did not succeed," she added quickly.

"I'm so glad you are safe," Gerry said. "It has been a real bad time. I have not heard from George for over two weeks now. The last time he called he was somewhere in the north and said he could not use their cell phones anymore because they were all being traced. That is how Superintendent Musgrove was caught."

"How do you know that?" The young police officer, resplendent in her new uniform, asked.

Then the whole story came out and, with it, tumbled out Gerry's intense loneliness. "Everybody I have met since coming over here is lying low, hunted as a criminal. My work colleagues are not colleagues at all, but seem set against me from the very first day. And I worry about George and the others so much."

"You love him, don't you?"

"Yes, I do." And then she changed the subject before the tears became a flood. "Have you seen Adam since you got back?"

"No, Miss Matthews, I only arrived back in the country on Saturday evening and I have been on duty pretty well since then. I haven't been back to my old flat in Stevenage yet. They kitted me out completely from scratch and put me in the

Holland Park Police Barracks."

"You are living in barracks? In a dorm?"

"Yes, well no, I have a bedroom I share with three other constables and we share a bathroom with one other bedroom, and all meals are provided in the dining hall. I suppose it is easy for a new arrival like me, but two of my roommates have been there forever. The cost is taken straight out of our pay so what is left is just spending money."

"You have to pay? It sounds dreadful, so impersonal. Do you have to stay there?"

"I think it is required for the first two years but I don't know for sure. It is certainly crowded. The rooms were designed for two people but they mostly have four in now, with bunk beds. So maybe they would allow people to leave to ease the congestion a bit. I'd have to ask, but it is too far to commute from Stevenage."

"I have a spare room. The rent would be nothing as it is paid anyway by the Society."

The deal was done by lunchtime and Brownie Browning was allowed to move in that very evening, after her shift finished at 6pm. It suited the authorities perfectly. Her possessions shocked Gerry, who had travelled over from the States with four suitcases and felt she was hard-done-by. Brownie owned nothing but a suit bag for her uniforms and a medium-sized, police-issue grip bag for underwear and nightwear. The first thing Gerry did was give her a pair of jeans and a sweatshirt so she could relax and wander about the flat barefoot. The second thing she did was insist that Brownie call her Gerry instead of Miss Matthews as had become her habit.

"We are flatmates and fast becoming friends," Gerry said. "You were very brave and organised when you took charge and got George and me out of the police station in time for the election. I couldn't have done that for anything. I want us to become friends."

"I did it for the movement," Brownie replied. "But I sure am glad I met you in the process." Her poor mock American accent, mixed with Essex, made them both laugh and Gerry, for a moment, forgot that her big day was coming up tomorrow. She would hear from Mr Pearson at 3pm. Deidre had not been in on Monday but the others had adequately deputised for her with their questioning and disapproving attitude to everything Gerry did. It was subtly done. No tribunal would ever find fault but, nevertheless, Gerry felt entirely alone in the office.

"Tackle it head on," Brownie had said when they shared breakfast on Tuesday morning.

"I have to wait for Mr Pearson's call first."

"That's what I mean. Start by tackling it straight on with your boss. Be prepared to stand your corner. You are in the right." Brownie stood up, drank the remains of her tea and looked for her jacket. "I have to go. I'm on long shift today so won't get back until just after 8pm but let's talk about it then."

Gerry could not settle all morning. She was scheduled to interview a top civil servant in the cabinet office, someone called Fernby, but every time she started to read the brief, rehearsals of the afternoon's phone call crowded into her mind. Finally, she forced herself to read Fernby's background as she walked east along Birdcage Walk towards Westminster, turning north on Horse Guards Road to walk past the Imperial War Museum and the Churchill War Rooms. She was early and stopped for a moment to consider what it would be like to be Winston Churchill during the war. Perhaps that too had been a lonely job. But surely not lacking in contact? Perhaps George would one day be known as a great Prime Minister, a saviour of the country just like Mr Churchill. Could she see herself with him on that journey in this strange land of wet and damp, where intense kindness came in fits and starts?

Fernby was, she calculated, fifty-seven years old. He seemed to have followed a classic civil service career, starting with public school and Oxford then, when in his early thirties, a six-year stint in Brussels before coming back to run Education and then Defence and finally the Exchequer before heading the Cabinet Office. Back in the old days he would have been knighted somewhere along that road, but that was disapproved of now and usually only granted to actors and pop stars in a glitzy twice-annual ceremony in the Royal Albert Hall. So much had changed in Britain. So much that used to be was whittled away, like a clarinet reduced to a penny whistle. This was what Deidre called progress. She could see the remnants of what it had been like and it made her sad. Sad, and angry too.

Fernby looked the part when she met with him in Downing Street at 11am. His pinstripe suit and silk tie looked like they were attached to him. She tried to do the trick her old boss in DC had taught her, of imagining any intimidating person naked, but it did not work. The pinstripes were like his skin. He had a hawkish, aristocratic face that did not suffer fools gladly; thin lips, thin hair, thin nose. Imperious was the word she was looking for.

She found Fernby in interview to be condescending in the extreme. It was quite simple: he was a big person and she was a little person. She was also American. The twenty-minute slot allocated to her seemed interminably long after the first opening question. Thankfully his phone went after six-and-a-half minutes and he had to leave.

"Perhaps another time, Miss, eh…"

"Matthews."

"Yes, Matthews. Perhaps another time." Said with perfect insincerity. They both knew it was not going to happen. But the burning indignation kept Gerry's mind from her upcoming phone call during the walk back to her office. Instead, she framed out a damning article on the Head of the Civil Service.

"Call for you on line two, Miss Matthews."

"Thank you." She had given up asking them to call her Gerry. The moment had come.

But it was not Mr Pearson calling from America. Instead it was another American voice from the Embassy a mile north and west of her, rather than 3000 south and west.

"Hi Gerry, this is Adam Forster, remember me?"

"Of course, Adam, how could I ever forget? And I have some news for you."

279

"I know. She is back in the country and in London and staying with you."

"How do you know these things?" Her worry about the call with Mr Pearson was put to one side for a moment.

"I have my sources." He laughed. "It helps to be number three in the Embassy of the richest and most powerful country in the world!"

They arranged for Adam to come around that night when Brownie got back from her shift. "Don't mention it to her, I want to surprise her."

After the phone call, Gerry worked on the article about Fernby. She knew it would be controversial but did not care. The newsletter she had taken over on arriving had increased its circulation tenfold and was still rising. She had received several visits from EurComm, patiently explaining that certain things were unconstitutional and inappropriate. Because she was a foreigner and a citizen of a major ally and defender of Europe she had managed to feign surprise and buy time. But that time was running out. Her articles were war-torn and she felt like a war correspondent. War-torn because of the battle to get them through Deidre and the others and onto the printing press. She had wisely taken control of the bank account early on and not argued when the printing press asked for a 20% price increase. In fact, she had hinted that this might be appropriate, thus buying an ally in her war for freedom. Several times she had bypassed Deidre as editor and taken her scripts straight to the printer.

The afternoon slid into early evening. Tea was drunk in the office but no one knocked on Gerry's door to ask her if she would like a cup. Asking her would have meant passing on the message that Mr Pearson had rung. It was not until her secretary came in to say that she was leaving that Gerry remembered the call that was supposed to happen. How could she have forgotten?

"Yes, Miss Matthews, there was one message. Mr Pearson

called at 3pm. I did send you an Outlook reminder." So she was in the clear but she knew that Gerry did not use Outlook.

"Cynthia, I am going to reorganise the office over the next few weeks. I think it wise to warn you that I don't think I need a full-time secretary. You have been invaluable over the last few weeks so I wanted to give you maximum notice to enable you to find another job." Take the fight to the enemy. Stand your ground.

"Goodnight, Miss Matthews."

It was quarter to six before Gerry got hold of Mr Pearson. When she explained the delay he was courteous as ever. "But Gerry, my message to you is not what you are going to want to hear."

"Sir?"

"You need to scale back on this attack against everything to do with the USE. The allegations Miss Harrington has made are very serious. I remember Mr Unwin-Smith very fondly, but he is officially an outlaw and you seem very close to him and his cause."

"He is my boyfriend." That was the second time she had said it.

"Then you need to be impartial. You should remove yourself from any professional comment concerning British and European politics. This could be a major upset to our relationship with Europe at a very fragile time. You have risked the position of the Society with a major organisation who we are working with every day on multiple levels. And a less generous interpretation could be that you have done this in pursuit of a man you are infatuated with."

Gerry argued for over an hour but Mr Pearson was firm. He would not risk the Society provoking an embarrassing incident at this delicate time. "There is one other change I am making. I want Miss Harrington to assume direct control. You are to submit all articles to her and not to bypass editorial by going straight to the printing press. It is entirely up to Miss Harrington whether she prints anything you write. Do you understand me, Gerry? I want you to concentrate on membership and Miss Harrington to concentrate on the newsletter and general management. She is now your boss, at least until I can get someone over there to restore order. I am sorry it has come to this, Gerry, but your actions have been reckless in the extreme, risking the good name of the Society for your personal objectives. Frankly, most people would have fired you at this stage but a little bit of me still believes in you and you have some good people back home speaking up for you. I think you have just lost your head and need to work in a structured environment to regain perspective. I want you to give me your word that for the good of the Society you will buckle down and accept Miss Harrington as your boss. Good, thank you. I am communicating the same message to her later this evening at her home. I will be stressing the need for structure." It was a devastating blow that put Gerry in tears as she left the office and walked home. She did not notice that the drizzle had stopped and the dark sky was lit to abundance with a thousand brilliant stars. She only thought that she had failed in the one thing she had tried to do to help George.

She did not remember anything of the evening arrangements until she got back to her flat at 7.45 to find Adam Forster waiting in the street outside, leaning against a lamp-post like a cartoon character.

"Something on your mind, Gerry Matthews?" he said as she approached. "I seem to remember making some arrangements just a few hours ago and already I have been forgotten!"

"I'm real sorry, Adam. I just had the worst phone call of my professional career."

"What's up?" Adam stood up now, peering at her with concern.

"Demotion, I guess you call it." As she took out her key and opened the door, walked up the stairs and into the flat, she told him about the call with her boss. Adam listened and thought but did not say much.

"But now we need to get ready for Brownie coming back. I want this to be a real surprise for her. She has been through a lot since she got taken away back at the beginning of September."

***

Constable Brownie Browning was tired from a long shift. She had been on the streets much of the time, assisting EurMilPo staff in their efforts to keep order. There had been an impromptu demonstration in Kensington High Street that afternoon and they had all been issued with riot gear. It had been a tense couple of hours but passed when the police and military police made a shield wall and cleared the street, detachments going down side streets to flush them out. At one point she had been sent down an alley under the command of a military sergeant who looked like he had never smiled. He used hand signals to give orders and became impatient with Brownie and the other police officers when they did not understand the military signals. But at the end, during debrief, he had smiled, as if his personality had been held in suspense while duty called, and said that she in particular had done well. "It will go on your record." He said. It was another step on her journey back.

She also did not notice the weather on her walk home, in fact so absorbed was she in thinking about the day's work that she set off first to the police barracks, only remembering where she now lived when someone stopped her and asked for directions.

Thus she was tired when she finally got to her new lodgings at 8.40 that evening. She was looking forward to putting on her jeans after a long bath. Maybe she and Gerry would share a bottle of wine and talk into the early hours. She was on late shift tomorrow so she did not have to rise early.

She did not recognise Adam when she entered the sitting room, only thinking it a shame that Gerry had invited a friend back instead of the two of them sharing the evening.

"Hi Brownie, it's me, Adam." She stared for what seemed like a long moment, the moment before the order to up out of the trenches and go over the top, or the moment before a young

283

couple learns the sex of their firstborn. She blinked several times and then, reality sinking in, she suddenly jumped across the sofa and flung herself at him, her heavy-duty radio dropping out of her belt and smashing the glass coffee table so that the two glasses of red wine, and the third empty glass that was waiting for her arrival, slid down the broken glass and added their own shards, now stricken red like blood at a crime scene.

"Adam!" was all that she could say. "Adam!"

"Great Scott, what an entrance." Gerry laughed as she made to clear up the glass.

They had takeaway Chinese that night, selected because it was the closest to the flat, just at the end of the next street. Adam and Brownie went to fetch it, linked arm-in-arm all the way there and back, their union re-forged in moments as if the last six weeks had never happened to Brownie. When they got back, Gerry had moved a new table from the hall into the sitting room and had laid out a new bottle of wine. "No more athletics now, Brownie!" Instead, Brownie went to her bedroom and changed out of her uniform, putting on her jeans and noticing a crop top that Gerry had left on the bed for her. Smiling the warmest of smiles, she returned to the sitting room as Adam opened the wine.

"You are so beautiful," he said. And he really meant it. For the first time he was seeing her out of uniform. The turquoise top, donated by Gerry, made her arms so jet-black in contrast, like a single stage light focusing on the star. Her bare feet were elegant with a high instep and each toenail painted bright red.

"Just for fun," she said when Gerry asked her if she went on duty like that.

Not surprisingly, they stayed up late that night, but something told Adam and Brownie to keep it light, to stop Gerry dwelling on the difficult conversation she had had with Mr Pearson. It was a reunion of the Great Escapers; only they dared not dwell on that either, for the sake of Gerry's feelings about the missing escaper. So they played silly games, they talked of their childhoods and of their dreams. Brownie had a past they would never have guessed at. She had been born in Germany when her soldier father had been stationed there and married a German girl. Her father was later imprisoned for a fight he did not start and dismissed from the army. He had opened a bookshop in Tilbury on a whim and ten years later owned ten stores. Then her mother was sent to jail for using the bookshops as a cover to distribute banned leaflets.

"We are quite a family of rebels," Brownie joked. "Which is probably why I never got any further than constable! They take family background very seriously but I gave them a sweet pack of lies about wanting to mend the dishonour the family had caused and turning my back on my family." They opened more wine and cooked bacon sandwiches that resulted in an argument about whether British or American bacon was better. Finally, Adam said he ought to get going. But he did not go anywhere that night.

Gerry woke late the next day with a heavy hangover. She could hear Adam and Brownie laughing in the kitchen; neither appeared to be any the worse for the late night. She rushed through breakfast, had a shower and dressed in her work clothes. She was happy for them but the contrast with her empty life was all the stronger. When she was ready to leave and Brownie was in the bathroom, Adam asked her whether they could meet later. "I have an idea."

"Lunch, then, at the pub just off Birdcage, the Queen's Head, 1pm," she said.

She got to the end of her street and thought, *Hang it, I am not going in to have Deidre gloat over me.* All she needed to do was to write out her resignation and she could do that anywhere. So she turned around and headed back to the flat. As she approached, she saw Brownie talking earnestly into her radio as she went the other way down Burrington Gardens, towards the police station. That was strange as she had said she did not start today until midday and it was only 10.30am. She followed the young policewoman, who was her lodger and friend, and got a little closer. Brownie was absorbed in her radio conversation.

"They're sitting ducks," Gerry heard. "Just need to move in when you are ready. No, I will keep out of the way. You never know when my distance might be useful. That's right. The main subject is supremely intelligent and hard, but not used to sudden action. We should get him by surprise. The woman is more moody and unpredictable. I can't say I know her too well. It doesn't matter that they are foreigners, we are in this all the way and it will cause a ruckus but we have to live with the consequences. No, this snatch is absolutely vital to our interests. Plan for success, prepare well, and move quickly when the time is right." Then she merged with other pedestrians in a crowd outside the tube station and her discussion was lost to Gerry.

What did this mean? Was Brownie double-crossing them? Had that weird place she had been to actually changed her, turned her from supporting the cause to undermining it? Could she have been brainwashed? She still seemed the same person but maybe you never could tell.

Gerry shuddered to think that the new friend she had taken into her home was planning a 'snatch' of her and of her own boyfriend, Adam Forster.

Gerry did not go back to the flat that morning, nor did she go to the office. Instead, she walked three times around St James' Park, trying to judge the circuits so that she would arrive at the Queen's Head for 1pm. Her mind trotted between the two tracks she was trying to run down: what to do about Deidre and what to do about Brownie. She had worked at the Society since she had left university and had always imagined she would work there forever. She did not want to resign but how else could she respond to the humiliation of demotion, for that is what it was, however sugar-coated it came out as? She had got no closer to a solution when she heard Big Ben chime once, the bell ringing out like a lunch gong across the cold streets. She had timed her circuits perfectly as the door to the pub was thirty yards up the street and Adam was holding it open for her.

If Gerry had no answers, her countryman did. After ordering lunch and drinks and selecting a table in the bay window looking onto the side street that ran up to the park, he told her of his idea. "You remember talking to me on election night about working together? Well I want to do that. I want to fund a newsletter that you will write, or rather the embassy wants to fund it."

"Why, Adam? And why now? I am just about to resign from the Society."

"Don't do that. We need you now to stay there."

"But Adam, I have been demoted! I can't just take that on the chin and carry on."

"Even for a higher purpose?" Adam mimicked Gerry's words on election night. "For the good of your country and of Britain too? In fact, it is for the benefit of the entire world order. We wouldn't ask you if it was not of vital importance."

"I don't understand. Why is it suddenly so important?"

"Because if we don't get this damn country organised real quick we are going to have a great big mess on our hands. And because we want to support the notion of an independent and strong Great Britain but we sure as hell don't want to upset the USE."

"You can't have your cake and eat it."

"Can."

"Can't."

"Can."

"OK, let's grow up a bit. How?"

"We keep the funding secret. Nobody knows about it. That way we don't upset the Brussels crowd but we help the London crowd. And that means we very much need you to stay in position at the Society and to be seen to toe the line."

"So I," Gerry added, suddenly serious about this idea, "don't tell anyone so the source of the content is never known? I play along with the Society's decision on this but all the time I am writing the articles that really matter? So, outwardly, I appear to agree to the changes at work and to Deidre's promotion, but really I am working hard for the liberation of this country with our government's secret approval? And it is me who is actually following the Charter of the Society, my employer, because I am seeking liberty on a massive scale?"

"Exactly!" Adam downed his drink and went to order two replacements. "I have a bit more news for you," he said when he got back, with a grin on his face. "Brownie and I are getting married!"

"What?"

"I asked her this morning and she said yes. You don't seem very pleased."

"Oh, I am!" she lied. Should she tell him what she had overheard? How could she? She would buy some time and think about it. "It's just that it makes me realise how much I miss George."

"Of course, I am sorry, Gerry. I should not have banged on about it. Can you forgive me?"

"Ad, my dear, there's nothing to forgive. I hope and pray everything works out perfect for you two."

They talked then more about the newsletter, as if they had exhausted themselves with emotions after their five-minute excursion into personal matters. Over a weak cup of coffee, they decided to use the existing printing firm because they knew that was the last place people would look. Gerry would be editor and one of the contributors. Adam would arrange the other contributors as well as all the logistics and money.

"Don't worry, I have a whole office full of staff with nothing much to do! This'll give them something to justify their extortionate salaries!"

"Publication date?" Gerry asked.

"Each Friday, starting in two days," came the reply.

"You want to publish in two days? That means getting copy to the printer tomorrow!"

"I figured you would have a backlog of articles that were too contentious for publication before."

"Well I do, for sure, but I've got also got some serious writing ahead of me!" she replied, adding, "Actually I can give you my first piece this evening. It is an interview with Fernby, the Head of the Civil Service. I just want to spice it up a bit first." Adam paid the bill with a credit card, stuffed the receipt into his jacket pocket, and they went outside into the street. There were a few brave people sitting at outside tables but there was quite a chill as they said goodbye and Gerry walked to her office, just a few hundred yards up the street and onto Birdcage Walk.

The short walk was not enough time to fully consider how to approach Deidre but Gerry's instinct took over. The Society was her life and she had not wanted to resign so maybe she had jumped too readily at the idea. How practical was it to produce a first newsletter in a day and a half? But it meant she was living up to the standards of the Society, even if blatantly breaking their rules. As she nodded to Joe, the doorman, who held the door open for her, she thought that the most important thing was to let Deidre think she had won completely so that in her triumph she would be blind to suspicion. Who was it that had said the best form of defence is attack? Well she would add to that phrase that sometimes the best form of attack is retreat. So she did just that.

"Hi, can I possibly see Deidre?" Deidre's secretary, who was so remarkably like Deidre but older, could possibly be her mother - only Gerry had read all the personnel files in-depth to try and understand her team and knew her to be a happily married woman without children, originally from Devon - looked up in surprise.

"I'll see if she is available."

"Thank you."

Gerry was shown into Deidre's office for the first time. It was a half-version of Gerry's office, partitioned down the middle to make two offices. The work was well done so that the partition looked natural, even though it carved through the big bay window, giving Deidre just half the outlook onto the park that Gerry enjoyed. But it made the room narrow and awkward, the desk in front of the window was large and took up most of the width. In front were two chairs, the upholstery dark red with gold sceptres marching in columns across the back and seat. Then there were three filing cabinets. It was a functional room, whereas Gerry enjoyed the extra space that allowed a sofa and some easy chairs around a coffee table.

Deidre was deeply involved in some work and did not look up until Gerry gave a little cough. "Good afternoon, Gerry," she said, using her first name for the first time in their acquaintance, as if sensing already the impending switch in roles. "What can I do for you?"

"I think you have probably had a conversation with Mr Pearson concerning some changes to responsibilities." Deidre had not asked Gerry to sit so she stood in front of the desk, feeling a little like a schoolgirl. "I just wanted to congratulate you and say if there is anything I can do to help please let me know."

"Thank you, Gerry. I will be sure to inform you if there is anything."

Deidre returned to her report and Gerry turned to leave the room quietly.

"Oh, there is one thing, Gerry."

"Yes?" Gerry was in the doorway and half-turned back to face Deidre.

"As I will be having a lot of meetings, well you can see that this office is not exactly suitable and I cannot always be sure of the availability of the conference room. Well," for the first time Deidre looked at her adversary and Gerry clearly saw victory in the shine of her eyes and turn of her mouth, "I think it would be appropriate to swap offices. Trot down to the doorman and ask him to get Janitorial to arrange it this afternoon."

"Yes, Deidre." Gerry moved further from the door into the secretary's office and then Deidre called one more time, this time so that her secretary could clearly hear.

"And Gerry, one more thing. I don't think it is appropriate that you call me by my first name given my promotion and your, shall we be kind and say, sideways move?"

"Yes, Deidre, I mean, eh… Miss Harrington." She closed the door firmly and went downstairs, seeking the doorman, face burning as she crossed in front of the lookalike Deidre in the outer office, enduring the undisguised smirk.

"How the mighty have fallen." The words chased Gerry out of the room.

Hatching Plans

The pub was nothing special. It sat on a street of Victorian terraces, firmly in working class territory. There was no sign swinging in front, for the buses would have knocked it down each time they passed. Instead, the 'King's Head' was in faded red paint on a long board above the door. Someone once had dedicated time and effort to making the sign attractive, with gold swirls and squiggles above and below the 'Finest Ales' and 'Bar Snacks Available', but no one had cared in recent times. Inside, there was a saloon bar with a half-dozen workers drinking their lunch, and a small snug. The snug claimed a tiny portion of the bar so that to attract attention George had to lean across the counter.

"Two large Scotches, please. Johnny Walker Red is fine."

"Are you who I think you are?" The young bar lady was slim, dark-skinned with a tiny waist, neck and wrists, as if every circumference had been tightened beyond recommendation. Her black hair fell in huge amounts, reminding George instantly of Gerry.

"Yes." There was no point in trying to come up with an evasive answer.

"I think you are wonderful." She had an accent that was foreign, but with a distinct Lancashire element. "All my friends voted for you."

"But not you?" George was amused by her choice of words.

"I was too young. I turned eighteen the Tuesday after the election."

"Well, a belated happy birthday to you." George picked the

two whisky glasses off the bar and turned towards Francine sitting by the electric fire at one of the only two tables in the snug.

"I would have done, voted for you, I mean. We are counting on you, Mr Unwin-Smith. We are all waiting for you."

Back at the table, George quickly ran through the bar conversation. "That's the problem, Fran. Every…"

"Francine, have a pretty name, use it."

"Sorry, that's the problem, Francine. Everyone seems to be relying on me to come up with a plan and other than a few snippets I don't have any idea what to do."

Francine downed her Scotch in one and rose to go back to the bar. But first she pulled a pen and pad from her bag and said, "Write down each snippet on a different page while I get another drink."

George, sipping his drink slowly, wrote on the first page: 'need an advantage'. On the second he wrote: 'Major Bellew' and underneath it put 'army support essential'. He paused a while before writing on the third blank page: 'support of the people'. Then on the fourth page he put down: 'Strengths and weaknesses' and was attempting to fill this out when Francine returned with the girl from behind the bar.

"George, this is Tracy Beck. She wants to talk with you."

"Hi." Suddenly she was a lot shyer. With Francine's prodding she started on her story and George was completely caught up in it.

"We don't have much time," Francine interjected after fifteen minutes. "It is a big risk coming here, especially during the daytime. But I wanted you to hear this." George's mind was racing. So Francine had planned this meeting with the young girl.

"He regretted it to his dying day," Tracy concluded her hurried summary of the whole of her adolescent existence, a childhood shattered by the choices made by her father. "He tried to undo it but it was a terrible thing to have on his conscience. We think, Mum and I, that it took the will to live right out of him."

"He became a Spider," Francine explained. "It was like the conversion of Paul on the road to Damascus! But then he died of cancer less than two years later." Tracy was crying now. George suddenly stood up and hugged her where she stood in front of the small electric fire that radiated a surprising amount of heat into the tiny snug.

"It's OK, Tracy, your father was a good man. I can tell. He did the right thing in the end." But over the top of Tracy's head he was looking at Francine, amazed at the depth of character that sat with a second empty whisky glass in front of her and a look of complete determination, her stubby nose and freckly face seeming to epitomise defiance itself.

They had to leave then, spurred on by the distant sound of a siren that George swore was getting closer. Tracy showed them out the back way, through the yard dotted with crates and empty bottles and a skip that looked like it was never emptied. They went through a gate into a warren of back passages running behind the houses of various streets, Tracy leading the way. She spoke in fluent French to Francine and George was able to gather that she was asking where they had left their car. A minute later they were back at the plaza of shops and getting into the car. Tracy made to shake their hands but George again hugged her after Francine led the way.

"It must be weird for you to be with the daughter of the person who captured you." George felt it a pointless thing to say, but wanted to stay with the subject. Francine did not reply at first, just slammed the gearstick into First and clashed the gears as she moved the car forward, not looking at the traffic stream, just joining it.

"She's half French," Francine said, as if that explained something. "Her mother is French and they run the pub together now that her father, Barry, is dead. Barry was Warrington-born and bred. He was a career policeman, worked his way up to Inspector. I couldn't believe it when he arrested me after offering a truce to discuss ways to ensure our rallies were peaceful." Another long silence, broken only by the clunking of gears.

"It was so sudden," she said eventually. "I was at the rally in Chester and had the meeting scheduled with him immediately afterwards. He was to escort me to Liverpool while we discussed the safety aspects of these big rallies. Then the next thing I knew I was in the back of a police car. I had done nothing wrong except to speak out for freedom. It was the start of a horrible time." Francine, George had come to appreciate, would tell a whole story but in parts separated by long periods in which she drove aggressively or otherwise occupied herself with a practical occupation. It was the way she coped. He thought of the nasty burn scars on her leg. Those obviously occurred at this time of captivity. It made his six-hour period of torture under the almost comical fat lady bulging out of her undersized black uniform seem so insignificant in comparison. Yet it had got to the very core of him. He desperately wanted to ask Francine about the torture and she seemed to understand this.

"I talked." She spoke after a particularly wild bout of driving through the streets of Warrington.

"Sorry?"

"I could not take the pain of fire. I talked. I gave names and details of movements and plans. I said anything to stop the fire."

"I understand."

"No, you don't. You did not talk."

"But I was only being tortured for a few hours."

"I talked after forty minutes." Then they drove in absolute silence until they pulled off the dual carriageway at the Blackburn turning. "That is what I meant the other day. Everyone has their strengths and weaknesses and it is the combination of all our strengths that override our individual weaknesses. There aren't any heroes, George. We all just muddle on and the total of all our muddles is what makes a difference. You do not need to get cross with yourself because you do not have all the answers. This is not the comic strips you read as a child, this is real life muddling through, all in it together." Francine drove on, deliberately taking a roundabout route to their destination for the night; a suburban detached house on an estate built on an old brewery.

"You know what the funny thing is from all this?" she added as she turned into the drive. "We ended up good friends. He was disgusted with himself. He had been told that I was being taken in for my safekeeping and he believed it, then he saw me being prepared for torture. He never forgave himself. He resigned from the police and bought the pub and joined the Spiders, and for two years until he died he was a local leader and a good one too. Now his wife and daughter are carrying on the work from their pub." She reversed into the dustbins out for collection and ended their conversation with. "*Merde.*"

George had a restless night. The sofa was uncomfortable and the house was modern and airless with the central heating left on all night. Eventually, he got out of the sleeping bag and lay on the top of it in his underwear. He had had a bath that night and his clothes had been washed, but his skin smelt of deep-down life on the road like a prison pallor hanging over him. He could not get Barry's betrayal out of his mind. In particular, the sudden switch in Francine's condition from free-ranging underground resistance leader to captive awaiting torture. It had been the same for him on the evening before the election. He watched the digital clock move on, each click a minute through the long night. He started counting the seconds in between the clicks until it reminded him of counting through the five-minute breaks in his torture regime. Then he turned away from the clock but kept waiting to hear the next click.

At 4.12am, still deepest night, he decided to go outside and get some cold, fresh air. He was surprised to find the kitchen door unlocked.

"Hi, George." It was Mandy. "I couldn't sleep, either."

He slumped in the garden chair next to hers, adjusted it so it tilted half-backwards, and stared up at the stars that echoed their light off each other, going back into the beginning of time. Had those same stars shone on the first grains, right at the beginning?

"We're running out of time, Mandy. I or we have to come up with some plan to give us an edge. We've lost 10% of our active members in the last three weeks through capture. We can't move around nearly so easily. We've got to strike a major blow before they smother us. And I can't go on much longer like this. I'm not cut out for this type of existence."

"It was Mark and I that got you into all this."

"No, you just issued the invitation. Well, you also made one hell of an impassioned speech about it as well. Actually, it was Gerry who really made me think it was the right thing. She's to blame so I'll have words with her next time I see her. If there is a next time."

"God, George, there will be a next time, and a next time after that, and a million more times." She realised the lie as she uttered it. She had thought the same of Mark; there would always be a next time. But George was too preoccupied to make the connection. Mandy changed the subject.

"Where did Francine take you?" So George told her the story.

"Good God, so let me get this right. Five years ago, Francine had a police escort led by Inspector Beck and he betrayed her?"

"That's right. He was told it was for her own safety but then she was tortured." It was then that the idea came to him, sitting on a patio in Blackburn at half-past-four in the morning, with the cold descending upon them like death waiting for an opportunity. But it did not come as a proper plan, just another idea with an inkling that there was something to this one.

"What if we managed the same thing?" he suddenly said.

"What do you mean?"

"Verdun is coming in a couple of weeks and we had planned a general uprising when he was here. So, what if we actually kidnap him?"

"My God, George, what an idea! But how could we get near to him?"

"The same way Francine was caught." Now the idea was evolving. "That's how we do it. We find a way to infiltrate his guard and then we snatch him."

"On his way from Dover," Mandy suggested.

"Perfect. Listen, how quickly can we get everyone together to work this out in detail?"

"A few days."

"Try and make it tomorrow. I know, let's meet in Chester, where Francine was arrested. She would find that appropriate. Can you organise that, Mandy?"

"Yes, first thing. I can check now whether we have a safe house in Chester then start contacting people around 6am. I'll let you know by mid-morning whether we can do it for tomorrow."

"Oh, see if you can get Major Bellew to come up for it, or else get him on the phone at least."

"Yes, sir!" Mandy saluted from the chair next to George.

George grinned his thanks and said he was going to try and get some sleep.

They did not wake him until 9.30, just enough time to grab breakfast before departing for the next safe house. Mandy gave him a thumbs-up, everything was on for tomorrow afternoon. George spent the day revisiting and reworking his nascent plan. Would they like it? It was simple, perfect, and they had nothing else anyway. It could easily be the game-changer they were seeking, provided they could remain undetected for the next two weeks while they planned out the detail. But first he had to get their buy-in.

The plan was formally adopted by the committee that ran the resistance during the afternoon of the next day, but only just. They met in a mothballed building materials factory just outside Chester; a monument to an earlier day, with rusting kiln, and pallet trucks lying around as if time had stopped still during lunch break. They used the boardroom and someone got the coffee machine from a secretary's office and made it work, along with china cups and saucers and bottles of water from the fridge, still running. They rubbed the whiteboard of figures charting the decline of the business, with roof tiles being imported at half the local production cost. George sketched his ideas on the whiteboard, standing like a company director making a marketing or product presentation. Perhaps one such director had made a desperate pitch to save the business. Would that director have been as nervous as George as he stood to outline his plans, not knowing if they would be accepted or laughed out of the room? This was his only option to save the resistance movement.

It helped that Major Bellew made it up for the meeting. He suggested several practical modifications that made eminent sense. He was confident of getting any amount of everyday army equipment. "I've worked the system since Sandhurst," he said.

Francine was a solid supporter, while Mandy really liked the lack of violence. But several others thought it had little chance of success. They talked all afternoon, with guards and scouts posted on each route to the factory. The vote came close to sundown and was hung at five votes each. Then George stood up.

"As Chairman of the Management Committee I am going to use my casting vote in favour of the plan. It is therefore carried by six votes to five."

"Bravo," said Mike Cunningham, Deputy leader of the Spiders. "I voted against but we are nothing if not a democracy and living by the rules we set for ourselves. I have reservations, but I will back George's plan to the hilt now that it has been approved. Let's get on with the planning. We have a lot to do and precious little time to do it."

They talked for another fifty minutes, making plans and delegating tasks.

"We'll meet again the day after tomorrow in Horsham," George concluded. Then they left, a half-dozen cars, Francine driving George at her insistence, George looking forward to the company but not to her driving.

Swiss Holiday

Sir Terrence was shaken by the news that his friend had advanced stomach cancer and would probably not last out the year. He had known Edward was seriously ill but the finality of the Zurich doctors was sobering.

"You should have told me, Edward," he remonstrated on a visit to the hospital. Sir Terrence, unwounded, had spent just one night in the hospital after their escape and was exhibiting all the energy that had characterised his long life and belied his age. Paul had been shot in the right arm but, other than a sling and an inability to drive currently, he was fine and staying with Sir Terrence at a friend's house outside the town. They would not leave while Edward Unwin-Smith was here in hospital, which probably meant they would be here until the end.

"Scott, it would not have made any difference. I wouldn't have missed the trip for the world. It was another dead end but at least we tried."

"What will you do now?"

"I suppose go home."

"But Edward, you will be arrested at the airport! I have a better idea."

"You always do," joked the professor. "Let's hear it then."

"The three of us take a villa for the duration and we get in whatever medical assistance we need."

"I have no money, Scott, I can't do that."

"Don't be silly, Edward. I have buckets of cash in Switzerland. It would give me great pleasure to do this and to spend the time with you. What else would I do anyway?" It was agreed and the following week Edward moved in to the luxurious house Sir Terrence and Paul had found. They arranged a housekeeper who, along with a young student seeking part-time work, did everything for them. Sir Terrence also arranged for a specialist to see Edward every second day at the villa and to have twice-daily visits from a nursing service. The pain was intense and debilitating now. The least Sir Terrence could do for his friend was to make his last days comfortable, entertaining, and trouble-free. The view from their house was spectacular; water, woods and mountains. It was cold but calming, a perfect setting for a dying man.

"Is there anyone you would like to see?" Sir Terrence asked over breakfast the first morning. "Other than George, of course, who even I can't get to right now!"

"Well, there is one person, actually. But he lives in America."

A few phone calls later and Professor Jay Stuttermann was on a First Class flight to Zurich, arriving at the villa on the morning of the third day.

Was it fate that made Professor Stuttermann available to take Sir Terrence's call that afternoon in early October? And was it fate that his university schedule had changed so abruptly the week before so that he could rearrange a few things and jump on a flight, reversing the journey his parents had made so many years ago when the war had ended and they could safely leave Switzerland to join a cousin in America? Being immersed in the holocaust and a specialist in tracing lost families from that period, having lived all his adult life with his Aunt Jessica until her death six years before, he was very aware of his own family history and appreciative of the significance of the trip he was now undertaking. But overshadowing all those neat-fitting thoughts was a deep concern for his friend who Sir Terrence had told him was terminally ill. This was the friend who had welcomed him forty years earlier, when he had come hesitantly to Oxford as a visiting academic. He remembered that three-year period of his life fondly. They had become firm friends, Stuttermann travelling back on several occasions and returning the hospitality numerous times. He had been there when Edward's wife had died of cancer. He had consoled Edward and comforted the young George. He had been there for her death and now, it seems, he might be witness to the last days of Edward as well.

They embraced, even though Edward was an Englishman, such was their affection for each other. They caught up, Edward doing most of the talking because of the incredible series of events over the last few months. Edward had heard nothing from George for over a week, since the Friday before he and Bertie had journeyed to Germany. At the time George had been full of hope, but since then there was only bad news; at least from official sources. There had been numerous captures of key people. For all Edward knew, his son could be locked up in some grim prison cell, tortured like last time, but without the American connection to assist. Sir Terrence had all sorts of feelers out but news was hard to come by and unreliable. Edward had phoned Gerry from his hospital bed, thinking she would have heard something if anybody was to hear. But she had not heard a word.

"I expect he does not want to incriminate or involve you in any way," Edward had said to her on the phone, sensing her loneliness and her courage in trying to deal with it.

"There is something big brewing," Sir Terrence said as they sat on the veranda with a fire burning in a big upside-down metal dish on a wooden frame. Paul was supervising the preparation of supper because he was fed up with Italian cooking and wanted something 'English rather than all this pasta!'

"Is that your intelligence?"

"Yes, but a lot of guesswork as well. Most avenues of communication are cut off. People don't use phones because they can be traced within seconds. But I don't know what this big thing is going to be. Nobody dares talk explicitly on the radios and they have to be relayed through various people to get to us all the way out here. People just refer to GF day, God knows what that is."

"Guy Fawkes Day," Edward said instantly. "Bonfire Night, 5th November. That is just a few weeks away."

"Of course. But I wonder what is going to happen."

"It's a strange day to choose," Jay said. "The Gunpowder Plot failed, as you know. Why link yourself to a failure from history?"

"Easy," said Sir Terrence, "the first thing about attack is to do the unexpected. You might expect that to be the last day that someone would select for an uprising or whatever is planned, hence you select that date."

They had Shepherd's Pie for supper that night, along with an excellent bottle of local wine. Their talk was dominated by GF Day. They simply did not know enough about it.

"Why don't I go back and find out?" Paul said suddenly. "Nobody knows who the hell I am."

"If you are sure?"

"I'm sure, Sir Terrence. I could fly tomorrow and be back in a day or two. I just need some way of contacting the underground and finding a way to convince them to trust me."

"The first is no problem. I can give you a couple of contacts," Sir Terrence said. "It's the trust bit I am struggling with."

They went through several ideas. Anything in writing was out of the question. They were not aware of any token or symbol he could take with him. And Sir Terrence was sure the passwords would have changed several times over the last two weeks while they had been out of the country.

It was Edward who came up with the best idea. "Scott, will Paul actually get to meet George?"

"Almost certainly, provided he can give the assurances we need to come up with."

"Then a verbal token is the best way, from me to George through Paul. I mean a message from father to son, something that tells George the communication is from me and that Paul can be trusted. Let me think. I know, tell him his father said he hoped to solve the mystery of General Stein and Joachim before the end and the end will come soon because of my stomach."

"Will do, General Stein, Joachim and reference to your

303

stomach cancer. Got it. I'm going to go and pack my toothbrush and arrange a flight. Goodnight, gentlemen."

After Paul left, Jay asked Edward what he meant by referring to General Stein and Joachim.

"The war-time Nazi general. He apparently surrendered to my father. You see, my father was a Major General under Montgomery. Joachim was Stein's young batman and he was murdered in a horrible way after the war."

"Bricked up in a cellar," Jay said.

"You know about him?"

"Yes, quite a lot, as a matter of fact. It is a fascinating series of events. Shall I tell you? I researched it about twenty years ago as a sideline to something else I was working on."

There was absolute silence as Jay Stuttermann took them back to the events of early 1945, when the German war machine was in its valiant death throes, shaking its fist bravely at the enemy as its body was severed limb by limb. It was a time of violence and destruction, crime and inhumanity, the veneer struck off altogether. But it was also a time of compassion and humanity and courage and kindness. It was a perfect example of the extremes of human behaviour clashing and vibrating through a Europe torn to shreds by ambition and the hatred that ambition inspired.

"Good God, to think I have been trying to find out about General Stein for years now and all the time my closest friend knew it all!"

"More importantly," Sir Terrence added, "I think we can use this to our advantage. For the cause, I mean. We need to think about this carefully."

As Edward went to bed that night he reflected that it was amazing what was stored in a human brain and also on the sheer coincidences involved. History was the sweep of events, gradual change building up, punctured every so often by more aggressive or sudden actions. But also there was a huge element of surprise from coincidence. If Jay had not been able to come over to visit, or if Paul had not volunteered to go back to England and make contact with the movement that George was leading, then the truth about General Stein would never be known and would have gone to its own grave when Jay eventually lay down for his. How much of history therefore depends on chance? He would have to discuss a modification of the hourglass theory with George as soon as he got a chance. He was scripting his conversation with his son when sleep took over and released his tired body from the grip of pain that dominated his waking hours.

Military Manoeuvres

The scene is a corner of Salisbury Plain, unused and overlooked. Small country roads criss-crossed the terrain while two mock-French villages stood in quiet decay, viewing their foreign surroundings. The weather added to the atmosphere, with sheets of icy rain giving visibility measured in yards and slippery mud everywhere, while the wind kept changing its mind, its angle, and its velocity. George sat in the front passenger seat of a Land Rover, wishing he was anywhere but where he was. His cheap map was waterproofed but the water had worked its way in on his last hike, so that contour lines smudged into an orange mud-bath to reflect the reality in brown around them. He had avoided hiking or camping all his life.

"I am an armchair adventurer," he had said, but this did not cut well with Major Bellew.

"Well, that is fine and dandy," he replied, "but we can't have any make-believe in this plan. You can imagine everything working out perfectly from in front of a roaring fire, but nothing works like trying it out for real. So, we'll do one more rehearsal today and then you get the hot shower and dry clothes."

"Something to look forward to."

"Yep, then we debrief, then you get the chance to sleep, hopefully in the dry."

"Who would join the bloody army?" Bertie shouted through the window. "Come on, let's get on with it."

Four hours later, the dozen men and women George and Bellew had delegated to be the section leaders were huddled in a disused barrack room. There had been no hot water and there were no dry clothes to change into. There had been nothing to eat but three packets of biscuits to share. Bertie had produced a bottle of Scotch and poured it into plastic cups. They sat in what probably had been the sergeants' mess, but the only evidence was a visitors' book with comments from visiting NCOs. They at least had some worn furniture, left behind when the base was deserted.

"Where's Bellew?" Nobody knew.

"We'd better start without him," George said. "I'll lead off. I thought we ironed out a number of problems today. For instance, we resolved the issue of…" George became aware that nobody was listening to him. There was a clattering sound beyond the door.

"Help me, mateys." Bellew's voice boomed through the door. "Someone open the door. I'm loaded down."

All twelve, George included, rushed to the door and helped the major through it. He had a double pack on his back, more slung over each shoulder, and was carrying six plastic bags, with a crate of beer bottles balanced on his spare fingertips. "Rations," Was all he said. "Plus some clothes, dry, for the benefit of wet bastards, morale for the improvement of. Lord, I'm all in!"

"Where did you get all this?"

"I told you I could get anything out of the army."

They stayed six days on Salisbury Plain, the longest they had stayed anywhere, and the biggest collection of resistance leaders. It would have been a goldmine for EurMilPo had anyone turned them in. But the major had been sure that nobody from the army would do so.

And they had not. George found it deeply reassuring that so many soldiers were behind the resistance.

"It's a mixture of things," Bellew had told him one day when they paused for hot tea from a giant urn carried into their private training ground by a couple of grinning squaddies.

"Here, soldier, come over here a mo."

"Yes, sir." They both came. Like a comedy duo, one was the height of the major, the other a foot shorter, the smaller man out of breath from carrying the urn at almost shoulder-height.

"Tell me what you think of the modern army. Don't hold back now!" Bellew ordered.

"It stinks, sir."

"Go on."

"Well, it started with that barmy Euroarmy idea and also the new oath of allegiance."

"Not even to the bloody Queen it is," said the taller man, evidently from Wales. "And everything changes every week and we don't know what our purpose is anymore."

"Do you know who I am?" George spoke up.

"No, sir," They chorused. Then the shorter one added. "It's enough for us that the major trusts you, sir."

"I am George Unwin-Smith."

"You mean the guy who should be Prime Minister?"

"Do you believe that?"

"Yes, sir," came the two voices immediately.

"OK, boys, off you go now and thanks for the tea." Bellew dismissed them, then said to George. "See what I mean? Everything is poised for change, just hanging in the balance. Unwin, you should be very proud of what you've achieved."

"Me? I've not achieved anything, at least I don't feel like I've done anything much."

"George." Bellew suddenly grabbed him by the shoulders so that George dropped his tea, the heavy-duty mug bouncing on the ground and spraying tea over his trousers. "What you've got to understand is that nothing would have happened without you. The resistance would always have been pottering about. The army would have remained disillusioned but moaned rather than acted." He stopped talking for a moment and looked into George's eyes, realisation dawning. "The trouble with you is that you've got some ridiculous bloody notion of leadership in your thick head. You've got to let that go because nobody can live up to it."

"Not you as well," George groaned in reply.

"Ah, well, George, you are standing up for democracy, yet you are trying to be a bloody dictator to yourself. Listen and learn, old man. Try using that famous brain a bit more agilely. You're your own worst enemy. Good Lord, you're not even listening to me."

"What? Sorry, I was just thinking about the plan." It was consuming him. It had to succeed.

***

They came in the middle of the night, as they usually do for maximum effect. The first George heard was the major banging on his door. "Up quick, armoured patrol reported heading for the main gate. We need to leave now by the firing range. Get dressed and wake the others."

"What are you doing?" George asked, surprising himself by how alert he felt when twenty seconds earlier he had been fast asleep.

"A few tricks to slow them down."

"Let me help you," George opened the door, dressing as he went, doubled up to pull on his boots, grabbing his wet-weather jacket. "Bertie, wake the others and lead them to the firing range and the far exit. There are three vehicles there. Take two and leave the third for us. Separate out and call every thirty minutes. Go now, Bertie, there should be eleven of you in total, make sure you have everyone." Then turning to Major Bellew he said, "What did you have in mind?"

"Some fireworks I've kept in reserve."

They ran from building to building with hastily stuffed backpacks of explosives and two submachine guns slung under their shoulders. "First we recce," Bellew gasped when they were within sight of the main gates.

"I see five, six, seven… eight heavy vehicles, plus a car. They are coming up the hill about half a mile away, coming slowly." The clouds had moved on, leaving a brilliant moonlit sky so that George could see and interpret the dark bulks moving up the hill towards their camp.

"You have excellent eyesight. So that's probably 120 men, fifteen in each vehicle. George, go back and check the others have left. I'll move over there and make some preparations." He pointed to a waist-high brick wall that ran around the main car park. George noted its location and moved quickly back to the sergeants' mess.

Five minutes later the force was at the main gate. There was a barrier but they smashed through it and drew up in an arc, left to right, just inside the gate. Bellew had established himself behind the wall and had two-dozen grenades lined up, but George had not returned. If they would only move to their left and go down the hill slightly to the main part of the camp then Bellew would be behind them and could do much more damage. For a moment it was very still, no movement and no noise apart from the engines at idle. Where was George? He could do with another arm to hurl the grenades. He could see now that they were Mark IV APCs, only twelve people in each vehicle so the odds were lessened a little. But they were still stacked hopelessly against him, especially alone.

They were clearly conferring. Bellew wondered what he would do if he were in charge: probably split the force to cover the most ground. But at the point when he expected a decision leading to movement, lights came on down the hill and then the Major heard Duke Ellington booming out from the officers' mess at the lowest point of the camp. Instantly, all nine vehicles turned to their left and rolled down the hill, away from Bellew. It had to be George; there was no one else in the camp. Bellew did not waste a moment, grabbing handfuls of grenades; he ran after the vehicles and expertly blew the tracks of the last four vehicles. Two crashed into each other and then slid into a building. A third one rolled over into a drainage ditch and the occupants scrambled out, clearly dazed. Bellew ran around them and sprinted for the lead vehicles. His next grenades fell short as the vehicles picked up speed. Then he gained as they reached the officers' mess. Men spilled out and encircled the buildings. Bellew stumbled in his mad dash to catch up, his foot hit a drain cover, and he was over in the mud. He tried to rise but his ankle was on fire. They saw him then, a young armed police officer pointed and cried to his comrades. Five men started to converge on him, forming a semi-circle, sub-machine guns ready. Bellew tried to get up and run, but his ankle gave way in a huge spasm of pain. He scrabbled along the ground, dragging his right leg behind him, but they were closing fast. If he could make it back to the wall he might be able to put up a defence. They were not firing, just moving steadily closer, twenty yards then ten. Bellew felt panic. He was still ten yards from the wall. He would not make it.

The explosion happened just then and was followed by two more. Bellew squinted towards the wall and saw George there, ready to throw a fourth grenade. But there was no target; the police officers had fallen back to their vehicle. George threw the grenade anyway and then jumped over the wall and grabbed the Major, hauling him back to the safety of the wall.

"My God, George. What a performance."

"No time, Major, we've got to keep moving. Can you make it to the mess? I've got Francine waiting there with the Land Rover. The others went on like you said. One more big effort now."

"I can do it."

The ankle was not broken, just sprained. George examined it in the back of the Land Rover while Francine drove like a fury across the old firing range and out the far side of the camp at the top of the hill. They drove down tracks, hard to see in the moonlight, so that each bump reminded Bellew of his injury and his escape also.

"Good God, Unwin, that was spectacular." He spoke through gritted teeth but the admiration was clear. "That was as neat a manoeuvre as I've ever seen!"

"It just sort of came to me," George replied. "It was like I was someone else. I didn't have to think about it. I just knew what to do."

"But the idea to turn on the lights down the hill and the

music. That was inspirational. What made you think of it?"

"I just thought if we could get them going down the hill we would divert them for a few moments from the firing range and the others trying to get away. And then I thought we could chase them from behind, which you did very effectively."

"You'll do, my man." The Land Rover bolted on through the night, another narrow escape, but things were coming to a head; they had to be, for how long could they keep going like this?

The Interview

When Gerry got back to her flat that evening, she was exhausted and drained. Adam was waiting for her, leaning against the same lamppost.

"Hey, I've got some great news." He spoke quietly. "Let's go inside and I can tell you more."

Gerry unlocked the door and went up the stairs, Adam following her two steps behind, like a shadow.

"What is it?"

"I've set you up with a meeting with someone from Future Perfect."

"What?"

"To interview them tonight. Get changed into some casual clothes while I make a sandwich for us both. We need to go now."

Gerry's mind was flooded with possibilities as she quickly pulled off her business suit and chose some black jeans and a black polo-neck sweater. Something made her choose black, like the night she was going to be moving through, she thought. Could it be George? What were the chances? Probably close to zero as he could not risk a meeting, surely?

They left the flat within fifteen minutes, Gerry selecting her long black coat to match her clothes. She noticed that Adam was in jeans also, but with a brown checked jacket and an open-neck shirt under his heavy wool coat.

"Where are we going?"

Adam did not answer but hailed a cab.

"Grosvenor Square." He gave the driver the instructions.

When they were settled in the back he said quietly, "We need to get a car from the embassy. They have one on standby for me all the time."

"No driver, I will drive myself." They climbed into a large Ford. Adam started the engine and eased the car onto the road.

"So where now?"

"A long drive, I'm sorry to say. We have to get to Salisbury, that's about two hours from here, maybe a little less if I can step on it."

"Who are we meeting?"

"You mean who are you meeting? I am not meeting anyone. I am just the driver here!"

"OK, so who am I meeting? Or should I not ask?" All the time she did not know for sure there was a chance it could be George.

"No clue at all!"

"Come on!"

"No, I really don't know, that's the God's honest truth. All I know is where we are going to and contingency plans."

With the diplomatic car they drove straight past all the roadblocks and police checks like superior beings bypassing ordinary folks standing in lines. Adam drove very fast, then slowed right down, then fast again, alternating at irregular intervals.

"Trying to make sure we are not followed," he explained. He then dialled a number and said. "This is formula one on for pit stop one." To Gerry he just said, "Contingency plan necessary."

"Are we being followed?"

"Yep, two cars as far as I can tell. So we need to do a quick change. Be ready to jump out when I stop the car, it will be about ten minutes." Then he turned off the motorway at a small exit that was badly lit, signposted to a series of small villages people would never be able to locate on a map, all with similar names as if designed to confuse. They drove through two of them where the only movement was centred on the pubs, all other stretches dead quiet. The third village, just a hamlet, came up. Gerry read the signpost: Murley Brigham. Adam switched off the lights and glided into the car park behind a shuttered pub called the Brigham Arms, the sign out front hanging by only one chain now. The car park was deeply dark and Gerry could see nothing.

"Out now! Just trust me, Gerry," Adam said as he placed a friendly hand on her shoulder and looked at the passenger door. Gerry looked across at him but only saw shapes and shadows. She opened the door as the car was still moving slightly. She expected it to stop and Adam to jump out and guide her to whatever form of transport was chosen for the next stage. But as she climbed out, Adam accelerated and said, "You'll be fine, I'll see you tomorrow."

"Are you leaving me here? In the dark?" But Adam was gone, the car heaving off into the darkness and disappearing, eaten by the night. She saw the lights turn back on about fifteen seconds later. Adam was going in the same direction as before, away from the motorway, two big cars following at a distance.

Suddenly she was alone in the pitch-black night, a light wind stirring up the leaves on the ground and shifting them in collections with sudden gusts. She could not see the closed pub fifty feet away. She felt panic rising as she stepped back in a puddle and felt her foot give way; luckily she was wearing practical shoes and could easily regain her balance but it felt as if she was stepping off a mountainside. Would her eyes get used to the night and use what little light was available to piece together her surroundings? At the moment she doubted it.

Then more action as a car, obviously hiding at the back of the car park, revved its engine quietly, no lights on. Just like Adam's car in reverse, it moved close and the passenger door swung open. "Get in quickly," said the voice from inside and she did, preferring the company of a stranger to the deathly-dark car park.

"Do up your seatbelt. We will be driving fast." Without any lights she could not see the driver but was thankful it was a woman.

Mandy drove very fast through a series of deserted lanes, sometimes crossing a main road but avoiding them where she could. She put on sidelights occasionally but most of the time only the instrument panel gave any shape to the world around them.

"Why all the mystery?" Gerry asked, thinking it a foolish question as soon as she said it.

"Security. But we should be OK now. You don't remember me, do you?" The voice was familiar for its clarity and energy, but Gerry was too shaken to recall where she had heard it before.

"No," she said simply.

"Mandy Fryer. We met on election night in Oxford. Do you remember?"

"Of course. I knew I recognised your voice, I just couldn't place it."

They talked on freely. Mandy was making good progress without detection and was gaining in confidence that they would make it to Salisbury.

"We've been moving around every few days, making plans, gaining support. I've seen more of the country than ever before!"

Gerry asked a lot of questions. She asked about their plans. She asked about what it was like to be on the run. She asked whether Mandy really thought they would succeed. And she asked when that would be. The only thing she did not ask was whom she was going to meet, because Mandy might tell her and then she would know that it was not George.

They pulled into Salisbury a little before midnight, drove straight towards the cathedral, and parked the car in a residents' spot on the roadside. Gerry could see the bulk of the cathedral just across what looked like a green but could not make out the detail. It gave an impression of permanence that was reassuring as, apart from Mandy's friendliness, she felt totally alone in this strange world.

"You'll see it better in the morning." Mandy said.

"Am I staying to morning?"

"Well, I think you should!" Gerry could tell from the tone that Mandy was amused. "At least, you probably will want to."

What could she mean?

George was waiting for her just inside the townhouse that looked over the cathedral as if it was part of a guard detail. He had the advantage of knowing who was coming but he was still shaken by her presence, with her masses of rich brown hair above a face full of character and a beautiful body clad all in black, offsetting her pale skin.

Gerry could not believe her luck. They embraced for a long time in the hallway before George led her to a sitting room to the right where they could be all alone. There they talked, catching up with each other's story until they got over their natural shyness and George led Gerry upstairs to a bedroom.

In the morning, George kissed Gerry on the lips. "I have to go in a moment, my darling."

"Hang about a sec." Gerry sat up, awake and anxious. "I have a story to write for the newsletter with Adam Forster. What do I say?"

"Tell them the truth."

"You mean everything we spoke about last night? Won't that put people off?"

"Trust me," George replied with a firmness he had not felt for a long time. "Write every word just as it comes to you. Be honest with your readers and the truth of the situation will shine out."

"I don't know. I'm not sure it is wise to hint at weakness. Let me think about it some more."

"OK, my love, just write what you feel is right deep down. God, it is good to see you again. I felt like a nothing when I left you in DC, like I could not even make a decision to kiss you! I feel like nothing can stop me now." George jumped off the bed and did a Tarzan-style beating of his chest until Gerry burst out laughing and then collapsed back on the bed. Then they kissed again several times, aware of their pending separation after such a short period together. "Gerry, take care, please don't do anything dangerous. It is just not worth it, nothing is worth risk to you."

317

"I just want to help in some way, George, and writing is what I do best, and if I have to tip my cap to Deidre the Dragon then that is what I'll do. And I will do it with great joy whatever they throw at me because I know it might help you in your struggle just a little tiny bit."

"Oh, I see, so it is just a tiny wee bit of help you are doing, is it? Some of those articles are incredible."

"You read them?"

"And afterwards I used them," George grinned.

"What do you mean?" Gerry asked earnestly, propping herself up on one elbow.

"Well, it is hard sometimes to get loo paper when sleeping rough. I find your articles the perfect solution!"

"You little so-and-so!" Gerry exclaimed.

"And that is another thing," George replied, moving backwards fast to avoid her flying arm.

"What this time?"

"Well, if we are going to be together you are going to have to issue the odd swear word from time to time."

"Bloody loony!" said Gerry, trying hard to sound English. They fell back on the bed again and George was seriously late for his next meeting.

"We will have lots of time together soon, I promise," he said again quite some time later.

And he was gone, leaving Gerry, under Mandy's care, to travel back to London. Mandy drove her to within six streets of her flat, public transport being too dangerous. They talked throughout the two-hour journey about George, the resistance, and plans for the future.

"I am writing an article for an underground newsletter about George."

"Great, make it punchy! We need all the support we can get. You know if it makes one reader in twenty stand up when the time comes, that is a whole load more support we can count on. Gerry, it is a really important thing you are doing. Think hard about it. You have to make maximum impact. We have to counter all the propaganda coming out of the state. You can make all the difference with this article."

"Well, thanks for piling on the pressure!"

"You're very welcome," Mandy replied. "Seriously, maximum impact."

"He's changed," said Gerry a few moments later.

"In what way?"

"Well, when I met him in DC he was almost diffident, like he wanted to dip his toes into everything but that was it. He has a real fine mind, one of the best, but didn't seem able to make any commitment in anything."

"And now?"

"Completely different. Like the same underlying personality but with purpose. It's like he's finally made some choices and found a way. Yet there is something else as well, like he is playing a part. I don't know. All I do know is that I love him, have done since we first met, and I want to do everything to help him."

"Well, think hard about the article then because we are at a really pivotal time right now. The more people you can convince, the more chance we have of success. I can't talk about the plan for obvious reasons but I do know that we need every single available person to be behind us when we press that trigger."

From the flat, she called in sick and then switched on her computer and began writing up her interview with the leader of Future Perfect.

She made the deadline by ten minutes. Adam read it in the back of the cab on the way to the printers. He thought it was ideal and worth the huge risks they had all taken. Adam had spent half the night driving around in the dark with his two black shadows always a discreet distance behind. Finally, at 1.50 in the morning they had recognised the futility of their endeavour and pulled back, drifting away, suddenly putting their full lights on, as if declaring their presence after the fact. Gerry hastily wrote this into the story, resting her laptop against a glass frame containing examples of early print placed in the foyer of the printers. Their first newsletter was going to cause a stir and just at the right time, too.

"Adam?" She should tell him about Brownie.

"Yes, Gerry."

"Nothing." Except how could she?

"Except…" She had to. "Adam, are you sure about Brownie? I mean, you barely know her."

"Gerry, I'm real certain, never been more certain. It was love at first sight!"

"She is a police officer."

"And a good one, she must be for them to give her a second chance after what she did."

"Do you ever think maybe…"

"I think I know what you are trying to say and the answer is no. We are very much in love. Her heart is as big as her smile and as genuine, too. Don't worry about her and me. Put it out of your mind."

"But…"

"Gerry, out of your mind, please. No more talk of this. We should go eat. Brownie finishes at 7pm so I'll text her to meet us some place."

"No Adam, you go. I want a quiet night, too much excitement for a small-town girl!"

"If you're sure?" Adam replied. "Gerry, you did a great job. This will help the cause no end."

"Well it is our cause, the cause of freedom, so thank you, Adam for setting it up."

***

Deidre rewarded Gerry for her absence with a further demotion on Friday morning.

After getting Janitorial to move her into the smaller office on Wednesday, she changed her mind and got her moved out of that same office on Thursday afternoon.

"Where am I supposed to sit... Miss Harrington?" Gerry asked.

"In the main office, Geraldine." This was a new development for Deidre, perhaps sensing that Gerry had always preferred the short version of her name. "I have some important work for you to do on the membership records. You are so organised and have such a sweet voice. I want you to phone each member and check their details; home address, phone numbers, dependents, that sort of thing. Then enter any corrections on the database. Do you think you can manage that?"

"Yes, Miss Harrington." What did she care about being humiliated? She had George and she was working secretly for the movement that he was risking his life for. She would bear anything for George, even Deidre's treatment, which hit at every professional fibre.

"And report each half-day, before lunch and before you go home, to Miss Crutcher, on your progress. I want to see you working through the membership records diligently, not flitting off again on some flight of fancy."

"But Cynthia is my secretary. I..."

"Miss Crutcher was your secretary. If you had managed to make it into the office yesterday or if you had checked the notice board this morning before charging into my office like a headstrong teenager you might have noticed that she has been promoted to Membership Manager. She is your boss, Geraldine, and your future in this organisation very much depends on pleasing her. Do I make myself clear?"

"Yes, Miss Harrington."

"Well, run along then. I have important work to do if I am to save the newsletter you have managed to virtually destroy." As Gerry closed the door, a little suspicion grew in Deidre's mind. Why was Gerry being so compliant? It was no fun if she did not fight back. It meant she had to keep finding new ways to humiliate her. "I wouldn't put it past that bitch to be up to something," she muttered to herself before returning to the article she was writing on how the USE promoted liberty in many forms.

Gerry, meanwhile, found her new desk under the stairs near the photocopy machine and with a sigh opened the membership records on her computer and picked up her phone, Cynthia watching from her own office to one side of the main room.

Twenty minutes later, the idea came to Deidre. She rose immediately, a tight smile difficult to keep off her face. She walked past her secretary in the outer office, left the door wide open and crossed the main office to the door to Cynthia's new office, four feet from Gerry's desk. She wanted the maximum audience for this show.

"Cynthia, there is something that has been worrying me," she said in a loud voice so everyone in the office could hear. "With Geraldine's recent job change I am concerned that she is sticking out like a sore thumb amongst the other girls."

"Whatever do you mean, Miss Harrington?"

Cynthia crossed her office to the door and looked at Gerry, a similar smile to Deidre's flashing across her face.

"I mean her attire, Cynthia. She is dressing like the executive she is not. She is dressing like you and I in her smart business suits. I think she is placing herself above the other admin girls, and this is disconcerting for the others."

She paused to let the words sink in, clearly enjoying the deep flush on Gerry's face.

Gerry just thought, *George, George, I am doing this for George*, and kept silent, eyes on her computer screen with the membership records in neat boxes. Nobody was working now. Deidre waited until she considered enough time had passed to build the suspense.

"Cynthia, be a dear and take Geraldine out this morning to get her some suitable clothes. Use the corporate card as a little gift to her. Guide her, please, in her choices and get her sufficient for a few days until she can get to the shops herself and replace her wardrobe appropriately." There was a gasp from the main office. Gerry kept thinking of George and Adam and the newsletter. She had to endure this.

"Come along, Geraldine," Cynthia said. "Get your coat and bag and let's go shopping."

***

Three hours later, Gerry was sitting in the break room having lunch. She wore a plain white top and a heavy pleated black polyester skirt with white tights and black flats. She ate in silence at a table on her own. She had just endured a presentation to Deidre of the 'new look Geraldine', including displaying her various purchases and getting approval.

"You'll fit in a lot better this way, Geraldine." As Deidre entered new levels of condescension, Gerry thought of George again. She would bear anything for him and for his cause. "Now, here is your new name badge for your new position. It is the new style we are introducing." Gerry took it but did not want to. It was three times the size of the old style she had devised. "Pin it on your top and make sure you always wear it. I objected to the idea of name badges when you insisted on them but, on reflection, it was one of your least bad ideas as it makes everyone's status very clear."

"Admin Assistant!" Gerry exploded on turning over the new badge.

"Yes, that's right. We struggled with the right job title. Miss Crutcher, your boss, came up with this one as you are basically starting from scratch and learning on the job, hopefully getting it correct this time around. Now we also have to talk about the flat you have been staying in."

"What do you mean?"

"Are you forgetting yourself, young lady?"

"I'm sorry, Miss Harrington, I just meant what do you mean about my flat?" She was clearly forgetting George and Adam in her anger. Control, she had to have control, and then get a plan together.

"Thank you, that is much better. Now, when you have your badge on I will tell you." Deidre and Cynthia were clearly enjoying this. Gerry fumbled with the pin, which was stiff and awkward to handle, thinking this was a huge price to pay. But it was George that mattered and if she had to go through this to assist him in some small way then so be it.

"Silly girl! You have it lopsided." Cynthia stepped forward and redid the pin so the badge was straight. "No doubt she will get used to it, Miss Harrington."

"No doubt, now enough of this nonsense and on to more serious things. Geraldine, you clearly cannot stay in the flat. It is enormously expensive to rent and you are not making any payment for it."

"I'm happy to pay, Miss Harrington."

"On your wages? Don't make me laugh! You were making a pretty packet as an executive but you keep forgetting that you failed miserably in that position. Cynthia, what does an apprentice earn?"

"7.25 euros an hour, Miss Harrington."

"So on thirty-five hours a week that comes to about 1000 euros a month, say 900 after taxes and pension contributions. The weekly rent on the flat is more than that. No, it is quite a hardship for youngsters to find somewhere to stay in London, but very luckily for you Miss Crutcher has a box room which she has very generously said she can make available for 600 euros, which should leave you enough for the bus pass and a little spending money as well. It also means you will come in and go home together so she can keep a good eye on your time-keeping so I don't have to reprimand you so often in the mornings. Please plan to be out of the flat by 20th November. I will leave it in Miss Crutcher's hands to make the arrangements about you moving in with her."

"Thank you, Miss Harrington and Miss Crutcher." *George, George, George.*

"That's quite alright. We like to help the juniors when we can, even the errant ones. Now we are going into your lunch break so off you pop. I don't want you complaining you have not had time to gobble up your lunch!"

As she finished the sandwich she had brought with her, sitting alone, fuming, a shy young girl who had never spoken much to Gerry came forward tentatively.

"I think it is awful what they have done to you."

"Thank you, Kirsten. But I will survive."

"I am the other apprentice in the office. I will show you what to do if you like," Kirsten had read Gerry's name badge. Gerry saw Kirsten's and noted three differences straight away, apart from the size. Kristen's included her surname whereas Gerry's just said 'Geraldine'. The second difference was the inclusion of 'junior' before the job title on Gerry's badge. Their determination to humiliate would stop at nothing. The third and most significant was the department Kirsten worked for - Newsletter, whereas Gerry was in Membership. That could be useful, as Gerry had no access anymore to the drafts of the weekly publication.

"Thanks, Kirsten, that would be real good."

"Well, to start with..."

Several others then came up, preventing Kirsten from launching into her list of daily chores. But Gerry met her eyes and mouthed "Later", to which Kirsten nodded enthusiastically.

"You were a good leader. Why did they do this to you?" This was Amie from Belgium, who had started the same week as Gerry, a long lifetime ago, it seemed.

"Because, well because I was not very kind to them. I rode roughshod over their principles in pursuit of my own."

"But they are wrong! And you are right."

"I don't understand. I thought you were all against me," Gerry was stunned.

Then Maria came up to their table. "Geraldine..."

"Gerry, please."

"Gerry, Miss Harrington said that you were self-seeking and ambitious and just wanted to help your boyfriend."

"I do."

"But she implied it was a bad cause. But we Spiders know better."

"You're a Spider? All of you are Spiders?" Gerry's despondency lifted like fog.

"Most of us are."

"I am now," said Amie. "I just joined the web!" The joke broke down the remaining reserve and for the first time since arriving in Britain Gerry realised she was making friends.

Playing the Part

"Kirsty, can you take a break now? I've been given ten minutes," Gerry whispered as she walked past Kirsten's desk on the way to the break room. Kirsty nodded and quickly saved her work on the computer.

"Do you have to ask for a break?" Kirsty said as they worked the drinks machine and then selected a table away from everyone else. "I just go."

"You don't have a boss like Miss Crutcher!"

"True, Mr Martin is a dream boss!"

"So, Kirsty, can you tell me what you do each day so I can learn? I want to get this right." Gerry had the germ of a plan she was determined to develop.

"Well, first of all I take Mr Martin's coat when he gets in and I hang it in the cloakroom. So you should do the same for Miss Crutcher. That means always making sure you arrive before your boss. His secretary looks after his coffee so next I check that the daily news upload happened overnight and then I check with the Print Supervisor whether there are any problems with the printer and the copy. If there are I have to schedule a meeting so they can sort it out." Kirsty gave a concise run down of a typical day, her confidence growing as she went through the familiar tasks.

"So at any time you can see the draft newsletter articles?"

"Yes, it is all on the drive. Anyone with access will be able to see it at any time."

"I would love to see it and maybe even be allowed to help you with some of it."

"Well, I probably should ask Mr Martin, but he did say it was fine to get you familiar with everything when I asked him if I could teach you the ropes. He said I, as the senior admin assistant, should try and help you fit in as much as possible."

"That's absolutely right! I would love that, Kirsty, I mean to be taught and guided by you. It would make my job meaningful again." Kirsty responded by reaching across the table and squeezing Gerry's hand.

"That would be great," she said, smiling.

***

"So this is where you two have got to."

"Mr Martin, I am sorry. I was just telling Geraldine about how things work, like you said for me to do."

"That's OK, Kirsty, but you'd better get back to work now." Then he turned to Gerry, winked, and said, "Miss Crutcher is out but will be back soon."

"Thanks, Mr Martin," Gerry replied as they filed past him. Her plan was beginning to take shape.

"Just a mo., Gerry." Mr Martin touched her gently on the arm. "Can I have a word?"

"Of course, Mr Martin." Gerry sat down again. Mr Martin waited until Kirsty was out of hearing then sat down in the seat Kirsty had vacated with a cup of tea from the machine.

"Call me Simon when no one is around."

"Sure, Simon, how can I help you?"

He cleared his throat, started to ask her a question, changed his mind then just blurted it out. "What they've done to you is unpardonable. I don't know why you are putting up with it and it is not my business, but you would have every right in walking out and starting a lawsuit for constructive dismissal. I just wanted you to know that quite a lot of your old managers are behind you."

"Thank you, Simon. That is real supportive."

"Can I be frank?" Gerry nodded, half-suspecting what was coming.

"You seemed very aloof when you first came over, almost like dictatorial and also, well, frankly biased for your chosen causes, or should I say cause in the singular? You didn't seem to want to listen to us and our opinions."

"I know, Simon. I realised that over the last few days. I was arrogant, pig-headed and conceited."

"You said it, not me!" Simon joked. He had such a warm shine in his eyes when he smiled; it was the first time Gerry had noticed it.

"It needed saying. Now, I better get downstairs before Cynthia gets back."

"There is one other thing," Simon said as he stood up. "I said it is not my business why you are enduring this awful humiliation they are meting out. It is not. But I just wanted to say that I read a fantastic article about George Unwin-Smith this weekend and it really moved me. I sort of know that writing style but I just cannot quite place it." They looked at each other with perfect understanding, then Gerry rushed down the stairs to Cynthia's office, while Simon sat a moment longer over his cup of tea. The truth was he would dearly like to know why Gerry was putting up with the humiliation piled onto her and why she was suddenly so friendly with Kirsty.

"Miss Crutcher, could I possibly see you and Miss Harrington for a moment?"

"Go and wait outside her door and I will see if she has time."

When Gerry was told to enter twenty minutes later, she adopted a slightly stooped stance, hoping it looked respectful. She stood in front of the desk that had been hers very recently, Cynthia sitting on a chair to one side, Deidre in the desk seat. Gerry spoke in a very small voice, hoping she was not overdoing it.

"Miss Harrington and Miss Crutcher, I have been thinking a lot about what you have both said to me and about my behaviour since I came over here. I want to apologise for the real poor attitude and for the problems I have caused. I just wanted to say that I accept that my mistakes mean you have had to take charge and that you are working hard to correct the problems I created by being so misguided and headstrong." Was she laying it on too thick? Apparently not, as they both smiled in appreciation. "I also wanted to thank you for the guidance on my dress and always welcome all suggestions now and in the future so that I can become a better employee and try and undo some of the damage I have done."

"Well Geraldine, this is a change of heart, certainly." Deidre found her voice.

"Yes, Miss Harrington. I am truly sorry for the trouble I have caused and so grateful for the chance to try and make amends. I've been listening to Kirsten in my breaks and she is going to hold my hand a lot to guide me in my new role. Mr Martin told her to do this."

"OK, Geraldine, carry on, but don't forget your membership records duties. Now off you go, we have some important things to talk about." Gerry thanked them again and left the room quickly, seeking out her new friend in the main office.

"Kirsty, its OK, I asked Miss Harrington about working with you and she said it was OK."

"You spoke to Miss Harrington?" Kirsty was impressed.

"Yes, now why don't you take me through the newsletter database and show me how it all works."

"Fine, yes of course. And afterwards do you want me to put plats in your hair?"

"Like yours, you mean? That would be lovely. We could be twins!" *George, George, George.* But now she had a plan.

Publication Day

Adam wondered whether one million copies of the inaugural newsletter would be too ambitious. But, after talking it through with Gerry, he went with it anyway. It meant an investment in printing and distribution of $800,000, the largest single expenditure item he had authorised on this posting. The deal was done secretly of course, so it was entirely cash, and US dollars had a great attraction with the new EurEx regulations in place. About half went on printing, the other half on distribution. None of the twenty-six writers, Gerry included as both contributor and editor, received a penny. The distribution money was spent on vans, petrol, bribes and more bribes. But it worked and the paper, eight sheets in tabloid format, was an instant success. The headline on the front page sold it. Next to a picture of George it said: 'Freedom or Die Trying.' And underneath it said: 'Exclusive in his own words: The Tortious Doubts of Resistance'. Adam read again the article written by Gerry in promotion of liberty. It seemed even more powerful now in print rather than on a computer screen as he followed the words, imagining them being spoken.

Last night I met again a man. He is known to all of you. He is George Unwin-Smith. George is an unlikely hero. His nose is too big to be a movie star. He is not suave like James Bond, nor is he tough like Clint Eastwood or John Wayne. He is lonely, frightened and worried. He is lonely because, despite many colleagues who show equal commitment to the cause of liberty, he has taken on the mantel of leadership and on his

shoulders rests the future of this great country. He is frightened because EurPo tortured him. I saw the result of this torture when he was rescued from 'police custody' on the eve of the General Election. He is frightened for those colleagues who have been captured and are experiencing similar or worse. He is worried for his country and its future. And he is worried that his plan will not be good enough to shake off the weight of oppression that lies upon this land.

George told me last night that he used to think that being a leader was easy and came naturally but now knows the reality of leadership. He has learned this the hard way. He has been lost, confused and desperate. He has faced failure. He has had to rely on others whereas previously in life he was an island. He has come to know his frailties: what he can do and what he must rely on others to do for him. He has learned about teamwork and how vital that is. He has learned that teamwork is everything and now he is calling on the greater team that is this country, once proud and free, to become proud and free again.

And that is the message that George gave me last night as we talked into the small hours. The resistance is a team. He is but one cog in that wheel. All the cogs add up to a huge wheel. He is frail. He is human. But the team together is strong, matching frailty with strength. Together they are invincible. Because of this they will win. But right now they need your support more than ever. George said to me late at night: "We were a free people and a free people we will become again!" I do not need to add anything to George's own words, other than to say watch out and be ready for the time is coming for action.

The paper hit the streets in London at 5pm on Friday, 23rd October. Vans had already charged their way across the country, with stashes hidden amongst the luggage on flights to Belfast, Glasgow, Manchester and Plymouth. The distributors were individuals who picked up a hundred copies at one of the many secret depots and took them out on the streets, returning for more when they had disposed of the first batch and if they had not been caught and arrested. 'Distributing illegal literature first offence' carried thirty days, subsequent offences rose through a scale to five years. A five-year sentence was virtually a death penalty because they worked on you hard for those five years, turning your mind towards how they saw things. Distribution was even more dangerous under Emergency Law. Penalties were doubled or tripled, shootings on the street happened from time to time.

It was a scary occupation. But the distributors kept coming and, this time, they kept coming back for more copies. Between the release at 5pm and 6pm not many were circulated. But after 6pm, as commuters dominated the travel routes, the pace picked up. The advantage of a copy in a commuter's hand was considered to be much higher because they often left them on the train to be read by others or took them home to their family and friends.

By 8pm half the copies had been taken up. By 10pm, despite dwindling numbers out on the streets, they were down to a few tens of thousands. By midnight they were all gone.

"I should have ordered more copies," Adam sighed.

For Gerry and Adam it was the culmination of forty-eight hours of frantic work. At 2am on Saturday morning they were toasting its success with a bottle of red wine. Brownie was sitting with her feet stretched over Adam's lap on the sofa. She had just got back from a long shift with overtime and was too tired to change or eat, or do anything but curl up next to Adam and sip wine.

"By rights I should arrest you both," she said on flicking through the newsletter. "I've been confiscating these all evening up in Notting Hill."

"Why don't you?" Adam asked.

"Only reason is I am too bloody shattered." She closed her eyes. Adam slipped off her shoes and rubbed her feet, jet-black skin clothed in jet-black stockings.

"I love every bit of you," he said.

"Bloody hell, stop being so soppy, Forster. Just rub and shut up." Another of her most beautiful smiles as she threw a cushion at his head and knocked over the bottle of wine. "Shit."

"Don't worry, I'll do it. I'm getting used to clearing up after you." Gerry threw down some paper towels and rubbed vigorously for a few minutes. "I suppose it doesn't matter much anyway as we have to be out of here in a few weeks."

"What? I've only just moved in." So Gerry told them the events of the day. Sometime during the narration she heard Brownie snore. She was fast asleep.

"Ad, I didn't want to mention it in front of Brownie, but I think I have a way of getting to the drafts of the Society's newsletters. Kirsty is a sweet girl and I hate to use her, but this is all in a much bigger cause." She explained her plan and Adam quickly approved.

"Just don't get caught," he said. "So that it why your hair is plaited. It looks real sweet."

"Stop it, Ad, or I will throw something heavier than a cushion. Seriously, what do you expect now?"

"I think there will be some disruption over the weekend but it is going to take something significant to make real change. I wish I knew what the resistance was planning."

"Well, I don't want to know because it might lead to George being hurt or…"

"Don't, Gerry, don't torture yourself. You'll be together soon." Then, after a long pause, in which they both continued to sip in silence, he added, "Gerry, thank you for taking this on. What it must be like to be so humiliated by such people is beyond me… Gerry?"

But Gerry was gently snoring, too.

Reconnaissance

Paul made a spy's textbook arrival into Heathrow. He had purchased some skis and appropriate clothing to match and, with his arm still in its sling, looked like a fallen skier returning early and alone rather than staying to watch the rest of the party having fun on the slopes and in the bars.

"Rotten luck," The EurImm officer said on scanning his passport, so that Paul did not even have to lie.

"It happens to the best of us!" Paul had joked in reply. Now he was heading in a black taxi into Central London. Sir Terrence had told him to get a hotel room rather than go to the mews behind Sir Terrence's London home. He chose one off Piccadilly that offered a room that was tiny, little larger than the bed, and clearly partitioned from a larger room in pursuit of as many euros as possible. But Paul was not here for his enjoyment, or for the sights, but for a purpose. As soon as he had dropped the ski bag on the floor he returned to the foyer and used the hotel pay phone to ring a number.

"Number 17 requests RV." He had rehearsed this with his boss. They both hoped it would work.

"Password?"

"Freedom." The phone went dead. The passwords had been changed. He dialled the second number he had memorised.

"Number 17 requests RV."

"Password?"

"Liberty." Same response. He dialled the third number and was, again, asked for the password.

"GF," he said, knowing it would never be a password but

that he had to take a risk to get their attention. He could hear a pause, then silence as the phone was replaced. *Damn*, he thought. He only had the three numbers and the fall-back plan to get into contact involved a lot more risk of detection.

The phone in the booth rang just as he was leaving. He grabbed it, catching his wounded arm on the booth door as he swung round.

"Bloody hell!" he said into the receiver.

"17?"

"Yes, sorry."

"Waterloo, 7pm, outside Gents, red tracksuit, black backpack." The phone went dead again.

Paul arrived at Waterloo at 6.35, used the Gents to check location and then spent fifteen minutes trying to be interested in the magazine rack at WH Smiths. At three minutes to the hour he walked over to the Gents again, saw a girl in a red tracksuit and black backpack and walked up to her. As he approached he was about to say something, but her look was one of warning. She brushed past him and made her way to the Ladies without any form of recognition. He waited for ten minutes, scanning the board of departures as if waiting impatiently for a train, then she came up to him and asked him where to get a bus. She stood close to him, touching his arm, as if she was unaware of personal space.

"What bus number for Stockwell?" she asked. She had a pockmarked face and flaming red hair.

"I think 17," he said in reply, catching on to her code. Then he pointed towards the bus sign overhead and she thanked him and left. He stared after her and then looked away, aware that he should not risk detection but frustrated that the rendezvous had been abandoned. Was security really that tight? Did she mean him to get a bus? Surely he was not meant to follow her? And was there even a bus number 17 running from Waterloo? He looked again at her red and black back disappearing across the concourse and then looked down, aware that he was staring again. Then he saw the train ticket on the floor. He was sure it had not been there before. He picked it up, feigning irritation at having dropped his ticket in case he had an audience. It was a pre-booked return ticket to Farnham, leaving at 7.25 that night. He glanced at his watch. It was 7.18. He looked at the departure board. There was a 7.25 to Farnham on Platform Six. He would take it and hope no police officer asked him why he was going there.

The police were at each barrier and appeared to be interrogating passengers on a selective basis. Paul slid in behind two youngsters with mock army-style jackets and boots. His hunch was correct. The police pulled both of them to one side and let him through with barely a look.

Bertie was there at Farnham station, waiting in the shadows. He had received a brief description of Paul on the radio and was looking for an athletic-looking fifty-year-old with short grey hair and his right arm in a sling, with the sleeve of his black leather jacket hanging loose.

"17?"

"Yes."

"Who sent you?" But Paul was not ready to give that information yet, so he replied that his ticket came from a girl in a red tracksuit and black backpack. That was sufficient for Bertie and Paul was taken to a car parked on the street outside the station. When they were in the car, Bertie said that he would have to blindfold Paul for the drive.

They arrived in pitch-blackness twenty minutes later. When the blindfold was removed, Paul could still see nothing, but he sensed and heard that they were on a farm. He was taken indoors and led into a typical farmhouse kitchen with an Aga and a worn table in the middle of the room. He recognised no one around the table.

"Why did you call?" Bertie asked.

"To give a message to George Unwin-Smith from his father."

"What is the message?" When Paul told them, Bertie left the room with a nod to one of the others. "Look after him." They gave him a cup of tea and some biscuits but were not inclined to talk. They reminded Paul of wartime resistance fighters, grim determination emanating from every pore. Paul drank the tea and ate the biscuits. He took a second cup but refused another biscuit. It was a long wait, made longer by the silence from the others. They were not aggressive, just purposeful.

Eventually, Bertie was back. Paul quickly finished his third cup of tea and followed him into the large drawing room at the front of the house.

"George! You are safe, thank goodness."

"Paul, I never expected you. Is my father OK? And Sir Terrence?"

They spoke for an hour. For the first ten minutes it was all about George's father and a little about Sir Terrence and Professor Stuttermann. Paul related the rush to get out of Germany and immediately George thought about Aunt Jessica.

"My God, he was shot twice? Is he really OK? The bastard who shot him will pay for this."

"George, your father is very frail. I wouldn't hide that from you. The cancer…"

"You know about that?"

"It came out in the hospital. I don't think he would have told anyone if it had been up to him."

"I only found out at Oxford General in the same way," George said. "My God, I want to see him."

"You can't, George, it would be a risk too much. He will be very reassured to hear from you through me."

Then it was George's turn to talk and Paul's to soak in the intelligence. George outlined a few of the ideas but not in detail in case Paul was detained on the way back to Switzerland. "Secrecy is everything right now," he said. "If our plans get out they are so easily countered. So I am just telling you the barest outline. We are strong and growing but ultimately we will not succeed because they will just send endless more troops in. We have to make a big strike now."

"George, I don't want to know for myself, but your father and Sir Terrence?"

"They are just going to have to understand. We've all put so much into this plan we cannot risk it now."

"When did you come up with the plan?" Paul was trying to think of what they would ask him back in Switzerland.

"Only ten days ago. We've known we need to do something but what and how eluded us until I had an idea ten days ago. We've reworked it and honed it and rehearsed it endlessly since then. I think it is going to work but, my God, am I nervous!"

Towards 11pm, Bertie interrupted to say that to catch the last train to London they would have to leave right now.

"Travel safely, Paul, and relay the little I've told you to my father and Sir Terrence. Give my best to Professor Stuttermann and please give my love to my father." Tears came into his eyes and suddenly he hugged Paul, Paul knowing it was for his father, who he might never see again.

"I will," Paul said. "And I will tell him you are in great health. Goodbye for a little time and, for God's sake, look after yourself."

Bertie was much more chatty in the car on the way back to the station. They were tight on time so he drove quickly.

"George has changed," Paul said as they sped out of the farmyard.

"In what way?"

"Grimmer, more practical, less about theories."

"Needs must! This is sink-or-swim time, Paul, we have to make it work."

Paul had to run over the bridge to get on the train and did not say goodbye to Bertie properly. By one in the morning he was back in his hotel room but unable to sleep. The scale of what the Future Perfect was planning was clearly incredible. If it worked, well, it would change the whole country, in fact the whole world.

Paul was back in the rented villa within thirty hours of leaving it. He had left the skis on the luggage belt, uninterested in retaining them, and desperate to get the news to the others. He announced first that George was well and sent his love to his father and his warm regards to the others. Then he gave his general assessment of what he had seen of the underground movement.

"Very well organised, lots of determination, a sense of purpose. I think there are thousands of them. I met with Bertie Graves. He drove me from the station to the house where I met George. Do you remember him? He was a top adviser to David Kirkby and then turned and came over to us. He won a seat in the elections, somewhere in the south, I think. He told me that they don't have a headquarters, rather that George, Bertie and a few others move from cell to cell, usually at night. He said there were over 1,000 members in that cell alone." Then Paul moved on to a brief outline of the Guy Fawkes plan and, just like him the previous night, they listened in silence.

***

Late that night, Edward could not sleep. The pain was increasing and his body weakening. The nurses were in residence now and tried to keep him in bed, but Edward wanted to spend as much time as possible with his friends on the veranda, warmed by the upside-down-dome fire and drinking a little white wine while they talked. He returned to the veranda to find Sir Terrence stoking up the fire.

"I thought you might not be able to sleep so I wanted to resurrect the fire."

"That's kind of you, Scott. Will you sit with me for a while?"

"Nothing I would like better." When Sir Terrence said something, you always knew he meant it. "A little wine?"

"Thanks."

"Is it bad tonight?"

"The pain is quite bad but there is something else. I feel my body weakening. It's like the extremities are closing down segment by segment."

They talked about George and the movement as the sun started its slow preparations for another day. The air was cold, thinly populated by particles, fresh, dry, light and wholesome.

"You know what to do," Sir Terrence said into a silence while Edward's eyes flickered closed.

"It is my one remaining work and now I have the facts."

"But you cannot publish. The story will die with you and us. It is how it has to be."

There was a long silence. Finally, Sir Terrence leaned forward and put his hand on Edward's shoulder as he slumped in the chair. "It is how it has to be," Sir Terrence repeated. "It is too valuable to George," he added gently. There was no response at all. They sat in silence.

"Scott?"

"Yes?"

"Will you get Jay to witness a new will?"

"I can be witness."

"I need Jay."

Sir Terrence was back in three minutes with Jay in his pyjamas. Sir Terrence had paper and pen.

"Tell me and I will write it down."

Sir Terrence started with: 'This is the last will and testament... I, Edward Peter Unwin-Smith, being of sound mind... do leave my possessions as follows.'

Then Edward spoke up.

"100,000 euros to my Oxford College." Sir Terrence wrote it down.

"All my other possessions to my son, George." So what was new about this?

"Except all my workings and study papers on General Stein and my father, General Unwin-Smith." Edward paused as Sir Terrence scribbled like mad. "These I leave to my good friend Sir Terrence Scott, to do with as he thinks fit in the interests of the United Kingdom of Great Britain and Northern Ireland." That was why he needed Jay to be a witness.

Edward signed his name, Jay likewise, then Edward with a sigh gave up on the life he had loved with one last command to both men present to give his never-ending love to his son.

For a long time afterwards, Sir Terrence and Jay sat on the veranda while the sun danced through the shadows and spoke of hope.

Whenever the sun comes up there is hope.

Boots and Feet

Gerry was looking forward to work on Monday morning. The newsletter, her newsletter, had created turmoil all weekend. All the police had been on overtime, Brownie had barely been back to the flat. They were charged with tracking down the perpetrators before the promised second edition the following Friday. As Brownie admitted on one of her two brief visits back to wash and change, they had little chance of achieving this as no one would talk. Gerry was secretly pleased to see Brownie exhausted and defeated but somehow drumming up the energy to return to work. The more occupied she and the rest of the police were, the less opportunity they had of snatching her and Adam.

Gerry had befriended her, offered her lodging in her flat, yet her reward was a pending kidnap and that meant more time in the cells. She shuddered to think of that. She could not understand how Adam could be so complacent about Brownie. But maybe he knew something she did not, because Adam was no fool. He would not be so calm if there was a real risk of being snatched.

It was so complicated and Gerry did not know what to think. She had to just concentrate on what she could do to help George.

She was looking forward to work on Monday morning because she could anticipate the panic as Deidre's beloved USE was made to look foolish and fragile again, and it happening just before Verdun's visit, starting on Tuesday week. It was perfect timing. If he cancelled his visit he would look weak, but what chance did the USE president have of making an impact under these conditions? Adam's timing of the newsletter had been bang on.

They tried, of course, to keep the turmoil off the news channels and off the internet. But you cannot lie to the public when the streets are alive with unrest, demonstrations and disorder. So the official channels spoke of a quiet weekend getting ready for President Verdun, while the unofficial channels gleefully reported chaos everywhere.

And it was not just London. In Liverpool there was almost civil war; not much better in Belfast or Glasgow. Police barricades were overturned in Oxfordshire; a police station in Inverness was taken over by the public. Citizens' arrests were made of EurMilPo staff across Britain, as if ordered by some all-seeing central command. One whole platoon was kept confined to a pub in Somerset all weekend, the detention organised by a retired Army major with a particular, well-justified hatred for the military police. Regulars kept watch in fours, guarding the exits, even though each of the eighteen captive soldiers was securely strapped to pub chairs.

In Anglesey an armoured vehicle was taken over and driven across the bridge to the mainland, where it became the centrepiece for an improvised street party before being delivered to the underground movement on Sunday afternoon. As John Baker described it on his pirate news channel, "The people are rising and there ain't nothing nobody can do about it!"

This was the joyful scene that Gerry considered as she walked across St James' Park early on Monday morning. It was a situation she had contributed towards and was delighted to be a part of. It made her feel that she was included in the struggle that George was at the centre of. When she received a hand-delivered card on Sunday morning, which just said 'Thanks from Big Nose', she was overjoyed. She could not wait to see Deidre's panicked face and hear her shaky voice as she tried to work out what on earth to do. Would she guess that Gerry had had something to do with it?

Adam had visited on Sunday evening and they had eaten salad and sardines, all that Gerry could quickly throw together.

"It's real important that you remain undetected, Gerry," he said. "I know it is tough for you to buckle down under the Deidre Dragon but that is the most important thing you can do right now. She will be pushing her own newsletter out tomorrow afternoon and it is vital that we know what is in it and what, therefore, we need to counter in our next edition. It is vital that you are not suspected."

"I think I probably am already, Ad. She has to suspect something when I've just accepted her authority lock, stock and barrel. But I needed her to bless my spending time with Kirsty. I think she fell for that, but she will be suspicious if she sees all the fight gone out of me."

"You're right, Gerry, but we just cannot risk you getting fired. We must have access to their newsletter. It has become the single most important vehicle for expression of the establishment since our friend Deidre grabbed back control. I know it is real awful but we need you to give us at least one more sight of the newsletter before you walk out of there. One more week is all it is going to take."

Gerry nodded, wondering what would be thrown her way during the coming week. At least she had the pleasure of the consternation and confusion created by her own newsletter.

"Ad, I hate to raise this again, but I feel I must. I overhead Brownie talking on the radio the other day. She was talking to someone about…"

"Kidnapping a pair of foreigners," Adam interjected. "Don't worry about it. She saw you, you know, I mean following her. She told me about it."

"She told you about the plans she was making?"

"Yes, well, she told me a little bit of them. But I am sworn on my mother's life to secrecy so you are just going to have to take my word for it that it's nothing sinister!" Then, on seeing

Gerry's disappointment, he added, "Believe me, Gerry, there are a lot of lives depending on this, George's included. Brownie told me the little I know because, well I shouldn't even go into that."

So they had finished their sardines and salad and talked about other things.

***

Gerry had dressed carefully that morning in a brown and yellow check wool-effect dress chosen by Cynthia. It had a neat white collar, matching cuffs and large brown fake buttons down the front. She had plaited her own hair, in a very similar in style to Kirsten's, and wore her large glasses instead of her contact lenses. She looked the part. On the way out she bumped into Brownie clattering up the stairs, exhausted from a long shift.

"Excuse me, Miss," Brownie reversed back down the stairs to the landing.

"Brownie?"

"My God, Gerry. I didn't recognise you. You are so different You look so pretty."

"Hardly."

"No, seriously, you look really nice. That dress suits you. I just always expect you in some expensive business suit. You look really nice. And the glasses and the hair too. Wow, I'm going to have to watch Adam around you."

"Do you really think so?" Gerry was shocked. She had wanted to look defeated, humiliated, ground-down, in order to make it easier at work, not pretty or attractive.

"Yes, I really think so! You look so soft and feminine. The dress is perfect on you. Honestly, it is a great improvement. I'm going to have to stop Adam from coming round here!"

"Don't be silly. I'll see you later," Gerry said, completely puzzled at Brownie's reaction, thinking hard as she walked down the street to the tube station. She tried to check her appearance in a few shop windows as she went, then was disturbed in this task by a builder's crew, who whistled and made cheeky remarks from their scaffolding. At first Gerry thought they must have been teasing someone else and stopped to look over her shoulder.

"No darling, it's you is the love of my life," shouted one of the builders, showing an acute understanding of the questioning in Gerry's mind. "There's nobody else for me. Marry me!"

"No way, sir!" she yelled back, suddenly flattered by the attention. "Go marry your cute buddy. He looks like he has the hots for you."

Nobody had catcalled her since university.

Gerry opened the office front door, noticing the absence of the doorman. In fact, he had not opened the door for her on Friday either. He was in, though, sitting on a chair at the table where he sorted the post. He glanced up and said, "Morning."

"Hi," said Gerry, not sure how to deal with his apparent offhandness. "Is something up?" In reply he looked around, winked at her, and said in a low voice that he had been told not to treat her with deference following her demotion. He had explicit instructions not to hold the door open for her or to start any conversation other than saying a brisk 'good morning', but he did not feel happy about it.

"A lady is a lady, I always say. And you are looking very pretty today, Miss. Do you mind if I'm forward enough to say I like your new hairstyle and the glasses are fab? I always knew there was a real beauty under there just waiting to get out. I don't agree with what they've been doing to you one jot and it makes my blood boil. But it takes real class to take it on the chin like you've done. Us mere mortals down here think the world of you, only we daren't show it for fear of our positions."

"Thank you, Joe. It will take more than a few bad apples to spoil my pie."

To which Joe suddenly burst out laughing, shaking so that the table wobbled, then hastily losing himself under it when Deidre came down the stairs, Joe mumbling something about lost post for the first floor suite.

"There you are, Geraldine. What time do you call this?"

"Its 8.47, Miss Harrington," Gerry said, holding her watch up in front of her face and seeing Joe from under the table make a rude gesture towards Deidre. Gerry reflected that Deidre had never been in before 9am before the changes.

"Before you wile away what's left of the morning," Deidre replied from the first half landing, "come and see me in my office. I have an assignment for you." She swept back up the stairs so that Joe could climb out of his hiding place, still chuckling away.

Gerry quickly hung up her coat and made her way to Deidre's office. She knocked on Deidre's secretary's door and explained to Deidre's office mother that Miss Harrington had summoned her a few minutes ago.

"I'll see if she is available. Wait here. Yes, she'll see you in twenty minutes. No, she said to wait here, Geraldine, she doesn't want you wandering off and forgetting about your appointment." The stress on the 'she' made Gerry take notice; something was not quite right. "Here, straighten your dress a bit while you are waiting. You want to make a good impression, don't you?" It was not said unkindly and Gerry hastened to do as bid. She looked down at her new dress but could not see anything wrong with it. Deidre's secretary, seeing the confusion on Gerry's face, rose and came across to her. "It's the collar, dear," she explained. "These type of collars often ride up. You need to iron them in the morning before you get dressed. My niece had one just like this. I always had to straighten it for her. Here, let me."

"Thanks, Janet."

In reply Janet smiled, took Gerry's hand and squeezed it. "You know I said you needed to come down a peg or two but I didn't mean for you to be treated the way she treats you."

"But I thought you were in it together."

"Far from it. I can't stand her. But you were 'Miss Hoity Toity' yourself, in case you have forgotten."

"Yeah, I was," Gerry replied without thinking. "But I was taken down a whole bunch of pegs!" They laughed quietly, not wanting to be heard from Deidre's office, another communion hidden behind fear of Deidre and her newfound power.

Then Janet added, "You know you're quite a looker when you get out of those bloody awful overpriced suits!" This caused Gerry to laugh again. "What did I say?" Janet asked.

"Nothing really, it's just that you are the third person who has said that today and it's barely 9am."

"The truth will out," replied Janet, then quickly going back to her desk to answer the phone from Deidre.

Gerry has to wait over half an hour in Janet's office, but Janet pulled up a chair for her and they chatted together, both keeping an eye out for Deidre. Finally, Gerry was summoned in, only to find Cynthia, Simon and Kirsty already there, taking the only readily available chairs. Gerry was not invited to sit anyway.

"What's with the new hairstyle, Geraldine?"

"Kirsty showed me on Friday after work. She taught me a few things about office procedure and then showed me how to do it. I thought it was real sort of nice and just wanted to try it out today. I was practising over the weekend because I wanted to do it right today." Every time she volunteered subservience, she saw it as a risk. Had she gone over the top? Luckily, Deidre and Cynthia both seemed drunk on the humiliation they had meted out, senses blind to the deception she was engaging in.

"Do you like working under Kirsten?" This took Gerry slightly by surprise; she had not seen herself in that role. She answered, "Yes, she is a great role model and I'm learning a lot already," and was rewarded by a big, self-conscious smile from the girl she had befriended on Friday.

"Good, because you are going to do a lot more of it from now on."

Deidre's plan took Gerry totally by surprise. She clearly was not the least flustered by the weekend events, more like she relished the fight.

"Geraldine, I want you to take part in a delegation to the

main parade next week in Parliament Square in support of President Verdun. This is a delegation of the Society and should be taken very seriously. You will meet up with similar delegations from the Civil Service and other interested bodies and then march, en bloc, to Buckingham Palace, where the Queen will be waiting to meet him and his wife."

"Thank you, Miss Harrington."

"Kirsten has been tasked with organising it, reporting to Miss Crutcher, who has overall responsibility. You will work under Kirsten and do all her fetching and carrying and running around. There is a lot to organise in a short period of time. Do you understand?"

"Yes, Miss Harrington. Thank you for the opportunity. I appreciate the chance to do something useful." Gerry, heart beating wildly, saw a different opportunity to everyone else.

"Off you trot then and don't let the side down again, Geraldine."

"I'll try my hardest, Miss Harrington. Thank you."

Outside, Kirsty took Gerry's hand and whispered, "I don't have the first idea what to do. But I am so glad we are doing it together. Gerry, you are so beautiful today. That dress is gorgeous; it is like a new you. Did you really want to copy my hair?"

"Yes, of course I did. You have been a great inspiration to me, Kirsty. And don't worry about the delegation, I've organised a heap of such things before. I'll guide you for sure. We'll be a team! Now, what about taking a quick look at the draft newsletter first, just to set the scene."

Second Edition

On Thursday afternoon, Simon Martin got Gerry's attention. "I know what you are up to."

"What?"

"Come to my office at 6pm when it's quieter."

"I can't. I have so much to do this evening." It was the day before the second edition was due to go out and she was behind with two articles and a host of editorial tasks. The deadline for the printer was eight o'clock the following morning.

"Gerry, you are going to have to find time. This is really important and could be to your benefit."

It was closer to seven before Deidre and Cynthia left and Gerry was free to go and see Simon. He closed the door, even though they were the only ones in the office and if anyone came back in the doorbell would be set off automatically. He sat at the tiny round table and offered the other seat to Gerry.

"I've worked it out," he said to start the conversation.

"Worked what out, Simon?"

"The sudden devotion to Kirsty."

Gerry's heart went cold. "I like her," she said. "She's helping me a lot."

"Gerry, come on. She is eighteen years old and this is her first job. You are, say twenty-eight? OK, twenty-nine, and you have worked for eight years, is my guess. There is nothing she can teach you, zero, nada. I've watched you these last few days. You are making all the suggestions and she is lapping up your advice. You're not learning anything from her, that I am certain of."

She did not reply. There was no point. He watched her a moment and then went on, "The next thing I had to work out is why you're doing this. That is what I did not understand. It was Kirsty who put me on the right track, quite inadvertently, I would add. She is devoted to you. For that matter, Gerry, a lot of us think very highly of you."

"Thanks. What did she say?"

"Just that she liked helping you understand how the newsletter went together." He was spot-on.

"So? It has always interested me."

"Gerry, don't insult my intelligence. You are working so closely with Kirsty in order to get access to the drafts of the newsletter. My guess is that you are behind the other publication that made such a splash last Friday and you want to find out what the response from the Society is. Am I correct?"

"I am just a journalist, interested in such things."

"Gerry, let me put it another way. Deidre is one step ahead of you."

"What do you mean?"

"I mean that she anticipated your interest in the newsletter. She has fed you a lot of drivel through Kirsty. She has used Kirsty every bit as much as you."

"You mean the drafts that Kirsty has access to are not the…"

"… right ones, that is correct." He finished her question and answered it as well.

"Good Lord! And to think I thought I was being so clever. All the time I've been fed a pack of lies with Deidre and Cynthia laughing up their sleeves."

"They have certainly enjoyed themselves recently. But that could also be their downfall."

"How?" Could there be some hope after all?

"Well, I am the newsletter manager," Simon replied. "I have access to the real version."

"And?"

"I won't give it to you. I want to be able to look Deidre Harrington in the eye on Monday morning and say that I know nothing about it. However, I am going home now and that will leave you alone in the office. I keep all my logins and passwords in my diary. Usually, I take that home with me but I seem to have mislaid it somewhere. The last time I saw it, it was in the top drawer of my desk, but I seem to be getting so forgetful."

"You're a real gent, Simon."

"And you, Gerry Matthews, are a veritable lady. I'll say no more other than goodnight. Remember you have a lot of the staff on your side now."

"Not then but now?"

"That's right, not then but now you do. Goodnight, Gerry. Don't burn too much midnight oil!"

Gerry burnt all her midnight oil and then some more. She did not sleep that night. She did not even leave the office until 7.30am, just before the doorman came on duty, and with just enough time to get to the printers. She had called Adam early on and he called her back several times. Her excitement increased to new levels as she absorbed the propaganda put together by Deidre and then countered it with a complete eight-page newsletter. She had four appropriate articles from other contributors but had to scrap the rest as unsuitable. This was her chance to strike a real blow for George and for his cause.

"Adam, let's double the production run, two million copies."

"I don't know."

"Read it, Ad! It's a real sizzler. We have to max out on this."

Adam laughed in the back of the taxi and spent the next ten minutes reading the final copy on Gerry's laptop.

"Come on," Gerry called when they arrived at the printers. "We've got to get this to them pronto."

"Three million run, gentlemen," Adam said.

"Blimey, that's the biggest run we've ever done on anything."

"And a 10% bonus if you get all three million done by 4pm today." Then he turned to Gerry and said, "Now, breakfast for you and me and then bed for you while I keep up with progress on the print run." Gerry did not argue, but when Adam dropped her back at her flat after a lavish breakfast in the embassy she could not sleep. She paced the floor, remembered to call in sick to the office, then called the printers to check on progress.

***

The printers earned their bonus with seconds to spare. Three million copies hit the streets at 4.30pm, with a distribution effort that dwarfed the previous week. There were bundles at every station entrance. One enterprising person sold them outside the House of Commons, until led away by police to cheers from the crowd that had formed. Meanwhile, every city in Britain was receiving copies with the first bundles from the printing press going to the hard-to-reach fringes in the north and in Scotland, across in Belfast, and to the extreme South West.

Brownie's shift finished at 7pm, by which time over one million copies of the newsletter were in the public's hands. Her shift had been a twelve-hour one and she was exhausted. She unlatched her belt and flopped on the sofa just as the phone rang.

"It's for you, Brownie," Gerry handed her the phone. Minutes later, Brownie was buckling up her belt to go back onto the beat.

"I'll see you when I see you."

"Take care, Brownie." Gerry found it so hard to think of this cheeky, lively woman plotting to do harm to her and Adam; Adam who she was engaged to. It seemed like a bad dream. Adam had been so reassuring when Gerry spoke to him about it and all her instincts told her that Brownie was genuine. She jumped up from her armchair. "Just a second, Brownie. They can wait a few minutes for you." She ran to the kitchen and made a salmon sandwich and then opened a bottle of beer that Brownie had bought. "You have to eat. Take five and get your energy back."

"Thanks, Gerry, I could eat a bleeding horse right now."

"You look like death. Sit down and eat slowly. You won't make it through the night at this rate." Gerry went to sit at the small kitchen table opposite where Brownie had slumped down, then thought better of it. Instead, she stood behind Brownie, took off her cap and started to massage her neck and upper back, marvelling at her beautiful, smooth midnight skin, but feeling the tension in her muscles.

"You're a gem, Gerry." Brownie closed her eyes, talking with her mouth half-full of salmon and bread. She sat quite still while Gerry worked some life back into her, Gerry surprising herself at how satisfying it was to feel the tension in another evaporate through pressure and manipulation.

"Drink your beer."

Brownie was thirty minutes late for her impromptu extra shift but she was alive again and ready for business.

After Brownie left, Gerry sat alone for a couple of hours. It was strange, she reflected, how the world was being turned upside down yet she, as one of the perpetrators, existed in isolation and in perfect calm. The massage on Brownie had been an instinctive desire to help someone she cared about and could not believe was against her, yet it had somehow raised Gerry to a new understanding. Giving was receiving. The world really was turning upside down, the veneer peeling away.

It was almost eleven o'clock when the doorbell rang. Gerry had drifted off to sleep over the last few minutes but was suddenly wide-awake.

"It's George," came the voice on the crackling intercom. "I've only got a few minutes." They embraced in the hallway and then George asked her where the bedroom was.

"I had to come when I read the newsletter. It was fantastic. Francine is outside, waiting to drive me back. I can't risk more than a few minutes. I just had to see you again before the day, before Tuesday. Gerry, I love you."

"I bloody love you too, George!"

Afterwards they had little time for talk.

"Will it really be over on Tuesday?" Gerry asked.

"Yes, it will. I can't tell you what is going to happen but the plan is a good one, dare I say it is the best, as it was my plan originally!"

"So what will we do when you are Prime Minister and busy running the country?"

In reply he kissed her again and finished getting dressed. Only when they were outside, walking together to Francine's car, did he say, "Firstly, I am yours. Everything I do is for you and to be with you and to share with you. Nothing else matters, Gerry, I just want to share my life with you. Will you marry me, Gerry Matthews?"

"Yes, George Unwin-Smith, I will marry you. Yes, yes, yes."

Procession and Possession

George had been waiting all night, waiting with nothing to do. Every plan was made, every contingency catered for. Perhaps a cooler leader would have retired to bed and slept soundly, or partied to the small hours, slept briefly before waking as fresh as a new-born. But George was not cool, had never been cool. He sat, mostly alone, sometimes with others, going over and over in his mind the plan. Such that when Mandy came to him at 4am to summon him to breakfast, he was still sitting in the armchair, his mind working furiously. He looked as pale as death.

"It will be OK," she said, squeezing his hand. "It won't be so bad once we get moving."

"It's the responsibility," he replied in a monotone.

After breakfast they changed, checked themselves thoroughly, and lined up beside the vehicles they were using that day. They were just outside Gravesend, in a manor house owned by a member of the movement. They could hear the traffic on the A2 when the wind blew from the north. Large lorries were bringing fruit, vegetables and dairy products in vast quantities from the continent. But today there was no wind. There was no movement in the early morning. No sun, no sound, no movement; just heavy fog dampening sight and sound.

"Are we all ready?" George asked Francine L'Amour, who

would be in the next vehicle. She looked so different dressed in EurMilPo overalls, with a cap on her long, straight auburn hair tied in a tight bun.

They recognised the risk of so many senior members of the movement in just a few armoured trucks. It was a risk they had discussed in-depth and decided there was no way around it. They had to have maximum presence for this to work.

"Yes, George, all is ready. Have you got your helmet?" Damn, how could he have forgotten such an elementary thing?

"It's OK," Bertie said. "I was looking after it for him." He walked out of the darkness into the torchlight, looking so different dressed as a police escort, with his own helmet covering his curly hair. He held the helmet up for George, who muttered his thanks, acknowledging the white lie Bertie had indulged in.

Then Major Bellew appeared from the same darkness. He was superbly dressed as a tank commander; his trade, after all. Over the next twenty minutes each member was checked by the major or by Musgrove to ensure correct attire, weapons, rank badges. Everything had to look genuine. Nothing should give them away.

At 5.40am nothing had changed in the world around them as they loaded up in their stolen vehicles and moved off, down the manor drive, and swung into the road. They headed north to the A2 and then turned east and south, heading for their destination. A2, M2, A2 and then south to Aylsham. There they stopped at a little before 8am. They had selected a disused factory on the industrial estate. Now the wait began again.

It was a cold day, the coldest since February. But it was also a day of damp fog that hung like old-fashioned skirts, heavy and layered. It was the perfect day for their plans, prayed for and now happening. Even when the sun's rays broke through the fog they had a brittle appearance, as if you could lean out of your armoured vehicle and snap the beams in two with just the right pressure in just the right place. Those rays were not substantial and could not be relied upon but they promised a clear, hard day when the fog lifted. Again, just what was needed.

Others rolled in to create a small force of two-dozen armoured vehicles and the same number of motorcycles. A total of 264 men and women. This was the task force.

George formally surrendered command to Bellew, who inspected each vehicle and person again. Then at 9.50am the first detachment of four armoured vehicles and four motorcycles left on Bellew's command, heading back up the London road. Four more detachments left at hourly intervals, Bellew taking the fourth one, until just one detachment was left. This was the vital one, containing George, Musgrove and Bertie.

At 2.20, after a lunch of packed sandwiches and beer prepared the night before, the four motorcycles left for their role as scouts. They returned several times and once Musgrove went in the sidecar as far as the outskirts of Dover. Each time they reported the entourage a little closer to Point X. Finally, at 3.28, the order was given and the big engines started up. They moved back to the edge of the road and waited, engines idling. There was tension like a longbow pulled back to the point of release. Nobody spoke. Then they heard the approaching engines, the noise growing, distorted and bent in the fog so that they soon seemed like wild animals screaming in the dark. Now was the point of commitment. George felt his limbs and organs go stone-cold, then his head flushed and burned. His was the main act today. He had to perform just like in the rehearsals. He had to get it right. But first Charles Musgrove had to do his bit. They shared grim, nervous smiles, both thinking how short their acquaintance was yet how well they knew each other: the greater the urgency, the more the essence of a character was evident. There was no time for deceit when fighting in a bitter civil war. Weaknesses and strengths were worn on their sleeves and how practical for everyone to know everyone's qualities so well and so easily.

Even though the noise was growing, the vehicles seemed distant, mirage-like in the fog, never quite getting to them and threatening to fade back into the mist. Finally, Musgrove gave the command and his vehicle moved forward into the road. The approaching escorts were forced to stop.

Musgrove talked in French for seven minutes and fourteen seconds, timed by George on his watch. George did not speak French but they had rehearsed it in English so many times he knew exactly what they were saying. Charles was describing the increased state of unrest in the country and how they had been sent as an extra armed detachment to ensure safety and security. George lost the French at one point but guessed that Charles was referring to Gerry's newsletter when he heard the word 'journal' said several times in a tone of disgust. He felt a wave of pride that his American girlfriend was playing such a significant part.

Musgrove waved the signal to the other three armoured vehicles and they all moved off, somewhat jostling for space around the president's car. Then Musgrove's vehicle sped up ahead of the others and turned across the road.

"This won't do," he said in French. "We need order. Because we know the road, we will go at the front and the back." It was agreed after a few minutes of discussion and the convoy moved off again, with the rebels' powerful vehicles firmly enveloping the original convoy.

The fog was still heavy but thinning when the next detachment joined, with a military police captain in the lead vehicle, explaining that they had been sent for extra security as the situation was deteriorating. The next detachment, headed by Bellew, spoke of trouble in northern Kent that they had to traverse in order to get to London. The fourth and fifth joined without any explanation or protest. It seemed that the British were panicking and sending all their resources out to protect the president.

The last detachment was special. The vehicles were bigger and the armament was heavier. Their leader was a bad-tempered Welsh man with cropped orange hair and hands so large that the stock of his automatic weapon looked like a toy gun. For added effect, they could all hear gunfire in the distance.

"That's Gravesend," the Welsh captain said. "Bloody hell in there." He insisted that because he had the better armament he go closest to the president's car. The fog was quite gone now and the sea of clearly visible vehicles around him made Verdun think of a regatta. He wondered where in this melee his captain of security was. If Verdun had been informed that he was trussed up with his lieutenants in the back of a lorry heading to Dover, he would not have felt so secure, but appearances can be deceiving. That was certainly George's intention when he had first thought of this idea and presented it to the others for consideration. They had worked on it endlessly since then, perfecting every detail to ensure success.

So, as they passed Gravesend and entered the outer suburbs of London, Verdun still felt secure and safe, surrounded by loyal members of EurPo and EurMilPo. He daydreamed about his visit to Buckingham Palace and how the aged Queen would feel obliged to be polite to him, feigning interest in his observations, secretly terrified of what further changes he would bring upon her greatly reduced kingdom.

"Fear is a great weapon," he said to his wife.

"And you are an excellent wielder of that particular weapon," she replied with some respect but a strain of disgust also.

"Look at the crowds cheering," he said in reply. It is strange how a man can so misread the situation as to see approval when condemnation and derision are the order of the day. There were a few cheering but most people along the side of the road did not hesitate to speak their mind.

One of those, as they got closer into Central London, was Gerry. Decked out like the dozen other Society workers in a light blue suit with a neat white USE sash that had 'Verdun' printed in gold on back and front, she was seen at first by Verdun as another supporter. But then into a split-second lull in the multitude of noise, she stepped forward into the road, tore off her sash, and stamped it into a puddle. Her clear mid-western accent rang out.

"Damn the President, damn Verdun!" That was the extent of the speech, for Cynthia Crutcher rose to the challenge. Jumping quickly out into the road, she put her weight into a rugby tackle that downed Gerry spectacularly. Then, rising first, Cynthia stamped her winter boot down on Gerry four times, then a fifth, breaking her right arm and striking blood on her face and head. Then others in their party had Cynthia in an iron grip and two policemen took her away. Gerry lay in the puddle where she had been downed, her normally clipped-back hair lying like compasses points in all directions, her quiet sobbing evidencing both that she had been hurt but also not severely.

If George had seen her he would, without doubt, have jumped down from his vehicle and come to her assistance. Someone would have recognised him and, for sure, cried out his name. Then his cover would be blown. An enterprising police officer on the wrong side might have caught him and taken him away, where he could look forward to the special re-education they had planned for him, the same that Andy was enduring right then. But history turns on such tiny things and this was one of them. George's vehicle was just ahead of Gerry when she stepped out into the crowd. He did not hear her damn the president and he did not see the brutal attack. Thus the future was saved from the present by a click or two on a stopwatch.

George's original plan culminated at Parliament Square. He had often envisaged the final scene taking place just where he had waited all night with Mark and Mandy and the others. But Bertie had insisted it take place outside Buckingham Palace.

"It is a constitutional matter, George," he had explained. "And many more people will be able to see it outside the palace gates." And the others had agreed and George was outvoted.

The lead vehicles turned around in two semi-circles, peeling off as if foot soldiers on parade. Then George's vehicle came up and stopped. The Queen, Prince Charles and others were on the balcony. George stood up and bowed. The crowd hushed, suddenly sensing that history was happening and they were its witnesses. Then George's car turned at an angle and stopped. It could still be said to be facing the Queen but it was also addressing the crowd around him. Verdun's Peugeot had to stop, as there was nowhere else for it to go. Verdun waited for the door to open. He imagined the rest of the journey would be on foot. He suspected nothing, although his wife seemed anxious.

George was handed a microphone and stood on the bonnet of his vehicle. This was his moment. This was the climax of all his efforts, all he had gone through with the others. He took a deep breath. He had spoken many times in public but never quite like this.

"Your Majesty, your Royal Highnesses, Mr President, Lords, Ladies and Gentlemen." The quiet was like that of a church, everything from outside deadened within. So the police formed the walls, the crowd the congregation, and the palace balcony the altar. George was the archbishop, but dressed incongruously in police fatigues. "My name is George Unwin-Smith." A cry went up that could have been 'Amen'. "I was elected a Member of Parliament in the recent elections but, along with many others, have not been permitted to take my place." These opening lines were why he had wanted it to be in Parliament Square with the Houses of Parliament as the backdrop rather than the Palace. But he accepted that the others had voted for this alteration and had adapted his speech accordingly. "I was denied my chance to serve you, the people, the free people of this great country, by a corrupt authority that I and an overwhelming majority of the Commons were elected to rid ourselves of. We stood up together through much danger and we stand together now today. We will remain standing together until we have righted the many wrongs this country has suffered and undone the many things done by other people to this country." Another huge 'amen' from the crowd. But George did not want to go on too long. He was coming to his point.

"Mr President, you had planned to stay a little over twenty-four hours in our country. You may still be able to go home at the appointed time. But you will not go home until we have received guarantees from you and every nation of the USE that we are a free people able to rule and govern ourselves. Mr President, I hope you will consider yourself a guest of the free people of Great Britain and Northern Ireland for as long as it takes. You are an honoured guest and Her Majesty confirmed to me yesterday that you are most welcome in her home for as long as it takes. Now, with no more delay, I, on behalf of the British people, welcome you as a foreign dignitary and would like to escort you into the palace." It was the end of the speech, except for one final sentence.

Turning back to the crowd, George waited for a hush and then said, "Remember always that you are a free people and a free people you will remain."

Met with a resounding 'amen' that burst through the clouds and raised the roof of the very sky above them. Then one elderly gentleman started singing *God Save the Queen* and it spread like a strong breeze across a wheat field. After that they sang *Jerusalem*.

***

Hilda Rheinalt only heard the end of the speech on a hastily brought-in television set in her Berlin apartment. "*Nein.*" Was the only word to leave her lips. "*Nein, nein, nein.*" It could not be.

***

It was late at night, long after the state dinner, that George heard of Gerry, quite by accident. He rushed immediately to St Thomas' where she lay asleep, her beautiful face bruised and cut, her hair cropped on one side to facilitate the large white bandage and sticking plaster applied to her bare scalp. Her arm was already in a cast. He sat there until she woke early in the morning.

"I love you."

"I love you, too."

"Even like this?"

"Even more like this."

"Sir, could you spare a minute?" It was a flustered civil servant, probably hauled out of his bed to help handle the chaos that was around them. "It is just that President Bruges is on the phone for you, Sir."

"Bertie will handle it," George said, turning back to Gerry. But Gerry told him to take the call so he did.

"George, this is Edouard here. I saw your magnificent speech earlier, such panache, such style."

"Will you go along with our demands?"

"We will of course, my dear George. I... how do you say it? I admire your courage and conviction." The man clearly knew when to acquiesce.

"Thank you. Will you please announce this to your sister nations so that they can follow the lead your great country is taking? Thank you. Now I really must get back to my important meeting. Goodbye and thank you, Edouard."

Gerry made progress and was allowed back to her flat two days later. George insisted on taking her back himself, despite the voices everywhere waiting to be heard by him. But he could not stay long so it was Brownie who took on the role of carer. "I got assigned to protection duties and George put a word in for me so I got allocated to you," she said. "But you will need to lend me a few clothes."

"I'd be delighted to, Brownie." Gerry's good left hand gripped her shoulder as Brownie leant over her to fiddle with the bed covers. "I don't think I need protection but if so I could not ask for a better protector!"

Later, Gerry got up for a while and they sat together in the sitting room for half an hour. Gerry wanted to talk about the kidnapping plans. Presumably she could now be open about it? But she did not know how to start the conversation.

Finally, Brownie said it for her. "Gerry, you want to know about the conversation you overheard with my sergeant and me, don't you?"

Gerry just smiled and nodded her head. Sometimes talking was not necessary.

"You thought I meant you and Adam, didn't you?"

"Yes, I did. Can you blame me? There were so many different secrets."

"Gerry, you stupid thing, I don't blame you one jot. Let me tell you a little more to make it a bit clearer, although there are some things I will not be able to tell you."

"You sound like a female James Bond!" Gerry joked.

"Something like that," Brownie replied seriously. "How old do you think I am?"

"Twenty-four, maybe twenty-five?"

"I'm thirty-two, Gerry, so either just lucky or baby-faced, not sure which one. The point is that for the last eight years I have been an undercover agent infiltrating the police as a slightly dozy, not-going-anywhere, constable. That is quite a good assessment of who I was back in '16, I suppose. But something infuriated me about events that year and I went to a few meetings here and there. The next thing I knew I was approached by Mr Musgrove. He was just back from a posting to Brussels and had been promoted to Chief Inspector. At first I thought he was trying to date me!" She stood up, crossed over the room and took off her heavy police belt so that she could sit on the sofa next to Gerry, with her feet curled up at her side. "I am actually now a major in our command structure. I've worked very closely with Mr Musgrove, who is my CO. My job has been to infiltrate and undermine the police force in preparation for the great day."

"So you have spent eight years patiently working for the liberty of your country? That's longer than I've worked for the Society. It rather puts me in my place!"

"Not at all! I've not had my face stamped on by some crazy lunatic."

"I'm not going to press charges, Brownie. I guess it's enough for me that she's lost her job. She was fuelled by, like a brainwashing."

"That's what they tried to do with me on my little 'holiday'! I had to pretend it was successful in order to get back into London, where I could be useful. Then they wanted me to shadow you to get to your contacts. What they would have given for Mr Musgrove or Mr Unwin-Smith! I had to deceive them and pretend I was working for them. They were delighted when you offered for me to move into the flat. I had to pretend that their 're-education' had really worked!"

"And I thought they had succeeded, especially when I overhead you talking on the radio. It was the Verduns you were talking about, right, and your sergeant must have been in the underground movement too?" Brownie nodded. They fell silent for a moment, both thinking back over the last few days.

Then Gerry simply said: "No harm done and it was all in a good cause." She reached up and gave Brownie a short kiss on the forehead but banged her broken arm in the process. "Oh dang it!"

"That's the nearest to a swear word I am ever going to get from you!" said Brownie with another of her enormous smiles.

***

Verdun was feeling a variety of emotions. His wife tried to list them in order of size. First was mortification at his capture and at becoming a token in the resulting exchange. Next was anger, quickly followed by fear. This was the emotion he used to such good advantage on others, now it was turned back on him. Lower down the scale was regret at not building bridges with these people, such that he had now become a mere pawn in the game. Then there was determination, chiefly the determination not to be a victim any longer than was necessary. Finally, at the bottom of the list, was just a modicum of guilt. But not guilt born of remorse, rather the type that apologises when caught, the 'I'm so sorry' type.

Bertie had set him up with a small office in the palace where they were staying. Chief amongst the office arrangements were three hotline phones pre-programmed to dial the USE leaders but nobody else. There was also a screen giving constant up-to-date news so that Verdun could witness the extent of his humiliation, stoking the bonfire of emotions and feeding it moment by moment. Then there was the old-fashioned word processor so that the secretary transferred for the duration of Verdun's stay could type his minutes and take the calls. There was no internet, nothing that could not be controlled. Major Bellew had advised that a bodyguard be set up to ensure Verdun's protection and his security. Surprisingly, Andy volunteered to front it.

"You didn't go through what I went through," he argued. "The brainwashing, the indoctrination was unbearable. You need to let me do this to put my own mind back in order."

"But you are our treasurer, our statistics man," George said.

"So what?" Andy replied. "You were our intellectual vision but you became a man of action and had your moment. I want my turn. I don't want to have to tell my grandchildren that I added up the numbers. I want to play a meaningful part." So George had appointed him and directed him to select a team to work around the clock, allocating them the nearby offices to be hastily converted to bunk rooms.

The memos to and from Verdun flowed from dawn well into the night, such that the secretary became one of a trio on shift duty. The memos to the USE national leaders cajoled, persuaded, ordered and threatened them in rough cycles as his hopes of freedom rose and fell each day.

"Good morning, Mr President," Bertie said on entering his office on the Friday morning. "I hope you are making progress." Andy and two others in near-identical black suits lounged by the door, taking turns to rise up and walk around the room every few minutes.

"Some," he muttered in reply, "some." He needed all thirty-two national leaders to sign a special amendment to the treaty of Berlin and thirty-one of those thirty-two leaders wanted something in return. And when they sometimes learned what another country had gained, they would up their demands, sometimes doubling or trebling them. Thus Portugal got a new motorway, while Poland early on won a dispensation from the ban on state aid so as to help its troubled steel industry. France got the biggest concessions. Chief amongst them was a new airport outside Paris but close behind, ranked by economic journalists as a real coup, was an agreement that Brie could only be manufactured in France, its original homeland.

Thus, thirty-one leaders fought for gain, many also relishing the precarious state Verdun found himself in, nicely put by *The Sun* in its headline on Wednesday. Next to a grotesque cartoon of the man ran the words 'President or prisoner?'

The thirty-second national leader was Hilda Rheinalt and she threatened all the hard-won gains of the other thirty-one because the only word she had to say on the subject was *'Nein'*.

"Mr President, it does seem like you will be with us for quite some time to come," Bertie said on hearing the latest from Germany. "Of course, it makes no difference to our independence, it would just be nice to be friends with our continental neighbours."

"I don't think, Monsieur Graves, that she will ever agree."

"Then make yourself comfortable. Perhaps we should replace the word processor with a billiard table or a chess set? What do you and your wife prefer in this regard?"

"I prefer my liberty, Monsieur Graves."

"Rich comment from someone who has enslaved whole nations." Bertie did not reflect that he had been part of the same establishment until very recently.

***

Back in Number 10, George was having considerable difficulties with his own emotions. He shared little of those held by the President of the United States of Europe; a little anger, and, of course, regret over Mark, or rather that it had been Mark and not him. But by far the most dominant emotion was depression. He had, after all, just heard of his father's death in the villa outside Zurich.

Sir Terrence and Jay Stuttermann had flown to London on

Wednesday afternoon, as soon as they had confirmation of the extraordinary events culminating in the seizure of Verdun. They had been briefed by Paul, himself briefed by George, to expect something spectacular on 5th November but the scale of the achievement had left them speechless.

Except they did need to speak as they needed to inform George of the death of his professor father, his only living relative and the man he had looked up to throughout his thirty-two years in this world. They met in the flat at Number 10, Terry Rose having quickly moved out and gone to ground somewhere in his native Yorkshire, refusing all interviews and doing endless crosswords and jigsaw puzzles, half expecting the police to knock on his door.

George had known immediately that all was not right because his father was not with them. But hope is the hardest emotion to kill and thank goodness that is the case, for without hope there is nothing. Hope and love march by our sides as we make our mistakes and wander off-course. But pretty soon George only had love to console him, as Sir Terrence told him of the last moments of Edward's life and the message that he carried of enduring love for his son. This was a message that crossed from the past to the present and it was these words that George could hardly bear to hear because it was the final death of hope.

He would never see his father again. He would never share his guidance; never sit with him on the garden bench, warming his hands on a mug of coffee. He would never share his research and deeper thoughts. His father would never again make bluff jokes or rise to stoke the fire. Now he would be a memory, almost like an institution, or a dry set of facts on the internet, or on a memorial stone at his Oxford College.

For a while he would be a memory, while others still had known him, but then, as time wore on, he would just be a fact. He had once lived and now was dead. His grains were in the lower half of the hourglass and new grains were piling steadily on top.

Sir Terrence and Jay decided not to tell George of the late

changes to the will. There was plenty of time in the days ahead: one stage at a time.

Sir Terrence, ever practical but with an extraordinary sense for other people's feelings, took charge of the arrangements. The body would be flown back on Thursday. The funeral would be on Saturday in Oxford. Edward would be buried next to his wife, George's mother, who had waited over thirty years for the reunion. Paul would accompany the body and would stay on at the family home, if George so chose it, to take care of everything until George had decided what to do.

George sat alone all that night in the flat at Number 10. He had not wanted company and had refused their offer to stay. He knew there was a polite clamour of people waiting for decisions but, although occupying Number 10, he did not feel like a prime minister, more like a squatter who had spied a way in through an ill-fitting window. Nothing seemed right anymore. Before, everything had been simple. He had to win in the struggle and that was all that mattered. They had often speculated on first steps in government and it had always been assumed since Mark's death that George was the leader. But that had been when his father was alive.

He wished he could call Gerry but it was 4.20am. Finally, he decided to text her; that way she would not be disturbed and could answer as soon as she woke up. His text was short:

have bad news; want to talk when you can.

The reply came straight back. At first George thought it must be some automatic reply saying Gerry Matthews was not available and would answer as soon as she could. But it really was a reply from her, equally short:

know the bad news, can you come now?

"I haven't slept since Sir Terrence and Professor Stuttermann came around to see me earlier," she explained when the car dropped George outside her Kensington flat. "I wanted to call

371

you but you did not give me the new number and Downing Street would not put my call through."

"I asked not to be disturbed."

"Come here," said Gerry tenderly, seeing the anguish like an epitaph chiselled on his face. He came to sit on her bedside and then threw himself into the folds of her body and wept for a long time. She stroked his light brown hair, much lighter than hers, and wondered what colour hair their children would have. "The grains of sand keep flowing," she said, but his weeping was too much to hear her.

***

George was a cardboard cut-out throughout the next few days. It looked like George, it sounded like George, and it moved like George, albeit without the intellectual energy and clarity of thought everyone had come to expect. But there the resemblance ended. There was nothing to the cardboard figure: no beating heart, no churning of emotions, no clicking of intellect. He responded when spoken to. He attended the funeral, wonderfully organised by Sir Terrence and Paul. He listened to the tributes from Jay and two other colleagues but did not really hear them. There was a wall between him and the world around him. Sometimes he felt that he was on the other side of the Heaven and Earth divide and was actually with his father, but that was nonsense for no father spoke to him, no father chided him and urged him to attend to the problems of the day.

And there were many problems.

He could not find anyone suitable to take over from Fernby and run the Civil Service, in great need of reform. He did not know what to do to resolve the Verdun situation, nor who to appoint to the multitude of positions from Cabinet downwards that were now vacant. His days were filled reining back from the daydreaming that dominated: the harking back to the resistance, when everything had been dangerous but simple and there had been everything to live for. But had he not spent

372

much of the resistance period harking back to the past also? Was he just a fake? Every time he tried to make a decision now, he just met a hundred conflicting consequences. What was the point?

It was Dennis who stepped forward into the vacuum. His first visit to George on Friday morning had left him very concerned. He came back that afternoon and quietly resolved a few urgent problems. He took the CVs of the contenders to replace Fernby home with him that night and selected two candidates, who he met after the funeral on Saturday, explaining to them that the PM was indisposed. George was delighted when on Sunday morning he was presented with the chosen person, a middle-aged tough lady called Brenda Howard, who reminded Dennis a little of Mrs Thatcher. She was head of the Foreign Office and only made one stipulation on her promotion, that being that her deputy at the Foreign Office, Maria Wilberforce, take her place.

"We were great friends at university," George commented about Maria. "She is as sharp as they come."

"We will need all the sharpest minds over the next few years."

It was only later that George reflected on Dennis's use of the plural pronoun. It set George thinking.

Sunday also saw Dennis making recommendations for the final ministerial places and George signed without comment. Dennis attended the first cabinet meeting at Bertie's insistence, as an observer. Strangely to everyone except George, Francine L'Amour was absent. She had said she was not interested in government and had achieved her life's aim with independence. She was going back to Bordeaux to write her memoirs and make her marriage right.

But it was a mixed bag around the table. George was nominally in charge but Bertie ran the proceedings while Dennis seemed to provide the real leadership. The new cabinet had a smattering of Spiders, seeming out of place in the establishment. Mandy surprised everyone by turning up in a pin-striped suit with a generous skirt that came down below her knees, a silk neck scarf and much shorter hair cut in a bob. "Got to look the part!" she said, secretly anxious that Dennis would take her place at Environment and leave her with some junior role.

"We are so lucky to have you, Mandy," said Dennis, shaking her hand warmly. It was as if he had read her mind. George noted again the 'we'. Mandy saw how genuine Dennis was and was reassured. She would probably let her hair grow out but would keep the new clothes for the time being.

"The main problem we face," Bertie started, sensing that George was not going to lead off, "is Chancellor Rheinalt refusing to agree to the terms of the release of President Verdun. The longer we keep him, the more we look like common kidnappers. The plan was for this to be a quick thing."

"But if we release him now we run the risk of being seen to be capitulating."

"Exactly. And we do not have long to sort this out. I think we should meet again on Friday and be ready to thrash out a solution. I don't think waiting to Friday will cause a major problem, but we must be prepared to work out a solution then so everybody please concentrate on this key aspect. Are we agreed, then?" That was Dennis. George had not said a word, nor did he rise when the others left, just stayed sitting at the cabinet table, staring at a frozen spider's web outside the window. It was Mandy who came back for him, no words, just a communion of shared loss. She sat next to him and took his hand and held it for a long while until the shadows became longer as the short day retreated in the face of the cold, starry blackness that divides and defines our days.

Mind over Matter

"You're getting restless, aren't you?"

"No, I want to be with you. I'm fine," Brownie replied.

"I don't doubt it, Brownie, but I can see it with my own eyes. You've been cooped up with me for a week now and you need to be part of the action. You've lived and breathed the hope of freedom for too long to be sitting quietly with me while so much is going on out there." When Brownie did not reply, Gerry added, "Admit it now!"

"OK, I admit I would prefer to be out there with the action but I have been a police officer for fourteen years now. Police officers obey orders. I would not dream of leaving you."

"So you're sticking with me to obey orders?" Gerry teased and got a cushion blow across her head, striking her damaged face so that she flinched and put her hand up.

"My God, Gerry, I didn't mean to hurt you!" Brownie dropped the cushion and scrambled onto the sofa. "Are you OK?" But Gerry was laughing and Brownie could not help but respond the same way.

"Well, you might be obeying orders but frankly I am feeling cooped up myself and I don't have anyone to obey, unless, of course, I still have to defer to Miss Harrington." Gerry smiled, then added sadly, "I haven't seen George for several days."

"Nor me Adam," Brownie replied, then more slowly as the reasoning worked through her mind, wild ideas being proceduralised in order to validate them, "I am ordered to protect you. I am not ordered to keep you a prisoner in your flat. I could still be protecting you if we went out and saw

George and Adam, maybe lunch together?"

"Call him now," Gerry replied. "Then I'll phone George."

But best-laid plans do not always work out. Adam's office was not helpful. He was out of the country. She called his mobile but just got voicemail.

"When will he be back?" Brownie called his personal secretary.

'We are not at liberty to say."

"This is his fiancée, Brownie Browning."

"I'm sorry, Miss Browning, but I cannot inform you." Then his secretary added more kindly, "I really don't know myself. He was suddenly called away to DC for a briefing yesterday. He went straight from the office to the airport when he got the phone call. I expect if the meeting happens today he will get a flight back arriving early tomorrow morning. I'll tell him to call you as soon as I hear from him."

They were a little luckier with George. He could not make lunch but had a little time for coffee at the Houses of Parliament. Could they be there at 2.30? A car would come for them. Gerry rushed to get changed, Brownie helping her with her arm in the sling before slipping into her own bedroom.

"Why the uniform?" Gerry asked when Brownie emerged as the doorbell rang to announce the car waiting below.

"Because I am on duty, silly!" Brownie replied, checking her radio then briefing her sergeant as they tumbled down the stairs.

"Yes, I know, Sergeant, but Miss Matthews arranged it with the PM. There was not much I could do," she lied, winking at Gerry.

Neither had been to the Houses of Parliament before but their trepidation was unwarranted. They were taken directly to the entrance, where Bertie was waiting to vouch for them. After security, Bertie took them up to a small and virtually deserted dining room. George was not there.

"WPC Browning, perhaps you would like to meet the police

detachment we have here? I could take you," Bertie suggested tactfully.

"Yes, sir, I should report to them." She picked up on the hint and smiled when Bertie held the door open for her.

George entered the dining room three minutes later, a stream of people behind him with files and papers. They embraced, then George pulled back a chair for Gerry and they sat down.

"It is so good to see you," George said.

"Well, I was feeling quite neglected," Gerry joked.

"I'm sorry. Frankly, I am really struggling. I can't stop thinking about my father."

"I know." She leant over and squeezed his hand with her one good hand. "I want to help you as much as I can."

"It's not just that," he said after a moment's reflection. "I am lost in this world. I have a trail of people behind me the whole time asking for decisions and clarification. I just can't cope with it. But how are you, Gerry? I have really missed you over the last few days."

Gerry reported that she was recovering steadily, getting bored, needing and wanting to play a part in the rapid developments, and becoming firm friends with Brownie, who was equally bored and frustrated.

"We could get a role for her. I know. We've just formed the Verdun Protection Team. I'm headed there right now, after this meeting with you. Perhaps she could switch over if you are going to be OK? I'll try and get you more involved in the politics as well. I really need you, Gerry."

"Sort out Brownie now. She needs to be involved. I can wait another day but she can't and I don't need her anymore." So George called an aide over and instructed him to assign Brownie to the Verdun Protection Team.

"With immediate effect?" George asked Gerry.

"With immediate effect." The aide nodded his understanding and backed away.

George had barely sat down and now he had to go. After one aide with an urgent query came to interrupt him and Gerry, the floodgates were opened. They kissed quickly but passionately, a hasty date set for midnight at Downing Street - "I'll send a car around." - and Gerry was on her own again, waiting now for Brownie to return.

"I've got you a new job," Gerry said proudly as Bertie walked them down to the waiting car.

"What is it? Talk about friends in high places!"

"Working in Buckingham Palace," Gerry replied, enjoying the chance to tease her friend, whose face fell.

"You mean Royal Security Duties?" That was a moderately appealing prospect, not ranking as exciting.

"A bit more than that," Gerry said. "It's only protection duty for President Verdun."

"Wow, you're an ace!"

"I'll tell you all about it in the car on the way home." But Gerry did not get the response she had expected when she elaborated in the back of the large Mercedes winding its slow way back through the busy streets in the direction of Kensington. It started out with Brownie delighted at her new role. But then she heard who was in charge, who her new boss was to be.

"Bloody hell," she said, forgetting herself, then recovering. "I'm sorry. It's just that I know Andy Durrington."

"So do I, at least a little. Isn't he the Treasurer for Future Perfect? A great big man? I met him in Oxford on election night."

"I met him more recently. He was on my re-training course. Gerry, they were brainwashing everybody and I did not like the end product in his case. He claimed it had not got to him but it took me a huge effort to withstand it. I think he succumbed."

"But that is all over now. Even if you are right, he can't hurt anyone now."

Brownie did not reply, just sat staring out of the window as the shops and shoppers flashed by. Several minutes passed. Perhaps she was turning over Gerry's point in her mind, seeing the sense of it. But then she leant forward, knocking urgently on the plastic screen. "Driver, stop."

The car came to an instant halt, causing horns trailing away down the queue of cars. "We need to go to Buckingham Palace."

"My orders were to take you back to Kensington." The driver half turned so that he could see Brownie out of his left eye. "I've got to take you there."

"I'm a police officer."

"I can see that but orders are orders."

"Driver, I'll take responsibility for this detour," Gerry spoke up, seeing the urgency in her friend, not understanding it but reacting nevertheless.

"Will you sign a route variation form?"

"Yes."

"Well, let me get to a safe parking place and find the forms. I know I always have a few in the car in case of just such incidents as this. Are you sightseeing, Miss? Is she your bodyguard?" He indicated towards Brownie, but both of them had had enough.

"I am George Unwin-Smith's fiancée and WPC Browning is a member of the Verdun Protection Squad. She has determined that we need to go to Buckingham Palace and that is enough for me. Think, friend, where Verdun is being kept. That's right. Now get us there pronto and you might just save your job."

"Yes, Miss." There was no more delaying, no more hesitation.

"At least we might see George again," Gerry said as the car shot along a bus lane, government lights flashing.

"He's there? Oh my God."

"What? Why?"

"I don't trust Durrington. Whatever he was like when you knew him, I had a bad feeling about him. The retraining..." Her voice ran out, but no more explanation was required.

"Sir, I have a pass for WPC Browning, issued by the PM." The guard was reluctant to let them in, despite Brownie's uniform, but the pass resolved the problem. Or passed on the responsibility. He examined the pass long enough to see the PM's signature and then handed it back.

"We need Verdun's quarters," Brownie said.

"Jones, take these ladies to Verdun's rooms, use the jeep. The car and driver stay here. Stay with them, Jones."

"Yes, Sergeant. Come along, ladies."

Seven minutes later WPC Browning, Private Jones and Gerry Matthews stood outside the main Verdun office. They knocked.

"Wait." But WPC Browning turned the knob and entered.

"I bloody said wait!" Andy Durrington screamed as Brownie entered.

It was then she saw the gun.

It was pointed directly at George's head.

George was tied to an office chair, a tea towel stuffed into his mouth, his eyes bulging with warning. In one corner the duty secretary was huddled under a table, not daring to move. Her vision was fixed on something and led the new entrants to look across the large room to the opposite corner, where two bodies lay slumped on the ground, thick, dark blood seeping out over the carpet like sea wetting sand. Two crumpled black suits; bloodstained white shirts where the knife had entered; drained, lifeless faces like memorials to the dead. The top body still boasted the knife that had ended both guards' lives. One knife, rapid movements, two dead bodies.

There was nobody else in the room except Verdun, shivering by the window, shaken not so much by the cruelty of the attack but by the speed. He had been expecting a rescue, but he had pictured himself driving away sedately in the back of a large car, taking a call from an aide or two. "Yes, I was held captive by the resistance movement but our forces got me out. I will be with you as soon as the plane lands. Call an Emergency Meeting. No, I am alright, a little shaken but I will live."

Instead, he was startled to smell the blood, he could almost feel it dampening down the air, adding to the humidity of that heavy winter's day. All his ambition was gone now. He would have traded everything he had built up for a janitorial role in a quiet forgotten museum with a dedication to something equally obscure, as he wished to be. If only he survived this, he would want nothing more. No more power plays, no more manipulation, no clever manoeuvres.

His prayer was for survival.

Private Jones was not armed.

WPC Browning was not armed.

Andy Durrington had two handguns, one pointed at George bound in the chair, the other at the new entrants.

"Why, Andy?" Gerry asked.

"I know why," Brownie said. "The re-training. It gets most people. They can turn the most fanatical rebel into a rabid supporter, who sees only his or her duty to the state."

"Shut up!" Andy shouted, almost screamed. His job was to get Verdun out of there and safely to the City Airport, where a plane was waiting to get him away: if he killed the rebel leader also, so much the better. He adjusted the aim at George and put pressure on the trigger.

Except something bothered him. It did not seem right to kill George Unwin-Smith, the architect of his superiors' troubles, but somehow not a criminal or a terrorist. He had worked with this man, supported him. From some dim past memory, he pictured his laptop issuing out statistics about George and his party. It was like a chronic attack of déjà vu. He frowned, the lines multiplying on his forehead as he struggled to reason. It was a mistake to hesitate.

For it was then that Private Jones made his move.

And WPC Browning was right behind him.

Jones pushed Gerry down to safety with his left hand and sprung across the room, directly towards Andy, using the leverage from Gerry's body to launch himself.

He got halfway there, past the secretary's desk and out into the open area between her desk and Verdun's, where Andy was standing. Gerry and George watched as his face caved in with the impact of the bullet, then the back of his head blew off and George was smattered with blood and brain. Gerry was untouched as Jones had pushed her under the desk, but as she looked over the top she saw every surface littered with scraps of brain and skin. It was a battlefield on a minute scale. Jones was still standing but he had stopped mid-way across the floor, as if he had slammed into an invisible wall. Then very slowly he slid down that wall into a heap on the floor. Then the sound of the bullet from Andy's gun registered with everyone.

Jones was dead on the floor, but WPC Browning was moving against his left flank. She jumped onto the secretary's desk and launched herself at Andy's left side. The second shot hit her in the arm but momentum meant she continued coming. She hit Andy before he could fire again and they rolled on the open floor between the desks, merging with Jones and then rolling away again. No assistance from Verdun for Andy.

But Gerry tried to help her friend. She picked up a metal wastepaper basket and slammed it down on Andy's head, just as the third shot hit their ears.

Then suddenly everything was silent. There was no more action and no more accompaniment of noise. Andy's body lay, face-down, on top of Brownie's, length-on, as if they were lovers in some sick parody of life, no movement except a trickle of blood; inevitably where there is a wound there will be blood. Gerry stood motionless, unable to process the last fifteen seconds. She noted the deep, dark red spreading over Brownie's white shirt, her jacket sleeve having been completely torn off in the struggle. The blood seemed to be exploring the best route out of the body, like water making new tracks across open ground. It pooled on her forearm, then more appeared at her shoulder, and then a patch spread from the elbow. Gerry could not take her eyes off the spreading blood. Was it Brownie's welling up from her wounds or Andy's dripping down from above?

Somewhere in the back of her head was a clamouring noise, an almighty pump churning up her own blood, as if to add to that spilled already.

Then there were cries from outside, breaking in on their silent world where death blanketed them in shock and uncertainty. The door burst open and four soldiers ran in, automatic weapons ready.

"Down on the floor now!" Everyone complied instantly

except George, who could not move.

"Five bodies!" one of the soldiers called. "No, four, one is still alive. Get an ambulance." Gerry was lying face-down behind the secretary's desk. The tangle of Andy and Brownie was just in front of her in the carpeted space between the desks. By raising her head minutely she could see them both, but which one was alive? Or was it one of the others who hung on to life? That would mean Brownie was gone.

"It's Jones." One of the other soldiers called, bending over the body of his colleague. Gerry's heart sank for the implication if Jones was alive was that Brownie was dead. But how could Jones be alive? She had seen the bullet crash into his face, blowing away the back of his skull like a drunken driver. "He's been shot dead," the soldier called. "Who the hell did this?"

"Listen to me," George spoke up as soon as one of the soldiers pulled his gag out. He explained in ragged jerks while one of the soldiers untied him. He explained what had happened, how Andy had flicked out a knife and killed the two guards in an instant, before pulling the two firearms and ordering Verdun to tie and gag him in the chair. Where had Andy learned to kill like that? He closed his eyes, tormented by the replays, then opened them to find Gerry, up from the floor and standing beside him. They embraced, supporting each other, finding strength to give to the other when there was none left for themselves.

The medics arrived and tended to Brownie. She was unconscious and had a flesh wound in her right arm but otherwise was unhurt, just covered in Andy's blood. It had mainly been Andy's blood. Then the police moved in and everyone had to leave. But not before they watched Andy's body being zipped up in a black body bag, his name scrawled on the front, and then lifted onto a gurney, then the same process three more times.

From now on it would all be routine for Andy; nothing unpredictable remained.

"He is at peace now," George said, thinking of the man he had known, the terrible waste, the cruelty veiled behind the routine of the re-training camps.

"Those responsible never pay the price." He looked at Verdun for the first time since the soldiers had come in. The man sat upright, not touching the back of the chair, arms on his lap, as if removing himself from the scene, distancing himself. But strangely, George felt no revulsion - just pity, almost sorrow -for the man who could not see the consequences of what he presided over.

Gerry was comforting the secretary, who could not stop shaking. Someone made hot, sweet tea, but someone else skipped straight to the brandy. She gulped it down.

"My God," was all she said. "My God. My God." With each utterance it was like escaping steam, steadily reducing pressure.

George instructed a cohort of soldiers to escort Verdun to alternative rooms and stand guard until relieved. He had nothing to say to the man who had orchestrated this catastrophe. He only hoped it had not been planned this way. One look at Verdun's grey face told him no deaths had been planned. But he bore huge responsibility.

The medics took the secretary away and sent a nurse after Verdun. They wanted to take George and Gerry to hospital to check them out, but Gerry wanted to walk in St James' Park. She wanted to see the green of the grass and watch the birds fly from bare branch to bare branch as the sun wound down behind the tall buildings around, bringing an early dusk, a city dusk.

"We'll get a cab to the hospital to see Brownie," she said. "But let's walk for a few minutes first."

So they walked out of the palace and into the park, at first just side by side but then holding hands, then arms around each other. They did not talk, other than to nod a greeting to a tramp choosing his bench for the night. They let the birds do the talking. And the wind and the light, sweet rain like mist that tried to cleanse their very souls.

They walked past the offices of the American Society for the

Advancement of Liberty. Gerry broke the silence, pointing up to the double bank of windows on the second floor.

"My old office," she said.

George said nothing, but gripped her more tightly. Nor did Deidre say anything, watching from her new office windows above, her life filling again with the bitter envy she could not control, suddenly wishing she were Gerry and not Deidre, ignorant of what Gerry had just been through; ignorant of everything.

Rewriting History

It was late on Thursday evening that Sir Terrence and Jay Stuttermann returned to Number 10, Sir Terrence holding a slim folder under his arm like a sergeant major's baton. The folder contained the last will and testament of George's father. Now was the time, they both thought. It was two days since the attempt to free Verdun and everything had settled back into stalemate, Frau Rheinalt refusing to give way.

Gerry was with George, the bruising on her face still massive and turning a multitude of mixed-up colours, reminding her colleagues of a puddle of autumn leaves in the park. George made an effort and offered them Scotch, which they all took when Gerry handed them around.

"To victory in our struggle," Sir Terrence said.

"To victory." They chorused back, the American tones outgunning the British. They were even on paper, at two-a-piece, but Sir Terrence's voice was a solo effort, as George did not speak.

"How are you doing, Gerry?" Jay asked.

"OK. I guess. The pain gets real bad but I am just happy to be alive... oh, George, I didn't mean it like..."

"Don't apologise, Gerry. I have to get over my father's death and you can't tiptoe around me forever. Well, you can if you really want to." As he spoke, he sought the reassurance of her hand in his: physical contact as an emotional support.

Sir Terrence noted George's joke and wondered if his task might become a bit easier.

"There is something I want to say to y'all." George

deliberately mimicked the American phrase and they smiled, more from pleasure at his slight re-emergence than from appreciation of the humour. "I've been thinking a lot about my future."

Suddenly, everyone was a lot more serious. Sir Terrence thought of his experience at the end of a gun barrel. George had faced the same just two days earlier. Sir Terrence always held that it had been the making of him, but everyone was different. And George's fiancée had been there in the room as well. That could not have been easy.

George passed around the bottle before continuing.

"I don't want to be Prime Minister."

"What?" came the American-dominated chorus.

George told them of all his worries. It was not just that his father had died but also that he did not feel like a politician and did not relish running a country. He was an historian by nature and that is what he wanted to do with his life. "I want to write popular books, books that bring history alive and ask the right questions. I want to research into so many areas." They talked about it for a long time. Gerry agreed with George, as did Jay. Sir Terrence was gradually won around, but was concerned for his country and its future. It was an irony, Gerry considered, that by far the oldest person in the room had the greatest concern for the future.

So, gradually, they worked out a plan. It was the plan that George had started to consider last Sunday when Dennis had introduced Brenda Howard to him, who had made such a strong start in her first week.

"I think Dennis should be PM." It was the second shock of the evening. But, again, as they talked it through, over a third Scotch, and pancakes cooked by Jay and Gerry, 'American style', it started to make sense.

"It's a sound idea," Sir Terrence said. "You have a fine mind, George. They are going to miss it on the political stage."

"But that is my point. I am good at ideas and concepts, but I am useless at the hectic everyday punch-up of politics. I need to think things through carefully rather than go on instinct.

Take the example of the capture of Verdun. I had the original idea..."

"And a brilliant idea too," interrupted Sir Terrence.

"Yes, but that is my point. It was just an idea. I could have developed it into a theory or an argument or an essay but what I could never make out of it is an operational plan like we needed and got through the efforts of everyone else. That is a skill-set I just don't have. And I need peace and quiet to let these brain cells tick. I just can't work in a chaotic, constantly changing environment. I realise now that that is why I could not get on in business. And even my time as editor of the magazine was great fun but it was too hectic for me. I am my father's son and not my grandfather's grandson! Gosh, that was quite a speech!"

Deep in conversation about future plans, they had forgotten the last will and testament of George's father,. They had forgotten the purpose of their visit completely, until George reminded them by saying that his historical career would kick off by completing his father's unfinished work on General Stein.

"Ah, we may have a problem there," Sir Terrence spoke up. He then let Jay tell the story of what he knew about General Stein and General Unwin-Smith, events that had taken place almost eighty years ago and had become close to being lost from history forever. As George listened, he kept thinking of his father and the pride he had in his own father, and how badly he wanted to complete this work.

"But it does not stop there," added Sir Terrence. "For when your father understood the implications of this remarkable series of events, he had no real hesitation in making his decision. I say no real hesitation because he badly wanted to publish this work but knew its value to you and to our country. This brings me appropriately enough to the new will he made just before he died, which was witnessed by Jay. I'll read it to you."

Afterwards, George just said, "He knew me so very well." And perhaps Edward had used the will to reach out to his son one final time, from the bottom of the hourglass to the top, to guide his son, to imprint upon the next generation some of the lessons learned from the past.

"He was guarding you against your better self," Gerry said, suddenly understanding much more about the man she had barely known. "He knew you would publish for his sake but he was looking out for you and the greater good. Even as he died he displayed extraordinary selflessness. You should be very proud of your father, George. He won't go down in history as a great man but he was quietly great."

"I am very proud," George said.

They worked out a plan that evening, honed it before presenting it to a hastily convened inner circle the next day. Bertie loved the neatness of it. Mandy was concerned for George and his father's work, but saw the sense behind it and thought it would work.

"Who will go to Berlin?" Jay asked.

"I will, of course," replied George, once more in charge. "And it needs to be the rest of you, as well. Jay, you need to come as witness to the will. Sir Terrence as benefactor, and the rest as representatives of the government. And you, Gerry, I just need your strength and wisdom by my side as I do this. Dennis, could I have a word in private?"

Dennis, like any politician would be, was flattered beyond belief.

"I'll have to talk it through with Audrey," he said.

"She's here now," George replied. "I took the liberty of asking her to come here. I didn't tell her the reason but I think she suspects something is up. I'll leave you here to talk and will be in my office when you have finished. Please come and see me."

***

Before Dennis could even broach the subject with his wife, Audrey took him in her arms. "I want this for you, Dennis. I want you to take a cabinet post. I don't want you if it is just half of you. I want Dennis Shepherd the politician, the man who makes a difference. That is the man I married all those years ago and who I want to stay married to."

"Audrey, dear, but you don't understand. I..."

"I do understand, dearest. You either take the post of Home Secretary and have a wife who loves you to pieces or you lose both." Her large grey eyes imparted both the earnestness of her position and the humour with which it was portrayed.

"But..."

"No buts, dearest, you have a choice to make, all or nothing."

"Audrey, just stop talking a moment. Listen instead, will you do that?" She nodded, suddenly aware that it was something else. Dennis continued, a strain of humour in his own voice now. "I have not been offered the post of Home Secretary or any other position working for George."

"What, then?" She was anxious for him. Her new love for him stretched back over the forty years since they had met at Cambridge and became one continuous bond: for better or worse.

"I have been offered a different position altogether."

"Well tell me, husband, or I am going to walk out anyway! You are teasing me and that is unconscionable under the circumstances."

So he told her and then they held hands and kissed. "You will have to give up the company directorships, I'm afraid, but the charities are fine, and the university too. In fact, you will have more time for the university, which is what you always wanted."

"We will live here then?" she asked.

"Yes, do you have a problem with that?"

"Well, we are certainly going to have to decorate! These colour schemes are so..." She did not finish because Dennis took her in his arms again.

***

The contingent left early on Saturday morning, but did not go to Berlin. Instead, Sir Terrence's jet flew them to Dusseldorf, where they got a helicopter to take them directly to Hilda's sanctuary. Sensing the importance of this visit, yet knowing nothing about its content, she had suggested meeting there at the weekend rather than in the glare of Berlin. She had asked, even demanded, prior knowledge of the discussion points but none had been given. It was not how Hilda liked to do business.

They arrived at 10.45. Sir Terrence and George were offered bedrooms in the main cabin; the others were allocated comfortable bunks in the guardhouse.

"It's the most we ever have had here," Hilda was clearly nervous. She liked to know all agendas in advance and had almost not agreed to the meeting, but her instinct told her it had to happen.

"Well, let's get straight down to business, Frau Chancellor," Sir Terrence said.

"Please call me Hilda, Sir Terrence."

"Gladly, but you must call me Scott in return!"

"Agreed." She tried to smile but appeared lost.

They sat with apple juice from the local orchards; pressed, the caretaker's wife informed them, only two weeks earlier by her husband's cousin. It was delicious, so unlike the long-life version sent over to Britain. They used the big polished dining-room table, although they could equally have sat on the floor like teenagers. There were no papers between them, just the will kept in Sir Terrence's jacket pocket. George and Gerry sat next to each other, opposite the big window that looked onto the porch and then over the clearing. The bare trees were bending in the wind like drunks trying to get home. The ground below was swept completely clean of leaves so that bare roots ran like roads on a map out from the base of each tree. George looked at his host; the 'Frau Nein' Bertie had nicknamed her after their last visit. She sat now more on the edge of her chair, much less confident.

"Jay, I think you had best tell the story." So Jay did and, for George, it was like going back thirteen years, to the fireplace where Aunt Jessica held court and commanded silence from her audience. So her nephew now kept his audience quite still and quiet as his strong New England accent gave nothing away of his German-Jewish heritage.

"It all goes back to the closing stages of the war," he started. "The allies were on the offensive and already inside Germany. It was clear that Germany would lose. They were formidable fighters and they threw everything at it but the combined resources of the allies in the west and Russia also in the east was like a steadily tightening grip on the Fatherland. One of the major generals was George's grandfather, General Unwin-Smith. He was a good, strong general; perhaps not one of the world's most brilliant, but one who looked out for his men and carried them with him. They would go anywhere for him. And he was a thoughtful man, very like his son and grandson." Jay looked at George but saw Edward instead, the friend he had known for over forty years but who now was gone. Was this what it was like for each generation? First, life seems to stretch on forever, then suddenly someone you know dies and the whole world turns in an instant to something so much more fragile. But he was keeping his audience waiting.

"Then, on the other side, we have General Stein." He looked at Hilda as he spoke, wondering what was going on in her mind. She looked reined in, as if controlling her emotions by pulling back tightly on every possible outlet for them; mouth pursed, eyes glazed, arms folded, fists clenched, no doubt knees clunked together, but he could not see below the table. "General Stein was, without doubt, a brilliant general. He had won his spurs, as it were, in the invasion of France and then gone on to great things in Greece, North Africa and Italy. He was in command of a division in the last few days of the war and was causing the allies quite a lot of problems. He was an older man but with a young wife who adored him. Her name was Hilda," everyone looked at Hilda Rheinalt as the name was mentioned. She blushed and studied the table, "and she was at the front, or close to it; never far from the husband she had married at seventeen."

One chapter at a time, thought Jay as he held out his glass for some more of the fresh apple juice. Hilda shifted in her chair but avoided all eye contact. Deep inside she had known the agenda would be this, just had not admitted it to herself. Gerry watched two squirrels outside, playing amongst the trees, unaware, it seemed, of winter descending, just out for fun.

"Well, the essence of this story is quite extraordinary. General Stein suddenly leaves his division behind and literally walks into the enemy camp to attempt to surrender, but not his whole division, just him." George could not help noticing how the nephew, Jay, switched tenses just like his aunt had done, and how it brought the story to life through a mad mixing of the tenses, all the past happening now.

"*Nein*," said Hilda, banging both fists on the table. "*Das ist falsche.*"

"No, Hilda, as you well know, it is the truth. General Stein may have panicked but he undoubtedly sought to better his own life at the expense of the safety and liberty of his men. He went to the allied positions and tried to trade information on the deployment of his division and what he knew of the other divisions. He wanted to escape war crime charges and start a new life with allied blessing. That man was out for himself, without a shadow of doubt. When General Unwin-Smith sent him packing, refusing his surrender, he went back to his division and his wife but was haunted by his actions."

"You can't prove this," Hilda said, rallying.

"I can and will right now." He went to George's bedroom and returned with a leather briefcase. He tipped out the contents on the shiny table-top: a diary and two single pieces of paper, along with a Nazi identity card. "This is General Stein's diary and this is an account written in General Stein's own hand."

"This is ridiculous. Why would he write a confession himself?" Hilda asked, recognising the handwriting from old papers she had in her study in Berlin.

"Because Joachim Fielder, his young batman, insisted he do it, supposedly as security for him and his sweetheart." That must be the old lady they had met in Waldenbuch, Sir Terrence thought. It seemed like years ago but was only a few weeks before. "See, Hilda, here is a confession from General Stein and also a statement from Joachim. I found these at his family home twenty years ago when I was investigating another resident of Waldenbuch, who had been a friend of Joachim's. It says here in General Stein's own hand that Joachim felt threatened by the general when he got back from the attempt to give himself up to General Unwin-Smith. Joachim knew exactly what had happened and he feared for his life. So he stole General Stein's personal diary and then forced him to write the confession, on pain of revealing the diary to the world. It's all here in black and white, and I have had the papers checked for age and authenticity." Hilda took the three articles and scanned them, hoping to find some loophole, some way of undermining the case against General Stein, her countryman. But it was a watertight case. She had seen other diaries written by him in earlier, happier years, and knew immediately that this one was genuine.

"There is a little more to this, however." Sir Terrence took up the next chapter, standing up as he talked so that his height bore down on Hilda sitting across the table. Some people grow stunted with age but Sir Terrence seemed to get thinner and straighter, challenging gravity and time to try and drag him down. "Joachim thought he was safe with the diary and the signed confession. We presume he had promised to return the diary on receiving the confession but later changed his mind and decided to keep it. We will never know for sure what happened but General Stein was dead within days. I met Joachim in February 1945 on the battlefield and I know he was not capable of murder; he could not pull the trigger to kill an enemy officer. He was a boy. So the suggestion that the general killed himself is probably correct. Maybe when Joachim refused to return the diary, the general knew it would get out at some stage, it was just a matter of time. Look at the confession again. It is suggestive but does not actually incriminate Stein. It was cleverly written by a supremely intelligent man. So on 7th

March 1945 General Stein commits suicide."

"No!" Hilda could not accept it. "He was murdered. He would never take his own life."

"It is a debatable point but not an essential fact for this narration." Jay took over again. "The fact is, he died within a few days of attempting to give himself up and so create favour for himself. It was only George's grandfather who prevented this happening. A lesser man would perhaps have accepted it and even publicised it for advantage. General Stein behaved in an appalling manner in an attempt to secure his own freedom and future. Nobody knew this for sure except General Unwin-Smith and young Joachim. The British general died of natural causes in late 1957 when his son, Edward, was a child. But General Unwin-Smith would never have spoken to anyone about this. Stein's secret was safe from that corner. Joachim, however, was a young man at university with a whole lifetime ahead of him. He got drunk one night and stupidly alluded to what he knew about General Stein. Six days later he had disappeared and they found him bricked up in a cellar at the university in Stuttgart. He starved to death in October 1948."

"The big question is, who killed him - and we do have the answer. But you know already, Hilda, don't you? You don't need to wait for me to tell you, do you?" Hilda did not answer, just stared at her reflection in the table-top. What was she seeing, wondered George: history as she wanted it or as it happened? Or perhaps there is no real history, just whatever is required by the individual. Tell a lie enough times and...

"*Es ist Verklich,*" Hilda suddenly said. "*Ich glaube das mein Mutter hat...* that is, I have always been thinking that my mother did a terrible thing. She blamed Joachim for her husband's death..."

"Joachim was a boy," Sir Terrence said, uncharacteristically aggressive in defence of the young soldier he had met across a rifle barrel all those years ago. "I knew him. He was incapable of doing anyone any harm. So..."

"So, just let me finish, Sir Terrence. It is true, there is no point denying it. My mother was General Stein's wife. She adored him and was never the same again after his death. She married Dr Rheinalt and they had me as their only child but she did not love my father." Here she stopped a long moment. The wind whipped up, as if to blow the falsehoods away, clattering at the windows and doors, rustling through the tiles, building into a frenzy. Nobody in the room moved, in contrast to the bustle outside; all waiting for Hilda to continue. "I grew up with the perception that General Stein was my father. Of course, I knew he was not but the way she talked about him at every opportunity, the way she referred to what he would have done or said, the way my real father, the doctor, was side-lined. He was really just someone to provide a roof over our heads." She stood up and started to walk randomly about the large open-plan room that formed the main part of the cabin. All the others stayed motionless at the table, knowing the outcome but willing Hilda to say it all, as it really happened. She swung her arms then clasped them behind her back as she walked, struggling with a lifetime of suppression.

Then she said in a very small voice, quiet but also thin, something that would be blown away by the rising wind in an instant if outside. "I have always suspected my mother of causing the death of Joachim Schmidt. She was… well, she was not a balanced person after my father, I mean General Stein, died. She blamed Joachim for his death."

"But it was not just that, was it, Hilda?"

"*Nein.*" The voice was quite a bit stronger now. "I have also suspected that she was motivated by fear of his losing his reputation as a great general and a great man. I think that Joachim got drunk and foolishly talked about what he knew and my mother panicked and thought the man she had loved so completely would have his reputation destroyed if this got out. So she paid some henchmen to do that dreadful thing to Joachim. I don't know whether she ordered that particular death or whether the henchmen were sick enough to think it up on their own. But I do know that my mother went quietly mad when the general killed himself. I think she was capable of ordering the awful fate that happened to young Joachim."

"Hilda, there is a little more and then we are all done," said George, suddenly seeing it all completely clearly.

"What do you mean?" asked Jay, thinking the story complete with Hilda's confirmation.

"Hilda knows and she will tell you."

"Yes, George is quite right. I have played a part in all this. I am not a murderer, of course, but I suppose you could say I am an accessorise."

"An accessory," Sir Terrence corrected.

"Yes, an accessory. I was not even born when Joachim died and obviously I had no part in that." Another pause while Hilda slowly poured the remainder of the apple juice into her glass and gathered her strength. "But I am guilty of a similar crime and the irony is I am not even a relative of General Stein. You could not say even he was a stepfather because he was dead before I was born. I am guilty of the crime of covering this up for all the long years I have known it because I saw General Stein as my father and did not want his name brought into disrepute. I have known about this since long before my mother died in 1979. I heard things as a child and confirmed them through my own research as an adult. I could have brought my mother to justice as a murderer but I did not."

One more time, George prompted her. "And the reason you did not?"

"Not for love of her. I ended up hating her for what she did and for how she was. It was such an awful crime. But she did it for love and hate and revenge. These are powerful emotions. I did it for pride, for family pride. I did not want it known about the surrender of General Stein and the way he was prepared to desert his men. Yet he was not even my father. He was not even related to me but somehow I grew up thinking he was. That is my only excuse."

Hilda Rheinalt slumped back in her chair and closed her eyes. The others filed out without a word and crossed to the bunkhouse, where the caretaker and his wife brought them a light lunch of soup that no one felt like eating but did warm and nourish them. They did not feel like talking amongst

397

themselves; there seemed little point, all had been said already.

Except for Act II, that opened late that afternoon when Hilda sent a message to them that she wished to reconvene.

Hilda had prepared well. She welcomed all of them back with bottles of fine *dunkelbier*, as dark as Gerry's hair, with a fruity, malty taste and healthy bubbles hurrying to the surface where they exploded in tiny sprays against their cheeks as they drank. There were pretzels, salty and hot, along with cold meat, bread and tomatoes. The caretaker's wife started to tell them about the tomatoes, fresh from their garden, but Hilda waved her away to prepare for the next course. They returned with hot pork in pasta, sitting in gruel. It was delicious.

"*Maltacha*," Hilda said. "A delicacy of Baden-Württemberg." It was served with white wine that filled their mouths with its flavour, such that it could be a meal all on its own.

Hilda had prepared well and was preparing her guests equally well.

The conversation was light but not too light. There were no jokes, more observations. They skimmed over a range of subjects, no one daring to get too deep. Thus they ranged from the recently-held Olympics to China's invasion of Taiwan, from the earthquakes and forest fires plaguing California to entries for the following year's Eurovision Song Contest. At a hint of controversy, someone always moved the conversation on. Until the schnapps came out once the supper was cleared away.

"Let's sit by the fire, there should be just enough chairs if we squeeze together." There was not quite room so Gerry sat on the floor on a cushion, using George's legs as a chair back. The fire was an electric one, despite the woods and abundance of trees around them. Hilda had an elaborate chair with arms shaped like claws, which she turned around from the dining room table to face the others. It was deliberate, so that she looked down two feet on everyone else. She poured eight glasses of schnapps and each person took a glass as they found their places.

It looked like Hilda was holding court. She had prepared well.

"I do not want this information to go out any further." Her voice was completely recovered from the trauma of earlier, the lightness of casual supper conversation equally absent. She was serious and intent on her goal.

"Professor Unwin-Smith was gifted the additional research done by Professor Stuttermann and he then left the full amount of that research, including his own work, to me in his last will and testament." Sir Terrence patted his jacket where the will was waiting to be produced if required.

"I am not interested in ownership," she replied. "I am only interested in discretion and security."

"And I am only interested in the truth," Sir Terrence replied.

"Nonsense!"

"What?"

"Sir Terrence Scott, you are the leading financier of the rebel movement in sector 8. You have recently become friends, I understand, with Professor Unwin-Smith and Professor Stuttermann. You turn up here with representatives of the rebel government that has seized power in sector 8. You and your sidekicks are responsible for the kidnapping of Alois Verdun, the President of USE. I cannot believe that you would come all this way to enlighten me on ancient family history. Also, your people have stated categorically that I knew all this anyway. No, my dear man, you are after something else, so out with it and let's see how unreasonable and impractical your plans are. Then we can maybe look for some common ground."

Her analysis was perfect. "You have described our position very well," Terrence replied, trying to gather his composure. "We do want something for the guaranteed secrecy of this embarrassing information. And what's more, you know exactly what it is we require, only you want us to say it first so that it comes across as a request and gives you the upper hand."

"Don't play games with me," Hilda said, angry at his response, respect for him rising with her ire.

"Then don't play games with us," Dennis interjected. "This is an impasse and we have not even got as far as mentioning the subject we all need to talk about. I have an idea." Everyone turned to Dennis, squashed into the middle of the sofa, Bertie on one side, Mandy on the other: the government contingent. "Hilda, is your caretaker still here?"

"Yes."

"Call him."

Hilda rang the bell and the caretaker's wife appeared.

'Yes, Frau Chancellor?"

Dennis spoke up. "Frau Bucher, we need either you or your husband to do a small service for us."

"Of course, sir."

Then Dennis explained his idea. Two pieces of paper were fetched, one for Hilda and the other for Dennis. They each wrote a few words before folding the papers and handing them to Frau Bucher.

She then read them both, nodded cautiously and said, "They are in agreement. Shall I read each one, sir?"

"Yes please."

They had both used remarkably similar words to describe what the British party wanted in return for the guaranteed secrecy of the Stein story. The rules of the idea were simple. Each party had to put down what they considered the British wanted and could not then raise any new points after this. Thus, if either side downplayed the requests they could easily be outmanoeuvred by the other. The slight difference in words just reflected the attitudes. So, while Hilda had written 'Independence for sector 8', Dennis had written 'Complete independence for Great Britain and her dependent territories'.

"*Nein*," said Hilda.

"I own a publishing company," said Sir Terrence. "And a printing press. Copies of this book could be rolling off the line within days."

"*Nein*," said Hilda.

"Your choice," said Dennis, hauling himself up out of the low-slung sofa. "Thank you for the hospitality. Supper in particular was delicious."

"*Nein*," said Hilda.

"Scott, can we get the helicopter back to Dusseldorf tonight?"

"Let's see if we can reach an agreement," said Hilda. She had most to lose and she had blinked first.

The deal took all night, Hilda fighting every square inch of the way. It was 4am before they finally drew up and signed an agreement between the two countries, Jay and Gerry acting as witnesses. Hilda would have a press conference later that morning in which she would agree to the independence of the United Kingdom, free of the USE completely. It was agreed that she would be presented as the great broker who had brought this about. Verdun would be released immediately after the press conference and would hold his own conference, with Hilda and others in Brussels on Sunday afternoon. Great Britain would formally gain her independence at 3pm on Sunday 13th November 2024.

It went entirely according to plan. Verdun was full of praise for his German colleague and together they wished the great nation of Britain all the best in the future, as friends always.

On Monday morning, George went to see the Queen and shortly afterwards Dennis was invited to set up an administration. George and Gerry shook hands with him on the steps of Downing Street before catching a cab to Paddington and then the train to Oxford.